THE

STEAM CATCHER

FOR MY PARENTS

Pat and Bridie O'Sullivan

THE
STEAM CATCHER

Jim O'Sullivan

© Jim O'Sullivan 2024

ISBN 978-1-8384052-6-7

Published by Rymour Books
45 Needless Road
Perth
PH20LE

A CIP record for this book is
available from the British Library
BIC Classification FF

cover and book design by Ian Spring
printed by Imprint Digital, Exeter, Devon

Acknowledgements

Without my friends and family, I doubt *The Steam Catcher* would ever have been completed let alone published. So, thanks to Stuart Campbell and Lee Healey for their endless encouragement.

Thanks to Ian Spring of Rymour Books for his support, advice and for championing *The Steam Catcher.*

To my siblings, Joan, Noreen, Mike, Mary and John, thanks for your love, help and support down the years.

Thanks also to Jean Anderson (my primary school teacher) Rob Brien, Molly Fitzgerald, Bill Harding, Simon Hackwell, John Henderson, Paul Holland, Pete and Sarah McCormack, Barbara Mautterer, Ian Mollison, Stewart Reid, Eddie Smith, Julie Slinn, Gavin Smyth, Mark and Philippa Walsh, Zoe Woodward, Paddy and Meritta Wiggall and Paddy's dear Mum, Peg.

Russell Gardner and Rob Hughes supped a pint or two while sharing their encyclopaedic knowledge of motorbikes and motorbike racing. Hawick Museum brought to life the legendary motorcycle racer Jimmy Guthrie, the inspiration for the racing passages.

The information provided by the archivists of Gloucestershire Heritage Hub and Cheltenham and Gloucester Museums have, I hope, helped me bring early twentieth century Gloucester and Cheltenham to life.

Kerry County Museum, Tralee, provided invaluable insights into 1920s Kerry and the life of the great explorer, Tom Crean. The staff at Mons Memorial Museum, Doudou's Museum Mons, the Flemish Association for Industrial Archaeology and the Commonwealth War Graves Commission shaped my understanding of life Post-World War One in Flanders.

Any errors or inaccuracies are solely the responsibility of the author.

Finally, thank you to my beautiful, wonderful wife Diane for her support, love and patience. I owe her everything.

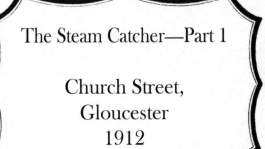

The Steam Catcher—Part 1

Church Street,
Gloucester
1912

CHAPTER ONE

The crowd of mourners outside the Tallow's crumbling house must be ten deep, with a fair few on tiptoe, craning their necks to get a better view. One or two I know but mostly they're strangers, rich and poor alike, drawn here by young Georgie Tallow's murder.

Ever since he was found floating face down in the docks last week, Georgie's slaying has left us all wondering what black-hearted monster could kill an eight year old boy. The devil's work say some, a madman's hand say others, which explains the fingers pointing at Dad given he wanders the streets all hours shouting and bawling in the Irish. Seeing the police in and out of our house leads more people to suspect "Mad Joe Casey" especially as Dad can't or won't say where he was the day Georgie perished.

Despite this, and Mrs Tallow refusing her offer of a few shillings towards Georgie's coffin, Mum still wants to pay her respects. Telling me to keep close, she leaves the house and pushes through the jostling crowd, stopping beside a sour-faced woman two rows from the front. "Close enough Tom," she says, grabbing my arm to steady herself. Now it's my turn to stand on tiptoe and peer through the sea of weaving, bobbing heads, only to stumble after a clumsy oaf lugging a camera pushes me into a young woman.

"Sorry," I mutter.

Smiling, she answers, "No bother, bound to happen with us packed in like sardines." Her smile fades as she nudges the older woman beside her and whispers, "Mad Joe's missus." The pair of them ogle Mum, who pretends not to notice but grips my arm all the tighter.

Thankfully their interest wanes when the two coppers outside the Tallow's front door move aside. The hubbub dies down. Children are shushed. Cigarettes ground out. Expectation grows. The moment's pure, crisp silence is shattered by sobs and shouts of "God Bless," as the pinched faced Mr Tallow (for once wearing a collar and tie) and his eldest son, sixteen year old Ned, carry Georgie's coffin from the house. They're followed by Mrs Tallow and the other seven raggedy, stick-thin Tallow children, the youngest two clinging to their mother's threadbare black dress.

"Could I take your picture?" the pushy cameraman asks Mr Tallow. "There's great interest in your son's tragic end." Ignoring him, Mr Tallow sets off for the Mariners Chapel in the docks but within a couple of paces draws to a stop. "Looks like Mad Joe's come out to play," says a man behind us. "Never seen the like."

Head bowed, revealing the Sacred Heart tattoo on his crown, Dad, barefoot and wearing only his trousers, stands in front of the coffin. He raises his head, fixes a shrew-eyed stare on Mr Tallow and asks, "Did you see them?"

"Please Joe, just let me bury my son," answers Mr Tallow in whisky befuddled tones. There's a flash of light followed by a whiff of rank smelling smoke. The cameraman straightens, looking pleased as punch.

"They were here. On this very spot," Dad insists. "I saw them. Honest."

"Let me head on Joe."

But Dad stands his ground, only moving after Mrs Tallow, giving lie to her careworn frame, slaps him twice about the face, shouting in shrill, heartbroken tones, "You did it! You killed my darling boy!"

Her lie joins the other lies spread by those who wish us ill. They're here today these men and women, useless articles the lot of them, no doubt enjoying the spectacle, unashamed their deceits are souring the day poor Georgie is being laid to rest.

I'll admit there's been times when I believed the lies as I've witnessed Dad's dark, blathering rages which saw Mum hurry me, my younger sister Florrie and our little brother Stanley upstairs to spare us a hiding. But now's not the time for doubt as the coppers, their truncheons drawn, order people to step back and afford the Tallows some peace.

The older copper glowers at Mum. No words are needed. "Let's get you inside, Joe," she says, draping her black shawl around Dad's broad shoulders.

"I saw them, Sal. The Three Sisters. They've come to protect me." He rubs his smarting right cheek and starts to count on his fingers, something I've learned to fear as it usually ends with a fit or a fist. Sometimes both.

Ignoring the hateful looks, spittle flecked jibes and clenched fisted anger surrounding her, Mum guides Dad towards our house. Florrie and Stanley both in Sunday best, look on from the front step. Both are aghast, with Stan wringing the life out of his cap. His best pal's death has upset him more than he's letting on and Dad's latest shenanigans have made things worse for him. For all of us come to that.

∘ ∘ ○ ○ ∘ ∘

"Told you to keep an eye on him," Mum hisses at Florrie as she takes Dad inside.

"Couldn't stop him Mum," Florrie answers, upset to have copped the blame.

After calming Dad, Mum still wants me to attend the funeral on her behalf. Madness in my eyes. Much better to stay home and avoid those sly looks and harsh words that will follow me to the Chapel. But I've no choice. Mum's mind is made up. I leave the house and slip among the shuffling back markers, hoping nobody will recognise me.

"At least the rain kept off," says the elderly man behind me. "Explains the turnout."

"No surprise, Grandpa," answers the woman beside him. "Doesn't bear thinking about what poor Georgie endured. I know the Tallows aren't everyone's cup of tea but they don't deserve this. No-one does. Haven't let the children out of my sight since."

"Who was the fella who stepped in front of the coffin?"

"Mad Joe Casey," she mutters darkly. "Everyone thinks he had a hand in it. Just seen for yourself. Why would an innocent man beg for forgiveness? At the poor boy's funeral too. Ever since he shipped up here, there's been something fishy about him. Irish for starters. Makes him a liar. Dare say he'll cut your throat for ten bob."

Again I wonder if Dad has it in him to kill Georgie and this notion dogs me all the way to the docks where hundreds watch Georgie pass beneath a guard of dockers and enter the Chapel. A wheezy organ starts up and 'A Mighty Fortress is Our God' drifts over us. A few mourners sing but most stay quiet and look on, their coats and jackets drawn tight against the bitter wind.

Still wary of being spotted, I slip into a maze of stacked crates and barrels piled beside the dock gates and disturb a rummaging terrier. Quayside, a ship's horn blasts and a cloud of black smoke and cinders funnels skywards, forcing a flock of wheeling gulls to change tack. Perhaps the ship is sailing to Antarctica to help my hero Captain Scott in his quest to reach the South Pole. What I'd give to be part of such an adventure.

The crowd parts to allow a horse drawn wagon to pull up outside the Chapel. Two swarthy, hard-looking men buttoned up in filthy coats, and shod in muddy boots, jump down from the Dray and walk towards the stacks. Fearing the worst, I slip further into the warren, and brush a stack of crates making it rattle and clink.

"What was that? one of the men asks. Heart in mouth, and scarce able to breathe, I duck down and hear their hobnails scrape on the cobbles. Three more steps and they'll be on me.

The terrier, clasping a rat in its jaws, darts between the men and scuttles away. "Just a ratter," says the other man. Seconds later, two trails of steaming

11

piss lap at my boots. I stay put. Can't risk them finding Mad Joe's son. No telling what they'd do to me.

"Pauper's grave for the boy?"

"Fourth one this week," comes the answer.

"Pint afterwards?"

"No time. Two more to be dug by day's end."

"Business booming then."

"Not on parish rates."

'Eternal Father, Strong to Save' pours from the Chapel. "Look lively, they're coming out," says the first man. The pair hurry back to the Dray. Within five minutes, the chestnut mare hauls the rattling carriage towards the dock gates. "Rest In Peace Georgie," I whisper watching the cart turn onto Commercial Street with the Tallows and what looks like the whole of Gloucester following.

The docks spring back to life. Steam cranes hiss and clank, stevedores curse and goods wagons rumble past me. Collar up, cap pulled low, eyes cast to the cobbles I step from my hiding spot wondering if I should take my chances and seek passage on the departing ship. Distracted by thoughts of adventure, I bump into a woman. She's of a similar age to Mum but taller and better dressed. She's onto me straight away and barks, "You're Mad Joe's boy. Some nerve you've got showing your face after what your pa did."

Turning to the lank haired slip of a girl beside her she says, "Keep away from him. He's afflicted. Like all them Caseys." I know the girl. Used to sit behind her in school. She opens her mouth as if to speak but thinks better of it.

Antarctic adventures forgotten, I run. Even strangers know my fate. Maybe I should keep running. Away from Gloucester and Dad's madness. Where I end up doesn't matter.

CHAPTER TWO

When he brought the pistol home last year, Dad threw open the back door, ran into the kitchen with a cloth covering his face, like one of them American bank robbers and shouted, "Your money or your life!" Mum almost fainted with the shock while us three kids fell about laughing.

Now he's pointing the pistol at the young doctor and yelling, "I'll shoot if ye come any closer."

The doctor and the two uniformed orderlies retreat to the landing. All three reek of piss. Dad's aim with the chamber pot has been deadly. "Reckon the loon's one of them Fenians," one of the orderlies mutters.

"Nobody mentioned a gun," the doctor says in his broad Scottish accent while wiping his trousers. Judging by the stains he's copped most of the pot's contents. "Did you know he was armed?" he asks me.

"He bought it from some fella in the Hauliers. Don't worry though it don't fire. No pin." Hearing this they run back into the bedroom.

"English bastards, free Ireland!" Dad roars as they wrestle him to the floor and rip the gun from his grasp. Moments later he's brought out, lashed to the parlour chair the doctor had asked me to fetch. I'm reminded of the picture in the tatty atlas we keep on the kitchen mantelpiece, beside Mum's bible and the Charles Dickens book, of that chubby maharajah dressed in fine silks and a turban being borne by slaves, like he's born to rule. But Dad's trussed up in a straitjacket, effing and blinding while fighting his bindings.

"Back up," instructs the doctor. The men reverse, knocking into the dusty photos of grim faced Queen Victoria and King Edward hanging from the wall. Leaning over the banister, I can see Mum and Florrie in the hall next to the spindly copper who arrived with the doctor. Next to the copper is Dad's mongrel terrier Murphy, who starts to whine as Dad is carried down the stairs.

After being set down in the hall, Dad says to the copper, "You're that sniper, from McBride's Commandos."

"Sniper?" the baffled copper mutters.

"I deserve it. I killed those poor children." The copper's interest pricks. "Kitchener's orders. No food or water for camp inmates. I'll pay in hell for my omission."

"Which children?"

"South Africa," Mum tells him. "Joe was a guard at one of those camps they put the Boer women and children in. The memories haunt him still."

"I see," the copper says. But I doubt he does. He'd have a much better idea if he saw Mum cradling Dad at night singing the lullabies she once sang to us.

To our surprise Dad sings, "But if I should die on a foreign land, and be buried so far, far away, no fond mother's tears will be shed o're my grave, on the Shores of Amerikay". Hearing the familiar air, Stan crawls out from his hiding place, under our bed, and joins us.

The doctor hands the policeman the pistol and points to the forms resting on Mum's bible. "Did you sign the order Mrs Casey?"

Mum looks at him, hoping for reassurance. "You sure it's only for a few days doctor?"

"Yes. The urgency order confers power of detention for seven days, after which your husband can come home."

"Don't, Sal," Dad pleads. Caught in two minds, Mum looks at him and then Florrie, me, and Stan.

"Mrs Casey," the doctor urges, checking his fob watch.

"Please, Sal," Dad begs. Wiping her eyes Mum crouches before Dad and wraps his bound hands in hers. "It's for the best, Joe, just for a few days. So you can get some rest."

"Please, Sal."

"Mrs Casey," says the doctor, growing impatient. Mum dithers a while longer and whispers, "Sorry, my darling." She signs the forms and hands them to the doctor.

Murphy whimpers and the floorboards creak as Dad is picked up and carried outside to a black wagon parked in the street. Despite the early hour, a handful of neighbours look on, no doubt pleased Dad won't be disturbing them. For a few days at least. Old Ma Clayton seems happiest of all. No surprise there, as our brassy neighbour is often round complaining to Mum that Dad's ravings are bad for business, which involve her letting shifty looking men into her house at all hours. Some nights, men knock at our front door and ask for Old Ma, only for Mum to send them packing and give Old Ma a mouthful the next morning. Not that it does much good. The men are back the next night and every night after.

I'd wager a week's pay Old Ma has spread more tales about Dad than anyone else these past few days.

"Happy now?" Mum snaps.

"Delighted," Old Ma answers, drawing on her cigarette.

"We'll return the chair," says the doctor as Dad is loaded into back of the wagon.

"Sorry about the chamber pot doctor," says Mum.

Dad hollers, "I served the king, the empire! I possess the Lionheart's soul!"

"Shut up, you Mick bastard," an orderly shouts, "Cover us in piss would you?"

With Dad loaded, the doctor and the second orderly squeeze in beside the wagon driver who blanches at the stench. The wagon sets off. Murphy gives chase before Mum calls him back. I can't believe I'm watching Dad, *my Dad*, being carted off to the asylum.

"Good riddance," Old Ma says, grounding out her cigarette. Mrs Tallow, sporting a fresh shiner, looks on from her front step. Ned slips past her and sets off for the docks where he's landed the plum job of apprentice clerk at the customs house. Sixteen going on sixty he is.

"When's Dad coming home?" Florrie asks Mum.

"When he finds some peace, Florrie."

"How long will that take?"

"Soon, as sure as God's in Gloucestershire," Mum answers while drawing the three of us to her. Everyone is crying. Except me. I never cry. Makes me a cold fish Florrie reckons. Not that I care. Best not to feel things.

Rain drums against the kitchen window and the wind whistles up through the floorboards swelling the cinder pocked matt in front of the fire.

"Right," says Mum, wiping her eyes and forcing a smile, "Tom we've still your birthday to celebrate."

"Changed my mind."

"Nonsense! It's not every year you turn thirteen. Doubt Captain Scott would be impressed with you giving up. I'll get your birthday rashers on while you go outside and make sure everything is still ship-shape."

There's a knock at the door. "What now?" Mum says wearily.

CHAPTER THREE

I catch the spindly policeman unawares. He stutters and seems to have forgotten why he's knocked. "Can I come in?" he asks.

"S'pose." He takes off his helmet and steps inside. Mum's waiting for him at the foot of the stairs. "What now?" she asks, "Haven't you had your pound of flesh for the day?"

"Sorry Mrs Casey," he answers while wiping his thin moustache. He holds up the pistol. "I wanted to ask you about this."

"I told the doctor," I tell him, "Dad bought it off some fella in the Hauliers a while back. It don't fire though. Doesn't have a pin."

"Noticed that. But having a gun in the house is unusual, even for round here."

"All sorts of chicanery goes on in the Hauliers," Mum says, "Proper den of thieves. You should be bothering the landlord, not us."

"I shall, but first I'd like to take a look around your house."

"Your lot have already rooted through everything."

"But the pistol is new evidence."

"And if I say no?"

"My sarge will be back with a search warrant and we'll tear the house apart."

Shaking her head, Mum opens the parlour door. The copper nods, goes in and soon comes out looking none the wiser. I follow him upstairs and watch him search both bedrooms. Again he finds nothing, but before going downstairs, he straightens the pictures of the king and queen.

"Find anything?" Mum asks. He shakes his head. "I understand your husband lost his job at the docks."

"After a misunderstanding with another man."

"Which led to this man suffering a broken leg." The revelation surprises me, Florrie too by the looks of her.

"Joe wouldn't hurt a fly," Mum answers. I haven't heard her lie before. Thought her faith forbade her.

"We know he was hanging around the docks the night Georgie was killed."

"Who told you that?"

"Can't say."

That'll be Old Ma.

"Joe often goes for a walk to clear his head. But as to him being on the dock's, I couldn't say." She steps towards the copper. "I must have told you lot all this a good half dozen times now. Caused us no end of trouble having you lot traipsing in and out."

"Just doing our job, Mrs Casey."

"Hounding an innocent man more like." Her angry tone catches the copper by surprise. "You should be asking questions much closer to home."

He frowns. But I wonder what he'd think if he saw Mrs Tallow's shiner. After a few pints Mr Tallow is well known for flying into addled, foul mouthed rages so bitter even grown-ups steer clear of him. Hearing his Dad barrelling down the road effing and blinding, Georgie, keen to spare himself a leathering, often snuck over to ours to wait for his Dad to fall asleep before creeping home.

Mr Tallow has taken to the bottle even more since Georgie died and now most nights, he staggers home the worse for wear threatening anyone and everyone in sight.

"We're casting the net wide," the copper answers. "Mind if I take a look out the back?"

"Suit yourself."

Opening the back door, the copper points at the flimsy tent puckering in the rain soaked breeze. "What's in there?" he asks me.

"That's where I'm spending my birthday. To honour Captain Scott."

"Bit tougher in the Antarctic than Gloucester. Polar bears for starters." He steps into the rain and pokes his head inside the tent but quickly retreats and says, "Think something's died in there." He wipes his nose and spots the Triumph propped against the yard wall, "Your dad's motorcycle?"

"Yeah."

He runs his hand over the bike's fuel tank. "Fine machine. Wouldn't mind one myself. How could he afford such a beauty?"

"He helped a fella a while back."

"What fella?"

"Dunno, but Dad said he was a true Irish Patriot."

"What does that mean?"

I have no answer, so I try to act as if butter wouldn't melt by shrugging my shoulders. He kicks the front tyre and twists the throttle. "Odd, a docker owning a gun and a motorcycle." He slowly raises the pistol and draws a bead on me. I flinch. "Reckon there's more to your dad than meets the eye. Thank your mum for her time." Smirking, he lowers the pistol and drags open the back gate and sets off along the alley.

He'll be back. They're not going to let us rest. Guns, motorcycles, madness. They can twist this story anyway they like. Dad's in peril. And my big gob has just made things worse.

CHAPTER FOUR

Dad closes the back gate. I'm gutted. He's forgotten my birthday. Again. The gate opens and there he is with Murphy beside him. "Thought I'd forgotten, Tom?"
"No," I lie.
*   "Catch."*
*   I snatch at the sixpence arcing towards me but it slips between my butterfingers and lands against the Triumph's front wheel. "Happy birthday," he says dragging the gate shut and heading off to the docks.*

I duck and go inside the tent, actually the tarpaulin that covers the Triumph, and gag on the stale, fetid air. After all that's happened, spending my birthday under canvas aping Captain Scott now seems a nonsense. I should abandon the Great Gloucester Antarctic Expedition. But I can't let Scott down. Besides, Mum has knitted me a new balaclava, and I've stashed five bob and six chocolate bars beneath the fire grate in our bedroom. What's more, every night last week I kicked the bedclothes off the bed to get used to the freezing Antarctic while ignoring Stan and Florrie's moans about the cold. Feint hearts both. Definitely not cut out to be explorers. Although to give her her due, last night Florrie, who's the one for words in our house, read out loud the page of the *Times* she pinched from the library detailing Scott's plans, while I stared at the photo of Scott and his men aboard his ship, the Terra Nova. "The British Empire in Human Form," the *Times* calls him. They're right. He is.

Now determined to press on with the Expedition, I return to the kitchen which reeks of frying bacon. Mum leaves the sizzling rashers to squeeze the life from me. She smells of bacon, grease and talcum powder. Although I'm now thirteen, I still enjoy her hugs. "Happy birthday Tom," she says, handing me my birthday tuppence. "Don't fritter it."

"Thanks, Mum."

"Sorry you've ended up working in the Tannery. I know your heart was set on the docks, but all this palaver with your dad put paid to that." She hugs me again. "By the way, given what's happened to poor Georgie, I want Florrie and Stanley to join your expedition."

My heart slumps. Why she thinks these two jokers should tag along is beyond me. After all, I'm thirteen, working, and have smoked eight cigarettes, the last three without throwing up. Having those two moaning and squabbling beside me isn't how explorers go about their business. "Why?" I ask mournfully.

"I'll only fret if you're not together." By the look on her face it's clear neither the king nor the almighty will change Mum's mind.

○ ○ ○ ○ ○ ○

Stan's baby face turns puce after I tell him Mum's plan. Slinking beneath the bedclothes he groans and says, "Got stomach ache." First I try to change his mind with a Chinese burn and then by pinching his ear. Despite yelping with the pain he doesn't budge. Even the offer of a penny or the promise of an extra rasher can shift him. I give up and fish under the fire grate for the Expedition's provisions. The five bob is still in the small canister but only two of the six chocolate bars are left.

"Did you nab my chocolate Stan?"

"Must've been Florrie."

"Liar."

"I'm not. Leave me alone, I've got stomach ache."

I want to belt him, force him to admit his thievery but think better of it. I go down for breakfast. A plate piled with thick slices of bread, slathered with butter and jam sits on the table and sugared tea steams from chipped mugs. Murphy hangs around hoping for a morsel. Florrie sits at the table reading her library book. "Happy birthday Tom," she says with a smile, a sure sign she's up to something.

"I've told Florrie what's occurring," Mum says with her back turned to us, tending to the rashers. Florrie rolls her eyes. "Looking forward to it, aren't you Florrie?"

"Yes, Mum," Florrie answers while shaking her head.

"Stan's poorly," I say.

"What's wrong with him?" Mum asks.

"Says he's got stomach ache."

"Upset about Dad and poor Georgie no doubt." Handing Florrie her flipper, she says, "Florrie, you dish up yours and Tom's breakfasts while I go and see to Stan."

Florrie tips three rashers onto my plate and two onto hers. After setting the skillet on the hob she whispers, "I want paying for going in that tent."

"No chance!"

"Mum won't let you out on your own, not with Georgie's killer on the loose."

"No chance!"

"In that case..." She clasps her belly and begins to groan, her face growing redder by the second. I'm sure she's going to keel over until I see the glint in her crafty blue eyes. Even though she's kippering me I have to admit she's good at faking stomach ache. But still I plead, "Have a heart, Florrie."

The groans get louder. Mum calls out from the landing, "Have you caught Georgie's bug as well, Florrie?"

"What do you want?" I whisper. Smirking that annoying smirk of hers, Florrie straightens, tidies her smock and says matter of factly, "Chocolate. Fry's too, nothin' rubbishy."

"That's blackmail."

"I know."

"And it's my birthday."

"Happy birthday Tom."

○ ○ ○ ○ ○ ○

Handing her the Fry's chocolate, paid for by frittering my birthday tuppence in the corner shop, I wonder if every little sister enjoys blackmailing their big brother. Probably. Sugar and spice and all things nice? My arse.

"I'm not going in there," Florrie says scrunching up her face. "It stinks."

"It'll be fine when it's aired," I answer flapping a tea towel around the tent, which only makes the stench worse. Florrie and Stan, now miraculously recovered after the promise of Fry's chocolate, step inside, both wrapped up in their hand-me- down overcoats, balaclavas and mittens. They side-step a puddle and perch themselves on the upturned crates in front of the bucket housing the fire. "Does Antarctica really smell like this?" Stan asks, pinching his nostrils.

"Yes," I lie.

"Reckon we'll be poisoned by dinner time." He sniffs, and then asks, "Can Murphy tag along? He can hunt for food."

"What can Murphy hunt in the Antarctic?" asks Florrie, her face a mixture of bafflement and wrath.

"Polar bears, penguins and whales."

"Don't have Polar bears in Antarctica and I doubt Murphy could catch a whale."

"Murphy can catch anything. He's the best ratter on the docks."

"Suit yourself," Florrie sighs. Defeated by Stan's stupidity, she takes off her mittens and opens her library book.

○ ○ ○ ○ ○ ○

"What's the book?" I ask as Murphy pokes his snout inside, sneezes and retreats to the yard's greasy cobbles.

"Room With A View."

"Who wrote it?"

"E M Forster."

"What does the E M stand for?"

She flicks to the front of the book. "Edward Morgan."

"Captain Scott's middle name is Falcon."

"Fascinating." The tent walls flutter. Florrie's eyes dart from Stan to me and then outside. "Don't expect me to stay if it starts to rain."

"What'll we eat?" asks Stan.

"Murphy can catch a whale. If not, pop to the kitchen and ask Mum for something."

Gobsmacked at their lack of gumption I reply, "Captain Scott can't nip to the kitchen, we'll just have to stick it out, 'til teatime at least."

"I'll starve," whines Stan.

I hand them another square of chocolate each. Provisions are dwindling. Starvation beckons. Murphy watches a dozen or so gulls wheel over the house. The rain returns. Water trickles down my neck. We've been under canvas for barely five minutes but already my excitement is wilting. Perhaps I'm not cut out for the life of an explorer after all.

"Definitely going to catch my death," Florrie grumbles, tucking her balaclava inside her coat collar. I arrange the newspaper and kindling in the bucket, strike a match. It flares then dies.

"Are those matches England's Glory?" Florrie asks, watching me strike another.

"'Course. Gloucester's finest."

"They're made from Norwegian wood. That's where Scott's rival Amundsen is from." She has me again. Always ten times smarter. I let the match burn down, unsure if lighting a fire with a match made from Norwegian wood is betraying Scott. "Hurry up Tom, it's freezin'," Stan pleads.

"Can't," I say, resigned to spending an honourable, if bitter, rain-lashed day without food, fire, or proper shelter.

"In that case." Florrie snaps her book shut, leaves the tent and hurries into the house with Murphy in tow. To avoid the dripping water, I lean forward and pull Dad's overcoat around me and watch the rain bounce off the cobbles.

"Georgie would have liked this," Stan burbles with his mouth full of chocolate. "He loved adventures."

"If you know what happened to Georgie, best tell Mum."

"Told the police everything I know." Even with his face half hidden beneath his balaclava I can tell he's afraid. "We'd just finished a game of five an' in out the alley. I won. Then Old Ma shoos us off. So, Georgie went home and I came in for tea."

"What time was this?"

"Not late. It was still light."

"Any strangers hanging around?"

"This fella left Old Ma's and booted the football along the alley. Big bloke, built like a heavyweight." He leans forward, lifts the balaclava onto his forehead and throws up into the fire. The thought that Stan could have perished along with Georgie takes the breath from me.

"Best get you inside Stan."

"Sorry Tom, didn't mean to spoil your birthday."

"Tha's all right. Wasn't in the mood for it truth be told."

"Will Captain Scott understand?"

"Expect so."

∘ ∘ ○ ○ ∘ ∘

I can't sleep. A gust of wind funnels down the chimney, reminding me of the banshee. Stan is buried under the blankets, gripping his football and muttering in his sleep. At least we've more room now that Florrie sleeps with Mum. All the same, it's weird not hearing Mum singing to Dad to ease his night terrors. Some nights she'd sing for hours on end and pleaded with Dad not to go out. But he always did.

If only Dad had stayed in the night Georgie died. He'd still be home, I'd not be working in the tannery and strangers wouldn't tell me to fuck off back to Ireland, even though I was born in Exeter.

Outside I hear footsteps and a man's voice. Old Ma's phlegmy cackle sets off Murphy. I get out of bed and from the window, watch a man drag Old Ma's back gate behind him after which she closes her back door. In the pitch black the man, now little more than a shadow, moves off.

Perhaps one of Old Ma's visitors killed Georgie, maybe the strapping fella who kicked Stan's ball. Or maybe Mr Tallow's killed his boy in a drunken rage. Not that me wondering will make much difference. Everyone's convinced a madman killed Georgie. Nice and easy to understand. Outside Christian virtue and all that. Dad's got no chance.

I catch my reflection in the window and stare at it for a minute, maybe two wondering what the first sign of madness will be. A look? A thought? A movement?

Despite the Great Gloucester Antarctic Expedition not going to plan, I'm still set on joining Captain Scott. But I know I won't. My life was decided the moment they fished Georgie from the docks. Working in the tannery while protecting Mum and my annoying younger brother and sister from Georgie's killer, with madness stalking me.

The banshee wails.

CHAPTER FIVE

"Welcome to our odoriferous trade Master Casey," the foreman, a sweaty, mutton chopped man with few airs and even fewer teeth told me on my first day at Wakeman's Tannery. "You'll earn your money here." He's right too, as most evenings I come home reeking of dung, my eyes stinging, my hands and arms burning. For all I know, my breath stinks of death. After dinner and with barely the strength to climb the stairs, I fall into bed and while Florrie slathers carron oil on my skin to soothe the burns, I try to stave off the thought of returning to that stench and filth in the morning.

When Dad lost his job, Mum was too proud to ask the parish for help meaning I had to leave school and find work. Nobody on the docks would employ a Casey and as the brick works, flour mills, and carriage works, weren't hiring, I'd no choice but to start in the tannery. But I was proud handing Mum my first wage. Prouder still when she handed me back two half crowns. Feeling coins jiggle in my pocket made me feel grown up. I bought gobstoppers for Florrie and Stan, and figuring every explorer has to start somewhere, I splashed out on a tuppenny map of Gloucestershire for myself.

"Time's getting on, Tom," Mum says, handing me my slice of bread and dripping. As usual she waves me off from the back step while Stan plays football in the yard. Dad gave Stan the ball on his seventh birthday, claiming it had bobbed all the way to Gloucester from somewhere called Montevideo. After finding Montevideo in the atlas, I decided he was fibbing.

I head towards the city centre, each footstep harder than the last, thinking myself Captain Scott trudging towards the pole. The cattle market outside the train station heaves with livestock brought in for auction. The cattle grow uneasy when a piercing whistle announces a train's arrival and a cloud of steam and cinders curls over the station. I reach up and grab a handful of steam for luck and hurry on hoping the foreman won't clock that I'm late.

For once I'm in luck. He's nowhere to be seen. I slip into the beamhouse and to lessen the stink, I stuff my nostrils with shreds of cotton and set about collecting the hairs scraped from the dirt-soaked hides, making sure to separate the more valuable white hairs from the coloured hairs. It's filthy, fiddly work, sifting through rendered flesh and sinew, but woe betide me if the foreman discovers I've let just one white hair slip by me.

All morning I keep my head down and work like a dervish, ignoring the jibes about Dad from the pale, dead eyed men fleshing the hides, pleased that my misfortune distracts them from their backbreaking labours.

The foreman arrives looking the worse for wear and in a foul mood. I worry he'll have me shovelling shit into the bating pits or mixing fresh limescale for the fleshing tanks. But for once he's in a generous mood, pleased I've bagged two sacks of hair. "Good work Master Casey," he says picking over the pile of dark hairs with a stick. "We'll make a tanner of you yet."

He rubs his whiskers, and belches. "Heard about your pa," he whispers, resting his spidery hand on my shoulder. I flush and stare at the floor, aware the other men are watching. "Madness is hard to take for those left behind. Head over to the bark mill and help old Bateman grind up this morning's delivery." He has a heart after all. It's the cushiest job in the yard. "But if you're late in tomorrow, you'll be shovelling shit for the rest of the week."

○ ○ ○ ○ ○ ○

Walking home for once free from pain, I linger outside the Hippodrome in Eastgate Street to stare at the pictures of strong men, midgets, illusionists, conjurers, and singers. Best of all though is the picture of a man dressed in seal skins, whose act is a tribute to Captain Scott. Scarce able to believe my luck, I step into the carpeted, gaslit foyer, its polished brass and glass a world away from the tannery's colic stink. I ask the bored looking woman in the booth the price of a ticket.

"What age are you?"

"Just turned thirteen."

"In that case tuppence."

"Only got a penny on me."

"Well, when you've got another one, you can buy a ticket." I turn tail and run home, a crafty plan forming; retrieve a penny from the grate; head back to the Hippodrome and buy a ticket. Ten minutes to run home, a minute to recover the penny and another ten minute run back to the Hippodrome. In just over twenty-one minutes I'll be marvelling at Captain Scott's exploits. What will be in the tribute? Snow and tents? Definitely. A penguin? Maybe. A whale? No chance.

In Southgate Street, a motorcycle overtakes me. It's a Triumph. The same make as Dad's bike. Captain Scott is forgotten.

"What's that contraption?" Mum asks as Dad leans the bike against the yard wall.

"Freedom Sal."

"Freedom? When we struggle to feed the kids and pay for coal."

"Cost me nothing. Did a good man a good turn."

"Good for you. Sell it."

I sit on the saddle and grasp the handlebars. "Fancy taking her for a spin, Tom?" Dad asks. I almost burst with excitement.

"Watch out for coppers," he whispers, straddling the bike and then paddling. The back wheel spins, the engine splutters into life and dies.

"Fecker." Dad squats by the engine, fettling knobs and levers. He remounts and paddles again. This time the engine starts, its note thick and hoarse.

"Hang on!" he says, stamping the bike into gear. We roll along the alley and turn into the street. Neighbours watch us scoot by. Children run alongside. For the first time in my life, if only for a moment, people notice me. Dad's shirt ripples in the breeze and tears squeeze from the corners of my eyes. The speed and noise terrifies me and I cling on for dear life as we hare along a narrow, pitted country lane. We stop on a hilltop and look over the city. I can make out the cathedral, the docks and the river Severn. Far-off hills rise and fall, a world waiting to be found.

"What do you make of her?" Dad asks.

"She's brilliant, Dad. Where'd you get her from?"

"Helped a patriot."

"What did he do?"

"Didn't ask. Best not to know. He needed help that's all. He'd made a mistake. You're not a man until you've made a few. The bike was payment." I wonder how desperate a man must be to give up such a wonderful machine. Dad hums "The Shores of Amerikay," then says, "People talk about fate and destiny Tom. That's in fairy tales or for people with money. For the Irish, our destiny, rests in our own hands and even then, daresay we'll have to fight for it."

The motorcycle's a sign. When I get home Dad will be sitting in his chair holding the tatty atlas, waiting to tell me where the ships he's worked on today hail from. Then he'll pick out the places he's been to in India and Africa during his army days. He'll speak of sea voyages, boxing matches and battling Zulus, Arabs, Fuzzy Wuzzies, and Boers. Savages all, in his eyes, bent on wielding their spears and rifles, refusing to bend the knee before the British Empire. He'll point to pictures of people the English, even poor ones like us rule over; Chiefs, Emirs, Fakirs, and chubby Maharajahs carted around on big chairs. Perhaps he'll tell yarns from Ireland, about the Great Hunger, about the little people and giants striding the bogs. Maybe he'll scream like a banshee and send Murphy bonkers and have Ma Clayton banging on the wall.

"I'm a proud son of Erin," he'll say. "Ireland's freedom is a just cause, but the British Army made me the man I am."

"What do you mean, Dad?"

"That, Tom, is the definition of a contradiction." Again I won't understand him.

The stories and songs came to an end when the voices began. "His Blue Devil," Mum calls it which she blamed on the things he'd seen out in South Africa. I found this hard to fathom, as to my mind, serving the king and the empire in faraway lands seems to be the *best* thing anyone could do. What can beat adventure and war? Besides, even though I was a tot when Dad returned from far off Africa, I didn't think him mad when he tickled me or pulled a funny face or sang one of those mournful Irish tunes that moved him to tears.

I want to believe. The motorbike *really is* a sign. It won't be the Dad who came home a month ago soused as a lord clawing at his face, his shaved, bloody head sporting the sacred heart tattoo while begging to the Three Sisters to intercede for him. *That* Dad's long gone. It'll be our *old* Dad. The sane, kind, funny one.

I swerve around strolling couples and earn funny looks from shopkeepers closing up for the night, but I keep running. Dad's home and everything can go back to normal. I pass the Nelson and turn onto Llanthony Road. Home in two minutes. My heart sinks.

Alf Fenwick and the Bridge Gang are loitering on the corner of our street. Alf delighted in tormenting me at school and still does whenever our paths cross. Why he hates me is a mystery. But I can't be caught. I have to get home. Head down I charge but Alf grabs me and then pins me up against a wall. Screwing up his ugly, big-nosed, fat face he says, "Still stink of shit, Casey." His pals laugh. "Still stink of shit, and your Pa's off his onion." He digs me in the chest. I try to break free but he's too strong. "Mad Joe Casey and his stinking son." His spit peppers my face.

"Kill him," Alf's weaselly mate Ted Pugh mutters. Alf punches me once, twice, three times, all the while shouting, "Stinking Irish bastard!" The punches sting and I can taste blood. Someone shouts. Fighting back the tears I see my best pal Jack Jefferson, squaring up to Alf. Jack's not afraid of anyone, not even the Bridge Gang. "Pick on someone your own size Fenwick," he says.

Jaw set, fists clenched, Alf moves towards Jack, but Jack drops him with a sharp left while Florrie sets about Ted Pugh screaming, "Attack my brother, would you!"

"Get her to stop," Ted cries as Florrie pulls off his cap.

"I'll stop when I'm ready," Florrie answers now tugging at Ted's wiry hair.

"Police! Scarper!" someone hollers. As the gang run off, a doubled-over Alf hisses, "Next time, Casey."

CHAPTER SIX

Jack lives in a boarding house run by his mum on Commercial Road. Does a good breakfast, by all accounts. His Dad's Jamaican, and a sailor who once gave me a shark's tooth, swearing he'd wrestled it from a man-eater in the Caribbean sea. That night I slid under the bedclothes and pretending to be a shark, stabbed Stan's foot with the tooth. He screamed and let go of his football which fell off the bed and bounced on the floor. Mum came up to see what was going on, laughed at my antics but still smacked me. The tooth went missing a few days later.

When he was younger, Jack got picked on a lot, like the time the Bridge Gang tried to scrub him white with a wire brush. He managed to deck three of them, before they forced him to the ground and scoured his face until it bled. I thumped Ted Pugh in school the next day. Got caned for it. But I didn't care. Dad always told us to stick by our mates.

Nowadays Jack's the biggest and toughest kid round here. Brave too, much braver than me. Swears like a trooper when the mood takes him. Every swear word too; shit, bollocks, fuck, all of them. If war broke out, he'd be a hero. Nothing scares me when I'm with Jack. Not even Dad's madness.

As the three of us high tail it from the copper, I ask Florrie, "Is Dad home?"

She shoots me an odd look. "No. Why would you think that?"

"Just thought he might be."

"Fool."

To my relief Jack says, "Fancy heading down to the docks?"

"Got to get back and help with the dinner," Florrie answers. "Besides, after what happened to Georgie, I thought you weren't allowed to go there."

"We're not," Jack answers, wearing a sly grin. Captain Scott can wait. I'll stick with Jack.

In the docks I've met Bretons, Sicilians, Prussians, Belgians and Norwegians, although I hate them now. I've bought onions from Basques, apricots from Egyptians and cocoa once from this giant Senegalese who could lift a hundredweight sack with his teeth. The whole world comes to Gloucester. A few times Jack and me have snuck aboard a ship only to be chased off. Other times we'll clamber inside an idle steam crane and pretend to load cargo or cadge a lift on a wagon and ride around the quays waving to everyone like royalty.

"What were you and Florrie up to?" I ask while we wait for an empty coal wagon to pass through the dock gates.

"Nothing. Just bumped into her outside the Library." Wanting to change the subject he goes on to say, "Must've been scary seeing your pa get carted off."

"After Georgie's funeral, the police told Mum she either sent him up to Coney Hill or they'd ship him off to gaol."

Thankfully Jack keeps quiet as we head towards the Victoria basin where a gang of stevedores unload a cargo of timber from a single funnelled merchant man. As they're on piece rate, the men run from ship to shore with dozens of planks balanced on their shoulders. "Ship's from Oslo," says Jack. "Timber for the match factory." That scoundrel Amundsen pops into my head. "My uncle worked there until he got phossy jaw."

"What's that?"

"The chemicals in the matches turned his bones brittle. The company sacked him and threw him and his family out of their tied cottage. They're staying with us at the minute, although Mum hopes not for too long as she wants to let the room."

"When's your Dad home?"

"Any day now Mum reckons. He's on a merchant man carrying timber from Brazil."

"Long way off."

"Last time he was there, he heard about a tribe of forest dwelling dwarves covered head to toe in tattoos who could stare a man to death."

"Really?"

He nods. "I'm going to go there someday. Australia too, Aden, the Indies, Spice Islands everywhere. Fancy it?"

"Course," I lie, knowing I'll never leave Gloucester.

"Sorry 'bout your pa," a stevedore shouts. Ashamed, I follow Jack towards the north quay where he skims stones but without much joy as the water is choppy owing to a fresh breeze. Chilly, I button my jacket and watch the smoke drifting from the brick factory's chimneys. I raise a hand to my aching mouth and shiver partly because of the cold, but mostly because of my run in with Alf Fenwick and his mates.

"Let's go into Waterman's warehouse," says Jack. I don't want to but can't have Jack thinking me a sissy. Lying empty for ten years after a fire, the three storey warehouse on the west quay has fallen to rack and ruin. Weeds sprout from the roof and chimneys whilst the heavy chains sealing its smoke-blackened doors have grown rusty. They say the warehouse is haunted by the ghost of Billy Stephens, a bargeman's son who went inside in 1893 and never came out. Old timers swear blind they've heard Billy pleading to be rescued.

"Heard there's loot in the cellars," Jack says, trying a near-rotten side window, "Find the treasure, buy meself a brig and set sail for the mysterious Orient." He tests another window. This one opens. He climbs in. I dither. "You scared?" he asks.

"No," I lie.

I crawl through the window and drop down onto a pile of torn-up wooden pallets. The air reeks of bird droppings. Pools of stagnant water stretch out before us. In the far corner, a spiral staircase winds its way through charred floorboards towards the roof, where roosting gulls squawk at the sight of us. A few yards away, wisps of smoke rise from a dying fire. Empty grog bottles mark the path to a set of stone steps leading down into the cellars. Somewhere in the murk, I hear a shuffle of feet followed by a rasping cough.

"No one would ever think to look for a murderer in here," Jack whispers as he follows the bottles towards the stairs. Reaching the top step, he presses a finger to his lips. Perhaps he's waiting for me to say something, but I won't be the first to back out. We descend, the light fading with each step until we're standing in a pitch-black tunnel. A sour breeze blows. Again I want to turn tail, *this is madness*, but Jack sets off, his hand brushing the damp brickwork. "How far we going?" I whisper, already struggling to make him out in the gloom.

"The bend up ahead."

A door slams. Footsteps pound. The echo booms. *It's Billy Stephens.*

"Sod this," says Jack, bolting for the stairs. Heart in mouth I turn to follow him but stumble. Tiny, sharp claws scuttle over my left hand as a bottle smashes against the wall inches above my head. "I'm comin'!" the ghoul hollers.

"Hurry, Tom!" Jack shouts. I stand and sprint towards the stairs. Another bottle flies past me and shatters against the wall. Taking the stairs two at a time we reach the surface and dash through an ankle-deep pool of water towards the gaping window.

"I'll skin ye both!" brays the ghost. Like a shot Jack climbs out, and I've barely got my head and shoulders through the window before I'm grabbed by the ankles and hauled back inside. "Jack! Jack!" I shout clinging to the window's rotten frame. Jack grasps my shoulders and pulls for all he's worth. But he's a boy against a man. Inch by petrifying inch, I'm pulled back inside. In desperation, I kick out. The phantom groans and lets go of me. I scramble outside.

"Fuckers!" the phantom hisses. Too scared to look back, Jack and me hare off and only stop running when we reach the Anselma.

"What was that?" Jack asks, gasping for breath.

"Banshee. Ready to carry us off to hell, like Billy Stephens."

"Didn't know banshees had Gloucester accents. More likely an old tramp or dosser."

But I know what I heard.

After resting, Jack decides to board the Anselma; a long abandoned two-masted brig that once plied between Gloucester, Hamburg, Oslo and Antwerp. To grown-ups she's just an aged wreck waiting for the breakers yard, but to Jack and me the Anselma's been a whaler, a buccaneer and a ship of the line fighting the French at Trafalgar. Lately she's conquering forty-foot waves in the Southern Ocean as we sail for the Antarctic. Jack always gets to be Captain Scott while I have to settle for first lieutenant.

A bargeman, a known drunkard, swore blind he'd seen Georgie Tallow plunge into the dock's waters from the Anselma. Others claim to have seen Georgie's ghost hovering over the water. Like Billy Stephens, I know the story to be a nonsense, but all the same I whisper a prayer as we board.

A football rolls toward me. *"We was playin' five and in."* There's an empty feeling in my stomach.

"Look who's here!" Jack says. I daren't look.

Stan is sat against the forward mast with his knees drawn up to his chest. He's shaking like a leaf and wears a haunted look. "You all right, Stan?" I ask. In an instant he's hugging me. "Florrie sent me to fetch you home for tea. Thought you'd be here. That's when I seen him."

"Who?"

"Georgie. On the forward deck. Just for a second. Then he jumped overboard. Even heard a splash. Reckon I'm cursed, Tom."

CHAPTER SEVEN

Stan's quiet as a mouse walking home and bolts upstairs when we go inside. "What's wrong with him?" Florrie asks, standing at the hob stirring the pot of mutton stew.

"Reckons he saw Georgie's ghost on the Anselma."

"Georgie's ghost?"

I nod. "Do you believe in them?"

"What?"

"Ghosts."

"Course not. Just tales made up to scare children and stupid people. Why, do you?"

I don't think it wise to mention Billy Stephens. I pick her book up from the table. "The Water Babies? What's that about?"

"Children seeking a better life. You should read it."

"Can't see the point in books. Besides, where'd you learn to flatten Ted Pugh?"

"Watching Dad give you and Stan boxing lessons."

"Jack told me you and him were in the library earlier."

"Nothing wrong with educating yourself."

"What's he doing in the library?"

"The same."

"Sailor's got no need for books."

"Whatever gave you that notion?"

"All Jack needs to know is the position of the stars and how to navigate in a south westerly."

"Jack won't go to sea. His uncle's finding him work in the match factory."

"His uncle's been let go."

She looks surprised. "He never told me."

"Doesn't tell you everything does he?" I'm pleased to know something about Jack that she doesn't. "Where's Mum?" I ask.

"In the parlour, with a visitor."

Mum keeps the front parlour for best. She's scrimped for years to furnish it. So far she's bought two armchairs, a table covered with a linen doily, and three dining chairs (the one Dad was lashed to, still hasn't been returned). On the doily stands a photograph of Mum and Dad on their wedding day. Mum just seventeen looking nervous, while Dad is stiff-backed and proud in his Royal Munster's uniform.

Two vases, one blue the other dark green sit, on the mantelpiece guarding my sister Alice's bonnet and my brother Albert's blanket. Born after Florrie and me, Alice died aged six months. All I remember about her is that she cried a lot and we laid her to rest in Exeter cemetery. Mum still lights a candle on her birthday. It's a day on which we've learned to be quiet. Even Stan.

I remember Albie sitting on Mum's lap, laughing as I leaned from the carriage window to catch a handful of steam on the train that brought us to Gloucester from Bristol. Albie perished aged four from a malaise on the brain. Mum cried a lot that day. Dad too. Even though I tried my best, I was too young to feel sad. Mum visits his grave once a week but complains it's getting harder to find amongst the brambles and weeds in the pauper's cemetery.

The parlour door opens and Mum follows a man into the hall. She's been crying. "Thank everyone for their kindness, Dermot," she says shaking his hand.

"Sorry it's not more, but money's tight at the minute. But your Joe's a good sort. Helped a fair few of us down the months." Dermot looks at me. "I'll keep my eye out for work for you on the docks, Tom."

Chuffed to bits, I open the front door. Pastor Davies stands in front of me. As usual I turn queasy upon sight of the founder of the Gloucester Female Mission. He'd arrived from Wales last summer to preach about the evils of drink. Mum is among his dozen or so devotees meaning most Sundays I'm dragged along to listen to his doom-laden prophecies. I never listen, prefer to daydream, although I did enjoy the time a fractious derelict manhandled the pastor outside the Barleymow pub while accusing him of thievery.

After Dermot leaves us, the pastor steps into the hall and booms in his rich Welsh tones, "I come to offer my ministry's succour, Mrs Casey."

"Most kind Pastor, but there's not much you can do for us." The pastor raises his right hand. Mum falls silent. "Mrs Casey, your husband's descent into madness demands we rally round, and being on personable terms with the relieving officer, I have taken the liberty of contacting him to come and assess your circumstances. View this as insurance against even more straightened times that may enfold you."

"Thank you pastor. But I hope matters will not reach that point. Tom has already found work and Florrie will soon start with me in the laundry. We'll manage. Tea? Tom, take the pastor's coat and then make a fresh pot. Best cups." Murphy waddles into the hall, looks at the pastor and growls.

"Lively little fellow, isn't he?" the pastor mutters nervously. Good judge of character, Murphy.

"Take Murphy out Tom," Mum now flustered, orders. I lead Murphy into the kitchen where Florrie asks, "What's he doing here?"

"Gloating."

"I'm starving."

"Have to wait until he leaves. Otherwise he'll help himself to the stew and there's barely enough to go round." Outside, Stan kicks his football against the yard wall.

"Did Stan mention Georgie's ghost?" I ask.

"Course not," Florrie answers. "He just wants some fuss."

Hard woman, Florrie. Even at the age of twelve.

○ ○ ○ ○ ○ ○

As I hand him his tea, the pastor smiles, revealing stained buckteeth. He drinks the scalding brew in three gulps, smacks his lips, and says, "Tea's beneficence should never go unheeded. My mother, a wonderful nurturing soul, believed it should be consumed speedily to ensure all its nutrients are absorbed by the body as efficaciously as possible." He sets the cup down. "Mrs Casey, as I was saying, everyone knows that mental illness is contagious and therefore the public should be protected. My own contention is that madness is the inability to control or moderate one's passions. The means to reform is in discipline and godliness. The asylum provides you respite whilst offering healing for your husband."

"I hope so, pastor. It wasn't easy letting them take Joe, but he'd changed beyond recognition, suspicious of me, the children, everyone. A month ago, he came home gripped by a vile rage and tormented by voices as black as tar."

"What were these voices saying?"

"That he'd pay for letting the Boer women and children starve to death in those camps."

Narrowing his eyes, the pastor replies, "I cannot believe the *British* Empire would ever stoop so low."

"He swore off the drink."

"Alcohol truly is the devil's buttermilk."

"But the blue devil still wouldn't leave him in peace."

The pastor leans forward wearing a pain wracked expression. "Mrs Casey, I cannot comprehend the agonies you are suffering. I know the asylum's superintendent. He is a good man, for a Methodist. If any medic can cure your husband, it is he."

"That is a comfort."

"I will detain you no longer." He stands and by habit straightens his grubby waistcoat and pats down his hair. "Will you be attending next Sunday? You are a living testament to the need for temperance amongst the feckless and the labouring classes. A veritable beacon."

"Of course pastor. Tom also." Her words sting more than Alf's punches.

∘ ∘ ○ ○ ∘ ∘

The screeching banshee trapped inside the chimney keeps me awake. Outside Old Ma bids her visitor goodnight. Stan fidgets.

"Keep still, Stan."

"Can't sleep."

"What's wrong?" I ask, thinking he's still upset from the Anselma.

"Is Dad mad?"

"Course not."

"You're not leavin' are you?"

"No. Go to sleep."

"Why did Georgie die?"

"His time was up."

"Are you sad he died?"

"Course. Why?"

"You didn't look it."

"Just cos I didn't look sad didn't mean I didn't feel sad."

"Am I gonna die?"

"Only if you keep asking stupid questions."

"I swear I saw Georgie's ghost."

"All right, Stan. Now go to sleep."

"Will it come for me in the night?"

"No. But if it does, I'll protect you."

"Promise?"

"Promise."

"Night."

"Night."

A few minutes later Stan is wittering in his sleep. I'm at the window staring down at the Triumph wondering if she can reach Antarctica.

CHAPTER EIGHT

The seven days are up. Mum and me, wearing our Sunday best, set off at eight sharp to fetch Dad home. As we passing the infirmary, a sharpening drizzle dampens my spirits and we trudge on in silence until Mum decides to shelter beneath a tree just outside Gloucester. The rain-soaked driver of a wagon hauling silage, nods as he passes. Mum waves back, after which she holds her hand out feeling for rain. "Just spitting," she mutters, and sets off at a fair lick ordering me to keep up.

A mile or so on, a glowering, red-bricked tower rises above the hedgerows. "Thank goodness," Mum says, "My feet are burning."

With every sodden step the asylum looms larger like a scowling beast, and I recall Alf and his mates endless taunts about me ending up here. And now here I am, certain that if I go in, *they'll* never let me leave. I slow down and stare up at the stern, sheer building rearing up before us. "Come on slow coach," Mum says.

A plinth sits over the main door bearing the words, "Bear ye one another's burdens."

"Can't I wait outside Mum?"

"You'll catch your death in the rain. Besides, Dad will be pleased to see you." It takes the pair of us to heave open the Asylum's oak front door. We step into a high ceilinged foyer. A plain faced woman wearing a high collared, grey dress sits at a desk scribbling into a ledger. The bored, heavyset, blue-uniformed orderly sitting beside her stirs.

"Yes?" the woman asks Mum, while looking her up and down.

"We've come to bring my husband, Joseph Casey home," Mum answers a touch nervily.

"Who?"

"Joseph Casey. He was brought in a week ago." She steps towards the desk beckoning me to follow with a flick of her wrist. The woman runs her finger down the ledger and turns over a page. Her finger stops halfway down. "Here he is. Casey, J, admitted on the eighteenth of November. Imbecility."

She pushes another ledger towards Mum and glances at me. "You sure about the boy accompanying you? He might be unnerved."

"Tom can cope."

You sure, Mum?

"Very well. Sign your names, please."

 38

As Mum writes our names in the visitors book, the woman tells the orderly to take us to Room 9. Looking surprised, he gets to his feet, grunting with the effort. The woman returns to her ledger as the orderly unlocks a green door to the left of the desk and tells us to follow. Expecting an axe-wielding nutter to charge us, I dawdle.

"Keep up Tom," Mum orders, already ten paces ahead, her shoes clacking on the corridor's wooden floor. I hurry after her, my eyes scouring the row of doors lining the hallway, certain evil lurks behind each one.

At the end of the corridor, the orderly unlocks a gate and we step through. My nerves start to settle. Everything seems normal; rattling window panes, people talking and mothers soothing their babies. Outside the rain has stopped and patients, wrapped up in pale blue coats and caps, are at work in the gardens. Bored looking orderlies watch over them on. Perhaps Mum is right. The asylum is a place to rest.

Two women, both older than Mum, and wearing identical high necked dowdy dresses, approach us. "Ida, Ivy," says the orderly, nodding to the pair, who giggle and whisper to each other when they spot me. Passing through another gate, the orderly thanks a young man mopping the floor for sliding his bucket aside to let us pass. The man doesn't answer and carries on with his chores chuntering to himself.

After unlocking another gate the orderly stops four doors along and knocks on a white door with a brass number 9 affixed. A key turns. The door opens a little. "Yes?" asks a man the other side of the door.

"Here to see Casey."

"You sure?"

"Yep," he answers with a shrug of his shoulders.

We go in.

My Dad is trussed up in a straitjacket and behind a table jammed tight against the wall. His face is covered in cuts and bruises. Dad tries to stand but can't shift the table. Mum hurries towards him. I hang back.

"Close enough, missus," says the orderly.

"Why's he bound?" Mum asks.

"He tried to harm himself last night."

"For the best," Dad says, "Fuckin' Boers. Bastards." He looks at me. "Who's this fella, Sal?"

Looking confused, Mum answers, "This is Tom, Joe. Your son."

"I have a son?"

"Your eldest."

"Eldest?" Purple-faced rage replaces his confusion. "Fuck off or I'll chin ye. Fuckin' donkey walloper." Now a fearful cuckold, he shivers and whispers, "Sal, you've brought the sniper." He spits at me. It lands short. "Fuck ye sniper, do your worst. I'm a free-born Irishman. I'll never run from the English." Again he tries to break free. But the table won't budge.

Mum skirts the table, but the orderly grabs her by the arm. "Please, missus. No further."

"Get your hands off her!" Dad shouts. "Touch my Sal again and I'll gut ye."

"It's all right Joe," Mum says.

I want to be gone.

Dad headbutts the table. Three times. The orderlies rush forward, pull the bloodied table away and tip him onto the floor. He looks up at me through wild, blood-hot eyes and rasps, "Anytime sniper."

"You'll have to leave," the orderly shouts.

"I'm staying put," Mum answers.

"Please missus," pleads the orderly who brought us here.

Another man enters and the three of them pin Dad to the floor. Part of me wants to fight them off. Another part of me wants to run. Mum tries to pull one of the orderlies off Dad, tearing a button from his tunic. She's picked up and carried outside. I follow. Dad shouts, "Sal! Sal! My Sal!"

The door is locked from the inside. Mum tries the handle but the door won't open. Inside Dad curses his captors. "Please," Mum begs the orderly.

"Can't, missus. Sorry."

Mum shouts, "I'll be back Joe! Trust me, my love, I'll be back."

"Don't let them take me, Sal!"

The orderly mithers to himself about the missing tunic button, smooths his jacket and unlocks the gate. "This way," he says trying not to lose his rag. The fight having left her, Mum doesn't argue and we move away. The racket in Room 9 fades with each step.

The sun has gone in, creating a furtive, prickly mood. Shouts go up, doors slam and footsteps echo. The two women we saw earlier now cower when we pass. The gardens lay deserted save for an old man sawing a tree branch. The baby has stopped crying.

We reach the green door but the orderly struggles to find the right key. Desperate to be gone, I edge closer to Mum all the while expecting Billy Stephens' ghost to haul me into one of the cells. I'm so on edge, I almost jump out of my skin when Mum takes my hand. "Not a word of this to anyone, Tom," she whispers. "That wasn't your Dad we saw today." She carries on talking, but I'm not listening. I've glimpsed my future; locked in the asylum, trussed up in a straitjacket and beaten down by uniformed brutes.

I can't breathe, with Mum, a hazy apparition talking ten to the dozen. The pastor's wrong. The asylum isn't a sober, orderly place run by Methodists, but a jail holding madness back. Finally, thankfully, the orderly finds the right key and unlocks the door. We hurry into the foyer.

"Mrs Casey?" says the doctor who'd taken Dad away. He's standing beside the stern-faced woman who now looks crestfallen. Mum steps towards him. "Is it right to treat a man who served the Crown so cruelly doctor? Like a wild beast?"

"I apologise, Mrs Casey. You should not have witnessed that."

"And what if I hadn't seen it? What else would you be doing to him?" I'm sure she's going to larrup him. But the doctor's weariness spikes her anger. "Please understand, Mrs Casey, your husband's moods are impossible to predict. One minute he appears fine, the next he is angry, sometimes violent to himself and to the staff. If I had known you were coming I would have made you aware of this so to allow you to prepare yourself."

"It's the brutality of his surroundings and your staff that I should have been prepared for, doctor. How will he get better if you treat him like a caged brute?" The doctor looks stumped. "At least tell me you know what ails Joe."

"My initial findings are that your husband suffers from prolonged bouts of demented schizophrenia."

"So he's not mad?"

"Madness is not a term we use. He is exhibiting prevailing feelings of suspicion and paranoia. We have already observed further deterioration in his mental capacity that can see him become emotional, distressed and hysterical."

"Then let me bring him home. I can look after him. You promised he could come home in seven days. Today is the seventh day."

"It's not that simple, Mrs Casey. Your husband resides in his own world, wrestling with invisible voices. In order to assist his recovery, he needs plenty of rest and to undergo more treatment, including possible chemical restraint to augment the physical restraint."

"So you lied."

"I acted in the best interests of your husband, you, your children and for society's wider good."

"Enough of this footle. We've been through too much to be parted. I vowed to look after him, in sickness and in health. Only God can separate us. Not you."

"That is very admirable, but if your attendance does more harm than good, I can bar you from visiting."

"You wouldn't dare."

"I hope matters will not go so far. But you should know, last night the director signed an order extending your husband's stay for a further four weeks."

"I won't allow it."

"I'm afraid there's nothing you can do."

"Joe's not some piece of flotsam to be tossed overboard and forgotten."

"Please understand, Mrs Casey, this is in everyone's best interests. Visit your husband next week. Hopefully he will be responding to treatment and we can begin at the very least to think about him coming home."

"So I can see Joe next week?"

"Of course."

Under the doctor's gaze we leave. "If that doctor thinks I'm going to give up, he's got another thing coming," Mum mutters. "Fifteen years we've been together. Even the Boers couldn't part us. No matter what state he got himself into, your dad always found his way home to me. He will again. Mark my words Tom."

"Yes, Mum."

"Come with me next week to see him. You heard the doctor. Dad will be in better spirits."

I heard no such thing. But I won't come. Don't want to see Dad all trussed up, battered and bruised. Like Scott, he'll have to endure. A different set of hardships, perhaps harder, but he must overcome them, for Mum's sake if nothing else.

CHAPTER NINE

Owing to Mum's feet, the walk home takes ages and we stop every few minutes to let her rest. But at least the rain keeps off. By the time we reach the cathedral it's almost mid-day. We go inside. The cathedral offers a peace and stillness at odds with the asylum's rage. Even the odd, echoing cough sounds heaven-sent.

"Fifteen when I first met your father," Mum says while staring up at one of the giant stained glassed windows. "Thought myself the luckiest girl in the world when we began courting. Me a plain little thing, and Joe so handsome. Funny too. A real charmer, the sweetest words dripping from his tongue. Thought all my dreams had come true. My dad took against him though."

"Why?"

"In his book, Irishmen are thieves or liars. So marrying an Irish soldier, and one a few years older, seemed to be the worst of all worlds. He thought I could do much better for myself. But when love stirs, you become reckless. Dad was furious when he found out we'd wed. Banished me from the house and forbade my mum, sisters and brothers, from having anything to do with me. Even when Joe left for South Africa, leaving me with you, Florrie and Alice, to look after, he wouldn't relent."

"He sounds stubborn."

"Florrie takes after him. But I do miss Mum." Taking my hand she says, "She helped bring you into the world. Two days you took to come out of me, as if you'd a notion how hard life would be. Last time I set eyes on her was seven years ago, at Exeter station while waiting to set off for Bristol. She writes on occasion but she'll never visit. Too afraid of what Dad might do if he found out. I was the only one who stood up to him. Caught a tongue-lashing and the belt a few times because of it."

"Why did you leave Exeter?"

"Your dad returned from Africa a different man. Haunted, broken, unable to settle. So we upped sticks and moved to Bristol. And when that didn't work out we moved here, with your dad promising me the life of a princess. Some dreams don't come true though. Marrying him was the best and worst thing I've done."

The cathedral bells strike midday. She grips the pew in front and hauls herself up. "Best get our skates on, the pastor's expecting us."

I'd forgotten about the Mission.

THE STEAM CATCHER

∘ ∘ ○ ○ ∘ ∘

It's three o'clock and I'm standing outside the Leopard pub with Mum and the other Mission members. Two of them struggle to keep the Mission's banner upright in the breeze. The plain green standard shows two golden chubby Angels, blowing trumpets with the words 'Temperance' and 'Godliness' pouring from the spout of each instrument.

The pastor clears his throat. It will be the fourth time I'll hear his sermon as we've already picketed the Talbot, the Barleymow and the Wheatsheaf. A few strolling families stop to listen. As usual I don't understand his blathering and fancy words; idolatrous, intoxication, and indolence. He wants to smite this and smite that and asks the angel of something-or-other to save the feckless and waifs. All the while Mum and the other Missionaries nod in agreement.

To my horror, Alf Fenwick and a couple of his langers appear. "Off his onion Casey!" Alf shouts. Mum, forgetting her station, shouts back, "I'll be round to see your Mother, Alf Fenwick!" Her outburst draws the pastor's ire. Alf and his pals sidle off, laughing, at which point the Mission burst into 'Crown Him With Many Crowns'. Mum thrusts the hymnbook under my nose and tells me to join in. Two men, worse for wear, fall to their knees, doff their caps and slur, "Pray for us, Father."

"I shall."

"Pray for a few pennies to turn up so we can afford another round," one of them says. Laughing, the pair help each other up and stagger on.

"Pay no heed," the pastor orders. His mousey, pooterish wife strikes up 'Abide With Me'. We all join in. When the singing stops, the Leopard's portly landlord pokes his bald head through the bar doors and asks. "Scuse me pastor, I know you're being worshipful, but saving drinkers' souls must be a thirsty business. Can I offer you and these upstanding ladies in your company some refreshment? Alcohol-free of course. On the house."

"Emlyn," says the pastor's wife, "remember your sacred vow to never cross the threshold of such a den."

"Thank you for reminding me, dear."

"Couldn't somebody else go? I'm parched," says one of the banner holders.

"No female Missionary may go," insists the pastor's wife. "Stoked by strong liquor, those men inside will be bent on fornication and wantonness."

"Tom can go," Mum says, to everyone's surprise. Handing me a penny she whispers, "Drop this into the wish bottle."

Inside the pub, the fug of cigarette smoke stings my eyes. Some men recognise me and nod. Dropping the penny into the wish bottle, I wish Dad home.

Moments later, with the landlord holding the bar door open for me, I bring out a tray laden with glasses of ginger ale. The pastor reaches for a glass but his wife grabs his wrist. "Emlyn, accepting a libation from such a place is how the corruption begins." The sheepish pastor leaves his ginger ale untouched.

With thirsts quenched, I return the glasses. The landlord asks, "How's your pa?"

"On the mend."

"Glad to hear it. He's a good man. A valued customer." He beckons me closer, the smell of fags and beer about him. "Can you remind the pastor of the twenty bob I agreed to cough up if he stayed clear of here but picketed the Goat and the Hauliers." He slips me a shilling. "Not a word to anyone." Confused, I nod and go outside to see the pastor loping off in lanky strides with his flock struggling to keep up. I have to run to catch him.

"Pastor, the landlord asked me to remind you about your agreement. Something to do with twenty bob a week?" He stops dead, and says, "Onwards to the Hauliers Arms ladies, young Thomas wishes to ask me about a passage in the scriptures." Mum looks relieved.

The pastor smiles his toothy smile. "Thank you for reminding me, Thomas. The landlord is a man of faith, but the hours of his trade preclude him from regular attendance. We have an informal arrangement to allow him to worship in a more temporal manner. Could you keep this matter to yourself?" He hands me a shilling. "For your troubles." I wonder how many more arrangements he's made with other landlords.

We reach the Hauliers Arms, the haunt of thieves and scallywags, whose landlord allows pinched loot to be sold in return for a cut. I wonder if the police have heeded Mum's words and questioned him about Georgie's death.

The banner is planted and the trumpeting angels unfurled. 'Nearer to Thee my God,' is belted out but at the start of the second verse, a spittoon flies from the public bar and clatters at the pastor's feet. The banner crumples and the pastor's wife sits on the kerb after suffering a palpitation. Despite the ungodliness outside the Hauliers, it is agreed that the day has been a success with two or three consciences pricked about the perils of drink.

Reaching home, Mum sighs as she sits and asks Florrie to heat a pan of water so she can soak her aching feet. Stan's in the back yard playing football.

"Who brought that in?" Mum asks, pointing to the small bag of coal sitting by the fire.

Filling the kettle Florrie answers, "Stan. He said now that Dad's gone we all need to muck in."

"I hope he hasn't pinched it. Last thing we need is a thief in the family."

I take the atlas from the mantelpiece and go upstairs. I retrieve the canister holding my money from beneath the fire grate. With the two shillings I've earned today, in all I've nine shillings and sixpence to my name. More than enough to reach the South Pole. I open the atlas and study the half drawn map of Antarctica wondering how long it will take for me to find Scott.

My plan is coming together.

CHAPTER TEN

It's still dark. Ice frosts the bedroom window. Sound asleep, Stan lays curled around his football. I slip out of bed and get dressed, pull on my other jumper and reach for my balaclava and gloves. I empty the canister and creep downstairs, praying the creaking steps will not betray me. The kitchen is in darkness. Murphy lying by the fire, jumps up to greet me.

I think about taking a slice of bread and dripping for the journey, but desperate to get away,. I step into the yard and heave the tarpaulin off the Triumph.

"Where you off to?" a half asleep Stan asks, watching me wheel the bike into the alley. Murphy is beside him.

"Taking the Triumph for a spin."

"Can I come?"

"No. Go back to bed."

"Please."

"No."

Sulking, Stan heads inside. I mount the Triumph, put on my balaclava and gloves and begin to paddle. The engine won't start. I dismount and stare at the machine, its pipes and levers a mystery. Fool. I haven't turned the fuel tap on.

I remount and paddle again. The engine starts. I put the bike in gear, twist the throttle and set off. The engine dies. After five minutes of fiddling and cursing, the engine fires and I pootle along the alley towards Southgate Street which lays empty except for the ramshackle houses and pubs lining it. I switch on the head lamp and head south towards the Antarctic.

Despite the balaclava, extra jumper and gloves, the cold cuts through me. But I press on and leave Gloucester, still heading south along a narrow lane surrounded by woods. Despite the cold and the jarring ride, it's thrilling to follow the narrow beam of light thrown out by the headlamp. The woods thin as I crest a hill. I pull up and with my breath hanging in the freezing dawn air, I take one last look at Gloucester. It's exciting but scary being on the edge of the unknown. My stomach rumbles.

I should've brought the bread and dripping. I won't reach Antarctica without breakfast. And I'm freezing. Despite my advancing lunacy, Mum still needs me. Best go home, stock up on provisions and strike out for Antarctica next week or the week after. No rush. Captain Scott's going to be ages yet. Am I a coward? Probably.

Freewheeling downhill, the engine fires and I head home. It starts to rain forcing me to crawl along at barely walking pace, but I still manage to tip the bike while rounding a muck-strewn bend. "Like the smell of shit do you?" says the farmer bringing his herd up for milking as I scrape cow muck off myself.

The farmer gives me a push, and I set off with his collie running alongside until I reach the junction with the main Bristol Road. I should have followed that route to begin with. Next time.

Murphy yaps as I push the bike into the yard. I'm soaked to the skin. Mum is on the back step. Stan's behind her, smirking. Mum's hand catches the top of my head. Despite the sodden balaclava, my ear stings.

"Where have you been?"

"Took the Triumph for a run."

My other ear stings. "Gallivanting about the county? What if you had an accident? How could I afford the infirmary? Haven't I enough on my plate, without having to worry about you taking off on that device?" Waving at the Triumph she says, "There's a place that sells these things on Westgate Street. I want it gone."

"But what'll Dad say when he gets home?"

"Leave that to me." She goes inside. Stan sticks his tongue out. I throw a punch but he ducks and I hit the doorframe.

CHAPTER ELEVEN

Outside Williams motorcycle shop, a tall man wearing a ten guinea suit and reeking of pomade is smoking a cigarette. "Where'd you get this beauty?" he asks as I dismount the Triumph and rub my bruised knuckles.

"It's my dad's. I'm here to sell it."

"Where did he get it from?"

"He helped a fella."

"Nice to hear. We could all do with a bit more of that spirit." He circles the bike. "Does he know you're selling it?"

"He's gone away."

"How long for?"

"Not sure. A fair while though." He rocks the bike back and forth. "Seems in reasonable nick. This model has the German magneto."

Clueless, I nod and tell him, "Barely been ridden these past few months."

"Since your dad went away." He smirks, opens the shop door and calls out. A balding, crafty looking man in greasy overalls appears. "This young man wants to sell his dad's Triumph 3 ½. Take her for a run out." The mechanic nods, wipes his hands on his overalls and mounts the bike. He sets off towards Gloucester Cross. Suit man invites me to take a look around the shop.

The smell of oil, rubber and metal greets me; the scent and promise of speed. Among the motorcycles for sale, is a Triumph, the same model as mine. The price tag hanging from the handlebars shows twenty-two pounds. The patriot was generous to a fault.

Another bike catches my eye. It has dropped handlebars, sits low to the ground, and sports a purple teardrop fuel tank with a huge brass headlight perched on the steering column. More animal than machine. "Beauty, ain't she?" suit man says. "Rudge. Bored out to seven horsepower. Had eighty-five out of her. Sit on her if you like." I straddle the bike and stretch along the fuel tank and grip the handlebars wondering what flying along at eighty-five miles an hour feels like.

The mechanic returns. He dismounts and touches the Triumph's cylinder head with the back of his hand and then draws out the spark plug and sniffs it.

"Well?" suit man asks.

"She is in good nick. Compression fine, not too much oil on the plug."

Suit man weighs me up. "You sure she's yours to sell?"

I nod.

"Ten pounds, no questions asked." Ten Pounds! A fortune!

"Fifteen," I say. The mechanic stifles a laugh. I ignore him and say, "You said yourself she's in good nick, good compression, no oiling."

"Eleven."

"Fifteen."

"Twelve. My last offer. Doubt anybody else in Gloucester will take it off your hands."

"Is that a fair price?" I ask the mechanic. He glances at suit man.

"More than fair."

"Twelve pounds it is," I answer. We shake hands.

"There's something else," says suit man. "You strike me as a lad with an eye for motorcycles. I'm looking for an apprentice. Interested?"

"What's the pay?"

"Twelve bob a week." *Twelve bob!*

"Will I get to ride the bikes?"

"Do a good job and we'll see. What's your name?"

"Tom Casey."

"You working, Tom Casey?"

"Over at the tannery."

He screws up his face. "You're well shot of that place. Monday morning, eight sharp. I don't like malingerers."

∘ ∘ ○ ○ ∘ ∘

Florrie is sitting in Dad's chair reading while Stan pets Murphy. Mum is at the sink peeling potatoes. She sets the knife down, wipes her hands on a tea towel and asks, "Well?"

"Twelve pounds."

The three of them look at me with disbelief. Even Murphy seems taken aback. "Twelve?" Mum gasps. I nod and one by one, set the pound notes on the table.

"Never seen such a fortune," Florrie mutters.

"We've staved off the parish," says Mum.

"Got a new job as well," I tell her. "Apprentice at the motorcycle shop. Eleven bob a week."

Mum and Florrie reel around the kitchen. Murphy yaps while Stan goes outside to play football. Maybe our troubles are coming to an end, and maybe Dad will be home soon.

There's a knock on the front door. Could it be?

"Pastor Davies," says Mum says opening the door. She looks surprised. Following Mum into the kitchen, the pastor eyes up the pound notes. Again just being near him makes me feel sick.

"Let me share our good news, pastor," Mum says struggling to hide her glee. "We've sold Joe's motorcycle."

He smiles. "My prayers have been answered."

"Heaven sent. Enough to keep our heads above water for a good few months."

"The godly are never forfeited in Jesus's plans."

"Amen, pastor. Tea?" He nods.

"Best cups, Florrie."

Closing his eyes the pastor says, "Oh Lord, bring your blessing upon this household. A family until recently in dire straits, who by adhering to the scriptures have kept the darkness from their door." He takes Mum's hand. "Your good fortune is most deserved."

"Tom's also secured employment at the motorcycle shop." The pastor smiles at me. My stomach churns. Catching herself Mum says, "Forgive me pastor, in all the excitement I forgot to ask why you are calling. Not that it isn't always a pleasure to see you."

"As it is to cross your threshold, Mrs Casey." He straightens his waistcoat and runs a finger along his shirt collar. Outside Stan's football thumps against the yard wall. "I had wished to raise the Mission's banner with you. Not literally, of course." He sniggers, and again eyes the money. "I think the banner needs to be more eye catching and possessing greater spiritual oomph. My dear wife thinks the sermon on the mount would make a fine setting with the inscription reading, 'Free thyself from intoxication and Jesus will enter thy Hearts'.

"Beautiful sentiments," Mum answers.

"I'm glad you concur, Mrs Casey. Of course such an undertaking will not be cheap and with the Mission's funds stretched."

Mum raises her hand. Now it's the pastor's turn to fall silent. "Fate and fortune have combined pastor. I am in a position to help." Florrie pours the tea looking daggers at the pastor.

"Please, Mrs Casey, you have the children to think about."

"Pastor. Your crusade to help those weighed down by drink must be supported." She hands him two pounds. In one swift movement he takes the pound notes and stuffs them into his trouser pocket. "Bless you, Mrs Casey. Our work can continue with a renewed vim." After drinking his scalding tea in two mouthfuls he turns to me and says, "Thomas, in your father's absence a great burden has fallen upon you. Please be assured I am here to offer my counsel." It's all I can do not to throw up over him.

○ ○ ○ ○ ○ ○

"A great burden Thomas," Florrie says mimicking the pastor's Welsh accent after he leaves.

"What does he mean?" I ask her. "I'm not Dad. I've no stories to tell or songs to sing."

"You're a fool sometimes Tom. We couldn't cope without you, Stan especially."

"Stan?"

"He worships the ground you walk on."

"But being a man means being strong, tough, a provider."

"There's other qualities Tom; steadfastness, loyalty and honesty."

"I'm none of those. I'm a boy pretending to be a man, without a clue how to provide for my family. All I'm certain of is ending up in Coney Hill. Everyone knows madness runs in families."

Florrie shakes her head and studies me. She's up to something. "How many secrets have you got?"

"One or two," I answer, hoping to sound mysterious even if my one secret is stashed in the fireplace.

"Dad had serious, big secrets. Much bigger that yours or mine. Remember when he came back from Africa?"

I'd turned five when this silent stranger turned up out of the blue. It took weeks before I'd worked up the courage to speak to him.

"He's been trapped by his secrets ever since. In Africa, Ireland, Exeter, Bristol and now here. But he couldn't run from his past forever. That's where his demons lie. You don't share his past so how can you share his madness?"

I want to believe her. After all, she reads books. But best of all she has certainty.

CHAPTER TWELVE

The mechanic is slumped over his workbench. He plays skittles most Sundays, which means he's hungover most Mondays. I pass the spot where Dad's Triumph stood, before a posh bloke from Monmouth bought it, and by habit whisper, "Morning, Dad."

I still can't believe I work in a place where nobody cares that I'm Mad Joe Casey's son. True, the mechanic can be a miserable so-and-so at times, but I love watching him working on the bikes, marvelling how odd-shaped bits of metal with strange names like magneto or piston, can make a machine go faster than a galloping horse.

Thinking the coast clear, I mount the Rudge, grip the handlebars and imagine hurtling along the roads at near one hundred miles an hour. "What you up to?" the mechanic asks, wheeling a bike through the showroom. He looks like death warmed up and even though he's ten feet away I can smell the stale beer on his breath. "Boss'll have your guts for garters if he catches you on that."

I clamber off, expecting the bollocking to carry on. Instead he lights a cigarette, rubs the sleep from his eyes and says, "Need you to take this Blackburne for a run out."

After firing the Blackburne up he says, "Bring her back in one piece."

Delighted finally to get the chance to ride, I put the bike in gear and set off. Straightaway the steering pulls to the left. Outside the Hippodrome, distracted by the handling, I brush a trick cyclist trying to drum up an audience. He falls off and hollers after me. I pretend not to hear and ride off, fighting the heavy steering.

Reaching Gloucester Cross I have to turn in a slow, wide arc and force a gang of navvies digging up the road to leap clear. With their curses ringing in my ears I set off on the return leg of barely a mile but fraught with slow, wobbly danger. I crawl passed the Hippodrome aware of the cyclist's glare and have to swerve to avoid a postman stepping into the road without looking. All the same he has the nerve to shout after me.

"All right?" The mechanic asks as I pull up outside the shop.

"Steering seems off." Best not mention the cyclist, navvies or postman.

He wheels the bike into the workshop where he dismantles the Blackburne's steering column. "As I thought, the column bearings are shot," he says, handing me scored steel balls. "No lubrication. Shoddy workmanship's always the case with Blackburne's. Triumphs are the way to go. Remember that."

Pointing to an engine sitting on the bench he says, "Reckon you can strip and rebuild that?" I nod even though I'm clueless where to begin. Lighting a cigarette he says, "You've got two hours. I'm going for a kip out the back."

Although nervous to begin with, I'm soon caught up in this measured, precise world and its heady scents of petrol, oil, and metal. Drawing on the hours spent watching the mechanic, I dismantle the engine, noting the sequence in which I've removed each part. I hold some parts up to the light and admire them. Most people would see lumps of metal but to me they're more beautiful than the Crown jewels.

"Not bad, Casey," the mechanic says, inspecting the rebuilt engine. I'm chuffed. "Looks like you forgot about this." He holds up a tiny spring. I'm crushed. He laughs. "Just kidding. Good job. Got a Rudge to reassemble tomorrow. Fancy giving me a hand?"

"Please!"

"You can head off home if you like."

I cross the road to avoid the Hippodrome where a strong man, his moustache slicked, neck veins bulging, lifts a giant dumb bell above his head watched by a gaggle of onlookers. There's no sign of the cyclist.

With time to kill I take a detour to the docks and sit awhile on the west quay watching a single-masted ketch being unloaded. The ship's lights glow in the early evening gloom as men run back and forth across its decks.

Today has been a good day, riding the Blackburne, rebuilding the engine and earning the mechanic's trust.

I glance over to the Anselma. Someone is portside, staring into the inky water. Behind me a shout goes up. I turn to look but hear a splash. Whoever was aboard the Anselma has disappeared. *Georgie's ghost?* Time to go home.

There's a group of kids outside the house chanting over and over, "Mad Joe's in Coney Hill, looney, looney, looney." They scarper when Florrie comes out and manages to scrag the ringleader, Fred Tallow, by the collar. She marches him across the street and knocks on the Tallow's front door. Mrs Tallow answers. No words are spoken as Fred bolts inside and his mum shuts the door in Florrie's face.

When Mum's not working or visiting Dad, she spends her time at the Mission falling ever deeper under the pastor's spell. It's left to Florrie to cook, wash, clean and look after Stan, all the while holding down her job at the laundry. Like Mum, Florrie won't brook cheek. Even Jack has caught the back of her tongue once or twice. "No doubt the cheeky beggars will be back tomorrow," she says to me outside the house. "At least the Tallows are talking to us again. Sort of."

"How long's this been going on for?"

"A few days. Stan got into a scrap with Fred after Fred taunted him about Dad. Red rag to a bull. Ever since, Fred and his mates have been goading Stan. I've tried speaking to Mrs Tallow, but, well, you've just seen for yourself."

"He never let on."

"Doubt you'd have noticed if he did. All you think about is your precious motorcycles these days. Mum's the same, caught up in the pastor's weasel words."

"When Dad comes home, she'll be back to her old self."

"When will that be?"

"Soon."

"Hope so. We can't go on like this."

∘ ∘ ○ ∘ ∘

As Florrie dishes up tea, Mum comes in. As usual after visiting Dad, she's wrapped up in the asylum's darkness and her strong, proud features have frayed a touch more. Without speaking, she takes her Bible down from the mantelpiece and goes into parlour, only returning after we've finished eating. "Put your coats on," she says, "We're going to the Hippodrome."

"Thought the pastor considered it to be a place of intoxication and licentiousness," Florrie says.

"What he doesn't know won't harm him. Chop, chop, before I change my mind."

I hope the cyclist isn't performing.

∘ ∘ ○ ∘ ∘

While Mum queues up to buy tickets, Stan, Florrie and me study a poster announcing the turns; Monsieur Velo, Cycliste Extraordinaire; Chief Tomahawk, the Cheyenne Legend, Moira O'Shea, singer of laments, Giggles McKiernan and his funny bone, the legendary escapologist Mysterio. Best of all though the tribute to Captain Scott, back by popular demand.

Mum is puffed out by the time we reach our seats in the near empty but still smoky dress circle. To my relief, Monsieur Velo is leaving the stage as Stan and Florrie peer over the balcony to watch two drunks cause a kerfuffle in the stalls. I study the rosy-cheeked cherubs floating around the gilded ceiling, playing fiddles, strumming guitars, and blowing into flutes, and wonder what life would be like if I could fly.

The lights dim. Florrie and Stan sit either side of me as Chief Tomahawk arrives on stage. Chubby and wearing a feather head-dress, and a buckskin tunic and britches he shuffles from side to side while chanting a strange but soothing tune. "Rain Dance," Stan whispers. How he knows this is beyond me. The chanting drags on, the drunks heckle and my worn, squeaky seat grows uncomfortable. Thankfully the Chief falls silent and his squaw, Running Wolf, stands before of a sheet of plywood painted with strange symbols. "Totem Pole," Stan mutters.

Running Wolf's braids droop as she lowers her head. From fifteen feet away, Chief Tomahawk hurls an axe. The plywood flexes as the axe buries itself in the wood inches from Running Wolf's head. The Chief hurls half a dozen more axes all the while whooping and hollering. Each axe lands nearer to Running Wolf than the previous one. Unable to watch I close my eyes, expecting to hear a blood curdling scream. "You can look now, scaredy cat," Florrie whispers as Running Wolf now shorn of her braids steps away from the splintered plywood peppered with six, bristling, glistening tomahawks.

"Thought she'd lose her head," Stan says watching the Chief and Running Wolf shuffle off stage, singing their strange, earthy song.

The Strongman, all bulging muscles and tight leotard, first raises a giant set of dumb bells above his head. He follows up by using only his teeth to lift first two and then four nervous looking men laying on a pallet. Stan is agog, even more so when the Strongman folds in a half a bicycle frame, iron bar and finally a cast iron skillet. Even the drunks' applaud. I wonder if the bike belongs to Monsieur Velo.

Giggles McKiernan struggled to raise a laugh while Moira O'Shea's songs bored Stan and me stiff but had Mum in floods of tears, especially the lament about a couple forever parted by war.

A tall, imposing man wearing a fur jacket and leggings hauls a sled on stage. He climbs out of the straps, lowers his hood and takes off his goggles. He sports a fine beard. I shush Stan who's still prattling on about the Strongman. The Explorer is alone. Strange. I was sure he'd pitch a tent and have a penguin or two with him. Stranger still there's a sadness about him. Scott would never be sad.

He waits for silence before saying. "Ladies and gentlemen, tonight I had planned to pay tribute to that great Englishman, Captain Robert Falcon Scott. Alas, I have just received tragic news. Captain Scott is dead." The world slows. A blur of confusion fills my mind. "Scott was the best of us, an Englishman who endured unfathomable hardship with stoicism and fortitude. He and the brave men who perished with him have stirred our hearts." His voice faltering, he continues, "Scott, Oates, Evans and Wilson. Men who gave their lives for England. There are no words. But please join me in singing the National Anthem."

Throttled by sadness and struck dumb I can only stare at the Explorer. *How did Scott die? Where did they find him? Did he reach the Pole? Did he beat Amundsen? Does this mean I'll never leave home?* The questions spin and tease me right through the anthem and as the Explorer straps himself to the sled and hauls it off stage in slow, grief stricken steps.

Whatever spell traps me is shattered by the crash of cymbals. A plume of dense white smoke draws our eyes back to the stage where a short, wiry man wearing a top hat and cape now stands. Amid more crashes and flashes he makes a girl disappear from a cabinet, puts a man in a trance and saws the girl who disappeared a few minutes earlier, in half. Everyone watches in rapt silence until a voice bellows, "Now ladies and gentleman, the great Mysterio will perform an escape so dangerous his mortal soul will be in peril. If you are of a nervous disposition please leave the auditorium now. If however you wish to witness the Eighth Wonder of the World please stay."

Mysterio departs the stage as two burly men wheel a tank full of water onstage. A minute or two later the magician returns wearing just his britches and shirt. The men bind his legs with chains and place a straitjacket on him. "Dad wears one of those," Stan says as Mysterio is raised into the air before being lowered headfirst into the tank.

"Barely a minute to free himself or he perishes." The voice booms. Scott forgotten, I see Dad fighting his bindings and picture Georgie clawing at the water in the docks. A crashing cymbal tears me from memory as Mysterio wriggles and squirms while trying to escape the straitjacket. Florrie's fingernails dig into my wrist as the conjurer first frees his right and then his left arm before yanking the straitjacket over his shoulders and letting it sink to the bottom of the tank.

He sets about the shackles, his long black hair streaming in the water. He's a blur of motion, hands tearing at the chains with plumes of air bubbles drifting around him. Drums roll, cymbals crash, the smoky haze grows ever thicker. Mum leans forward, giddy at the awful sight before her. Mysterio's grip weakens, his frantic efforts slowing until he falls still and the air bubbles tail off.

"Save him!" Florrie hollers.

"Please!" shouts Stan.

A stage hand grabs a large axe propped against the tank and readies to smash the glass. But miraculously Mysterio slips his shackles and clambers to the surface. He's helped from the tank and chest heaving, he accepts the applause with a series of deep bows his face hidden beneath the shock of sopping, black hair.

"A man who cheats death, a contortionist without parallel. Mysterio!" Booms the voice.

The stage curtain drops. The house lights go up.

"Is Dad an escapologist now?" asks Stan, squinting in the brightness.

"If you want him to be Stanley," Mum answers.

"I do."

"Then he is."

"I'd like to be one."

"Work hard, say your prayers and you never know."

"Do you think so?"

"I do, Stanley."

"Tom wants to be an explorer." I want to belt him. Don't want anybody knowing. They'll just scoff at the notion.

"I can see that," Mum says, "Although he's quiet, there's something extraordinary about our Tom." Embarrassed, I don't know where to look.

"Will he be as famous as me?" asks Stan.

"Nearly. Now, who fancies a bun?"

○ ○ ○ ○ ○ ○

Stan, his mouth caked in icing sugar, re-enacts each of the Hippodrome's turns as we walk home but comes unstuck with Mysterio. Worse still when we reach home, Mum sends him to bed for trying to bend the skillet in half. He's still wide awake when I go up and has his shirt on back to front with his arms threaded through the sleeves. "I'm practicing my escapologmagism Tom. I found one of Dad's jackets."

There's a knock on the front door. Odd for this hour. I go downstairs.

Mum's at the door, one hand on the latch, the other holding her lamp. She's on edge as if she knows who's outside. There's another knock. This one louder, more persistent.

Mum opens the door. Two suited men are standing outside. Both bruisers.

CHAPTER THIRTEEN

"Is this the home of Joseph Casey?" demands the older of the two in a broad Liverpudlian accent.

"Yes," says Mum.

"I'm Detective Sergeant Manning, and this is Detective Constable Wilson from the Special Irish Branch of the Metropolitan Police." Without waiting to be asked, they step inside. Manning gestures to Wilson to go upstairs.

"Where's he going?" Mum asks as Wilson turns on a torch and climbs the stairs.

"Searching for evidence."

"What evidence?"

"He'll know when he finds it."

"What's Joe supposed to have done?"

"Conspiracy and aiding and abetting a murderer."

"How? He's in the asylum. He's not well."

"So he claims."

"Ask the doctors up there, they'll tell you."

"We did. Yesterday. He's either a loon or a very fine actor."

"So it was you," Mum says anger now replacing her unease.

"What do you mean?" Manning answers, not quite so cocksure.

"They wouldn't let me see Joe today. Locked him in a padded cell. Hysterical they said. What did you say to him?"

Manning's poise slips a little further. Torchlight heralds Wilson's return. Stan, still with his shirt on back to front, follows him.

As Wilson searches the parlour, Manning asks Mum, "Does the name Cornelius Danaher mean anything to you?"

"No. Should it?"

"On the fourteenth of May last year, Cornelius Danaher shot two policemen in New Street, Birmingham, whilst committing a bank robbery to secure funds for the Irish Republican Brotherhood."

"Who are they?" I ask, guessing who Dad's Irish Patriot was.

"Fenians," Wilson spat from the parlour door. He's holding Albie's blanket.

"Give that to me," Mum shouts, snatching at the blanket. But Wilson doesn't let go. The blanket splits. "Whoops," Wilson says, handing over the blanket to Mum. She folds it and raises it to her cheek, once more lost to us in her grief. Florrie lunges for Wilson but I hold her back. Murphy snarls. Wilson levels his torch at Florrie forcing her to shield her eyes with her right hand.

In the murk Manning, once more in control, brushes his overcoat and continues, "Constable Warwick died of his wounds, while Constable Evans lost an eye. Danaher fled the scene on a motorcycle and subsequently left Birmingham by barge, on the evening of the fourteenth. The barge arrived at Gloucester docks on the evening of sixteenth, where upon he was smuggled aboard the German brig, the Hanover, which sailed for Kiel that evening. We want to know who arranged Danaher's passage aboard the Hanover."

"What's this go to do with Joe?" Mum, now back with us, asks.

"Your husband is known for his Republican sympathies."

"Nonsense. He served in India and South Africa under Lord Kitchener."

"He's been heard mouthing seditious oaths in Exeter, Bristol and now in Gloucester."

"What seditious oaths?"

"About a free Ireland."

"Joe is a loyal servant to the Crown. It's his duty that's landed him in the asylum."

"Your husband's political sympathies have been corroborated. And we have established that he has owned a pistol, and a motorcycle, and was working in the docks the night Danaher fled."

"The pistol don't fire," I pipe up.

"Irrelevant," says Manning waving away my words. "He bought a gun. Why?"

"Dockers come across all sorts of things. I played cowboys and Indians with it. Didn't mean any harm."

"Does that make us subversives as well?" Florrie says, looking Manning in the eye. "You going to arrest us for playing cowboys and Indians?"

"Bright as a button aren't you?" He answers. "Ever had your mouth washed out with soap?"

"Please, sergeant, we want no trouble," says Mum.

"Neither do we, Mrs Casey." He takes a breath. "Now, where did your husband get the funds to buy a motorcycle?"

"It's not what you think. Joe's not like that. He's a good man."

"No doubt." He wipes his mouth and breaks into a dishonest smile. "Did Cornelius Danaher lay up here?"

"No."

"Do *you* share your husband's political sympathies?"

"Ireland holds no interest. My time is taken up with raising my family, caring for my husband, and my faith."

"So you've never discussed the Irish question with him?"

"Of course not."

In the kitchen, while Wilson searches the pitch-black yard, Manning points to the Bible, the Charles Dickens book and the tatty atlas on the mantelpiece. "Who's the reader in the family?" he asks.

"Me," answers Florrie.

"Dangerous things, books. Can give you all sorts of ideas."

"Perhaps you should try it then." Half smiling, Manning retrieves a creased letter from inside his jacket. He holds the letter beneath the gaslight beside the mantelpiece and reads, "Furthermore, I worry my daughter has fallen under the spell of this wild man Casey, who since returning from Africa continues to spout poison about the king, empire and Britain with particular bile reserved for the position of Ireland."

"Who wrote that?" Florrie asks.

"My dad," Mum whispers.

Manning continues, "I pass on my concerns after reading about the constables' shooting and the murderer's escape via Gloucester docks, where my son-in-law now works. It is entirely possible that he is caught up in this enterprise." Manning studies Mum, her dad's words hanging between them. "You see, Mrs Casey? Even your father thinks your husband's a traitor."

"I never knew his hatred burned so deep," Mum says looking all at sea. "Please sergeant, Joe may have some funny ideas about Ireland, but all Irishmen do. He's a good man. He'd never harbour a traitor."

"Your father has his doubts."

"All clear," Wilson says, returning from the yard.

Manning lifts the Bible from the mantelpiece and runs his finger along its creased spine. "Always heartening to see the good book well thumbed." The dishonest smile returns. "Tell me, Mrs Casey, are you comfortable with shame?"

"What do you mean?"

"Your husband's banishment to the asylum must have caused a stir. I suspect those you thought were your friends have all but abandoned you. Just imagine what they'd think if you were led away in shackles in broad daylight. I daresay the people round here are wary of newcomers at the best of times. No doubt the youngsters have had a tough time. Bullied at school, picked on in the street. Menial work, with no prospects."

"We get by."

"Of course. But remember how your neighbours reacted to finding a lunatic in their midst. What would they say if that madman were charged with child murder? And what would they do upon discovering the madman *and* his family were also traitors. I'd doubt they'd take kindly to such news. After all, they've only their patriotism to warm the cockles of their flinty hearts."

"We've done nothing wrong."

"We'll see," Manning answers, savouring Mum's unease. "Shame, more than fear, loosens the tongue." He touches the brim of his hat. "We'll see ourselves out."

Wilson whispers, "Sorry for your loss."

"What's a traitor Tom?" Stan asks me after the coppers leave.

Dad, I think to myself.

CHAPTER FOURTEEN

Dear Mr Shackleton,

My name is Tom Casey. My sister Florrie brought home from the library an advertisement she'd pinched from a newspaper, The Times, I think. She wasn't supposed to but she's no chance of getting me to go to the library so thought it better just this once to steal. When she showed me your advertisement my heart nearly jumped out of my mouth. It says you are looking for men to undertake a hazardous journey to the South Pole. I'd like to partake of said hazardous journey as I'm desperate to visit the South Pole for reasons I shan't bore you with but they include a wish to honour the memory of Captain Scott. I've been in training for just such an adventure for many months, camping in our backyard and sleeping with the blankets off me at night to get used to the cold. I can also ride motorcycles, a skill you may be able to put to good use. I live near the Gloucester docks and like ships and have £2/7/6 saved up which I can put towards the cost of the journey, food, clothing and the like. I am five feet five inches tall and my teeth are in good nick. I can start at your earliest convenience, at least I think I can.

Thank you
Tom Casey (Aged 14 but 15 in November)
PS I'd like to be a hero.

The mechanic is hungover. Last night's skittles must have gone well. After lighting a cigarette he says, "Need you to take a Douglas for a run out. Cheltenham and back."

∘ ∘ ○ ○ ∘ ∘

There's a large crowd stretched along Cheltenham's tree-lined Promenade, a sight to behold in the summer sunshine, especially with all those posh people in their finery. I park up by the grand Queens Hotel and walk down the hill to investigate, stopping where the crowd is thickest. Across the road, standing beside a covered statue, is a group of men wearing fancy robes and hats. "What's going on?" I ask an elderly man, busy tapping his blackthorn stick in time to the nearby military band's tune.

"They're unveiling the statue of Edward Wilson to honour his sacrifice alongside Captain Scott." I didn't know Wilson came from Cheltenham.

As the music comes to an end one of the men in fancy dress steps onto a low platform and proclaims, "Today the townsfolk of Cheltenham have their wish granted in honouring Cheltenham's finest son, Edward Wilson, a man replete with pluck, fortitude and duty." He drones on and on, so much so, I stop listening, until after a round of applause the man says. "So I now call upon his worship the mayor to come forward to unveil Mr Wilson's statue."

A grey-haired man wearing a heavy gold chain and a fur-trimmed coat steps forward and tugs at a rope holding the tarpaulin in place. The tarp falls away to reveal a statue of a man dressed as an explorer. Goggles and everything. I close my eyes and pray Mr Shackleton's letter of acceptance is winging its way to me.

As the man has his photograph taken in front of the statue, the band strike up 'God Save the King'. They play more stirring tunes as a troop of boy scouts march past the statue, followed by a column of soldiers moving in perfect time, their boots beating out a steady rhythm on the road while their bayonets glint in the sun. Such a sight to behold. There can be no finer country to live in. Why Dad would betray England is a mystery. "Up the Glosters!" the old man beside me shouts, "You'll give the Kaiser what for!" I've heard the mechanic and the boss talking about this Kaiser fella and that war is brewing. I hope so. I'll join up to fight to defend those countries shaded red in the tatty atlas and show the world there's one Casey who's not a traitor.

"As long as the Hapsburgs leave Serbia and Bosnia well alone there'll be no need for our boys to march off," the old man's neighbour replies while stroking his plush, tobacco stained moustache. I wonder who the Hapsburgs are.

The band fall silent as the soldiers march passed the hotel and fall from sight. The crowd thins. I walk over to the statue and gaze up at Wilson. He looks brave, steadfast. English to his core. I can see why Scott chose him. *Please, Mr Shackleton.*

Wondering if I'd ever have a statue built in my honour, I return to the Douglas. An army officer is eyeing up the bike. He's barely twenty, sports a narrow moustache and has a broad, kind face. "This yours?" he asks.

"Sort of."

"Douglas. Made in Bristol. Does this one have the new mechanical inlet valves?"

"Course," I lie.

"Reckon she'd give my Rudge a run for her money." He points to his bike parked nearby. It's a beauty, all curves and menace. "Fastest production bike in the world."

"Depends on the rider."

"Boastful little beggar. Where are you heading?"

"Gloucester."

"I'll wager a shilling I can beat you to Gloucester Cross."

"Don't have a shilling."

"If you win I give you a shilling. If I win you don't have to give me anything. Fair?"

I've nothing to lose. "You're on."

"Good. We'll start outside the hotel."

The Rudge is faster and he's a more experienced rider, but I know the road, where its bends are tightest and its ruts deepest. I'll take it steady, let him lead out and catch him on the run in to Gloucester.

We wheel the bikes to the hotel's entrance. A group of people look on including half a dozen soldiers returning from the parade. The officer climbs onto his Rudge lowers his goggles and says, "Remember, first man to the cross."

Setting off, he weaves between motor cars and horse drawn carriages causing some horses to become skittish. I soon lose sight of him. Worried the race is over before it's begun, my crafty plan goes out the window and I give it full chat. Battered by stiff ridges of air, I struggle to keep the Douglas true, but I'm gazing along a tunnel, everything else fuzzy, of no consequence. Passing a pub, I round a goods wagon being hauled by two brindled drays and brake sharply to avoid hitting an old man ambling across the road. Near Innsworth, I glimpse the Rudge but again lose sight of it, until a mile on, outside Longlevens, I pass my opponent hauling the Rudge from a thicket beside the rutted corner I banked on being my friend. I round the bend gingerly and accelerate.

The busy Gloucester streets slow me. I look behind but there's no sign of him. Victory is mine, until on Eastgate Street I'm forced to swerve around a mangey dog who has run out into the road. I tip the bike over and slide to a stop. A sharp pain shoots through my right leg now trapped under the bike. But my only thought is to remount. I crawl from beneath the Douglas and after kicking the brake lever back into position, set off. The bright red Rudge flies by me.

He's already lit a cigarette by the time I pull up at the cross. His fuel tank sports a few dents and the headlamp is at a funny angle. "Hard luck, old man," he says. "You'd have licked me if you hadn't fallen off."

"Saw you in a hedge."

"Went into a corner too fast. Lucky to get back on." He throws me the shilling, which I drop. He picks the coin up and this time hands it to me. "I'll win it back next time. You're a talented rider. When war comes, the Signals will need lads like you. Look me up in the Bristol Depot; Lieutenant Chatterton." He grounds out his cigarette, lowers his goggles over his eyes, nods to me and sets off, the Rudge's exhaust note now sour after the crash. I trouser the shilling and set off for the showroom bracing myself for a bollocking over the damage to the Douglas but reliving the race. I'd ridden on instinct, knowing the right line to take for each bend, when to brake or to accelerate, my only thought to win. My aching leg is a badge of honour.

CHAPTER FIFTEEN

"Fevered," is how the pastor described the excitement at the start of the war. As usual I didn't know what he meant but wished Scott had lived to see such patriotic zeal.

Old soldiers dug out their medals, collectors rattled tins on street corners, and shopkeepers draped their windows with flags and posters supporting our boys. In the docks, warehouses and berthed ships were bedecked with flags and aboard the Anselma, Joe and me waged mock battles between our boys and the Germans. Our boys always won because Jack baggsied playing them and they had right on their side.

The boss bought streams of Union Jack bunting, which I strung up around the showroom. "Patriotism's always good for business Tom," he said, pleased with my efforts.

The mechanic studied the Daily Express to see how the British Expeditionary Force was squaring up to the Germans and soon considered himself an expert on the terrain of Belgium. He predicted the war would be over by Christmas.

The paper also had a story about Ernest Shackleton's Imperial Transantarctic Expedition had set off for the Antarctic. I didn't understand. I'd been clear in my letter to Mr Shackleton how much I wanted to go. At least he could have written back. I tried fooling myself that venturing to the South Pole was still daft, but as Florrie re-read the article to me that night, I couldn't help but marvel at Shackleton's bold plan to cross Antarctica on foot. Madness to some, but if the British Empire could defeat Antarctica, beating the Hun would be child's play. And to plant the Union Jack at the South Pole once again would avenge nature for taking Scott from us.

The next day a posh lad came in to pick up his serviced Triumph 3½ and told us he was joining up as a Despatch Rider. I thought of Lieutenant Chatterton, no doubt heading to war, proud to serve king and country. After the posh lad rode off, the boss said to me, "You've the makings of a Despatch Rider, Casey. If you become one, you can have your pick of the bikes here. At cost. I'll even throw in a spare set of tyres."

War *and* motorbikes. The life for me.

○ ○ ○ ○ ○ ○

Jack pokes his head through the shop door, making me wonder if something has happened to Mum or Florrie. "The Glosters are setting off. If we hurry we'll catch them."

I looked at the boss. "Back within the hour," he says.

There's a large, excited crowd outside Gloucester station. A military band plays, songs are sung and flags waved. Soldiers, some not much older than me, and bowed by the weight of kit, mill around saying goodbye to teary-eyed loved ones. To get a better view of them leaving, Jack and me walk along the tracks to a level crossing half a mile outside the station. Within the hour, the packed train rumbles by, covering us in steam. I stuff a handful in my pocket for luck and then wave the soldiers off. Some wave back. Some look unsure. Some look frightened.

"You Gloucester lads give the Kaiser a good shoeing!" Jack shouts his face flushed with excitement. As the train disappears from sight he says, "Fancy joining up, Tom?"

"When?"

"Tomorrow," he says.

"What about your Mum and Florrie?"

He shoots me a queer look. "They'd only try to change my mind."

"Reckon you're more afraid of Florrie than you are the Germans."

"Fancy it?"

"Go on then," I lie.

"The Recruitment Depot over on Barton Street opens at six o'clock. See you there."

"Fine," I lie again.

○ ○ ○ ○ ○ ○

There's a loud knock on the front door. The mantelpiece clock shows a quarter past seven.

"Can only be bad news at this time of day," Mum mutters. I open the door half expecting to see Manning and Wilson. Jack's Mum is beside herself, her proud, still pretty features despairing.

Mum comes to the door. "Whatever's the matter Mabel?"

"When did you last see my Jack?" Mabel asks me.

"Yesterday, watching the Glosters set off."

"Did you know he planned to enlist?"

"No."

"Are you sure?" I nod. Can I slink away without being spotted?

Stan shouts from the kitchen, "At school, the teacher said it was our duty to fight for the king and empire."

Mum shushes him.

"I've been to the Recruitment Depot," says Mabel. "But they won't tell me anything." On the verge of tears she continues, "Jack's just turned seventeen. He's too young to fight and die."

"Tom. Tea. Best mugs," orders Mum.

"I've no time," says Mabel," I'm heading to the train station to try and catch him."

"Can't understand why everyone's so upset. Jack's a hero," Stan mutters as he fills the kettle. "Teacher told us all about our brave lads defending the empire. But when we try to do our bit, grown-ups want us to stay home."

"Did you know?" Florrie asks me.

"He talked about it yesterday."

"Why didn't you tell me?"

"Didn't believe him."

"He'll get himself killed out there."

"No he won't."

"How do you know that?"

"He's Jack." Normally Florrie would thump me or argue the toss, but for once she turns tail and runs upstairs in floods of tears.

"What did you say to Florrie?" Mum asks me after seeing Mabel off.

"Nothing, honest."

"Poor Mabel."

"A few lads round here have joined up."

"I hope you're not thinking the same, Tom."

"The boss thinks I've the makings of a Despatch Rider. Said I could have my pick of the bikes."

"Look at what war has done to your poor father."

"Made him a traitor."

Her slap stings my left cheek. "Sorry Mum, I didn't mean it."

"Then why say it?"

"I dunno. Everything's out of kilter."

"Enough to think your father could be a traitor?"

Now my pain turns to rage. "Those two coppers and *your* dad thought so."

"Do you know how much it hurts hearing you say that?"

My anger melts to shame. "Sorry."

"Now it's my turn not to believe you." She puts on her overcoat and best bonnet and tells Stan it's time for the Mission.

"We're hours early," Stan moans.

"Get your coat on!" Mum roars, struggling with her buttons. "If I don't leave now, I swear I'll regret my actions."

I should have signed up with Jack. At least Mum would have a good reason for being angry with me. Mithering to himself, Stan puts on his overcoat, picks up his football and pokes his tongue out at me before following Mum out.

"You all right, Florrie?" I shout. No answer.

Everyone is leaving, Dad, Captain Scott, Jack and now Mum. Why can't things stay the same?

Needing to get away, I take the tuppeny map of Gloucestershire from inside the tatty atlas and spread it out on the kitchen table. I run my finger over the map and plump for a village south of Gloucester. It's Sunday. The showroom is closed. Nobody will know.

Inside the showroom a fuelled Triumph 3 ½ stands by the back door. I wheel her out, fire her up and set off, hoping the ride will stop Jack's bravery from gnawing at me.

∘ ∘ ○ ∘ ∘

Bunting is stretched across every street of every village I ride through. Apart from the odd yapping dog or old countryman standing by his front door enjoying the morning sunshine, I barely see a soul while trying to figure out why I said such hurtful things to Mum. It's all right to think them but not say them. If only Shackleton had taken me on. No risk out there of my loose tongue causing upset. Antarctica is safer than Gloucester.

I'll have to face Mum's fury all over again when I get home. Needing to think, and feeling sorry for myself, I pull over and dismount.

A boy and a girl both roughly my age, are cycling towards me, the girl struggling to keep up. The boy stops to wait for her. When she catches up, the girl smiles at me. She's out of puff and red faced but is the prettiest girl I've ever seen. "What you doing round here?" she asks after catching her breath.

"Hunting German spies." They both look surprised. "Been trailing one out of Gloucester all morning." Pointing to a house half-hidden in a copse a short distance away, I ask, "Who lives there?"

"Nobody since old Mrs Everitt died last year," the girl answers. "Doubt you can do much spying from there though."

"Why?"

"You can't see the road for starters."

"Cunning. That's what spies are. Found a Hun spy in a cowshed in Stroud last week. He had a knife on him. Big one. Sharp."

"What was he doing in Stroud?"

"More to Stroud than meets the eye."

They ride off, both staring at the cottage where my made up spy lurks. The girl returns. "If you like, we can keep an eye on the house for you."

"Thanks."

"When will you be back?"

"This time next week."

"What's your name?"

"Tom Casey."

"Millie Dawson." After Antarctica, compression and magneto, they're the prettiest words I've heard. Pointing at the Triumph she asks, "What's it like riding one of those things?" Now my lies catch in my throat. Tell her the truth. "It's freedom. The air rushing past with nothing bothering you."

"Doubt I'll ever get the chance to find out."

"If you like, I could take you for a run."

"Really? I'd like that."

"This one's a Triumph. Best bike money can buy. I plan to ride around the world on one."

"What an adventure, where will you go first?"

"Your house."

She giggles. "You're fresh, Tom Casey."

"And you're pretty, Millie Dawson."

She flushes. "Next week, then?"

"Next week." Calling to her brother to wait for her, Millie sets off. I stay frozen to the spot, watching her.

It pours all the way back to Gloucester, but the rain doesn't bother me. All I can think about is Millie and her shiny blue eyes, dimpled cheeks and strawberry blonde hair. But after returning the bike in the shop, these bonny thoughts soon thin with the dread of going home to Mum.

Running into Alf Fenwick would be a blessing. If I arrive home sporting a fat lip there's half a chance she'll forgive me. For once I head home hoping to run into the Bridge Gang.

CHAPTER SIXTEEN

The mechanic was wrong. The soldiers weren't home for Christmas, nor spring and judging by the papers befuddling maps, the stalemate in France and Belgium means they'll not be home anytime soon. Not that the mechanic's bothered. He's earning a pretty penny from selling offal from the workshop and gives me a few bob every week to keep quiet. I've quite a fortune now stashed in the fireplace.

The docks heave with ships laden with cargo bound for the Midlands munitions and engineering factories. The dockers work all hours and the pubs are doing a roaring trade. The pastor also has reason to thank the Kaiser as he can now point out alcohol is unpatriotic *and* sinful, although Mum's devotion to the cause of sobriety has cooled, as the new banner still hasn't been presented to the Mission yet.

Jack's Mum is still beside herself and whenever I bump into her, the dark look she gives me chills me to the marrow. Florrie hardly said a word to me for months, convinced I'd put Jack up to enlisting. She took against the war, profiteers in particular. "The working class are fighting the rich man's war," she told me one day, waving a pamphlet in my face. "Jack's out there risking his neck whilst these charlatans fleece us. Landlords double rents while butchers hike the price of meat. Even the price of tea has tripled. Where will it end?"

Thinking about the mechanic's side line, I answer, "Best be quiet, Florrie. Lot of lads from round here have gone off to do their bit."

"Then they're fools. Besides, why should we worry about the people round here? They've never taken to us."

"People don't like you spouting off. It's not patriotic."

"Patriotic? Look at where Dad ended up."

"That's not the army's fault."

"Then whose fault is it? Mum's? Yours? Mine?"

"Remember when we spoke about Dad's secrets?" She nods. "I've been thinking and reckon you're onto something. One of them is the key to Dad's madness."

I've surprised her. She wasn't expecting this from me. Neither was I to be honest. Since my row with Mum, I've tried to avoid thinking, as it only leads to trouble.

"But what if Jack comes home mad?" she says.

"Jack's too brave for madness."

"Can you keep a secret?"

"Course."

She retrieves an envelope from her library book.

Hello Florrie,

I hope you are not angry with me for joining up but seeing the Glosters leaving the station that morning I thought I ought to do my bit. After all it is tyranny we are facing.

The soldier's life is set fair with me even if the uniform doesn't fit! And I have a blister on my big toes from all the square bashing! But not as raw as your feet were that time we walked up Painswick Beacon.

It is a relief to finally be in France and facing the Hun. I have made some good pals in the regiment. All good Gloucester boys. The food could be better though! Still we've all got to make sacrifices.

I miss our talks Florrie. I miss you. You are in my thoughts and when I pine for home, which I do on occasion I think of you and my spirits improve.

Tell Mum not to worry. Tell her I will write soon. You are not to worry either Florrie. Everyone thinks this shindig won't last much longer and I'll be home in no time.

Got to go now my sweet Florrie.

Your Jack.

Putting the letter back in its envelope, Florrie's expression darkens. "There's poor Jack risking his neck for the country while greedy bastards profiteer."

"Takes all sorts."

"I want him home."

"Jack can handle himself."

Shaking her head she answers, "You've seen how people round here look at him. His teachers, the police, Alf Fenwick. How's he faring in the army?"

"It's the *British* Army. Any man who serves is a hero and is treated like one."

"Who says?"

"The king, for starters. And General Kitchener."

"Only a fool would believe that Tom. Look at us. We're outsiders. The English hate us for being Irish, and no doubt the Irish hate us for being English. Now imagine if you're black."

I have no answer and leave for work planning to ask the mechanic if he had any kidneys going spare. They normally cheer her.

CHAPTER SEVENTEEN

I open the back gate still mooning over Millie. She's yet to spot the spy but doesn't seem too bothered, probably because I took her for another spin on the Triumph. She even kissed me goodbye, on the lips too. Her lips tasted of honey. I felt gooey for most of the ride home and can't wait to see her next Sunday.

"Where you been?" Stan asks from the backdoor step.

"Out."

"Why didn't you take me?"

"Didn't want to."

"Reckon you will next time."

"Why's that then?"

He held out his hands. My stash of soot-stained coins nestles in both palms. I snatch at them, but he pulls his hands away in the nick of time and says, "I'll tell Mum you been hiding money from her. You'll be for it then."

"I'll give you a shilling."

"And take me out on a motorcycle?"

"Fine."

"I want to go where you went today."

Wondering what Millie will make of a spy hunter turning up with his little brother, I answer, "All right. Now give me my money."

"Don't believe you." I lunge for him, but again he's too quick and scampers across the yard, stuffing the coins in his pockets. He pulls open the back gate and scarpers. I give chase, the money now less important than belting him.

Despite being a couple of years younger, Stan soon stretches out a lead and is already outside the Mariner's Chapel by the time I reach the dock gates. He threads a path between dockers and sailors, ducks under a crane, and hares across the swing bridge towards the Anselma, the gulls scattering. Lungs burning, I board the ship to see him climbing up the rotten rigging.

"Come down, Stan. It's not safe."

He looks down at me, smiles and points towards the city. "I can see Dad. He's waving."

"No I'm feckin' not," whispers Dad.

"Dad! Dad!" Stan shouts.

"Just like his dad, a nutter," says Alf Fenwick. The rest of the Bridge Gang are with him. They've a new recruit; Fred Tallow.

"A nutter who kills children," Alf adds.

"My Dad didn't kill Georgie."

"Bollocks," Alf replies, "Everyone knows your pa killed Georgie, then made out he's mad to avoid the noose."

"He didn't," Stan shouts. "Honest."

"Maybe I did."

"My Dad reckons you Irish are born liars," Alf says. The others nod in agreement. "We're going to make you pay for what your dad did to Georgie. And that big darkie ain't here to protect you."

"Remember Tom, keep your chin tucked in and lead with the left. You have the Lionheart's soul."

Florrie's right. We're always having to fight. But it's not Alf I'm going to fight. It's Fred Tallow and like all the Tallows, he's thin, pasty. Smelly too. But being in the Bridge Gang has made him brave.

"Use the jab. Then follow with the right cross."

"Flatten him, Fred," orders Alf. Fred inches forward, his confidence draining, but unable to back down in front of his new mates. He throws a haymaker. I duck and land a left hook flush on his jaw and follow up with a gut punch. He falls and curls into a ball, groaning.

Alf catches me unawares with a rabbit punch to the back of my head followed by a kick in the shin. Reeling I take a wild swing and land a pearler on his chin. Alf stumbles, loses his balance and falls, striking his head on the balustrade with a deadening *thud.* Dander up, I move in for the kill, wanting to beat the living daylights out of this bastard who for years has made my life a misery. *"Fightin' Irish!"* I grab him by his shirt and raise my fist. But stop. Alf's out cold. Blood seeps from his mouth and ears.

"What you done, Casey?" Ted Pugh shouts above the screeching gulls. "You've killed him."

Stan is at the foot of the mast. He looks down at Alf and then at me with disbelief. "Tom," he mutters.

I have to get away otherwise I'll be strung up or thrown into Coney Hill. I abandon ship and run towards a group of stevedores unloading a single mast brig out of Cork. "Help!" I shout, "My mate's fallen from the Anselma's mast. He needs help." The dockers run towards the ship without giving me a second look.

Waterman's warehouse rears before me. Jack said nobody would ever find a murderer in there. I shin up the wall and scramble through the rotten window and land beside the pallets, scattering the roosting gulls. A fire roars. I skirt the stagnant water and follow the line of bottles, now much thicker, towards the cellar's steps.

With my hand brushing the brickwork I set off along the pitch black cellar, its smell stinging my eyes. I round the corner Jack and me reached last time and stop beside a cast iron door.

"This way to your madness Tom, your very own Hades."

I turn back and hunker beneath the stairs, gagging on the stench of piss and shit, wishing I'd enlisted with Jack. If I had, I'd now be a hero and not a killer on the run. I close my eyes, hoping that when I open them I'll be at home looking at the tatty atlas with Dad. But this is no dream. I've no choice but to run.

An hour, maybe two, passes. The warehouse falls dark. I hear footsteps and muttering and cursing. I peer around the steps and see a hunched, cloaked shape walking towards the stairs.

"Whatcha going to do, Tom?" Dad says, *"Police outside. Banshee in here. Your mortal soul or your neck?"*

Terror of ghosts bests fear of capture so I hurl myself up the stairs. The warehouse is quiet, undisturbed. I crouch beneath the window. Water drips. A rasping cough. Feet shuffling on the stairs. The cloaked phantom hobbles towards the fire and warms its hands. It sits, pulls the cork from a bottle, takes a long draft of grog and smacks its lips. I climb outside and dart along the quayside. The Irish brig's nightwatchman raises his lantern and shouts. I dare not stop and cross the canal lock and search the north quay warehouses, hoping to find an unlocked door. There's none.

Thankfully though, the chapel's doors are open. I duck inside, close the doors, throw the bolts and stop to draw breath.

The hunt for me will be on, the streets thronged with possess, just like they are in American cowboy stories. I've broken Mum's heart. Florrie's too. Stan will think it all a great adventure. Egged on by Old Ma the whole street will come for them. *Lay low. Think.*

Someone tries the doors. I freeze. A fella slurs, "Locked up for the night." Another man curses.

A church bell strikes one o'clock. Inching the Chapel door open, I slip outside and clamber over the locked custom house gate. A drunk, lurching home bids me goodnight and carries on his tottering way. The litter-strewn streets lay deserted as I take the back lanes towards the garage and slip inside, relieved to be out of sight. I rummage around the stores and find a half full canister of petrol and tip it into the fuel tank of a Triumph 3 ½.

Taking the mechanic's jacket and goggles, I wheel the bike into the alley and lock the workshop's door behind me. Where will I find sanctuary, north, south, east or west? I mount the Triumph and paddle. The engine fires but dies. I dismount, panic rising. Fool! The fuel tap, always the fuel tap. I paddle again. The engine starts. I open the throttle, stamp on the

22222222
222222

gears, hare along the alley and pull out onto Westgate Street. Find Jack. He'll know what to do. I head south not towards the Antarctic, but the war.

"The British Army will be the making of ye, Tom," says Dad.

"Shut up traitor."

The Steam Catcher—Part 2

The Great Pyramid,
Cairo, Egypt
1916

CHAPTER EIGHTEEN

From the top of the Great Pyramid I watch the blood red sun fall into the Nile and imagine opening the tatty atlas, pointing to Egypt and telling Dad of my adventures.

"Wish you well, Dad," I mutter, scarcely able to believe my good fortune. Sixteen going on seventeen and standing atop the world. I'm living adventures Florrie's books could never match.

After fleeing Gloucester, I'd arrived in Bristol in the early hours and a sleepy Bristolian directed me to the nearest army recruitment depot. It had yet to open, so I lingered in the doorway of a nearby hardware shop drawing odd looks from strangers hunched against the drizzle. In that gloomy spot, I relived that frenzied moment when Alf fell and struggling to understand why shame, excitement, and finally pleasure coursed through me. Uneasy with such barbaric thoughts, I strained to hear Mum reciting the Bible or singing with the Mission and caught my reflection in the shop window only for Dad to smile back at me.

"Proud of ye Tom. The noose or Coney Hill awaits. Either one will serve."

I cooked up Douglas Rudge, a twenty year old mechanic from Dursley, keen to serve the king and empire. Douglas Rudge was calmer than Tom Casey; braver too, less prone to talking tripe and getting into scrapes. Likeable Douglas Rudge grew on me, as did my hopes of evading justice.

At six sharp, the depot opened. First in line, I earned a welcoming nod from the wafer-thin sergeant unlocking the doors. Nobody batted an eyelid when I answered "Douglas Rudge" nor were they interested where I came from or my trade. In a small room off the main hall a doctor, still half-cut from the night before, told me to strip and walk and hop across the room a dozen times. After checking my sight, hearing, teeth, heart, and breathing, he asked if I'd ever had venereal disease. Having never heard of such an ailment, I answered no and he passed me fit for service.

The recruiting officer never asked me for any identification, preferring to spend his time admiring my motorcycle. "Can't go wrong on a Triumph, Master Rudge," he said, stamping and signing my short service papers. "You'll soon be in France, wearing the king's coat with a corporal's stripes." Douglas Rudge pocketed his papers and said goodbye to Tom Casey.

But I hadn't figured that before being shipped out to France I'd spend six weeks at a Royal Signals training camp outside Aldershot. Stuck here, the dark thrill of life on the run changed into the stomach churning dread of being unmasked every time someone hollered my new name.

Apart from loyalty to the king, I'd little in common with the other DR trainees. They were university types mostly, proper blue bloods, and the way they spoke, dressed, even ate, was foreign to me. So I kept my distance, rarely piping up as they griped about the Brass, the weather, the food or the lack of bike spares. My caution earned me the cold shoulder, with the barracks falling silent whenever I entered. New arrivals were soon set right if they were spotted talking to me.

I became the unwilling butt of japes. At first the tricks were childlike, pinching my bedding, letting down the Triumph's tyres, or draining the fuel tank. Ever worried about giving myself away I didn't protest, but my silence only encouraged the tormentors to become more brutish. After the Triumph's brakes failed on a right-hander during a run out to Southampton, I discovered the brake blocks had been loosened, as had the wheel nuts. Two days later, returning from the washhouse I found my tunic, cap, and DR's Brossard slashed to ribbons.

"What have I done to piss you off?" I bawled at them, "Ain't we here to fight the Hun?"

"Not with feral oiks like you Rudge," one replied, "You're not fit to wear the badge." Fuming, I flew at him but four or five others grabbed me and only the sergeant major's appearance spared me a beating. "What's occurring?" he asked.

"Rudge attacked me with this, sarge." My accuser said, holding out a knife.

"Did you, Rudge?"

I kept quiet and accepted the punishment of a week in clink.

"Welcome to my world, Tom. Locked away for no feckin' reason. Home's a distant memory now, son."

In the cramped cell, the joy of being Douglas Rudge thinned. Desertion crowded my thoughts and I grew homesick, longing for my old bed, Mum's stew, rowing with Florrie, lumping Stan, even the tannery's stench. To pass the time, I recited the pastor's temperance speeches and re-ran my race against Lieutenant Chatterton over and over, finding peace in those frantic moments.

Wary of the reception awaiting me, I returned to barracks relieved to see the Triumph still stood on the same spot. There and then I hatched an escape plan. Start the bike and ride off. So simple as to be fool-proof. Excited by my half-cocked idiocy, I straddled the bike, started her and pulled away. The bike ground to a halt. The drive belt had been severed.

More sabotage. The escape plan lay in tatters.

As I cursed my enemies, a Blackburne 499 pulled up. The rider removed his goggles and looked at me with an unsettling glare. He winced while dismounting and rubbed his left leg. He stood barely five foot, had a winnowy frame with his brown hair already thinning. His uniform was far too big for him. "You Corporal Rudge?" he asked.

"Yes," I replied, uneasy under his scowl.

"Heard the bed next to you is free."

Breathing easier I replied, "Last bunk on the left."

"Arthur Fletcher," he said heaving his kitbag over his shoulder. He entered the barracks and hobbled towards the far end of the dorm, ignoring the other trainees. The bedsprings squeaked as the kitbag landed on the bed. He sat down and muttered to no one in particular, "The ride up from Plymouth has shaken my sins loose."

"What happened to your leg?" I asked.

"Contracted polio aged four. Then five years since, a contrary mare shattered my thighbone as I shoed her back home in Devon. Smithy by trade. Been lame ever since. If I were a nag they'd have shot me long ago." Stifling a yawn, he stretched out and said, "Tireder than damnation. Wake me in time for dinner." He rested his head on the kitbag and fell asleep.

∘ ∘ ○ ○ ∘ ∘

Arriving at the cookhouse, Fletcher's lameness and baggy uniform drew odd looks, giving me hope that my tormentors would now turn on him. One fella limped to the tea urn and his pal repeated the trick, tottering like Charlie Chaplin for good measure. When a third followed suit, Fletcher squared up to him, despite being a good foot shorter. "Proper jasper ain't you?" he said, pulling his tunic's cuffs over his thin wrists.

"Just pulling your leg."

"What there is of it," added another wag.

Fletcher laughed. "Heard of David and Goliath?"

"Of course."

"Good." His left hook dropped the trainee. Fletcher sat and pointed to the uneaten pie on my plate. "You finishin' that?" Thinking it unwise to deny him, I scraped my pie onto his plate and said, "He didn't see that coming."

"Nobody does. A bantamweight's build but a middleweight's punch. Strength of Samson, me."

As the weeks ticked by a cagey friendship took hold between us. Fletcher's abilities with his tiny whirling fists protected me and whilst I never mentioned my past, he rattled on about a smithy's life and his adventures haring around the lanes of north Devon on the Blackburne. Under his patient and watchful eye I also learned to strip and reassemble the Triumph's engine in under an hour. Day by day Douglas Rudge's hopes of avoiding detection grew.

After completing training, we were both assigned to the Hampshire Regiment with Egypt our destination. Grateful that an ocean and continent would soon stand between justice and me, the days before departure dragged and my fears of capture resurfaced. I became even tighter lipped and convinced myself Fletcher was spying on me so kept an eye out for any sly glances or hurried whispers to the others. None came but my suspicions loitered, only calming when our troop ship, seen off by a brass band and heaving, flag-waving crowds, slipped from Portsmouth harbour into the Solent. As safety beckoned, I could have danced for joy, whilst the other men fell silent as home and loved ones were left behind.

"You're the only here who seems happy to be going," Fletcher said.

"Just proud to be doing my bit."

"Nice to see you've cheered up. You've been a miserable cur lately." He offered me a Senior Service and said, "When we reach Egypt, I'm buyin' a Fez. Always fancied owning one. Got the head for a Fez me."

∘ ∘ ○ ○ ∘ ∘

A chill breeze whips around the Pyramid and I button my tunic to stave off the cold. The scrape of hobnails on stone announces Fletcher's arrival.

"This Pyramid must've been a bastard to build," he said, rubbing his gammy leg. He took off his Fez and wiped the sweat from his brow. I lit two Players, handing him one and we smoked, while looking over Camp Mena far below, its perimeter fence lit by oil lamps.

"Kind of the Kaiser to let us do a spot of sightseeing," I mutter.

"Reckon we've found the quietest spot in all of Egypt. No calls to prayer, bellowing hawkers, braying donkeys, mithering camels or bastard flies. Even the sergeant can't be heard up here."

Reveille drifts up from the camp. Barked orders follow. Fletcher laughs. "Christ, he's louder than a Pharisee. Pity his poor wife and nippers having him hollering like that every morning. Drive me to drink, it would." Standing, he snaps to attention, salutes me and mimics a brash Cornishman. "Right then you ungodly urchins, which of you dared to give their loving mother a spot o' lip this evening? Who's not washed behind their lugholes?" He takes off my cap, ruffles my hair and barks, "Nits! In this house? Get your 'orrible 'ead shaved. All leave cancelled!"

"Hard man to please," I answer, smoothing my hair.

"Cornish. Strong willed as a temperance gathering but just as miserable. Bet he can gut a mackerel with one hand."

"Handy."

Fletcher throws his fag away and scratches his name on a block with his trusty lock knife. Handing me the knife I scratch, "Tom Casey, Gloucester, 1916."

"Race you down, double or quits," Fletcher says. Since landing in Egypt, we've taken to betting on everything, from peeling potatoes to swatting flies. Last week Fletcher had won a camel race around the camp after the cussed beast carrying me refused to budge.

"First one to scale the Sphinx wins," I answer.

"You part mountain goat? Haven't you done enough clamberin' for one night?"

"Want the bet or not?"

He bleats. We set off.

Fletcher took an early lead before slipping between the giant sandstone blocks. "Bastarding Pharaohs," he curses as I skip away. Within ten minutes I'm sitting on the Sphinx.

"What's the view like from up there?" asks a woman among a party of sightseers.

"Nice. If you can see in the dark."

"Mind if I join you?"

"Be my guest."

She scrambles onto the Sphinx's back, losing her hat in the process. Taking my hand, she sat next to me, sighed and tidied a loose strand of hair. She's sturdy and plain but possesses a lightness of spirit. Smells nice too. "Come here often?" I ask.

"Most weeks. Where are you from?"

"England. City of Gloucester."

"There's a town called Gloucester thirty miles from my home in Boston."

"You a yank?"

"Seems that way. Ellie Shaughnessy."

"Douglas Rudge."

"A pleasure to meet you, Douglas Rudge."

"Likewise. Here on holiday?"

"Yes. Strange as it may seem with war raging and all, my parents saw fit to pack me and my two sisters off to the Ancient World." Mimicking a deep voice she says, "War or no war Ellie, it behoves every American to see the world in order to draw on these experiences in later years." My Father is very forward in his thinking. This is our last night here so naturally my younger sister dared me to climb the Sphinx."

"Fair enough."

"Although the wine has emboldened me, I never back down from a dare. My sister would never let me forget if I did."

"My sister never put up with my shenanigans."

"That's a nice word." She giggles and repeats shenanigans to herself. "Excuse me, the drink has loosened my tongue, I'm not usually this vulgar." As if to prove it she sings in a pure voice,

"Oh band in the pine wood cease,
Or the heart will melt in tears,
Till the souls faint with longing
And the voices of old years"

"Nice song."

"It's from an old Civil War song. My father often sings it." She shivers. I take off my tunic and offer it to her. Thanking me she wraps the tunic around her shoulders.

"Smoke?" I offer her a Players.

"No thanks. But feel free."

I light my fag while she looks heavenwards. "It's so beautiful here, under the stars with the Pyramids rearing up to meet them."

"S'pose."

"Would I be bold in asking you for a kiss, Douglas Rudge?"

"Sorry?"

"Can I kiss you?"

"Why?"

"Because I am tipsy and you are handsome and gallant."

"Am I?"

"Yes."

"Very well." We kiss. Her lips taste of wine.

"Time to go, Ellie!" a woman shouts, "The Karnak leaves within the hour."

"My sister," Ellie whispers. She kisses me again, this time snaking her tongue into my mouth. She returns my tunic and says, "Good luck to you Douglas Rudge. Dare you to stay alive."

Befuddled by Ellie's boldness, I help her down where a well-groomed older man hands her back her hat and escorts her towards a car with her giddy laughter drifting on the breeze. I hope she'll look back, but she doesn't. As they drive off, Fletcher without his Fez, limps into view. He leans against the Sphinx's left front paw and says, "You sure you ain't cloven hooved like Old Jack himself?"

"Where's your Fez?"

"Lost the bloody thing when I tripped."

"Shame. You've a head for a Fez. Let's see your money."

"Bet's off."

"Why?"

"You said first one to sit on the damn beast. Well, here we both are by the creature's paws."

"Fair enough."

"You're not going to argue?"

"No."

"You're an odd one, Rudge. Jonah's luck with Job's patience. We've been pals for months yet I only know your name, that you're part Billy goat and a Fez don't suit you."

"Not much else to know."

"Oh yes there is, Tom."

CHAPTER NINETEEN

Every assigned DR had left camp at dawn to slog through the heat and sand, for over one hundred, knackering miles, ticking off festering checkpoints set in oases, abandoned wells, even a cave. To stave off mechanical failure, Fletcher had devised bodges to stop the bikes carburettors getting clogged with sand and the hot exhaust gases from cooking us. To try and keep cool we rode in shorts and loose shirts with sleeves hacked off at the elbow while under our topees, we wore linen gauze nets to ward off swarms of angry sand flies. Our crafty efforts were rewarded when we passed several broken down bikes and their stranded riders.

Seven hours after setting out, we rumble along Cairo's clogged streets where our filthy, sweat-soaked clothes and sunburned limbs earn odd looks from Egyptians and soldiers alike. We park up, find a bar to toast our success, and traipse around the bazaars. Fletcher haggles with a mouthy vendor over the price of a new Fez, whilst I fend off beggars and children flogging fruit. Nearby brothels spew out drunk Tommies and Aussie larrikins.

A few hours later at close to midnight, half cut but happy, we arrive in camp, our boisterous mood at odds with the sour looks on the faces of the men bivouacked next to us.

"What's wrong?" I ask the corporal.

"We've received our posting this evening."

"Palestine?"

He shakes his head. "No, mate. Gallipoli."

○ ○ ○ ○ ○ ○

"The Reaper's sharpening his scythe," Fletcher complains as we drink in our favourite bar the night before we're due to ship out. The place heaves with Tommies and Aussies drinking, cussing and singing at the top of their lungs. Cigarette smoke, sweat and hair oil fill the air along with a sense of desperation.

"Fuckin' Gallipoli," Fletcher sighs, "Our lads still haven't managed to fight their way off the beachheads. Winston's made a right balls-up. Christ knows what we're expected to do"

"Serve the king."

"He won't spare you an Ottoman's bullet." He drains his glass and asks, "You courting'?"

"No."

"A sweetheart?"

"No."

"Lost your cherry yet?"

I shake my head and take my time lighting a cigarette to hide my embarrassment. "We'll have to fix that. You'll need a warm memory or two to get you through Gallipoli."

"What do you mean?"

He tilts his head towards the flight of stairs that leads up to the brothel.

"I'm skint and besides you always speak fondly of your wife and children."

"I do. But I've got me urges and if I'm going to get me nut blown off in a day or two's time, honouring the commandments can wait." He hands me three shillings, "Come on! No dilly-dallying on the way. There be harlots awaitin'."

He pushes me up the stone steps. A woman wearing a near see through, flowing gown and a headdress garlanded with silver chains, sets down her fan and stands to greet us. As she took Fletcher's arm he winks at me and says, "See you downstairs."

Another, younger woman also wearing a loose fitting robe appears on the landing two doors down. The bracelets around her wrist slide towards her elbow as she holds up three fingers. I hand her the three shillings.

Her room smells of musk and incense which struggle to hide the fusty, belchy smell of the men who'd already lain with her. There's barely enough space for the narrow bed, its sheet tousled and worn, let alone the small table on which sits a terra cotta pitcher and mugs. Outside, chickens cluck and an Australian haggles over the price of a trinket. Downstairs liquored-up Aussies strike up the opening verse of 'Waltzing Matilda'. Not to be outdone, the Tommies bellow 'It's a Long Way to Tipperary'. Nervous and unsure what to say, I blurt, "You're beautiful."

"And you are handsome."

"Ta."

I sit on the bed and watch her undress. She steps towards me whispering something in her lingo. I wrap my arms around her waist and bury my face in her stomach, drawing in her scent. She strokes my hair. I feel exposed, not sure what to do. "What's your name?" I ask her.

"Sabra. Yours?"

"Tom Casey."

"A nice name. Do you want to begin?"

"Oh. Right. I see. Best get on with it then."

THE STEAM CATCHER

Sabra lays on the bed and watches me undress. I lay on top of her. She starts to rub my cock, thickening it until I think I'll burst. I shudder as she guides me inside her. Within seconds I'm finished. She moves from under me and says, "You will be a good lover. One day."

Still heady and revelling from the moment, I watch her wash under her arms and between her legs. Her back and arms are covered in bruises. "Who hit you?"

"Some men they drink too much." My blood boils at the thought of another man hurting her. She pulls on her robe and steps out onto a small balcony overlooking the street and calls out to passing soldiers. After dressing, I thank her. She turns and smiles but more out of pity than anything, I suspect. In the hallway I meet Fletcher buttoning his flies. "How d'you get on?" he asks.

"Sabra said I'd the makings of a gentle lover."

"My girl's name was Sabra. No doubt every girl in here is. Just remember her when you're fighting to get ashore in Gallipoli. Remember her scent, her taste, the feel of her skin, her squirming beneath you, being inside her. Remember you were at her mercy, and that you won't die a virgin."

As we leave the bar, Sabra shouts from her balcony, "Good luck, Tom Casey!"

"Who's Tom Casey?" Fletcher asks raising an eyebrow.

"Just a name I made up," I reply, angry with myself for slipping up. To my relief, Fletcher swears at an Aussie clutching a chicken for barging into us. Amidst the kerfuffle, Fletcher ducks and the Aussie's fist lands flush on my jaw. The chicken squawks.

CHAPTER TWENTY

Ten deep crowds cheer and hurl flowers over the Hampshires as they march towards the train station with Fletcher and me pootling along at the rear on our bikes.

"The chicken had a better jab than you, Rudge," Fletcher says. I've no answer but still seethe with him for ducking under the Aussie's punch and landing me with a shiner.

Reaching Cairo train station we load the bikes into a goods wagon and battle through the fly blown heaving carriages to find a seat. As the train moves off I lean through the window, catch a fistful of Egyptian steam and shove it into my pocket for luck.

We run north to Alexandria rattling through desert and scrubland, stopping to take on water at a small sun-withered station, its name written in squiggly Arabic. Even out here in the middle of nowhere, hawkers flog food and drink. Fletcher buys two oranges and hands me one. Peeling my orange, juice squirts into my eye. "You'll strike terror into the Turks' hearts," he says.

Six hours later, stiff-limbed, our shirts stuck to the slatted benches, we pull into Alexandria docks, unload the bikes and follow the infantry to the quayside where we're handed a cup of thin cocoa, a stale bun, and a lump of rank cheese. A plume of smoke drifts from the troopship's funnel as bearded, chipper Navy Ratings in dazzling blue and white uniforms prepare the ship for departure.

"Strange," says Fletcher as we loaf on the quay.

"What?"

"No Australians here."

Finally, it's time to board. Wary of damage to the bikes, Fletcher and me keep a beady eye on the rating overseeing their loading. "We off to Gallipoli?" Fletcher asks him. Pushing his tally back, the rating glances around him and whispers in a northern accent, "Not Gallipoli, chum. Mesopotamia. There's a division under siege somewhere up the Tigris. You lads are being sent there to relieve them. Then you're to press on to Baghdad."

"Where's Mesopotamia?" Fletcher asks.

"The land of the Arabian Knights," I mutter, remembering the tale Florrie once read to Stan and me. "Maybe we'll fly around on magic carpets."

"Course you will," The smart arse rating replies.

"The land of Adam and Eve," says Fletcher, laughing. "Makes us Cain and Abel, Rudge. Naturally, me violent nature points to me being Cain." He pats my shoulder and says, "Means that one day I'll kill you."

○ ○ ○ ○ ○

With little fanfare, we set sail. I catch a pocketful of steam and cinders trailing from the ship's funnel as the warm, brine tinged breeze ripple my shirt and hair. As Alexandria fades in the setting sun, a flag-strewn dreadnought, all howitzers and riveted menace, pulls alongside.

"How long will we be at sea for?" I ask. My stomach churns.

"A week, give or take," answers Fletcher.

"Christ."

"Don't worry. I plan to bury you at sea."

I close my eyes and whisper:

"But if I should die on a foreign land

and be buried so far, far away

no fond mother's tears will be shed o're my grave

on the Shores of Amerikay."

CHAPTER TWENTY-ONE

Standing in ankle-deep mud and lashed by torrential rain, we grow impatient watching the Arab labourers struggle to heave the last water wagon aboard the paddle steamer.

"Wetter than John the Baptist," mutters Fletcher as water drips from his topee onto his mackintosh. He slaps his neck to rid himself of another mosquito and then curses his luck for being here.

With the wagon loaded, we shuffle forward, desperate to get aboard and find shelter but are sent back to allow the supply mules to be brought on. One mule plants its hooves on the jetty's creaking planks and no amount of yanking or cajoling from its rattled handler can persuade the beast to budge. When the handler raises his whip, Fletcher shouts, "No need for that, mate." He strokes the mule's face, coddles its ear and whispers to it. Seconds later the mule follows him onto the steamer.

"What you say to it?" I ask him when he returns.

"I know a thing or two about fretful animals. Soft words and a fuss, that's all the beast needed."

"What words?"

"Secret words. Handed down over generations. Can't divulge 'em, even on pain of death. We swear on the sacred anvil."

"Cobblers."

"Maybe. But I saved the poor nag a beating."

With the mules loaded, the Hampshires lurch towards the jetty, but again are stopped to allow a company of Indian army seepoys to board. "Never right to let Indians go before Englishmen," grumbles a sodden Tommy.

Finally, to jeers, the bedraggled harbour master lets us board. Each man races to find cover under the steamer's canopy. Those who miss out must sit out in the open, fending off the pelting rain by wrapping their ground blankets and mackintoshes around themselves. But at least the rain keeps the usual swarms of flies at bay.

"Lash 'em tight," Fletcher tells me as we secure the bikes to one of the two barges tethered either side of the steamer. "Untrustworthy lot aboard. There's the smell of Somerset about 'em. Gaderene swine."

Swaddled in a tarpaulin, I again imagine opening the atlas and telling Dad my adventures. Thanks to the war, I *really* am an explorer, travelling to exotic, alien lands. Now I face another adventure, this time surrounded by strangers willing to lay down their lives for comrades trapped in the besieged town of Kut-al-Amarah. I'm proud to be part of such a heroic quest. Perhaps I'll earn a little redemption for killing Alf.

The rain stops as the steamer pushes off and takes up its position in our flotilla of paddle steamers, sternwheelers and tugs sailing up the Tigris. As the vessels meander around a shallow bend serenaded by the nervous, braying mules, I count ten vessels ahead of us and another four behind with most hauling barges laden with men and supplies.

"Can't say I'm sorry to see the back of Basra," Fletcher says staring back at the city. "Rougher than Ilfracombe on market day."

He has a point. Where the Egyptians had welcomed us with garlands, trinkets and food, the men and women of Basra glared and muttered oaths as we sauntered around its fly-blown, mud-baked streets. Fletcher thought it too risky to visit the ramshackle brothels ringing the port. "Just have to spill me seed instead. Certain to be a bountiful mandrake harvest round 'ere."

To stem the frenzied mosquitos, I cover my head with the linen net and scour the thick beds of swaying reeds and rushes lining the riverbank, hoping to glimpse the Garden of Eden. Pelicans circle overhead, as ducks bob in the flotilla's wash. Marsh Arabs paddle past in sleek canoes or larger sail-powered Mahailas. Some shout greetings, most don't. Not their war, I suppose.

∘ ∘ O ∘ ∘

"Can see why Eve nibbled on the apple," Fletcher says on the second morning as I watch an eagle haul itself from the river holding a wriggling fish in its talons.

"There's something beautiful about this place," I answer, watching the eagle soar skywards.

"One way of putting it. Shithole's another." He picks his misshapen teeth with a match and stiffens when a stocky, grizzled Indian sergeant wearing a bright orange turban and sporting a magnificent beard approaches. The three rows of medal bars stitched onto the left breast of his tunic tell of a hero. He salutes and says, "Sergeant Chatta Singh, forty first Dogras."

"Yes?" I ask.

"I am willing to pay for the pleasure of sitting astride your motorcycle." He swats away a gaggle of flies and holds out a coin in his left hand. The little finger is missing.

"Why'd you wanna to do that?"

"A kindly sahib major once permitted me aboard his Triumph motorcycle.

 94

I would like to do so again."

"Don't fancy the Blackburne then?" says Fletcher.

"Triumph only."

I shake Chatta Singh's hand and say, "You've taste sergeant. Go ahead."

After paying me, Chatta Singh sits on the Triumph, grips the handlebars and looks downriver, his bold, stern features akin to a ship's prow. Taking his lead, other Seepoys queue up. Climbing off the Triumph, Chatta Singh took payment from the first man and let him sit on the bike.

"Do you think it wise to allow a darkie to sit on your bike?" asks a rating taking depth readings. "Won't you catch something?"

"These lads are serving the king. Makes them all right in my book. Besides, I'm earning a few bob."

"Their rupees are worthless."

"Makes them happy though."

I flinch as a burst of machine gun fire from Lewis guns positioned either side of the steamer's wheelhouse slices the reeds. Waterfowl take flight in massed panic. We grab our weapons and take cover as machine-gun-fire erupts up and down the flotilla.

"Don't fret," says the rating, "Just our gunners keeping their eyes in. Can never be too careful with the Marsh Arabs. Hostile wallahs at the best of times."

○ ○ ○ ○ ○ ○

The days drag as we continue our rain-soaked voyage, passing near derelict villages and long-abandoned terra cotta mud forts stationed every few miles on each bank. Mahailas came alongside to offer food and fresh water. Each time they're sent packing.

I spend my time sleeping or staring at the riverbank, whilst Fletcher tinkers with the Blackburne or gossips with other Tommies. To keep dry we shelter under my tarpaulin now rigged between the bikes. Each morning Chatta Singh and the other Seepoys hand over a rupee to sit on the Triumph. "You'll be as rich as one of those Maharajahs at this rate," Fletcher half-jokes, but miffed that the Seepoys ignore his Blackburne.

"Maybe," I answer, recalling the morning Dad was carried from the house.

"There'll be no sin you can't afford to indulge in."

The lack of shelter and poor grub lead to grumbles spreading among the men with things made worse by the cramped conditions. On the fifth day, to raise spirits and quell discontent, extra food rations, along with a measure of rum are handed out. But being permanently soaked and deprived of sleep, tempers fray. Rows that would normally be settled with a handshake now break out into fights. The steamer seethes and for once Fletcher bites his tongue.

On the sixth day, fresh water grew scarce forcing the men to draw up the river's silted waters to slake their thirsts. Within hours many were laid low by vomiting and diarrhoea. Throughout the night, men squatted over the sides of the barges to relieve themselves. Rumours spread about a cholera outbreak. I hope we will put in at the next village for fresh water, but we plough on. Chatta Singh and his comrades stop queuing up for the Triumph.

For two days, I burned with a fever, passing nothing but fetid brown water, staring up at the tarp and gagging from the stench of shit caked along the barge's hull. Raging with thirst, I try to scoop up the river's water but each time Fletcher, also pain wracked and cramping, stopped me, saying, "That'll be like drinking Satan's piss. Better to go without for a day or two."

∘ ∘ ○ ○ ∘ ∘

"Back with us, then?" Fletcher says while cleaning the Blackburne's cylinder head.

"Looks that way," I croak. I'm washed-out and exhausted but at least the cramps have gone. "You all right?"

"God spares the virtuous."

"Nice to know your godly."

"Mother taught me the good book. Contains the answers to life's mysteries." He offers me his water canister. "Don't worry, its fresh, one of the tugs pulled alongside last night and delivered a few barrels."

The water is cool, nourishing, after which Fletcher hands me a Senior Service and says, "You were raving about that Tom Casey fella again. Who was he?"

"Just a pal from back home."

"Sounds like a wrong 'un. You were gabblin' about him beating people an' all sorts."

"A few years ago. He's calmer now."

"Are you, Tom?"

 96

CHAPTER TWENTY-TWO

Ten days out from Basra, we pull alongside a jerry-built jetty, already sinking into the mud. Despite the driving rain we're desperate to disembark and feel land underfoot.

As we prepare to wheel the bikes ashore, an eager, shiny-faced Lieutenant tells us to leave them and fall in with his platoon, as the bikes will struggle to pass through the waterlogged terrain.

"Don't fancy leaving my bike to these thieving Tars," Fletcher says, eyeing up a rating.

"Don't fret corporal, we'll only be gone for a day or two. The Turks have no stomach for a fight." Tapping my corporal's stripes he adds, "You'll earn these, though."

"How far is it to Kut, sir?" I ask.

"Little over a day."

Stepping off the steamer, Fletcher whispers, "If this jaunt's going to be so easy, why did we land so far away? Garden of Eden my arse."

Heading inland, thick, cloying mud churned up by forward columns stalls our progress. Still washed-out from my illness, I struggle to keep pace.

"More fun to be had wringing a chicken's neck," Fletcher gripes.

Two hours into the march, with barely three miles covered we reach a set of abandoned Turkish trenches. "What did I tell you?" says the lieutenant. "The Turks lack the stomach."

"Perhaps they're falling back to a stronger position, sir," a lance corporal replies. "I heard the Hun general who's leading them used the same tactics in France."

"Corporal, this is Mesopotamia, not Europe. The Turks lack the gumption of the Huns."

We push on and half an hour later, the battalion funnels into a narrow track bisecting two marshes. The stink takes me back to the tannery. Every few yards we're forced to free a supply wagon that has got itself stuck in the mire or has slid into the tall, billowing reeds either side of us.

"So much for us striding through paradise," Fletcher complains. "Muddier than Weston beach."

Threatening, ungodly mewls spring from the reeds whilst whining, diving mosquitoes drive us to distraction. A breeze whips up and flocks of screeching birds harry us, forcing us to swat them with our helmets, rifles, even fists. Shadowy, light-stepping figures flit amongst the reeds, withdraw but reappear minutes later. I'm edgy, my nerves not helped by the rumbling thunder and sheet lightning making its way towards us.

"Why the fuck are we here?" a Tommy behind me says as we heave yet another wagon back onto the track.

"To rescue our comrades," I answer.

"They're not my comrades," he spits back. "We've been sent here to cover up some General's fuck-up. Our lives mean nothing to them. So why should I give a fuck?"

"They'd come to your rescue."

"Like fuck they would."

Behind us someone starts singing 'It's a Long Way to Tipperary' only to be shouted down. It's gone midnight before we clear the marshes and reach a patch of open ground, where we are told to rest. Fletcher sits and sighs. "Payin' for my sins," he whispers in a dry, hoarse voice. "Shouldn't have laid with Sabra in Cairo."

"Really?"

"Course not."

Our spirits aren't helped when we're handed Huntley and Palmer tack biscuits and bitter black tea made with water drawn from the filthy Tigris.

"Where we heading?" I ask the Tommy next to me.

"Somewhere."

Moving off, a dust storm blows in from the desert, blinding and choking us. Bright bursts of light pierce the dust followed by the dull scream of shellfire.

"That's where we're heading," says the Tommy.

By sunrise the dust storm has blown through and we reach another line of abandoned trenches and take up position along the right flank. The trench is a disgusting mess of fresh human waste and rotting food that feeds a swarm of rats. But too exhausted to care, I fall into the trench and wring the last drops of water from my canister. Fletcher, his features caked in dust, rinses the grit from his reddened, sore eyes. "Can't take another step," he says, rubbing his thigh.

"Any idea where we are?"

"Bideford Sands, with a bit of luck. Could murder a pennyworth of chips, washed down with half a cider."

Machine gun fire rakes the trench. We both cower. "Found the Turks then," says Fletcher.

"Incoming shellfire!"

We flatten ourselves against the trench wall as shells burst overhead and shower us with shrapnel. Injured men scream.

"Enjoying yerself Tommy Boy?"

"You! DR!"

The lieutenant beckons me over and hands me a scribbled note. "Take this message to the major. He's towards the riverbank. We need ammunition and water."

I shove the note into my tunic pocket, sling my rifle over my shoulder and set off, but within fifty paces I'm lying face down on a duckboard. Dazed and half deaf, I get to my feet, the shellfire now dulled. The air clears to reveal the section of trench ahead of me. It has taken a direct hit. I scrabble over the ruptured earth, not daring to look at the dead and maimed, and press on. Fresh shellfire rents the air and shakes the earth. I scoot by men whispering prayers, checking their rifles and fixing bayonets. I ask one if he knows where the major is. A sergeant answers, "He copped a slice of shrapnel in the head."

"Who's in charge?"

"Major Attlee of the South Lancs, two hundred yards along."

Major Attlee doesn't cut a dash; short, frail with a clipped moustache. I thought him a clerk rather than a soldier. He pushes his cap back and scratches his thinning pate while reading the lieutenant's note. He gives me a weary glare and says, "No Ammunition. The water wagons are stuck behind us. Medics too. Tell him to do his best. But be quick, we're about to go over the top."

As I set off, shrill whistles blow all along the line. Ahead of me an officer scrabbles to the trench lip and roars encouragement to his boys, only to fall back with blood pouring from his throat. The men climb out from the trench and, bellowing for all they are worth, charge forward. Within yards they're snared in thick mud making them easy prey for the Turkish Maxims.

I run on, watching a rippling column of Tommies fall. The Indian brigades take up the assault, but again dozens fall upon reaching the quagmire. A third wave goes over but this time the men are waylaid by our fallen as much as the mud making them easy fodder for the Turks.

Whistles blow again. Now our Lewis guns rake the Turkish lines. The firing ebbs and alongside the smell of cordite, the cries and groans of the wounded fill the air. Two men, their filthy faces shot with terror and exhaustion, crawl into the trench pleading for water. Looking to our rear I spot an upended water wagon, so climb from the trench and keeping low, scuttle over the churned earth dodging terrified mules who've broken free from their wagons.

The wagon's driver and hauling mule lay dead, but the tank is intact. I fill half a dozen canisters, sling them around my neck, and crawl through the sucking, grasping mud towards our position expecting any moment to feel the sting of bullets.

Spared by the Turks, I slide into the trench, careful not to slop any of the precious water onto the blood-soaked duckboards. Even allowing each man one swig each, the canisters are soon empty. The wounded plead. I've no choice but to return to the water wagon. I'm not thinking, just acting, controlling my fear, just wanting to help my comrades.

"Definition of bravery Tom."

On my third excursion, I crab across the ground towards the spot where I'd left Fletcher and the lieutenant. Doling out the water, I look up and down the line for Fletcher. There's no sign of him. I ask several men if they've seen him. One lad pipes up, "The short arsed DR standing with the lieutenant?" I nod.

"They went over together. Neither made it back."

"You sure?"

He nods. "The pair of them fell right next to me."

Fletcher dead? Like Captain Scott and Jack, I thought him indestructible. I sink to my knees, deaf and blind to the suffering around me. I hope he received a quick death but fear for my future without him. Amid the shouts and cries for help, I hear, "Leave your knob alone, Rudge, and lend us a hand." Standing on the lip of the trench, mud splattered and bleeding from the head, Fletcher lowers the unconscious lieutenant to me and scrabbles down, wincing as he lands on his weaker leg.

"Thought you copped it," I say.

"Two parts Lazarus, three parts Judas, me."

"Where's the medics?"

"Few miles back. The brass didn't see any need for them to be risked as they thought it would be a walkover."

"So what do we do?"

"Not a clue, but I'm not leaving those poor lads out there to die. Comin'?"

He climbs out, and clutching a piece of white cloth, crawls towards a wounded Tommy. I follow. "Got you, mate," Fletcher says to the man. The Tommy garbles thanks as we drag him back to the trench.

All morning with the Turks looking on, we return to no-man's-land to bring more men back. "One more Rudge, we'll get one more," Fletcher keeps saying as we head over the top. But with no medics or medicines, all we can offer are sips of water and words of comfort as most of the lads we rescue suffer pain-wracked final moments, including the lieutenant. It's all we can do to stop the boldest rats from dining on the dead.

CHAPTER TWENTY-THREE

By the early afternoon, the medics pitch up with four carts to evacuate the wounded. Fletcher and me are pressganged into helping. Two Seepoys approach us carrying one of their own. The wounded man's filthy orange turban trails in the dirt. Chatta Singh lays on the stretcher with a blood-soaked cloth wrapped around his torso. A gaping wound stretches the length of his right thigh. His eyes are seared with pain as he grits his teeth and moans.

"Only English," the cart driver tells the stretcher bearers.

"This is Chatta Singh," one of the Seepoys answers. "He saved us from the machine gun. Please Tommies, find a doctor. Save him."

"Sorry mate, can't take him," The driver tells us as we help the Seepoys load Chatta Singh onto his cart.

"We're bringing him!" I bark.

"Means we'll have to leave one of our boys here."

"This fella's a hero. If needs be I'll throw you off to make room for him." The driver holds his tongue as we lift another wounded Seepoy onto the cart.

After piling as many into the carts as we dare, we set off, leaving dozens of stricken men behind. Fletcher and me dart between the wagons offering water and encouragement as the carts judder and buck over the muddy terrain that causes the injured men to cry out.

It's raining by the time we reach the marshes. Several men are already dead but are left among the living. Hidden from the outside world by the swaying reeds, I sense the slippery, light-footed marsh Arabs are enjoying our struggles. Again the mosquitos feast.

When a cart gets stuck every able-bodied man has to help haul it free. The first few times we release one, cheers go up, but within the hour a weary silence greets further successes. Progress at first is measured in yards and then in feet with the ever silent Arabs looking on. My excitement upon leaving Basra is long gone and replaced by fear of this hostile land and the brigands stalking us. I'm hemmed in, exhausted by illness and fighting, wary of looking at the dead aboard the carts in case Alf Fenwick is among them.

Head bowed, scraping along, I'm part of Captain Scott's doomed march from the South Pole, desperate to survive but knowing death waits. I stiffen my resolve by drawing on Scott's pluck, and I feel a surge of hope and energy. But another cart slides off the track. I just want this desperate adventure to end, grateful to Shackleton for heading off without me.

"Keep goin', Rudge," Fletcher says, sensing my despair while leaning into a stuck cart. We haul the cart free. Fletcher whispers his sweet, sacred words into the ear of the exhausted mule hauling the wagon. The mule strains against its harness and pulls the cart forward. "That's my babbie!" Fletcher shouts, coddling the mule's ear something he does to each passing mule.

By dusk the marshes are breached. At least half the men aboard the carts are dead, the survivors stricken and silent. Near the first abandoned trench, we come upon a column of men heading towards the front. The Tommies are taken aback by the rickety carts' desperate cargo and pass us without speaking, aware of what awaits them.

"Nearly there, Chatta Singh," I say after he cries out when the cart clatters over a rock. The other Seepoy lays dead next to him. Washed over with death, Chatta Sing says, "Donald Rudge?"

"Yes?"

"Your Triumph brought me luck."

"When we reach the steamer, you can take her for a ride."

"For free?"

"For free."

"You are a good man, Douglas Rudge."

"If you knew me better, you'd think differently."

We run parallel to the trench until the lead wagon driver finds a gap. With the mules straining we heave each cart up the short, sharp, slope rearing before us. From the summit the smoke from the funnel of a steamer ploughing the Tigris hoves into view. A beautiful sunset fills the early evening sky. Any other day you'd stop to take it in. The sound of shellfire drifts across the river.

"Fuck me," says Fletcher. "We made it."

Two hours later in near darkness, we draw up by a field hospital erected near the jetty. Exhausted, I sink down against one of the carts. A medical orderly hands me a water canister. I take a swig and then hold the canister to Chatta Singh's lips. He's dead.

○ ○ ○ ○ ○ ○

After unloading the dead and living, Fletcher and me sit beside Chatta Singh's corpse and watch a harassed, exhausted doctor assess each man, and issue sharp instructions to his orderlies and stretcher bearers. The living are taken to the field hospital, whilst the dead's details are noted down in a ledger after which a tag is tied to the breast pocket of their tunics. Their faces and torsos are covered.

"Who's this man?" asks the doctor. He sports a three-day stubble and dark rings circle his eyes.

"Sergeant Chatta Singh, forty first Dogras, doctor," I answer. "He single-handedly took out a Turkish machine gun. Saved his men from slaughter. We dragged him through a sea of mud so you could save him."

"You did your best, corporal."

"How many of the men we brought in are alive?"

"Just under a third."

"That all?" says Fletcher.

"It's usual for only a tenth of the wounded to make it back alive. You should be proud." He looks at me. "Can you chaps move the bodies to the cemetery? We need the space here for the next batch of wounded. After that get some food and rest."

∘ ∘ ○ ○ ∘ ∘

"What you got for us then?" A sweat-soaked Brummie gravedigger asks raising his lamp to us. He leans against his shovel, stripped to the waist, his face covered with a filthy cloth. Behind him stretching into the moonlit darkness lay rows of dead Tommies awaiting burial. Half a mile further on, bonfires light up the sky.

"Twenty-one Tommies and two Seepoys," Fletcher tells him.

"Set our lads down here. Take the Seepoys towards the bonfires."

The other gravediggers muck in and help us to unload the corpses. "They were good men," says Fletcher, waving away the hectoring mosquitos. "Make the graves good an' deep, with solid walls."

"No fears," The gravedigger replies.

Fletcher and me follow the cart carrying Chatta Singh and his comrade towards the bonfires. "Why do they burn their dead?" Fletcher asks. "Ungodly, if you ask me."

A handful of Seepoys also stripped to the waist but still wearing their turbans collect Chatta Singh and his comrade from the cart and bear them to two pyres. After lengthy incantations and prayers, the pyres are lit and the gathering flames consume the corpses. The smoke drifts across us, so I grab a handful and stow it in my pocket, while Fletcher coddles the ear of the mule hauling the cart. The driver, half lit by the fires encourages the mule on. The wind changes direction and again covers Fletcher and me in the choking smoke and offers further relief from the mosquitos. I trudge into the darkness and drop to the ground. To the sound of hissing, spitting wood I fall asleep and dream I'm in the tannery collecting hairs from soldiers' rendered flesh.

CHAPTER TWENTY-FOUR

I wake, dry mouthed and with a splitting headache. I squint in the morning sunshine. Fletcher nods. A fresh team of gravediggers are hard at work as thick black smoke from more bonfires drifts around us. Chatta Singh's pyre is now a smouldering pile of ash. I light two Players and hand one to Fletcher who shares his water canister with me. "If I make it back to Barnstaple, I'm never leavin' the place again. Not even as far as Bideford for Easter. Goin' to stay at home with the wife and children. Provide for 'em and love 'em for the rest of my days."

"You all right?'

"Had me Damascene conversion yesterday."

"You heard the doctor. A lot of those lads would have perished if it wasn't for you."

"Nearly shit meself doing it. All that muck and gunfire. Miracle we got out alive." Lowering his head, he sobs. I leave him to his grief and stand by Chatta Singh's pyre. *Anytime you want to ride the Triumph, just ask my friend.*

I return to the jetty where the wounded are being loaded onto a steamer. Beyond the jetty, the same doctor moves among the wounded issuing instructions to orderlies.

Starving, I queue for some grub and wolf down a plate of maggoty bully beef and a mug of the disgusting black tea. Feeling better for eating, I return to the jetty and find Fletcher aboard our barge running his eye over his Blackburne. A medic's armband has replaced his DR's Brossard. I offer him a biscuit, but he waves me away.

"Bikes are still aboard," he says. "The crew are Kent men. Trustworthy, the fellas from Kent." He hands me a medic's armband. "We're to help load the wounded."

"Where do we start?" I ask, fazed by the sheer number of men on the river bank.

"Him," Fletcher answers, pointing to a Seepoy. We carry the Indian onto the barge and lay him beneath the tarpaulin still slung between our bikes. I doubt he'll make it to Basra.

"Did you spot the Garden of Eden on the way out?" Fletcher asks, offering me a Senior Service.

"No."

"We'll keep our eyes peeled on the way back. Need something for our souls to cherish."

CHAPTER TWENTY-FIVE

Grand Place, Mons, Belgium May 1919

The threat of fisticuffs hangs in the air as the wine-addled Canadian and Frenchman square up to each other. "Five bob on the Canadian," whispers Timmings.

"You're on," I reply, even though it's a cast-iron certainty the Canuck will floor the bantamweight Frog. They circle each other. The Frenchman gets in first, landing a solid jab that knocks the brawny Canadian backwards. The Canuck charges, lifts his opponent and is about to drop him but pauses when the Dray's driver shouts encouragement to his team of horses.

From the crowded pavement, a Belgian woman clasping a rosary screams encouragement. "She'll do herself a mischief," mutters Timmings.

"We're honoured," shouts a Yorkshire Tommy upon seeing the blue and white DR Brossards on our left arms. "DRs getting their hands dirty for a change."

"Our intellectual heft is required," Timmings answers.

"What's the saint's name again?" I ask, looking at the gilded statue perched on the Dray.

"Waltrude."

A voice behind us asks, "Come here often, mate?" We lean into the wagon and heave with scores of men. Thoughts of that terrible procession from Kut fill my mind and I wonder what Fletcher would have made of things.

"Odd way to celebrate Mons's patron saint," says Timmings as he's manhandled by a Belgian. "DRs shouldn't be expected to undertake such physical exertion."

"Why are we, then?" I ask as the Canadian now beside me, hollers at the top of his lungs.

"I wanted to impress Ursula."

"Any other reason?"

"The locals believe if the wagon reaches the top of the hill, Mons is safe for another year."

"And if it doesn't?"

"Last time that happened was nineteen fourteen."

"Better get our skates on."

The cheering grows more frantic. More men fall in behind us and push, squeezing up like a giant bellow and trapping me. I've survived the Great War, but now I'm going to peg it pushing a statue of a long-dead saint up a hill. Mercifully, the crush loosens. More cheers break out, with fists raised in triumph. The Canadian flushed with beer and bonhomie hugs everyone around him as the chant of, "Et les Montois ne periront pas" goes up.

"That's Mons safe for the year," the triumphant Timmings says, straightening his tunic and wiping beads of sweat from his handsome, well-nourished face. Just to be sure I pat my tunic pocket and feel the necklace's knobbly outline. We squeeze through the crowds towards the Grand Place and return to the bar we'd left half an hour earlier. Ursula, the barmaid, sets two glasses of blond beer down in front of us.

"Merci beaucoops," Timmings says with a charming, impish smile. He'd been assigned to the corps three days before the armistice. We'd forged a friendship because he's from Cheltenham and we're the only DRs stationed here, the others long shipped off to Russia to fight the reds. Timmings is a rarity these days. He still sees the good in people. He also maintains a brilliant sheen on his tunic buttons, unaware that he'd offered the snipers a target." Keeps me off the fags, old chap, although I used to be a fag at school," he once told me. God knows what he meant.

It may have been the strength of the beer on this sticky, warm day, but I count my blessings for swerving Russia. With luck Celestine will let me stay the night.

"Now that we've saved Mons, what are your plans back in civvy street?" asks Timmings, brushing a loose thread from his sleeve.

"Not sure," I answer, returning to my usual state of unease. After years of war and evading arrest I've waylaid my optimism and struggle to sift the truth from the lies I've told to protect myself.

"Yet you volunteered to work with the coolies."

Being assigned to the 3rd Chinese Labour Corps meant safety in the shadows as nobody in the regiment wants to know about the morbid work those poor devils are paid to do.

After lighting his pipe he says, "Reckon you carry a dark secret, old boy. A broken heart perhaps, or maybe you performed a dastardly deed." The words set me on edge. Does he know something? He laughs, "I know! you pilfered from a Gloucester costermonger's and have been on the run ever since. You scoundrel."

"I liked haring round on a motorbike, choked and blinded by dust in the summer, drowning in mud during winter, all the while avoiding snipers, shells and GHQ staff cars."

"Steady on, you've said more to me in the past five minutes than in the previous six months. You're positively a chatterbox."

"All your bloody questions. What are you planning to do?"

"Off to Uruguay. I've an uncle over there who works for the Central Uruguayan Railway. A cove by all accounts, but he's assured my father he can fix me up. Latin America is ripe for men with ambition. That's me, all right. Hop on a steamer at Southampton then hightail it to Montevideo. By all accounts there's Senoritas by the bucket load." He sips his beer and continues, "The future is ours for the taking. One more year of service, and I'm off."

"I served the king, the empire and what did it get me?" I ask. "Two and six a day, and two stripes."

"Could you have made sergeant?"

"Two stripes were enough. Counted my blessings I wasn't shell bait. I'll never forget those lads' faces before they went over the top, hoping I carried fresh orders that stayed a push. Never did of course. Felt like the angel of death sometimes."

"Even though I saw a few days action, the war made life worth living."

"Count your blessings you missed the slaughter."

"Poor old Fletcher. Rotten luck to cop it." He pauses, aware he's struck a nerve "What lay behind that order?"

"The bastard major wanted to prove a point fifteen minutes before the whole shindig was due to end. Makes Fletcher's death all the harder to take."

Timmings taps his pipe into his hand, for once his bonhomie dulled. "The major ordered me to take that despatch. Fletcher took my place. Said he wanted to celebrate the armistice with a fellow Devonian in the battery. The sniper's bullet was meant for me." He raised his glass. "To Fletcher."

I also toast Fletcher but my actions feel hollow and weak.

"Were you ever wounded?" Timmings asks.

"Had the trots in Mesopotamia and had two rotten back teeth pulled in the winter of seventeen."

"Is that all?"

"The Turks were terrible shots while the Hun were creatures of habit. Their snipers lined us up in the same spots while their gunners' firing pattern never changed. Knowing these two things helped me earn my luck. And not having a sweet tooth."

Ursula set another round down in front of us. "Bon," she says with a warm smile.

"She is sweet on you," I tell Timmings. "I've never managed a smile from her."

"Perfectly understandable, old chap. I'm a Cheltenham charmer whereas you're a Gloucester ruffian."

I down the beer in three mouthfuls, wipe my mouth and say, "Heading off."

"Sweet Celestine?"

"The very same."

Letting my anger over Fletcher's death fester, I plough through the crowded Grand Place and run into the Canadian, now performing a lopsided can can with the Frenchman. He offers me his grog. I take a swig.

"I fired the last shot," he boasts, "On Armistice Day, outside Mons. I wanted to be the last one. Who'd have thought! an Albertan firing the last shot."

"Good for you." I answer, patting his broad back. A dozen others have told me the same already today.

"I'll never be forgotten." He puts his arm around the Frenchman and they start cavorting again. Everyone is dancing, joking and laughing. And why not? The war is over, we've survived, and thanks to our efforts with Saint Waltrude, Mons is safe for another year. I just wish Fletcher were here.

Reaching the hotel's grand, marbled entrance, I hop over canoodling couples and run up the three flights of stairs. A man leaving her room nods as I knock on the doorframe.

"Entrée." I step in. Celestine's smile melts my anger. "Rudge, if you would give me a minute."

I stand by the window and look over the Grand Place. A motley squadron of breast-plated cavalry lead a giant papier-mache dragon into the square. Celestine joins me and rests her hand on the small of my back. My cock twitches. "The Doudou. Tres bien!" she says. "Today Saint George will slay the dragon in the Grand Place."

"Doesn't look like much of a dragon. Besides, Saint George is English."

"But he also fought the dragon for Mons."

"Can't be right."

"Why do you English think only your history matters?"

"Because it does. To us."

"No matter. Are you ready?"

"I've missed you, Celestine." She smiles, revealing her even, salt scrubbed teeth. "You can stay the night, if you have money."

"I'd like that." I pull the gold necklace from my tunic pocket and hold it up. She smiles. "It is lovely, Rudge. Merci." She threads the chain over her head, admires herself in the wardrobe mirror and then throws her arms around me. I drink in her scent and stroke her soft auburn hair, wanting the moment to last forever.

"Tell her you love her."

"Can we watch Saint George slay the dragon?"

"Why not," I reply, disappointed.

"Fool."

CHAPTER TWENTY-SIX

I've been awake for an hour, perhaps longer. Celestine is still asleep, half buried under the blankets. I want to fuck but hold back. Instead, I open the bedside table drawer to look at the necklace and am surprised to see a dozen more such trinkets from other admirers. She shifts. I close the drawer, get out of bed and walk to the window. The sky is watery but cloudless. A road sweeper sweeps up rubbish near the bandstand, where Celestine and me had drunkenly waltzed on New Year's Eve. A handful of revellers are fast asleep there, probably the same men who were shouting and bawling last night, only falling silent when the Red Caps arrived and cracked their skulls.

I'll take the day off. The 3rd Chinese Labour Corp can survive a day without me. The coolies fill in trenches and dig graves to bury disinterred soldiers. Paid a pittance, they're flogged twelve hours a day, with many injured, after striking ordnance still laying in the earth. They live in a separate, fenced-off, barracks as the brass considers it unhygienic for Europeans to mix with them. The ones I work with seem decent sorts though. A fella called Tang performs magic tricks, whilst another nicknamed Petain, flogs bits of kit he's taken from the dead or found in the trenches.

Timmings and me take turns to carry the daily count of unearthed bodies to divisional HQ and return with a corresponding order detailing how many graves are to be dug. The brass never explain why two DRs were required for this task and we never ask, happy with our cushy detail that spares us a posting to Russia. Each day when I arrive with the tally, the adjutant's face drops and he complains about having to buy a few more acres of land from the wily Flemish farmers. Even dead, Tommies are worth a few bob.

I open the window, light a cigarette and wonder if Timmings' gift of the gab landed him in Ursula's bed last night. Probably.

A Harley Davidson sidecar combination sporting a Vickers machine gun, pulls up by the bandstand, disturbing one or two of the drunks. The rider and gunner dismount. Yanks in town for the Doudou. "Doudou," I mutter. Odd bunch, the Belgians. Everyone knows Saint George is *our* patron saint.

Across the square, outside the Hotel de Ville, Sikh Seepoys change guard. They remind me of Chatta Singh and the Maharajah from the tatty atlas. I hope Mum, Florrie and Stan have found it in themselves to forgive me. To my shame I can't remember their faces, or the sound of their voices but I wonder how they've coped with the disgrace of having a murderer in the family as well as a father locked away in Coney Hill. Madness stalks me still,

I'm sure of it.

"Don't fret, Tom."

A Triumph and its sidecar mounted with a French Hotchkiss machine gun, pulls up on the far side of the square. Rare to see a French gun mounted on a Triumph. Celestine stirs. I leave the window and join her in bed. She kisses me, smiles and strokes the Sacred Heart tattoo on my chest. "Café?" she asks.

"Please. I love you, Celestine." I flush and wonder how many other saps have told her the same. Judging by all the baubles in the drawer, hundreds.

"That is nice."

"How sweet of ye to say that."

She gets up, throws on her dressing gown and steps into the anteroom. She lights the single burner stove and prepares the coffee. I return to the window, wishing I'd kept my gob shut. The sweeper leans on his broom chatting to the Harley's passenger. Two more motorcycles pull up beneath me. The riders are clad in French tunics, British britches, and German boots. Their faces are covered with tank drivers' chainmail masks.

Celestine hums to herself while waiting for the water to boil. I've enough money for another hour, two if she's feeling generous. A Crossley lorry and armoured Rolls Royce arrive in the Grand Place, their heavy brakes squealing as they draw up outside the town hall.

"Sugar?" Celestine asks.

"Please." I answer, disappointed she's forgotten again. She hands me my cup.

"I've got the day off. Fancy going for a spin on the bike?"

"Today is soldiers' pay day, Rudge."

I'm a fool. How can a prostitute and a murderer share a future? This war will never end for either of us. What did Timmings say?" It is nothing more than a transaction old chap, don't allow yourself to fall in old amour, however pretty she is." Smart arse.

Wanting to be gone, I down the coffee and unlike the pastor, scold my mouth. Outside there's the familiar noise of a Vickers machine gun firing. I run to the window and watch the Harley's gunner rake the town hall, showering the Seepoys in shards of masonry. Three guards retreat behind the town hall's heavy wooden doors. The fourth stands his ground, raises his rifle but spins and falls, his body jerking as more bullets strike him.

The Hotchkiss opens up, spraying the Rolls and the Crossley. The Crossley's driver falls from the cab. His pal leaps clear and runs towards the town hall, but within ten yards he lies dead. Both machine guns now concentrate their fire on the Rolls, shredding the wheels and knocking out the gun turret. A third sidecar appears and strafes the square. I grab Celestine and dive under the bed as bullets shatter the window and lace the room, throwing up clouds of brick dust.

The shooting stops.

"Are you all right?" I ask. She nods but looks terrified. An explosion rocks the room.

Thick, black smoke billows from the Rolls' turret as the Harley's gunner rakes it again. The two other combinations draw alongside the Crossley. The Seepoys give fire from the town hall, but are pinned down by the Hotchkiss. Under cover from the solo riders, the gunners climb inside the Crossley and emerge seconds later carrying sacks of money. They climb back into their seats and their riders make for the side street running beside the hotel under covering fire from the solo riders who then follow.

Screams and pleas for help replace the gunfire's racket. The familiar stench of cordite fills the air. The raid has lasted less than a minute.

"Is it the Prussians?" Celestine asks, her eyes alive with panic.

"No. A robbery."

"What for?"

"Search me."

She throws on a dress, opens her bedside table drawer and picks out a Luger and cocks it. I must look surprised because she says, "Whatever it takes to survive, Rudge." Taken aback, I follow her outside.

"They're coming, Tom."

Downstairs in the hotel's ornate lobby, terrified shouts of "C'est les Bosch," ring out.

On the Grand Place, people run in all directions. A petrified café waiter grips his canopy's awning winch. Upended chairs and tables lay scattered. Celestine runs to the bandstand, stops and clutches the banister to stop herself falling. The drunken wastrels are all dead. Shot. The giant Canadian among them. The ground is littered with large calibre shell casings.

"The Sniper gets us all in the end, Tom."

Timmings arrives, his tunic askew and boots unlaced. "What's happened?" he asks.

"Been a robbery. Got to get after them."

"Are you all right old chap? You seem rather discombobulated."

CHAPTER TWENTY-SEVEN

I'm surrounded by whispering and coughing; and creaking bedsprings. My head feels as if it's been split open with an axe.

"Corporal Rudge?" asks a furrow-browed woman bearing a red cross on her pinafore. A man stands behind her.

"Where am I?" I ask.

"Field hospital. You received a concussion. Do you remember the robbery?"

I raise my left hand to the bandage wrapped around my head. "What robbery?"

"Yesterday."

"I've a friend, Timmings. Tell him to find Celestine, before he sets off for Uruguay."

A hard-nosed Red Cap looms over me. He reminds me of that copper Manning. "What did you witness, Corporal Rudge?" he asks.

"A robbery. Three sidecars, machine gun combinations and two solo riders. Maybe more, I can't be sure."

"Did they look like foreigners?"

"No, like soldiers."

"Recognise any of them?"

"Couldn't. They all wore masks. Strange thing though, they wore different pieces of kit."

"What do you mean?"

"French tunics, British britches, and German boots." I grab his wrist, "Please, I need to know if Celestine is safe. I planned to take her out for a picnic, down by the river."

"I'll make enquiries." He makes a note and asks, "What are your political sympathies?" I look to the nurse who gives nothing away. "Do you possess Bolshevik tendencies?"

"This fecker's come for ye."

"I serve the king, my country, the empire. I'm no traitor. I'm not my dad."

"What did he do?"

"Crown him, Tom."

"That's enough," interrupts the nurse, sensing my unease. "He needs to rest."

I try to get out of bed, but the nurse stops me. Everything is fuzzy, unclear. "Florrie!" I shout. "Don't let them take me, Florrie." The Nurse and Red Cap pin me down. "You fuckers can't keep a Casey down. I'm not going to Coney Hill."

"Game's up."

"Keep him still," orders the Nurse as she lifts my shirt sleeve.

"They want to poison you like they did me."

My forearm stings. I start slipping away. Everything, everyone even Dad, falls quiet.

I'm on the Triumph riding along a pitch black tunnel. Dad's riding along next to me. I accelerate. "You'll never lose me Tom, I'm in your soul."

Dad, Mum, Florrie, Stan and Jack shout and bawl from behind cell doors, their faces pressed against the bars. Steam covers me. I reach for a handful but it slips through my fingers. "I love you Celestine," But the words die as soon as they leave my lips.

Six Uhlan lancers stand before me with their carbines raised. I draw my Webley and let off a couple of rounds, hitting one of the Uhlans. His caparisoned horse veers into the next one, allowing me to cleave their line. They give chase. The bike slides from under me. The Uhlans, now aboard dragons, corner me. Fire bleeds from the dragons' mouths. I take aim with my revolver, only the gun is now a flaming sword. I am Saint George. I am England. But all I do is run.

CHAPTER TWENTY-EIGHT

Recuperating by the sea, honoured as a hero, is a welcome treat.

I start my day by leaving my well appointed pensione for a stroll followed by a dip in the sea. At first I could barely manage a handful of strokes but all the same, I relished the briny water washing over me. When I can't swim any further, I sink beneath the waves and claw my way back to the surface. The first few times I feared drowning, but now I enjoy falling from sight.

After a breakfast of boiled eggs and toast, in the company of travelling salesmen and holidaying Belgians, I leave the pensione, find a sunbed, and doze in the sun listening to the steam organs' gay tunes luring people to the funfair rides. Even the gulls sound soft and jolly.

The sweep of Ostend's golden sands draws red faced English day-trippers on the Ramsgate ferry, while the sea front's grand hotels and the Kursaal casino, speak of luxury and success, a lifetime from the war. Even the scaffolding wrapping shell-damaged buildings speaks of new beginnings. But I'm never more than a minute away from thinking about Celestine. I'm desperate to see her and again pledge my love. A hopeless infatuation I know, but I'm *sure* she has feelings for me.

In the third week of my stay, Timmings visited. "I knew you'd ask so I made a few discrete enquiries. Sadly there's no sign of la belle Celestine. She's like the proverbial will-o'-the-wisp."

As to the robbery; "Total mystery. The cocky blighters swan into Mons and pinched the battalion's wages. Over a thousand pounds. Everyone's keeping tight-lipped, but many chaps think the Bolsheviks are involved."

"Bolsheviks?"

"Lenin and his chums."

"Lenin robbed the British army?"

"Not exactly." He leans closer to whisper, "Revolutionary kindred spirits."

"Stop speaking in riddles."

"The reds are fomenting trouble everywhere, Germany, France, Italy, even here in little old Belgium. Haven't you noticed? Mons is plastered with hammer and sickle posters."

"Why would they rob the army?"

"To buy weapons to support the proletariat sweeping to power."

"The what?"

"The proletariat. The workers. You and me, in other words."

"You went to Cheltenham College."

"That's as maybe, Rudge, but they sound glamorous creatures. Not enough to stop me seeking out the Senoritas of Uruguay but intriguing all the same. Just imagine, a Workers' Paradise."

But all I think about is Celestine.

○ ○ ○ ○ ○ ○

The sun glints off the Triumph's new brass exhaust pipe. Timmings has been true to his word and kept the bike in fine fettle.

"Monsieur?" Standing by the coolie compound's fence, Tang beckons me closer and holds out his empty hands in front of him.

"What's the chink doing?" A passing infantryman asks.

"Magic."

Tang claps. An egg appears in his hands. "What the fuck?" says the soldier.

I hand Tang a franc. He trousers the coin and picks up a metal plate and launches it skywards. A revolver lands in his hand. The soldier scratches his head. "Never seen the like."

I hand Tang two francs. The Tommy walks away shaking his head.

The Triumph starts first time, the engine's lazy note a tonic. The bike zips along, skimming over the road, the onrushing air setting my thoughts free, even from Celestine and ingrained fear of the snipers. I pass a gang of coolies digging graves in a field already studded with rows of wooden crosses. Bodies stitched into canvas sacks are laid out waiting to be buried, while a masked priest oversees those being laid to rest.

Reaching Mons, I head for the Grand Place, parking in front of an abandoned shop daubed with a large hammer and sickle. Flower stalls fill the square with a heady, sickly scent. Stallholders and customers haggle. Groups of unemployed men, fags dangling on lips, hands shoved into pockets, watch passers-by, whilst well to do types sip coffee or beer under café awnings. Outside Celestine's hotel, an elderly woman enjoys an early afternoon snifter while watching a drayman struggle to lug crates up the steps into the hotel bar.

Celestine's window has been repaired, but the brickwork surrounding it is pocked with bullet holes. I enter the hotel and hoof it upstairs, smoothing my hair as I climb. I reach her door and knock. No answer. I knock again. There's a key in the lock. My heart races and my mouth dries. The door opens. A fat man wrapped in a dressing gown is surprised to see me. "Oui?"

he asks.

I look at the door number and then over his shoulder, hoping to see her. "Celestine?" I ask.

"Qui?"

"Mon amie Célestine habite dans cette pièce."

"Il n'y a personne du nom de Célestine ici."

Ignoring his jabbering protests, I barge into the room, hollering her name. But Celestine's not here, nor is her jewellery or the Luger. The room smells of this stale, sweaty fat man who smokes cigars and is in fear for his life. I step into the corridor confused, angry, hurt. Celestine loves me. I know she does. But where is she?

I catch the man's eye.

"Clout the fat fucker, Tom."

Seething I clench my fists. He'll do. Just his bad luck he's in Celestine's old room and not next door. He senses trouble and slams the door in my face and locks it.

"She left for Brussels a month ago," the smarmy receptionist tells me.

"Is she coming back?" He shakes his head. "Did she leave an address?"

He seems surprised I care. "They are gone. With the soldiers leaving business was poor."

I stand in the lee of the hotel. The elderly woman is asleep and the drayman eats a sandwich and drinks a bottle of beer in his cab. I walk to the hill we'd pushed the remains of Saint Waltrude up, stop halfway and look back at the hotel. The powerless rage takes hold of me again. I kneel and punch the cobbles. At least pain makes sense.

"Rest your weary bones," whispers Saint Waltrude. "I will grant you succour."

"Monsieur?" Asks a gendarme, standing over me.

"Tout va bien Monsieur, j'attends Celestine."

He helps me up, leads me back to the Triumph and tells me to go home.

After several hours of aimless riding, trying to make sense of things, I wind up back at barracks just as the coolie gravediggers return. One of them is on a stretcher and swathed in bloodied bandages. He'll need morphine, but chances are he won't receive any as the coolies aren't deemed important enough.

Outside the quartermaster's, a group of disinterred Huns, clad in rotted uniforms, lay on the ground. The air is putrid and thick with bluebottles. A stiff-backed priest, pressing a cloth to his face, passes among the dead offering prayers as a private searches for tags and other identification. Any money found will be shared amongst the troops on that day's detail.

A lorry draws up and masked coolies load the putrefied corpses. The lorry's gears grind as it sets off for one of the German cemeteries ringing Mons. The private divvies out the money amongst his pals.

I head for my tent, passing the coolies compound. Petain has laid out his day's booty of gas masks, satchels, a battered French helmet, nose caps, shell casings, rusted bayonets and a muddy .38 Webley. Soldiers look over the flotsam. "Jesus," one says, pointing to the rotting finger wedged in the Webley's trigger. Petain pulls the finger away and holds the revolver up for closer inspection.

"Dirty Chink bastard, no respect for the dead," the soldier says. "How much?"

"Dix francs."

"Cinq."

"Dix."

"Sept."

The soldier pays. Petain passes him the gun through the fence.

I find the brandy in my kit bag. I need to get drunk to force Celestine from my mind. Slinging the brandy in a rucksack, I return to the Triumph. The quartermaster shouts, "I hear your Celestine's left Rudge. I liked her too." My right hook connects and he falls.

"Great shot, Tom."

By force of habit I head towards Mons, but after a few hundred yards I stop, and tear off in the opposite direction, pelting along at break-neck speed, ignoring the rules I'd followed during the war to survive. To see crops springing from battlefields and herds of cows plodding along the patched-up roads, should be heart-warming, proof of life returning to normal. But normality means the lies I've lived for years are no longer of any use. Loving Celestine is the only true feeling I have. Without her what will I be?

I pull up outside a village on the Tournai road and down a third of the brandy. The alcohol burns, its taste angry, sweet, redemptive. I sit on a tree trunk and raise the bottle to my lips. "Idiot. Why did you think you'd be any different?" Seeing all the jewellery stashed in her drawer should have made me realise what a fool I've been for falling in love with her.

My thoughts are mushy and half-baked. I like this place. "Where are you Celestine? Dad? Mum? Florrie? Captain Scott? Jack? Fletcher? Who are you, Tom Casey? What became of you?" I can't scare up an answer for any of these riddles. I've been hiding for so long Tom Casey sounds fanciful, another imposter just like Douglas Rudge.

"My name is Tom Casey. I was born on the ninth of November, eighteen ninety nine. My mother's name is Sal and my father is Joe. He's mad. Maybe I am too. But I know I'm a murderer."

"Got a broken heart, have we?"

I spew a sharp, sickly gruel of bile and brandy. I stand but trip over a root, landing on my shoulder. Bursts of machine-gun fire carry over the air. Staggering to the roadside, I watch a column of motorbikes and sidecars approach. Each rider wears a mask and the gunners fire a volley into the trees, scattering roosting birds. A solo rider, with plaits of thick golden hair dancing in the breeze, train their revolver on me. I beg for a bullet to end it all. But there's no shot.

I mount the Triumph to give chase but after rolling forward a couple of feet, I topple over and trap myself under the bike. Soothed by the brandy's siren song, I stare up at the blue sky, flecked with scattering birds. The Triumph's growl trails off.

○ ○ ○ ○ ○ ○

"Up slowly," orders the officer while nudging me with his swagger stick. He would've been handsome, but his scarred, grey face has been worn down by war. "Name?"

A burning thirst and raging headache assault me. "Corporal Douglas Casey of the Royal Signals, sir, attached to the Third Chinese Labour Corps."

The officer scribbles my details onto a scrap of paper. "You smell like a distillery. Where are you headed?"

"Visiting a girl."

"Where?"

"Mons."

"Long way from Mons."

"She wasn't there."

"Where's she now?"

"Fuck knows."

"Fuck knows, sir."

"Sorry sir."

"So this girl is no longer and you get drunk."

"About the size of it. Then I see the robbers."

"How do you know they were robbers?"

"I witnessed the robbery in Mons. Same bikes, uniforms, masks, the lot."

"Which direction were they travelling?"

"West sir, towards France. I tried to give chase."

"But you ended up asleep on the verge. Unusual tactic." He sizes me up. "Any of that brandy left?" I hand him the bottle. He takes a swig and pulls a face. "Gut rot."

"Steady Tom, don't be hasty."

"You arresting me, sir?"

"My orders are to find and engage with this gang, not scoop up pissed DRs. They've just robbed a bank in Tournai. But we'll be hard pressed to find them in this woodland. Besides, good luck to them. Perhaps they've earned the right." He returns the brandy. "This stuff won't bring her back."

"Yes sir."

He follows his men into the woods, shaking his head and muttering, "Needle in a fucking haystack."

Still half cut, I ride on to Tournai. In the Grand Place, the chaos of the robbery is everywhere. "They killed four and made off with thousands," the estaminet waitress tells me. "We endured the Kaiser's terror, now our liberators rob us. Pity the poor teller they slayed, a wife and three children, the youngest born just last week."

∘ ∘ ○ ∘ ∘

While the bank robbers notoriety spreads, I spend every spare minute looking for Celestine, travelling as far as Brussels and Antwerp. But every brothel, bar and estaminet I visit earns me quizzical looks. Even so I'm still certain that our fates are entwined and that she's set me a test to find her and prove my love.

"You're like Tantalus old chap," Timmings tells me when I return from Charleroi after another fruitless search, "Endlessly torturing yourself over something you have no control over yet want more and more."

"Who?"

"A chap in a Greek myth. Come to think of it, I fancy there's also a touch of Odysseus about you." When I don't answer he says, "Go home and court a nice English girl."

"Nothing to go back to."

"There must be something."

"Tell him you're a murderer." I shake my head.

"Then maybe this will interest you. Got chatting to a chap in the bar the other night. The locals are organising a motorcycle race on Sunday morning. Mons to Tournai and back again, fifty francs to the winner. Why don't we fly the flag for the regiment? We're certain to nick the prize and we'll chalk it down to socialism."

"You still a red?"

"Absolutely. The ladies love a revolutionary."

CHAPTER TWENTY-NINE

A small crowd, huddled under umbrellas, has gathered outside the town hall to watch us set off. Most of the entrants are locals plus Timmings and me. Two Belgian made FN in-line fours pull up, their riders faces hidden behind goggles and scarfs.

"They'll take some beating," says Timmings. "Fastest road bikes in the world."

"The rain gives us a fighting chance," I answer, feeling the butterflies build, as they had when I raced Lieutenant Chatterton. I wish I still had his shilling for luck.

As we fettle and tinker with our bikes, a man wearing a mackintosh and bowler hat walks among us, revelling in his importance. The Belgians grow antsy listening to him.

"Wonder what's exercising them?" Timmings says.

"The roads are not closed for the race," replies a Belgian astride a Douglas. "So you must take your chances."

"Thought nothing different old man," says Timmings. He turns to me and whispers, "Not too dicey is it?"

"Just keep your wits about you."

"Cinque minutes," bowler hat man shouts.

I run through my plan. Start steadily, avoid risks as the rain will have made the unmetalled sections treacherous. Corner smoothly, open her up on the straight sections and pray to God I don't come a cropper on a waterlogged pothole. There's five miles of wood, which will shelter us from the rain but will also mask blind spots. Above all else, finish. If I beat the monstrous FNs, I'm in with a chance.

Shaking my hand Timmings says, "Good luck, old chap. First one home gets the drinks in. Let's show these blighters a thing or two." I nod, tighten my chinstrap and place my goggles over my eyes. Thick drops of rain smear the lenses. Already drenched, I take up my starting position on the third row, beside the two FN's. Timmings has drawn the front row, beside a Harley and an Indian.

A whistle blows. We lean into our bikes. A middle aged woman lowers the start flag. We push off. The other bikes pull away, but my Triumph won't start. The riders behind, pass me. I draw to a halt and examine the engine. Dolt! Fuel tap *again*. By the time the Triumph fires, I'm dead last.

"Stick to the plan Tom."

"What do you think I am going to do?"

Leaving Mons, I close down the two backmarkers despite being blinded by their spray. One runs off the road on a sharp corner and hitting a straight section, I overtake the other rider. The buffeting wind, rain and sodden surface make control difficult but I pass more bikes and start to reel in one of the FN's. Shards of blond hair hang dance around the rider's slender shoulders.

I throw the Triumph forward, taking a long, shallow curve at full throttle. All doubt cast off, I feel alive, no longer guilt ridden. I overtake the FN only for it to zip passed me on the next straight section. I try to get a tow, but the FN pulls away and starts to catch the group Timmings is scrapping with. He's stretched along his fuel tank, overtaking one bike at a time, patient but in control, a good rider. Even if he has shiny buttons and odd political views. On the next short straight the FN catches and passes him.

I reach Tournai's outskirts but the other FN rider, way out in front, is already on the return leg. Timmings and the second FN rider are two hundred yards behind the leader. My group enter Tournai's Grand Place. A lorry pulls out. The other bikes slow but I mount the pavement, squeeze through the narrow gap and then brake to avoid hitting a group of shocked, wide eyed nuns.

The return leg. I know where the bends are tight and the ruts deepest. The rain will help me. I have a chance.

Two miles on, sunshine has replaced the rain and the cobbles now throw up a blinding, relentless glare. The slim FN rider has pulled up on the verge. That leaves the other FN and Timmings. A Norton flies passed me, her pilot flattened along the tank. The Norton hits a puddle, jack knifes and catapults the rider over the handlebars while the bike cartwheels into a hedgerow. Shocked by the purler, I slow and allow the second FN to overtake me.

With Mons' spires looming in the grey distance, I decide to give it full chat. I'm on the floor, tumbling and sliding until I come to winded halt. Two Harleys and the mighty Indian manage to swerve around me. My Triumph lays in a ditch. The left brake lever and footrest are snapped, but there's life in the engine. Dander up, I remount and charge.

I catch the Yank bikes and we dice through Mons narrow streets, at one point pinning the morning's churchgoers against a wall. Like skittish colts, the bikes judder and kick up over the cobbles, their growling, strained exhaust notes bouncing around of the narrow street's buildings. I lead going up the slight incline towards the Grand Place and manage to keep the Indian at bay but the two Harleys catch and pass me on the finish line.

Timmings is sheltering in the bandstand and looking pleased with himself. "What kept you?"

"Did you win?"

He shakes his head."The FNs finished first and second. They've already scarpered. Didn't even collect their winnings."

"Think one of them was a woman."

"I know. Who'd have thought a woman would lick us? A dark day for the regiment." He lights his pipe, "All down to the blasted FN. We had the road craft, guile, and knowledge. Put us on their bikes and we'd win by a country mile." He draws on his pipe. "There is some good news though. As first and second have scarpered, I've been awarded their prize money as well as my own." In pidgin French he announces to the other rain sodden, mud splattered finishers that the drinks are on him.

At first Ursula is annoyed at having to open the bar, but as the stragglers return and our stories grow taller and songs more boisterous, her mood softens and she embraces the reverie.

Warming myself by the fire, I think about the female FN rider. I've seen her before, on the Tournai Road aiming a pistol at me. Timmings thrusts a glass of beer in my hand and as I drain it, Celestine hoves into view. Three glasses of beer later she's still tormenting my fragile memory. To clear my sour thoughts I go outside.

"There you are, old chap," says Timmings staggering towards me, puffing on a cigar while spilling his beer. "She haunting you again?"

"About the strength of it."

He clasps my shoulder. "Give it till May when we'll be heaving that bloody Dray up the hill again. If old Saint Waltrude can't offer you any pointers, give up. It will have been a year since you last saw her. Even you should realise that by then there's nothing to look for."

"Break the feckers' jaw, Tom. Teach him a lesson."

He goes inside to cheers followed by a Flemish rendition of 'It's a Long Way to Tipperary'.

I hang back.

But if I should die on a foreign land
and be buried so far, far away
no fond mother's tears will be shed o're my grave
on the Shores of Amerikay.

We're outside Ursula's bar basking in the glorious May sunshine. Ursula sets down two blond beers in front of us. Timmings kisses her hand.

"Charmer," I tell him.

"Manners maketh man."

"When you setting sail for Uruguay?"

"I sail for Montevideo's steamy bordellos this autumn."

"And Ursula?"

"I'll send for her in due course. A gentleman always keeps his word. There's still time for you to come with me. My uncle could use a man with your pluck. Chance to build a new life for yourself. Much better than this mad notion you've got in your head." He picks up the advert sitting underneath an empty glass and reads, "Join the Royal Irish Constabulary, the finest in the world. Ten shillings a day, plus bonus, free billeting and a month's paid leave. If you have the physique, good character and if you are or have been in the Services you can join the RIC today." He laughs. "You'll have fun chasing Fenians around Ireland's bogs. Your ugly mug will make great target practice for snipers." From his tunic pocket he hands me a timetable for the Royal Mail steam packet to Buenos Aires. "This may come in handy after your madcap adventure Rudge."

But Ireland makes sense. Douglas Rudge can stay in the shadows whilst Tom Casey purges Dad's treachery and Celestine's memory. Another simple, fool-proof plan. I pocket the timetable. There's no need to have a row. Not today.

Leaving the bar, we push through the crowd gathering around the Dray carrying Saint Waltrude's remains.

"Only us two in uniform this year," Timmings observes.

"No bad thing."

The old woman stands on the same spot clasping her rosary and muttering prayers with the same manic air about her. I smile at her and she prays even more fervently. Timmings claps me on the shoulder and says, "Ready to save a city old chap?" He's buffed his buttons again.

"Might as well." I reply, sensing Fletcher beside me.

The driver encourages his horses. Timmings, me, and scores of others heave the Dray forward. Saint Waltrude begins her journey once again.

CHAPTER THIRTY

June 1920 — Dingle, County Kerry, Ireland

The armoured Rolls leads the Crossley out from barracks and heads into Dingle. I'm in the Roll's passenger seat next to the driver whilst our gunner, a Gallipoli veteran, perches in the turret.

Reaching Dingle harbour, the smack of brine fills the cab. Tied up fishing boats bob in the restless water, while, quayside, women young and old, stand at tables gutting and beheading fish. Seeing us, they draw closer whilst shooing away a half starved mongrel. A barefoot woman hawks eggs and butter. Nearby a toothless old man hopes to scoop a penny or two by warbling in the Irish. I spot the pretty girl I'd spoken to last week, only now her hair's been shaved and her left cheek is swollen.

"Talking to the likes of ye caused that Collins," the gunner mutters in his thick Irish brogue. He gave me the nickname as he thinks I'm a dead ringer for Michael Collins, the Shinners leader. I struggle to see any likeness, but the joke has made the other men wary of me.

What if Dad hadn't left Ireland for the army? Would I be one of the young, bitter faced men looking on with malice, with no doubt one or two plotting our deaths? Maybe if I look hard enough I'll see myself.

A windswept, red-faced auctioneer moves among the crates of fish flogging them to mealy mouthed fishmongers from Tralee and Killarney. "You're the spit of them, Collins," the gunner says, "Why doncha stand 'em all a pint?"

We head out west passing Dingle's mournful cemetery and run along the coast road."Fuckin' boneshaker," the gunner grumbles as the Rolls clatters over jarring potholes outside Ventry, where a broiling bank of sea mist has cut visibility to a few feet. The driver, ever wary of a Shinner ambush, slows to keep the Crossley in sight. A pony and trap emerges through the fog. For a half second I think it's Saint Waltrude until I spot the milk churn. A farmer on his way to the creamery. We pull up in front of the trap's blinkered, champing nag and the captain steps from the Crossley, adjusting the holstered revolvers sitting on each hip. A scarred, dark soul, held together by whiskey and rage, he earned the Military Cross on the first day of the Somme for singlehandedly capturing a baker's dozen of Huns. A day later he's sliced by shrapnel, earning him a Blighty Ticket. But he stayed on, overseeing military jails and firing squads used for cowards and deserters. Ireland's war suits him.

As the milk churn is tossed from the cart, the farmer wisely bites his tongue and stares straight ahead as we head off into the fog. Tiptoeing around Slea Head, the mist splits long enough to let us glimpse the craggy, sheer outlines of the Blasket Islands erupting from the Atlantic. Why anyone would choose to hack out a life on a windswept island battered by the storms and ocean is beyond me.

The gunner sights along the Vickers as the sheds and boats tied up in the small harbour serving the islands, are searched. We find nothing so move on, the fog growing thicker.

Every day is like this. Patrol. Search. Question. If we're lucky we find something or someone, but most days we return to barracks empty-handed. In this grey, sodden, fog-bound world, studded by statues venerating the Virgin, everything seems twisted, half-formed. Even our uniforms are cobbled together from army and police stores earning us the name Black and Tans.

We're cooped up all day, in vehicles or in the barracks, spied on from near or far, ever mindful of snipers, mortars or bombs, hating living in thrall to the Shinners. If it were game of cat and mouse, who's the cat and who's the mouse is anyone's guess. At least with the Hun you were so close you could hear them speaking, smell their nosh and fags, even watch the steam rise from their piss.

But the Tans in my unit, veterans decorated for their wartime exploits, delight in this lawless, reckless combat, bolstered by good pay and a generous pension. In Flanders and the Somme, fear had sustained them. Here they run on hate and whiskey, kicking in doors, razing homes, meting out beatings and shooting man or beast. All in the king's name.

Living cheek-by-drunken-jowl for three months, tempers quickly fray and fists flail. Anything triggers a brawl; cheating at cards, pilfering, insults real or imagined, even aping accents. The gunner stands out in this regard. "Only rootless feckers wind up in this mouldy shite hole," he slurred, staring into a near-empty bottle of Powers, a week after we'd pitched up here. A southpaw, once his regiment's middleweight champion, he switches from delight to fury in the beat of a mottled gull's wing. Twice he's come for me. Why I've no idea, but both times I thought I was done for until seconds later he checked himself and cracked a joke. We're more afraid of him than the Shinners. It's no surprise the captain rates him. I already rue the day I steamed into Queenstown Bay to sign up with the Royal Irish Constabulary. Christ, trying to reach Antarctica on my Triumph would have been wiser. I was mad to think Ireland would help me forget Celestine and permit me to atone for Dad's treachery.

"Thank fuck," the gunner says, rubbing his backside as a herd of wandering Friesians force us to a halt. Engine fumes fill the cab. I press my face to the viewing slit to draw in lungfuls of the sweet, damp air and stare at a cow's incurious face. A weather-beaten farmer, cap pulled down, lips clamped around a fag, bawls instructions in the Irish and his dog snaps at the cattle's heels, forcing them to break into an ungainly trot towards a bracken-lined field. For once we don't stop to question the farmer and press on towards three giant headlands leaning into the bitter mist. When the Three Sisters come into view I whisper, "Protect me."

The first time I heard their name I thought the coincidence too great and I was sure I'd started on the path to madness. Dad's tales of suffering and magic are a lifetime ago, but I understand why this land, as hard as the hob of hell, sires such myths. Now I'm heartened to see the Sisters all the more since learning about the legend of two ancient lovers once sheltering there. I'll bring Celestine here. Then she'll understand.

The men fan out across the field and approach a farmhouse where information received from Tralee HQ indicates suspicious activity. Stepping from the cab, I stretch my stiff legs, light a crafty fag, cup it, and run my spare hand over the bullet marks pitting the Rolls's armour.

Sometime later the men seep through the fog empty-handed, their foot sore frustration plain to see. We drive on, the ruts shooting jagged spasms of pain up our arses, spines and necks, stopping to question loiterers and raid the odd farm. But there's no Shinners today.

∘ ∘ ○ ○ ∘ ∘

"Reckon them sheep have Republican sympathies, Collins," the gunner jokes as the sheep blocking the road ignore our horns. I climb out. From the Crossley a wag shouts, "Come by" and "Away to me," as I herd the sheep into a field, only to watch them hop over a derelict wall and clog the road twenty yards on. The captain, mithered by the delay, limps towards me pistol in hand and shoots dead the nearest ewe. As the other sheep scatter he rasps, "Get moving." Last night's booze still sits on his breath.

By early afternoon the fog has burned off and sunshine breaches the grey sky, dappling the dark green, waterlogged land, dotted with grazing sheep and cattle. In places, thick mud makes the road impassable, forcing us to deploy the ditching beams slung along the Rolls's running boards.

We raid a farm, outside the village of Camp before we cut south towards Annascual. Again we don't stop and the driver crunches the Rolls's gears and fights the juddering steering wheel as we wind uphill through steep, sharp hairpins towards Lispole where we'll set up a blockade and with luck have time for a mouthful of cold tea and a stale ham sandwich. After eating, the men deploy, their mood sour and resentful. They've had enough for the day. Someone will cop for it.

"Betcha this roadblock throws up fuck all," grumbles the gunner. "Same fuckin' rigmarole tomorrow."

By four o'clock we've stopped a lorry carrying seaweed; a handful of cyclists; and two pony-and-traps heading for Dingle.

A half-cut fishmonger, making for Killarney, pulls up. "Help yerselves to a couple of fillets lads." he says. As we stow the mackerel in the Rolls, a car heading from Dingle, accelerates, and tries to break through the road block, hitting one of our lads and forcing others to jump clear. The men open fire as the car swerves around the Rolls, shattering the car's rear window and peppering the bodywork. The car snakes across the road and tips into a ditch. Under fire, the driver scrambles out and finds shelter behind an abandoned, rusting thresher. Our lads close in but drop to the ground when he begins shooting.

I jump into my seat, scattering the mackerel and sight along the Hotchkiss. The Shinner takes half a step backwards, losing his cover. The gunner fires two short bursts. The Shinner falls. "Sweet Jesus, I've just killed a Patriot," the gunner says, making a sign of the cross. "May God have mercy on my soul."

A short, thickset man is dragged from the car's passenger seat and thrown to the floor. The men's blood is up. An execution is in the offing. The day will have been worthwhile after all. But for once the captain orders them not to harm the prisoner as he's dragged to the Crossley, blathering in the Irish and leaving a trail of blood on the tarmac.

"What's he saying?" I ask the gunner.

"Fuck knows. Only speak the King's English me."

○ ○ ○ ○ ○ ○

"How's our man doctor?" the captain asks.

Before answering, the doctor, a tall, athletic man in his fifties with a noble but worn air, wipes his hands on a towel and says, "Tibia and fibula are fractured. They'll need to be reset in Tralee hospital."

"And Mr Danaher?"

Danaher? The same name that copper Manning mentioned all those years ago.

"The bullet passed through his right thigh. I've patched him up as best I can but he needs to be in hospital too."

"All in good time doctor. By the way, did he tell you anything?"

"I'm afraid I can't tell you captain."

The captain leans forward. "Tell me."

"No."

"Fine," he says, his breath frosting the doctor's spectacles. "Expect a visit soon."

"If needs be. Good evening, captain."

"Evening, doctor."

With a look of tired despair, the doctor picks up his medicine bag, plonks the weathered homburg on his head and steps into rain lashed court yard.

CHAPTER THIRTY-ONE

Apart from one light in the kitchen, the barracks lay in darkness. The gloomy, single storey, stone building east of Dingle, can't have seen a lick of paint since being built. The roof leaks and clumps of the lime and horsehair plaster lay exposed. Where the plaster is still intact, crooked fingers of mould spread along the walls. The dormitory built for six, but holding twenty of us, reeks of stale men. Only the captain has his own quarters, a converted store cupboard, which sits beside the racks housing our arsenal of Lee Enfields, Thompson sub-machine guns, and Mills bombs.

Stodgy, tasteless breakfasts, dinners, and teas are rustled up on a worn out range in a kitchen no larger than a confessional, and the canteen also doubles up as a washroom, where two peat-burning stoves are on the go day and night, fighting the chill and damp. The one toilet, usually blocked or overflowing, sits in a small outhouse, accessed through the cell block. Crucifixes hang in every room, even the toilet.

"All quiet," the gunner says, returning from a recce around the ten feet high perimeter walls." What time is it?"

"Just gone three."

"Fuck. Another three hours." He pulls out a hip flask. "Fancy a nip?"

"No thanks."

He takes a sip and smacks his lips. "That's hit the spot." After taking another swig he says, "Fancy marching into Dingle, Collins? Find a couple of Colleens, dangle some gleaming shillings in their faces and watch their eyes open wide with delight. Their legs too."

"On your own there."

We wade through ankle-deep mud and climb inside the Rolls for a smoke." Jesus, that mackerel's rank," says the gunner. "Prince of fish mind."

Leaving the door ajar I hand him a Players and ask, "Why are you here?"

"The Peelers offer good money and a man has to work."

"Aren't you worried about revenge?"

"'Course. But there's fuck all in Ireland for rack rentin' hallions like me. Besides, I missed the Vickers' gentle song."

"Do you think we'll win?"

He smiles but can't hide the menacing glint in his flint hard eyes. "Not a chance. We're mercenaries, they're patriots. Whole country's at war with us. On their knees praying but still plotting our deaths. Young men attack us with rakes whilst old Bridgey down the boreen hides ordnance. Labourers dig traps and trenches. Quarrymen steal explosives. Farriers mould lead into buckshot. Jewellers repair weapons. Tailors stitch uniforms. They even have their children smuggling weapons and passing on messages sewn into their coats. So what do we do? Arrest people for whistling folk songs or reading the wrong newspaper. Sweet Jesus they're about to outlaw the bicycle in Ireland. That'll turn the fuckin' tide." He takes a drag. "Know what the Shinners' weapons of choice is?"

"No,"

"The Lee Enfield rifle. Home grown. That's the fuckin' English for ye, always keen to make a few bob even if it involves the departure of their fellow countrymen, even us upstanding men sworn to uphold the law of the land."

"What'll you do when this ends?"

"That'll not be anytime soon. Too much sport to be had yet." He crushes his Players against the Rolls' door. "But when it's finished and if by the grace of God, I'm still alive, I'll head west, to America. Maybe not on a coffin ship, but I'll gather up the family and scuttle off. May even go without them. They'd be better off without me anyways. Flanders turned me. Made me a killer. Got two brothers in a Shinners' Flying Column up in Cavan. They're the heroes whilst I'm the traitor. Tell me how that happened, Winston, me old chum? I fought the war to end all wars. Now a year later, here I am fighting my kin on England's doorstep."

I light another Players. "Why are ye here, Collins? Get a taste for war from the trenches?"

"I was a DR."

He scoffs. "Now I've heard everything. Why would a DR be fool enough to come to this place?"

"Had nothing to go home to. This seemed as good a place as any."

"You set the fuckin' bar low enough."

"Made a mistake coming here."

"Finally, some common fuckin' sense." He rubs his hands then blows into them. "So, where will ye head?"

"Uruguay."

"For feck's sake."

"I've a pal out there. Said he could fix me up."

"This land knows my rancid secrets and will slay me, given half the chance. And if the Shinners don't catch up with me, some befuddled Holy Man in a frayed surplus will tramp through the rain to proclaim my damnation. Catch the captain when he's sober, granted, a rare event, and hand in your notice. No shame in it. Most lads don't stick it. Do it though, otherwise ye'll meet a violent, untimely end."

"I'm proud to serve."

"There's only one thing to be proud of in war and that's to get out with your blood still pumping around your veins. One thing though."

"What?"

"That Danaher fella must be important."

Danaher. "Why say that?"

"Anyone else and the captain would have executed him on the spot."

○ ○ ○ ○ ○ ○

The daily patrol heads into Dingle. My last duty before grabbing a few hours' kip is to feed the prisoner. In the kitchen I pour a drop of cold, stewed tea into an enamel cup, find a slice of stale bread, and head towards the cells hoping the Danaher in the cells isn't the man Dad had helped escape justice years before.

"Time to meet an old friend, Tom."

Danaher winces as he sits up and struggles to draws the thin blanket tight around his shoulders with his one good hand. Dried blood stains his swollen, sweat soaked but intelligent face. His right trouser leg is split along its seam, revealing the bloodstained strapping on his thigh. I step into the cell and set his plate and cup down beside him. Fearful of a beating, he leans away from me, again wincing with the effort.

"Spare a fag?" he asks in a yank twinged Irish accent. I hand him a Players and light it. He sucks the smoke deep into his lungs, coughs and holds his ribs. "Some hero eh?"

"I know you"

"What?" I've caught him off guard. "How?"

"Say nothing, Tom."

"My dad helped you escape from Gloucester in nineteen twelve." He racks his brain and then nods slowly. "I remember. The Birmingham job. Escaped on the Barge. We barely spoke, just shook hands after he hid me in the ship's lifeboat. Your pa's a patriot."

"He's a traitor and you still need to pay for those two officers you killed."

"Two, was it? I thought it just the one." He shifts and grimaces at the same time. "They were casualties of a war not of my choosing."

"We sold your Triumph to a colonel in the British army."

"That'll break him."

"S'pose that makes me a collaborator." He takes another drag. "Tell me, what's the son of a Patriot doing in the British army?"

"Atoning for his treachery."

"What treachery?"

"My dad helping you, shamed my family."

"And you're here attempting to make good? By brutalising Ireland and her people."

Confronting him isn't working out." Honest, steadfast, and loyal to those I love."

"I feel the same towards Ireland."

"Not the same."

"Why not?"

"Ireland's part of the Empire."

"Says who?"

"The king."

"Does your pa agree?"

"Couldn't tell you."

"Why not?"

"Last I heard he's still in the asylum."

'Feckin' gobshite, why tell him that?'

My confession makes me hate Danaher all the more and I fight the urge to stove his head in. Better still, I'll fetch my rifle and shoot him. Make out he tried to escape or some such. The gunner will back me up. Open and shut case. Nobody will give a shit over another dead Shinner.

"Sorry to hear that."

"Why?"

"I've a Christian disposition."

"Why did he help you?"

"You'll have to ask him."

He sips his tea and screws up his face. "You forgot the sugar."

"Fuck off."

"Love to."

"Why were you in Dingle?"

"Coming home to fight."

"You should have fought in the war. Showed your loyalty to the crown."

"He's not my king."

"Course he is. He's the king of an empire where the sun never sets."

"One day it'll set over Ireland."

"We're not leaving. We saw off the Huns and the Turks. You'll be next."

"You've lost already."

"How do you figure that out?"

"You flog us, shoot us, and raze our homes. But that only makes us stronger, more determined to fight."

"I'm just doing my duty."

"And what if your duty oppresses the innocent? What do you do then?"

"Shut the fuck up."

"An Englishman's response to the colonies."

"I believe in England. The empire. I fought for it."

"Empty words."

"Not to me."

"One day you'll believe something different."

"Doubt it."

"Help me," he asks in a strained, fearful voice. "They're going to kill me. Help a fellow Irishman."

Now I'm knocked off kilter. If I help him, I can lessen Dad's suffering. It'll be easy enough, there's just the gunner and me here.

"Grub up, Collins!" the gunner shouts, bringing me back to sanity.

"Collins?" Danaher whispers. "Fine name."

"It's my nickname."

"A fine honorific."

"What?"

"A dandy nickname." He leans forward wincing with the effort to whisper, "Please, help me. If only for your pa."

"I'm no traitor."

Disappointed, he sits back. I lock the cell door and peer through the grill. Danaher takes a final draw on the cigarette and grab his ribs as another coughing fit erupts.

In the kitchen, the gunner slops porridge into a bowl. It tastes rank. "How's the prisoner?" he asks.

"Fine. Glad we're getting shot of him tomorrow."

He sniggers.

"What's so funny?" I ask.

"The captain has plans for him."

CHAPTER THIRTY-TWO

A slew of plates, glasses and beer bottles cover the mess tables. Cigarette smoke stings the eyes. The captain appears from his room with a crate of Powers. To cheers, he plonks four bottles on each table.

"Drink up, lads," He barks, pulling the cork from a bottle. "Proper soldiering at last. Cornelius Danaher in custody, another Shinner dead and more heads cracked. Grand sport." He downs a large slug of Powers and begins to sing a rousing version of 'Lloyd George's Beer'. The men raise their sloshing glasses to salute Lloyd George.

When it's his turn to sing, the gunner recites a mournful Irish lament. A loudmouth Geordie slurs, "Why's he singing a Shinner song?"

"I'll sing what I fuckin' well like," answers the gunner, shrouded in violent intent.

"But you're singing in the traitors' tongue." A punch up beckons. Everyone knows who'll win but that doesn't curb their gleeful, feral excitement. Sport. But the captain puts paid to things. "Enough now chaps. We've had a good day. No need to end it on a sour note."

"That's as maybe captain, but this fucker's decryin' me birth right. In me own land." He wears that distant, empty eyed look we've grown to fear.

"Quarrel's not with you." the Geordie tells him. "It's with that Shinner in the cells."

The gunner snatches a bottle of Powers from the table and leaves. The captain drains three more fingers of whiskey, leans back in his chair and listens to the Geordie strike up the first verse of 'Old Gallipoli'. The other Gallipoli veteran, a Belfast man joins in, but fearing for Danaher, I set of after the gunner.

"Where you off to, Rudge?" asks the captain, blocking my path. In the gloom, he's reduced to an unsteady silhouette.

"To check on the prisoner, sir."

"No rush. Have a drink." He hands me the bottle. I take a swig. "I must say our actions these past few days have stirred the blood, Rudge. At least the Hun looked us in the eye, stood toe to toe and slugged it out honourably. Not like these bastards. And after all we sacrificed for them in France."

"Careful, Tom."

"Perhaps we shouldn't be here sir."

"Didn't think you're the type to grasp the Irish Question, Rudge."

"More to me than meets the eye sir."

 138

"Sweet Jesus."

"If they didn't kill constables and torch police barracks, there'd be no need for us. Obey the law and we'll leave. If not, suffer the consequences. Don't you agree?"

"Absolutely sir. Loyal servant to the king, that's me."

"What about the gunner?"

"What about him? You know he gets lairy with drink."

"I do. So, I've set him a test. To prove his loyalty. We'll know soon enough if he passes."

○ ○ ○ ○ ○ ○

Danaher's cell door lies open. The gunner stands over him, a lamp in one hand, a bottle of Powers in the other. "Mr Danaher! Sometimes an Irishman prefers another Irishman's company." He offers Danaher the whiskey. "Don't fret, it's Irish whiskey."

"What you doing?" I ask. The gunner swings around and raises the bottle towards me. "See this fella, Mr Danaher," he says with a hard edge. "He hared around on a motorbike in the war, transportin' little bits of paper, whilst the likes of me crawled over the dead and slogged through filth."

"An Englishman's war," Danaher replies. "Not my war."

The gunner smiles. "May I say, Mr Danaher, you possess the wisdom of Solomon." He squats in front of Danaher and sets the lamp down on the floor, allowing his knotty shadow to crawl up the cell wall. He pulls a revolver from his belt. "But in this instance I'll be the judge." Danaher looks at me. "Yesterday, Mr Danaher, I killed a fine Irishman. By all that's holy I don't know why I did it. I didn't need to. Enjoyed it though. Strange, seeing I am a proud son of Erin. Even you Shinners could count on me."

He presses his revolver's barrel into Danaher's right thigh, making him squirm with pain. "But you bastards forced me to kill one of my own, leaving me with no country and making me a traitor. The question is. Am I guilty of treason?"

Without warning, he thrusts the barrel into his mouth, cocks the trigger and fires. The hammer clicks. No shot rings out. Pulling the gun from his mouth, the gunner smiles. "Seems not. So, if I'm no traitor, you must be, Mr Danaher."

Danaher gags as the gunner thrusts the barrel into his mouth. He pulls the trigger. Again nothing. "Fuck me, you may have a just cause after all," says the bemused gunner. He takes a swig of whiskey, returns the revolver to his mouth and pulls the trigger. Still nothing. The final verse of *Old Gallipoli* drifts in from the barracks. "Typical. Watched all of them poor Irish lads die in France, wept for their mothers and now the Holy Virgin spares me."

"Thas' enough Mick," I say. "What mad man gambles his life just for sport?"

"Says who? An Englishman with no future?" The gunner swivels and takes aim at me. I step back. "Good lad," he says before turning his attention on Danaher again. "One more turn Mr Danaher? Just to be sure we've both earned our Lord's forgiveness."

"Please," Danaher pleads before the muzzle is thrust into his mouth. His breaths are short, nostrils flared, panicked eyes fixed on the gunner.

The gunner cocks and fires. Nothing. "Sweet mother o'fuck, who'd have thought? We're both pure of heart." He pulls the muzzle from Danaher's mouth and studies it, like a child examining a favourite toy. "Two chambers. One bullet. Who's it going to be, Mr Danaher? You or me?"

He puts the barrel in his mouth and bites down. He squeezes the trigger. The blast is deafening. The gunner slumps to the floor taking his shadow with him. The revolver spills from his hand.

Danaher screams as if possessed.

∘ ∘ ○ ○ ∘ ∘

I can still taste vomit as I light a cigarette.

"Look like you've seen a ghost, Rudge," the Geordie tells me.

"Saw him do it."

Shaking his head, he says, "Must have been a sight an' half. Always knew the Mick was off his onion. Still had the Somme in his blood."

How far would I get if I ran? Who'd catch me first? The captain or the Shinners?

"So, Douglas Rudge wants to take his chances in England."

The gunner's corpse is brought out on a stretcher and stowed beside Danaher's driver in the Crossley. The barracks are silent, the bottles of Powers abandoned, except for the captain who pours us both a snort. "Feeling better?" he asks, handing me a glass with five fingers worth. Just the smell is enough to make me gag.

"A bit, sir. Came as a bit of a shock."

"I can imagine." He drinks two fingers worth, smack his lips and looks at me in his usual off-hand manner. "Think I'll write this up as an accident.

Don't want anyone sniffing around making life awkward for the men. I trust you'll keep what happened under your hat."

"Course sir."

"Good chap. Keep an eye on Danaher. Don't want anything happening to him."

The gunner's fading lamp lights up the ashen faced, disbelieving Danaher. He sits bolt upright staring at the splatter of blood and brains plastered on the opposite wall.

"Help me. Please," he whispers. An hour ago I wanted him to pay for murdering those Brummie coppers. But now I share his terror of this sealed, debased world we're caught in. I fight my rising shame for just thinking about betraying England. "Can't," I tell him.

"But you're an Irishman at heart."

Maybe I am. But I'm also a coward.

○ ○ ○ ○ ○ ○

"Here it is," the Geordie says reading the *Daily Mail.* "Depraved Fenian Police Killer hanged in Birmingham's Winson Green Prison."

"It says that Danaher was captured thanks to the brave and selfless actions of the Royal Irish Constabulary in County Kerry." He hands the paper to the fella on his left and says, "We'll be heroes back home. Could be worth a pint or two."

"And a fuck or two," adds the Yorkshireman.

"No mention of the gunner?" I ask. The Geordie raises an eyebrow. Nobody has mentioned him since. As if he's a curse. A bitter mood has gripped the men and egged on by the captain, they have found refuge in violence. Beatings are more savage, razings more frequent and shootings celebrated with more whiskey and song. But the violence only masks our fears. The Shinners are still out there watching and waiting. Danaher was right. A Vickers or Lee Enfield won't quell these people. Their land is chocked with centuries of suffering. There's no place for the king here.

CHAPTER THIRTY-THREE

As usual there's a large crowd for Annascual's monthly fair. An unsteady wheel of fortune spins, hawkers peddle sweets and biscuits whilst locals in Sunday best, stand bamboozled around a playing card trickster as a fiddler competes for their attention. A costermonger taps out a tune on two saucepans while a clatty beggar seeks alms from haggling farmers, shepherds and merchants standing outside a pub. A fish merchant does a roaring trade selling glinting fresh mackerel and herring while a wily old mongrel eyes the fillets with intent.

Everything, even the wheel of fortune, grinds to a halt when we pull up and dismount.

"Fix bayonets," orders the captain. Unease ripples among the crowd as the foot-long bayonets click into place. The bulk of the men are deployed to keep an eye on the locals, while the captain and the rest of us hurry towards a row of cottages, stopping outside the fourth cottage. The Geordie kicks in the front door and we pile in shouting and screaming.

The rich scents of pipe tobacco and burning peat fill the air. A kettle steams. Three lads charge upstairs while the captain, Geordie and me enter the kitchen where a silver haired man, about fifty, well-built with weathered features, fries rashers. A younger, heavily pregnant woman consoles a whimpering toddler.

A frayed Union Jack, a row of medals, and a ceremonial sword hang beside a crucifix over the mantel, on which sits a photograph of men wearing seal skins aboard a ship. One of the men is Captain Scott. The man frying the rashers, or a younger version of him, stands beside Scott.

"Eileen Crean?" the captain asks the woman. She nods. "We've received reports that you took part in a seditious act."

She answers, "I attended Thomas Ashe's memorial. Honouring the deceased is no act of sedition."

"A man who swore allegiance to enemies of the crown."

"He gave his life for his beliefs."

○ ○ ○ ○ ○ ○

Above us, floorboards creak, doors open and slam shut. Eileen Crean comforts the screaming toddler and watches the captain examine the military regalia on the mantel. "Did you serve?" he asks the man, while pointing to the Union Jack.

"I did and for twenty years before," he answers in a thick Kerry brogue.

"Where did you see service?"

"Royal Navy. Antarctica. Warrant Officer First Class. Once anyway."

"You're Tom Crean," I interrupt. "The Tom Crean who sailed with Scott and Shackleton?"

"The same."

Without thinking I shoulder my rifle and shake his hand." An honour to meet you, Mr Crean." He looks surprised, wary even. Facing the captain I say, "Sir, Tom Crean's a hero. He once crossed eight hundred miles of the wild Southern Ocean with Ernest Shackleton to save his stranded comrades."

The captain ignores me and picks up a silver teapot resting on the table. He reads the engraving on the pot's base. "Wishing you a long and happy marriage. Ernest and Emily Shackleton." He turns to Crean and smiles. "The great Mr Shackleton! Rudge is right Mr Crean, you *are* a hero." Setting the teapot down he whispers, "But while you were hopping about icebergs, I fought for my country's freedom."

"Sailed with a lot of good men captain, from all corners of the globe. Don't consider many to be my enemy."

"Shame I don't share your optimistic viewpoint." The captain tips the photograph onto the floor and stamps on it with the heel of his boot, splintering the glass case. Eileen Crean flinches. The child screams. But Crean keeps his cool.

"A hero. Nothin' more or less. And that's how they treat him."

"Torch the house sir?" asks the Geordie.

For once the captain is unsure. He looks at Crean who stares back with no hint of fear." Not today. As Rudge might say, wouldn't be right torching a heroes house." He nods to Crean and leaves. The Geordie follows. I stay put.

"What was Captain Scott like?" I ask. Crean runs a cool eye over me and says, "A good man, with a good heart. But stupid too. English. What do ye expect?"

143

"Rudge!" shouts the Geordie. I nod to Crean and leave, with the infant's sobs ringing in my ears.

Clothes, furniture and bed linen litter the road outside the Creans' cottage. Two men on push bikes speed up as they pass, eyes dead ahead. The dog runs off with a mackerel fillet, but the fishmonger stays rooted to the spot, eyes fixed on us. I clamber aboard the Crossley aware of the men's anger towards me. The captain takes a snifter from his hip flask and glances at me before giving the order to move out.

○ ○ ○ ○ ○ ○

The Geordie wakes me. "Captain wants a word."

I'm dragged me from my cot and out into the courtyard. The captain, in full regalia, sits behind a desk, oblivious to the rain. A flickering lamp lights his sodden, scarred features. A bottle of Powers rests beside the lamp. It makes for a mad, deluded sight. Satan in judgement.

Pouring himself three fingers worth, the captain drinks without taking his eyes off me, his endless fury plain to see. He sets his glass down, lights a cigarette and asks, "You a Shinner, Rudge?"

"Sorry sir?"

"Are you a Shinner?"

"I'm proud to serve my king and the empire."

A stomach punch winds me. "Well?" The captain asks.

"Well what, sir?" I groan.

A rifle butt strikes my knee. I buckle. The captain leaves his desk and helps me to stand. "Always found it hard to swallow that a DR would choose to come to Ireland. Don't think I haven't noticed. Always last to volunteer, always fumbling with your weapon, never shot or even struck a native, even when they're asking for it, which is to say all the fucking time." He grinds his fag into the mud and wipes the rain from his face. "Today you come to the aid of a known Fenian sympathiser and chose to undermine my authority, thus imperilling the lives of these stout, loyal men; *my* stout loyal men."

"Tom Crean's a hero, sir."

"He's Irish and therefore our enemy. Revealed your true sympathies today Rudge. I learned in France that there's only one course of action for remedying a traitor."

He signals to the Geordie who leads me towards the perimeter wall. I'm tethered to a large metal ring embedded in the plaster. Eight men all shouldering rifles, form up twenty paces from me. The driving rain drips from their capes They're the same faceless ghouls who chased me and Jack in Waterman's warehouse. The Geordie places a flour sack over my head. "Please, I served my country." He doesn't answer.

"Stand ready!" Bolt actions slide.

Time slows, each second precious. I think of Mum, Florrie, and Stan and see Dad struggling in his straitjacket. I'm in Coney Hill, my head in a shit-stinking sack doused by pelting Fenian rain. When the order is given, Englishmen and Irishmen will execute me. To think I came here to find redemption. But now both countries will have a hand in my death.

"Take aim!"

I don't want to die. It only took me a second to slay Alf Fenwick and another second to shake Tom Crean's hand. Two measly seconds to turn my life inside out.

"Shoulders back, Tom. Face them true."

"FIRE!"

Rain hammers the barrack's tin roof. I suck in deep breaths, coating my lips with the dregs of flour in the bag. A stream of piss trickles down my trembling right leg. Squelching footsteps approach. The Geordie takes off the hood as to a man, the firing squad roar with laughter. None of them take their eye off me. Fuckers. I fight my bindings but they only tighten. The Geordie levels the butt of his rifle to my face.

∘ ∘ ○ ○ ∘ ∘

My head is splitting. I'm confused and don't know where I am. A caterwauling chorus flies from the barracks. I can't make out the tune. But I sense the men are girding themselves. They'll come for me when the singing stops. I plead with the Three Sisters to keep the men singing: 'Shores of Amerikay', 'Lloyd George's Beer', 'Abide With Me'. Anything.

The cell door opens. "Shinner fucker!" a soused jailer shouts. I'm dragged outside and thrown into the back of the Crossley. Four of them set about me. The men egg each other on as the Crossley heads out onto the main road. The beating stops. A bottle is passed around and the hiding starts again. Boots and fists flail, the air blue with cursing. I curl into a ball. For all the good it does. After ten, maybe fifteen minutes, the Crossley stops. My boots are ripped from my feet.

"Fuck off to your Shinner mates!" the Geordie shouts as I'm dropped onto the rain soaked road. A bottle of Powers smashes inches from me, its harsh bitter scent filling my nostrils. Winded, I watch the Crossley drive off with the men bellowing 'Lloyd George's Beer'.

Taking off my tunic and shirt is a slow, pain wracked struggle. But I've no choice. Shivering with the cold, I tear my shirt into strips and use them to bind my feet. Putting my tunic back on and drawing it tight around me, I hobble east, away from Dingle through pitch black, fuchsia-lined fields and stumble along narrow, near invisible boreens, their stones tearing at my feet. I know what the captain's about. The Shinners find and then kill me. He goes on a killing spree in revenge. The bastard's clever. But the night is my friend and with luck, the rain will keep any Flying Column off my scent.

All my life I've had to run. Nothing ever changes. But as I told the captain, there's more to me than meets the eye.

○ ○ ○ ○ ○ ○

I ache all over, every shallow breath difficult. I cough up blood. My bound feet are shredded. I can barely raise my right arm whilst my left eye is all but closed. But I'm alive.

I check my tunic pockets and find the roll of notes inside the Royal Mail steam packet timetable along with Fletcher's lock knife. I set off for an abandoned farmhouse a half mile away, each step nerve wracked. I reach the farmhouse and collapse, grateful for the hovel's derelict shelter.

A road cuts inland from the coast bisecting steep bare hills dotted with sheep. Further off, I spot a black watered lake ringed by hills. A mile or so west of the lake stands a church spire threatened by storm clouds rolling in from the Atlantic. I'm somewhere west of Annascual, meaning Tralee train station is a day, maybe two days walk away. A fool's errand. My injuries and uniform will make me easy prey for the Shinners.

I skirt Annascual to the north and strike out for Tralee train station cross-country. But my injuries are such it takes me an hour to pass Annascual. Outside the village, I drink from a stream and spot a lone farmhouse along a boreen. A thin wisp of smoke drifts from its chimney. Hoping to find clothes, shoes and something to eat, I creep through a field towards the farmhouse, scattering a flock of grazing sheep. In the distance a dog barks. The farmhouse appears empty, its weathered whitewash speaking of neglect. A threadbare, sweat stained shirt and shabby trousers hang from a clothes line. Best of all a pair of socks. I stuff the clothes inside my tunic. The barking grows louder.

I peer through a small, filthy window and spy a pair of boots sat by the smouldering peat fire. The front door scrapes along worn flagstones and I'm greeted by the rich smell of burning peat. The kitchen is sparse, with no photographs or anything of sentiment on the walls or above the hearth. Except for a crucifix hanging over the fire. The farmer must live alone.

I pull the boots on. They pinch but they'll have to do. I snatch a half-loaf of soda bread and a lump of cold bacon from the kitchen table. A whining dog scratches at the front door so I slip out the back door and hobble towards a ramshackle shed, full of rusting, long abandoned tools. I change clothes and wolf down the bread and bacon.

Inside the farmhouse a man curses in the Irish. The windswept, gaunt, farmer steps outside and hurries down the boreen towards the road, ordering his dog on ahead of him. With the coast clear, I stash my tunic inside a battered milk churn, leave the barn and crawl through a field of looing heifers and bullocks. I reach the gate and look around. Nobody is following me. I open the gate and cross into the next boggy field, a Tinker seeking a better life.

○ ○ ○ ○ ○ ○

The Aureil, a French steamer, pulls away from a fogbound Queenstown harbour. Soot and cinders billow from the funnel smothering the deck. I catch a handful and stuff it in my pocket for luck before pulling my cap lower and jacket tighter to fend off the biting cold. I could seek shelter in the galley, but the thought of the stinking, cold grease that clings to everything down there makes my stomach churn all the more.

Two crewmen stand nearby, smoking and sharing a tale in guffawing French. The taller one, swarthy, with the build of a light heavyweight, glances at me and winces at the sight of my battered face. I offer him two quid for his boots. He raises his hands in refusal and leads his mate away from me. A freshening breeze clears the fog. The ship tosses and yaws in the swell. I grip the balustrade and throw up.

"You? Sailing to the South Pole?"

The Steam Catcher—Part 3

On the merchant ship
Aureil
September 1920

CHAPTER THIRTY-FOUR

I wake. The ship has stopped, a balm to my swirling innards. Gulls squawk and soar over brick warehouses with foreign-sounding names plastered on them. Crew members hurl thick ropes overboard to secure the ship to rust stained bollards. Ten minutes later, I plant my hobbled feet on Zeebrugge docks.

"Uit de weg!" shouts a drover guiding a herd of cows towards me. I step aside drawing curious looks from one or two of the doe-eyed milkers and limp on towards Zeebrugge train station.

Within the hour I'm surveying a rain soaked Ostend beach. A woman is walking her dog and two girls struggle to control their kite in the stiff breeze. Seagulls, their plumage ruffled by the breeze, peck at the sand searching for lugworms.

The last time I'd been here, the beach heaved with sunburned, paddling day-trippers. But now the steam organs are silent and the bellowing hawkers long gone. The air no longer reeks of waffles and Turkish tobacco. In hock to winter, the town lays half-dead like an aged aunt unaware that you've arrived to see her.

Ignoring the rain, I take off my boots and socks and walk towards the sea, scattering the gulls. The freezing water soothes my chafed feet. The dog splashes towards me, then runs off yapping as it chases the kite.

I tip-toe from the water, put on my socks and boots and head for the Promenade. The scaffolding has all gone but the bleakness makes me doubt the wisdom of returning. Before I'd been feted as a hero. Now this drifter's wartime service is of no consequence.

I follow a narrow lane into the town and come across a shoe shop. At least I can resolve one problem. The shopkeeper, a haughty, sour looking woman, looks aghast at the battered tramp leaving sandy boot prints on her carpet and I fear she'll holler for the police. But after I open the timetable, and show her my money, she delights in unearthing shoeboxes from musty nooks and crannies and I settle on a pair of boots so supple I scarcely know I'm shod. She points to my boots on the shop floor, "Nee, bedankt," I say, rustling up the little Flemish I know. "Alsjeblieft". I leave the shop, my toes enjoying their hard-earned freedom.

Free from pain and seasickness, I eat an agreeable meal in an estaminet a few doors along from the shoe shop. The owner, a handsome, middle-aged woman, widowed in the war, is delighted to be serving an Englishman out of season. Feeling like a man reborn, I seek out the nearby pensione she'd recommended.

I'll spend the night there, and head to Mons in the morning. But from the outside, the pensione looks like a doss house with tramps littering the front step, drinking. I move on intent on finding another room for the night. A few yards along, a row of Triumphs lined up outside a shop pricks my interest.

"Kan ik je helpen?" asks the short, chubby man standing in the shop's doorway. He hides his thinning hair with a careful comb over.

"Just looking."

"English?" I nod.

"You like Triumphs?"

"I rode one in the war. Despatch rider."

He shakes my hand and invites me inside. The shop smells of oil, rubber, rust and stressed metal. I close my eyes. I'm back in the bike shop in Gloucester. Most of the bikes are Triumphs alongside a handful of Rudges and Blackburnes. Abandoned engine parts lay everywhere with tools littering workbenches and spare parts spilling from stacked crates. Every bike looks to be in a dire state.

"Where they from?" I ask.

"I bought them at an auction in Bruges this summer. I thought I had found a bargain, but as you can see, they are all kaput."

"I can have a go at fixing them." A look of rapture that could have graced Saint Waltrude spreads across his face.

"I have no money to pay you, but you are welcome to stay in the room above the shop. It is small, but has a bed, fireplace, and stove. I stay here when my wife is angry, which is often."

"That suits."

"Gregorius Vandenbosch."

"Douglas Rudge."

"Pleased to meet you, Douglas Rudge." We shake hands. Even though he's at least twenty years older, five inches shorter, and four stone heavier, Gregorius' gusto reminds me of Timmings, right down to the shiny buttons on his suit jacket. "I knew good fortune would show itself to me today. Perhaps for you also?"

"Perhaps."

CHAPTER THIRTY-FIVE

I start each day with a brisk walk along the sands followed by a dip in the sea. Most mornings a black Labrador bounds along the water's edge to greet me while I dress. I'm on nodding terms with the dog's owner, a young woman whose right leg is encased in a calliper. After my constitutional, I return to my digs and eat a breakfast of bread, hard-boiled eggs, and coffee. The room, which I share with Troy, a handsome tomcat, unhappy to be sharing his bed with me, heaves with junk from Gregorius's efforts to make the largest fortune with the smallest effort. There are boxes stuffed with religious trinkets, miniature dolls, dirty pictures, kites, bottles of hair restoratives, potions to cure constipation, contraceptive contraptions and novelty clothes for pooches.

I eat dinner in the estaminet, where, after learning of my wartime service, the owner serves me a glass or two of wine on the house. I would prefer beer but keep quiet. Beggars and choosers and all that. Within a fortnight I'm sharing her bed and have the pick of her dead husband's clothes. To avoid any scandal, she insists I leave before dawn. I don't mind as I go for my early morning dip revelling in my good fortune of landing on pain-free feet. The arrangement also suits Troy, who has his bed to himself.

Some mornings Gregorius' wife, Magnhilda, visits the shop to chide him for his idleness while she struggles to keep a roof over their four children's heads. She's banned their eldest son, twelve years old, hair already thinning, from visiting the showroom as she fears he'll be taken in by his father's madcap schemes.

"A stern but magnificent woman Magnhilda," Gregorius once told me. "She can peel a potato using just one hand."

He loves to yap about his latest money-making wheeze; Mongolian coalfields or Cuban tea plantations. Lately, Malaccan rubber has caught his eye. The old, tatty atlas would come in handy to understand his far-flung notions. Indeed, the only peace I got from his scheming is when the fleshy local gendarme, his tunic straining to hold his girth, steps inside for a chat before taking his morning coffee in the estaminet. At first I skulked in the workshop to avoid the copper, but he never showed the slightest interest in me, or how I came to be working for Gregorius.

Within days I realised that it would be a tall order to get just one of the bikes roadworthy, but, as ever, working on engines was a pleasure, the simple intricacies of mechanical puzzles easy to solve compared to the

153

emotional conundrums we dream up for ourselves. But even though I was back in Belgium, any urge to find Celestine had all but disappeared, whether through the bikes or the estaminet owner's embrace I couldn't be sure. Timmings was wiser than his years. But *all that* time wasted pining.

But I'll admit I was surprised when after three weeks of trial and error, I wheeled a repaired Triumph outside. Gregorius murmured a prayer as I tried to start the long-dormant engine. After ten minutes of fettling, oiling and paddling, the engine sang. Heads appeared from windows and doorways. Two boys squabbling over a wooden hoop crossed the street to investigate. Gregorius, making a sign of the cross, looked heavenwards and says, "Thank you Lord for your intercedence and Douglas Rudge's mechanical knowledge."

Three days later while I'm cursing a sheared spark plug, Gregorius bawls, "Moeder Gods!" Expecting a foul deed, I step into the showroom. He's clutching a fistful of cash and showing a well-dressed man from the shop.

"What's happened?" I ask.

"We've sold a motorbike, Moeder Gods!" Magnhilda arrives to hand out her morning bollocking. But for once she's quiet, as Gregorius walks towards her with the francs in his hand. "Magnhilda mijn snoeptomaatje, ik heb een van de motors verkocht!"

He kisses her on the lips and whisks her around the floor. Then I saw something I thought I'd never see; Magnhilda smiled and playfully slapped him before taking the money.

Three more bikes were sold that week. Gregorius celebrated each sale by whirling Magnhilda around the showroom until the pair of them sat, out of puff and giggling, like courting teenagers. Within two months every bike that could be fixed had been sold with Gregorius now scouring Belgium and northern France for more. FNs, Triumphs, Harleys, Blackburnes, Rudges, and even a rare Swiss Motosacoche arrived, all in various states of disrepair. I adapted parts from one make to fit another make, falling back on Fletcher's bodges, but also surprising myself with my own elegant solutions.

I couldn't remember a happier time.

A month later, Gregorius handed me five hundred francs and said, "Rudge, you are a genius. You have the healing hands of a physician and the vision of a prophet. I have a proposition for you. Motorbike racing has become quite the thing. A Grand Prix was organised at Spa this summer, won by an Englishman on a Norton you will be pleased to hear. Why, even Ostend hosted a race a few weeks ago. Thousands came to watch. The riders are daredevils of the highest order. Young men will want to copy them and buy a motorcycle. And who will they buy their machines from?" He smiled. "Me! Everyone in Flanders will know the name Gregorius Vandenbosch. We will be famous and rich, opening shops in Bruges, Brussels and Antwerp. Maybe then Paris and Amsterdam. But we need to get them excited by the prospect of speed." He placed his hand on my shoulder and said, "Douglas, I want you to build the fastest motorcycle in the world, a motorcycle as fast as Mercury."

"Who?"

"The winged messenger of the Gods." Picking up a local newspaper, he leafed through its pages and translated, "Vandenbosch Motorcycles of Ostend to sell the fastest motorcycles in the world." The advertisement shows Gregorius, gurning like an imbecile, astride an FN.

"But that's not true."

"The war taught us not to worry about truth, Douglas."

155

CHAPTER THIRTY-SIX

Stepping from the sea, I shiver in the bracing wind while drying off, and return to the room where Troy greets me with a hiss before spraying a Triumph engine block. Eager to make the most of the early hour and empty roads, I skip breakfast and gather up my goggles, gloves and cap. The "Mercury" uses a Blackburne frame, FN engine, Triumph wheels, Motosacoche exhaust, and a Harley drive belt. It has taken weeks of trial and error and long hours in the garage, much to my lover's annoyance, but this latest version looks promising.

I ride onto the deserted beach. With the tide out, the damp sand holds firm. An onshore breeze whips across me, causing the white-tipped waves to break with force. I set off listening for signs of distress from the engine, but the note is crisp and sharp; a thing of rare beauty. I bring my weight to bear on the rear wheel hoping to stop the bike snaking and run true through any standing water. The speed builds with everything around me a sodden, sandy blur. For a few seconds Fletcher is alongside, bent over his Blackburne. He looks at me and shouts, "Faster, Rudge!"

The bludgeoning wind stings and a flock of seagulls take flight, forcing me to slow. The bike rolls to a halt, leaving a thin pimpled tyre track in its wake. My top speed was twenty two miles per hour quicker than the standard Triumph.

I leave the sands and set off along the still deserted coast road towards France, eleven miles away, my speed building nicely. Thoughts empty into nothing, all that matters are the few yards of tarmac ahead of me.

The French border guard steps from the customs checkpoint and raises a hand but I draw up before I reach him and check my watch. I've beaten my previous best time by almost three minutes. With a little more fettling the Mercury will match the FNs.

Better yet the ride back to Ostend is also completed in record time and I decide to treat myself with a juicy pork chop and all the trimmings in one of Ostend's fancy hotels. I even toy with the idea of inviting the estaminet owner, but think better of it. Best not give her any notions.

I return to the workshop, park and shake the stiffness from my limbs by strolling towards the casino. From its deserted terrace I look out to sea, shielding my eyes from the low sun. Dog walkers and couples stroll along the beach. I light a Players and spend an enjoyable half an hour plotting how to make the Mercury even faster.

The midday bells peel so I head to the estaminet for dinner. Outside the Parc Leopold, a man wrapped in a thick leather gherkin sits astride an FN studying a map. The bike's smooth, graceful lines dent my confidence in the Mercury. The rider nods to me and then rides off.

Near the café, Gregorius hurries towards me. Odd. He usually spends Sunday with Magnhilda and the children. "Rudge, I have been looking everywhere for you. I need a favour."

"What?"

"I have the opportunity of a lifetime, Douglas. My brother a spendthrift and a wastrel, but nevertheless my brother, has informed me of an investment opportunity in a copper mine in the Upper Congo that will guarantee enormous returns. I am meeting the mine owner's representatives in Bruges tomorrow."

"Won't Magnhilda be suspicious?"

"She thinks I am going to Ghent to buy motorcycles." He falls silent and tips his hat to a passing man and woman. When they're out of earshot he whispers, "I need you to visit the Bank of Flanders on Leopold Street for me tomorrow morning. To deposit the initial payment for the debenture. I must post surety before I arrive in Bruges. If her spies see me in the bank, Magnhilda will seek to thwart me. Would you do this?"

"S'pose."

"Good." He hands me a blue canvas bag and a business card, "Here is five thousand francs and the payment details for the banker's draft. When you have made the payment, send a telegram to the address on the card. And please Douglas, not a word to anyone."

"My lips are sealed."

"You are a good friend." He shakes my hand. "Now I must go. The tripe will be getting cold."

With the five thousand francs weighing heavy, I walk home, certain everyone I pass harbours plans to rob me. So it's a relief to reach the workshop unharmed. I stash the money in an empty oil drum, return it to its original spot and stack a second drum on top. Confident no robber will ever think to look there, I retire to the estaminet for dinner.

○ ○ ○ ○ ○ ○

Even though the large clock on her bedroom table shows five past nine, the café owner is still sound asleep. Deciding not to wake her, I get dressed and slip out the back door and run to the showroom where Gregorius is standing by the workbench looking worried. "Where have you been?"

"Went for a swim. Lost track of time."

"I can trust you Douglas?"

"Course," I answer, miffed that he could doubt my honesty. After all, haven't I rescued his business?

"Good. Remember to send the telegram after you have made the deposit." He looks at the Mercury propped against the workbench, low slung and all prowling menace. "Is this the machine you are planning to race?"

"Yes. I'm taking her for another run out after I've been to the bank."

"She is beautiful. As fast as Mercury?"

"Hope so."

The fat gendarme pokes his head inside and asks Gregorius a question. "He wants to know why the estaminet is not open," say Gregorius.

"Search me," I answer.

He checks his pocket watch. "I must go. Thank you again, Rudge. Don't forget the telegram." He shares a joke with the gendarme and sets off for Ostend station. Gulls wheel above the street. Rain hangs in the air. The gendarme leaves, stopping to speak to an elderly woman passing the shop and pointing towards the estaminet, presumably asking if she knows why it's still closed. The woman shrugs, so the gendarme heads for the parc, tapping the rails with his baton.

With the coast clear I retrieve the francs, wheel the Mercury out and set off for the bank, arriving just as its doors open. I've never set foot inside a bank before and breathe in the smell of polished wood, brass, and success. People whisper just like they do in church except for the angry old man standing at the kiosk arguing with a clerk. The woman in front of me checks her watch and sighs. Motorcycles are approaching. I retrieve the canvas bag from my jacket pocket and open it. Thick wads of banknotes present themselves. A fortune, enough to start a new life.

"Give it a go Tom."

The temptation passes when I take out the payment instructions and try to make sense of them. Two more kiosks open. The clerk, a man with a fine moustache and busy features, already bored with his day's labours, offers a weak smile as I hand him the payment instructions. After reading them, he nods and stretches out a hand for the money.

The blast of machine gun fire is deafening. Masonry rains down from the ceiling. Three masked robbers, all carrying machine guns, rush the counter while an accomplice stands by the door, keeping lookout.

"Quatre vingt dix!" one of them shouts, checking a watch.

 158

The woman in front of me screams. The timekeeper levels his machine gun at her. She falls silent. Now he shouts at the other customers who drop to their knees, raise their hands, and close their eyes. I pull the old man to the floor as the robbers fire a second volley, splintering the counter. Two robbers leap over the counter and rifle the tills.

"Soixante!" bellows the timekeeper, now running towards a heavy plain door beside the counter. He forces it open and hollers something in Flemish. Seconds later a tall, thin man and a red-faced woman both terrified, step from the room with their hands raised. The woman drops her handbag and its contents spill across the floor. She stoops to gather them up but freezes when the timekeeper places the barrel of his gun to her throat and forces her to lie down.

"Gendarmes!" shouts the lookout.

"Allez!" the timekeeper commands. The two others hurdle the counter and make for the door, slinging bulging canvas rucksacks onto their backs. The timekeeper rolls a grenade along the floor and shouts, "La lute pour liberer le proletariat vient de commencer." The grenade spews a thick white smoke, streaked with yellow and orange after another blast of gunfire. I press myself into the floor. My ears ring, muffling the other people's screams.

I stand, struggling to make sense of what has just happened, and go outside. Wisps of the grenade smoke follow me. The gang are on motorbikes and haring through the parc towards its northwest exit. Except one, who lays on the parc bridge, with the fat gendarme standing over him pointing a pistol.

"HALT!"

Two policemen level their side arms at me. Raising my arms I say, "They're heading for France. If you're quick you'll catch them." Instead they search me and find Gregorius' money.

"It belongs to my friend. He asked me to deposit it this morning."

I'm pushed to the floor and shackled.

"I've got nothing to do with this. I'm English."

CHAPTER THIRTY-SEVEN

The inspector, a tall, well-groomed man with kind eyes and a fine moustache, has come up from Bruges to lead the investigation. He speaks good English on account of his time in Birmingham before the war, where he worked as an engineer. He's a good listener, nodding sympathetically as I tell him what happened and the mistake his men have made in arresting me. All the while he smokes a pipe, stopping every now and then to tamp down and relight the tobacco. When I mention Gregorius, he scribbles a note and hands it to a gendarme, who leaves us.

"Let us see what Mr Vandenbosch has to say," the inspector says in a soft, helpful tone. "Hopefully he will confirm your story and we can put this unpleasantness behind us."

"He will."

The inspector smiles. I can trust him.

After the interview, a gendarme leads me to a cramped cell with barely enough room for one, let alone two beds. An unconscious man lays on the right bed, his face bloody and covered in welts. The only light comes from a small, barred window set high in the wall. A second gendarme steps into the cell and helps his comrade drag the man outside.

"Can't you see he's hurt?" I shout. The second gendarme, dead eyed and raging, steps back into the cell and works up a sweat setting about me with his baton.

"Be strong, Tom. They caged me too."

An hour, maybe two, later, the cell door opens and the gendarmes hurl the man onto his bed. He lands in a heap. Fresh, livid wounds scour his face. Both gendarmes spit on him, before locking us up. The coast clear, I help my cellmate drink from a cup of water brought to me an hour earlier. He retches and brings the water back up. After the fit fades, I lay him down on the lumpy, horsehair mattress and he rasps, "I know you." But before I can question him, he slips into unconsciousness.

○ ○ ○ ○ ○ ○

The inspector's first words to me this morning are, "Mr Rudge, every Belgian man, woman, and child, is grateful to you for your wartime service in the liberation of our country. Without brave men like you, our clocks would still be one hour forward and we would still have to abide by the strictures of the Bosch's martial law." He nods to the gendarme standing by the door. He steps forward and punches me in the face. The blow stings. "But, please, do not take me for a fool." I'm struck again. This time in the stomach. I'm winded. "You are a hero. Of that there is no doubt. But that does not make it acceptable for you to rob us."

"I'm no robber," I groan, staring at the table before me.

"Then explain this. You were found carrying five thousand francs outside a bank that had just been robbed of one hundred thousand francs. You were on a motorcycle, as were the gang who fled the scene. Witnesses saw you acting suspiciously inside the bank. One swears you assaulted him. Now Mr Laurent has implicated you."

"Who?"

"Your cell mate, Auguste Laurent. The man who slayed the clerk."

"I've never met him before."

The gendarme punches me again in the face."Please, Mr Rudge. The truth. How long have you been member of this communist rabble?"

"Have you found Gregorius yet? He'll vouch for me."

"Mr Vandenbosch died yesterday. Of a heart attack whilst on a train to Bruges."

"Dead?" I stare at the inspector, lost for words. "But he seemed fine yesterday." Despite my predicament, I feel a pang of sadness. Gregorius took me in, gave me a chance, and never judged me. He helped me to make a future for myself. But now he's left me in the shit. "Did you find the payment instructions I handed to the clerk?"

"No such details were found."

"Ask Magnhilda, his wife. She'll tell you about the money."

"Unfortunately the widowed Madame Vandenbosch confirmed that the money never existed. But if it did, she would like it back as she fears destitution. She also said you struck her as furtive, and, judging by your callous response to Mr Vandenbosch's death, I have to agree with her." He lays a dog-eared leaflet in front of me. "Can you explain why this was found among your possessions?"

"It's just a keepsake."

"Hook line and fuckin' sinker."

Shaking his head, he picks the leaflet up and reads, "The Royal Mail Steam Packet Company. Southampton to Sao Paolo, Buenos Aires, Montevideo." He looks assured. "Why would a humble motorcycle mechanic plan a voyage to South America?"

"A friend gave it to me."

"Or you planned to abscond there." He wipes his moustache and lights his pipe. "I should warn you, Mr Rudge, that this case is of particular interest to our prime minister. Although a wise man of impeccable Christian virtue, Mr Theunis demands those responsible are caught and dealt with in the harshest possible terms."

Sweet scented tobacco smoke drifts towards me." I do not wish to alarm you, but we are currently negotiating the lease arrangements to bring a guillotine from France."

Startled, I blurt, "But I'm innocent. Please, you must believe me. I'd only gone to the bank to deposit Gregorius's money."

"Or you were covering your fellow robbers escape." His chair creaks as he shifts position and drums the table with manicured nails. "I have ascertained that since your arrival in Ostend you ingratiated yourself with Mr Vandenbosch and several other townsfolk. For example, the charming estaminet owner told me that you forced yourself upon her, repeatedly." More drumming on the table. "So, why should I believe you?"

"Why should he Tom, Douglas, whatever it is you call yourself?"

"I'm telling the truth."

"That will be for the jury at Bruges assizes to decide. But you are a foreigner and everyone feels better for blaming foreigners. But I suppose you must hope. That is the point of justice. Even for aliens."

∘ ∘ ○ ○ ∘ ∘

I lay on my bed, fearful yet raging at the injustice of my situation. Locked up, condemned by circumstance and branded a murderer. Auguste is still unconscious. I rack my brains for a passage in the Bible that allows me to top him.

"Just place your hands around his neck and squeeze, Tom. Squeeze the life out of the fecker."

Auguste shifts. He opens his eyes and mutters, "Je ne dois pas ceder." His words prick my wrath. I picture Gregorius laying on a slab in some woebegone mortuary in Bruges. I'll receive justice for killing Alf, albeit executed for a crime I'm innocent of. In this tiny, rank, cell I share with a mute, I find solace in thinking that at least Mum will be spared the shame of my death. I'll pay for Alf's murder with the harshest sentence. Of being forgotten.

CHAPTER THIRTY-EIGHT

The weeks drag. The inspector asks the same questions and I offer the same answers and then receive the same thuggish beatings. Desolate thoughts fill my waking hours whilst nightmares haunt my sleep. My only company is Auguste, yet the savagery of his torture leaves him barely conscious and yet to explain where we've met before.

As the nights grew colder, I gave up my blanket for him and lay shivering on my cot, recalling the nights I'd kicked off the blankets at home to prepare for the Great Gloucester Antarctic Expedition. Some nights Auguste is so still, I think he's finally given up the ghost and perished. Then he wakes, his eyes darting around the cell while muttering, "Je ne dois pas ceder."

Despite dropping me in the shit, I grow to admire him for withstanding his ordeal. His fortitude may be my only hope of salvation.

One morning after Auguste had been led away for another hiding, the inspector steps into the cell. He's exhausted, skin grey, eyes sunken, once manicured nails bitten to the quick. "Laurent is a stubborn man," he says. "Apart from naming you, he still refuses to tell me anything. So, he is beaten. And then beaten some more. I am not fond of violence. It is futile." He lights his pipe and draws in a lungful of smoke. The tobacco's sweet aroma fills my nostrils. "Mr Rudge, do you remember when I told you that this robbery has angered the highest echelons of Belgian society?"

I nod.

"Good. I am pleased you listened. The guillotine is assembled in Bruges. I must say, from an engineering perspective it is a fine example of efficient, yet economic design. The French, as is their nature, were tardy in supplying it and as is their wont, they demanded more than we were prepared to pay. But I do not suppose you are interested in such bureaucratic wrangles."

"You'd be right on that."

"The whole of Belgium demands your death."

"I'm innocent."

"And as I told you, nobody cares. Laurent's testimony alone is enough to condemn you."

"I fought to free your country."

"And for that you have a whole nation's regard." He comes closer. Tobacco and coffee sit on his breath, his fatigue all the clearer. He whispers, "Get Laurent to tell you who his accomplices are, where they are hiding, and I will see that you are spared. And when all the fuss has died down, you can sail for England a free man, able to start again."

"Take the deal, Tom. Get the fuck away from this place."

"But he never speaks."

"The guards tell me you give him your food and blankets. He trusts you, Rudge. Exploit that trust. After all what is he to you? Save yourself."

"Maybe if you leave him in peace for a day or two I can winkle something out of him."

"A salient point." He stands and nods to the gendarme by the door. I curl up, expecting to hear a baton slice the air. Instead the cell door slams shut.

"Make something up Tom. What about that fella who wore the bowler hat in Mons? Land him in the shit."

I've never told anyone about the pastor's dealings with the landlord of the Leopard, the mechanic flogging rotten meat or the deranged gunner drinking on duty. Perhaps I should have. Might have made life simpler. Auguste killed a man. There's nothing wrong in betraying him. Mum would praise me for doing so. Get me back in her good books.

Yet something jars about informing. Auguste's constant interrogations don't make sense. Perhaps he hasn't betrayed anyone.

Maybe it's the inspector who is lying.

The cell door opens. The gendarme helps Auguste to his bed and lowers him onto it. For once he doesn't spit on Auguste but says in his guttural Flemish tinged accent, "Brave man," and then gently closes and locks the cell door.

I lay my blanket over Auguste. "Have you water?" he croaks.

Shocked to hear him speak, let alone in English, I hold my cup to his lips. He drinks, coughs, shudders and then asks, "Where am I?"

"Ostend police station. You've been here for weeks. I have as well. They think I robbed the bank with you."

"Why would they think that?"

"You told the inspector."

"He wanted me to name you, but I refused."

"The first night here. You said you knew me."

"In Mons. We raced. You rode a Triumph."

"You were on the FN?" He nods.

"Tell the inspector this. An Englishman won the Belgian Grand Prix riding a Sunbeam."

"Why tell him that?"

But he's asleep.

 164

"Sunbeam's are fine motorcycles, but this was not the answer I was expecting," the inspector says after I repeat Auguste's message the next morning. He leaves the room and orders the gendarme in. I drop to the floor and curl up before the first searing strike. As the beating continues I stare at the unconscious Auguste and repeat to myself, "Je ne dois pas ceder." The bastards don't even have my name.

With the thrashing over, the inspector returns. "I could have you killed, Rudge, toss your body into an unmarked pit and nobody would care. Unless you tell me the names of his accomplices and where they are hiding, that is where you are heading."

"Je ne dois pas ceder," I answer. The inspector leaves. I curl up and wait for the baton's caress.

CHAPTER THIRTY-NINE

Auguste swings his legs over the bed, strokes his fine, thick beard and then spits at the enamel latrine pail in the corner of the cell. He misses and phlegm trickles down the bucket. He stands and limps towards the pail to take a piss. "Morning Englishman."

"Morning," I reply, fearing another lecture on the need for revolution.

"Good, no blood today," he says, buttoning his fly. Despite the beatings, which stopped a fortnight ago, he is in remarkable shape, helped by his daily ritual of pacing up and down the cell one hundred times in the morning and one hundred times at night. He must have walked to Timbuktu and back by now. The walk completed, he drops to the floor and does twenty push ups. Only then does he sit on his bed and gobble down his bread and water. After eating, he says, "So, today we see Madame Guillotine. As good a way as any to go comrade. Cleaner than the firing squad. Buried too many who met their end that way. Did you serve?"

"Mesopotamia, France, and Flanders."

"I served in a prisoner battalion, digging trenches the Poilus fought in and the graves they were buried in."

"You didn't fight?"

"For the workers. The real enemy are the bosses and politicians who have pitted the working classes against each other. In nineteen seventeen, Russian workers pointed to a world free from war and poverty. Soviet Russia is the key. Our futures lie with Her. I escaped into the forests to work with men and woman who share my dream of revolution."

"Your duty was to fight."

"You look like a man who has had enough of duty."

"Did my bit. Do so again if needs be. Daresay most of the lads who perished would agree with me."

"The Germans are proud. This war will never end."

"Just let them try. We'll march foursquare behind the Union Jack. It's stood England in good stead."

He waves my words away. "The English, patriots and imbeciles in equal measure. March behind my flag, the Red Flag, towards a life free from tyranny."

"The empire's saved many from tyranny."

"You are a fool."

"You're a robber."

"For the revolution."

 166

"I'm being put to death for something I'd no part in."

"Most of us deserve punishment for something."

I see Alf Fenwick lying on the Anselma. Auguste has skewered me. "Is that why you're in here with me?"

He laughs. "For two weeks we watched the bank and the surrounding area. Every morning at nine o'clock the fat gendarme drank coffee in the same estaminet. On the day of the robbery, he is not in the estaminet but the Parc Leopold. My comrades escape, but he brings me down. How can that be?"

I keep quiet about my part in his downfall.

An hour later, we're shackled and taken into the station courtyard where a wagon is parked up. The inspector is with us. "You know he is innocent," Auguste tells him.

"It does not matter."

We reach the wagon.

"Don't let them take me, Tom. I can't go back to Coney Hill."

I refuse to budge so I'm picked up and thrown in.

"That showed 'em."

A few minutes into our journey, Auguste whispers, "Do you have faith in the workers?"

"Never given it much thought."

"Start now."

167

CHAPTER FORTY

We step from the wagon out onto the assizes' gilded courtyard, thronged with a jeering crowd seven or eight deep. We're led towards a set of stone steps guarded by two policemen. A photographer steps through the mob and the inspector delights in having his picture taken between Auguste and me. All the while Flemish insults ring in our ears.

Auguste, revelling in the attention shouts, "Rechtvaardigheid voor de arbeiders." Furious onlookers swat his guard aside and set about him. Shots ring out. Everyone freezes. A half-second of silence. Enough time. The inspector twists and falls. The two gendarmes hurry down the steps and fire into the crowd, wounding several, including my guard who falls and brings down the terror-struck woman bedside us. A stampede breaks out as people flee the courtyard. Some fall and are trampled.

The two gendarmes set about Auguste's guard. A masked gunman appears by the courtyard's heavy wooden gates and fires into the air, creating yet more panic. "If you want to live, come with me," Auguste says to me.

Leaving the courtyard, we race along a passageway and cross a bridge towards a covered fish market and weave among the bellowing mongers and their startled customers. Shouts, whistles and gunshots follow us. Auguste barges into one merchant who spills the crate of fish he's hawking. The trader opens his mouth to protest but thinks better of it after seeing the pistol in Auguste's hand.

Beyond the market, we reach a parked car. The doors are open. We dive in. Gunshot shatters the rear window and peppers the side panels, "Allez! Allez!" Auguste yells. We drive off, but not before the driver is hit in the arm. The car veers off course, narrowly misses a delivery wagon and strikes a bridge parapet. Under heavy fire, the driver manages to get us across the bridge and into a warren of narrow lanes. Minutes later we stop in a deserted side street beneath an imposing, steepling church.

Leaving the car we run along an alleyway that opens onto a street abutting a canal. In front of us sits a police wagon. I panic. Everything has been in vain. Gendarmes step from the wagon's cab. Auguste is still running towards the wagon. The gendarmes open the back doors and help Auguste and me to climb inside along with the two gendarmes from the assizes. One is squat, built like a welterweight, while the other's hard, intelligent features remind me of that bastard Tans Captain. Auguste hammers on the cab wall and we set off.

"Told you to have faith," he says as the wagon bucks over cobbles and tram tracks. After a few minutes the van stops. Auguste and the gendarmes tense. "Roadblock," Auguste whispers. "Silence."

Words are exchanged with the driver. Moments later the wagon's doors open. Two soldiers aim their rifles at us. A young officer stands between them. He seems uncertain, fearful. Auguste growls something in Flemish.

"Hout dat dier onder controle!" the officer shouts. The welterweight elbows Auguste in the ribs and then hands the officer a set of papers. After reading the dockets, he returns them to the welterweight and orders his men to lower their weapons. Auguste spits, earning another elbow to the ribs. The officer closes the wagon doors and shouts another order. The wagon's engine turns over. The welterweight cocks his revolver and edges towards the doors. We move off. Auguste winces and holds his ribs. The welterweight laughs. Auguste looks at me and says, "You're free to leave now Rudge."

"But if I do, won't the soldiers or your men shoot me?"

"Probably."

After an hour, we stop. The wagon rocks in a breeze. Heavy waves slap the shore. We drop down onto a deserted beach and our shackles are cut. A storm is closing in. Gulls wheel overhead. The wounded, shivering car driver, also disguised as a gendarme, is helped from the cab. Another lorry emerges through the dunes. A Harley and FN follow. The Harley stops fifty yards from us whilst the FN continues on with the lorry, the rider's blonde hair dancing in the breeze. The rider pulls up alongside Auguste and speaks to him.

"Allez! Allez!" Auguste shouts. I'm helped into the back of the second lorry and blindfolded. The air reeks of petrol. Others climb in. Revolvers are cocked. I expect the worst.

"Been nice knowing you Tom."

We move off to the sound of clinking crates and sloshing drums. I soon lose track of time, even falling asleep, only to be woken by heavy rain pelting the wagon's canvas roof. There are nervous, whispered mutterings in French and the odd sigh of relief when the lorry skids to a halt for the umpteenth time. Parched, I ask for water but receive none.

Several hours later the lorry stops and the wagon's canvas flaps are raised. The air outside is sour, rank.

"The ghosts of the dead are pleading for peace."

I'm helped down and my blindfold taken off. While my eyes adjust to the light, I hear laughter.

THE STEAM CATCHER

I'm standing among the ruins of a village square, its surface blistered with craters. Occupying one corner is a church with a shattered steeple. Diagonally opposite stands a garage, guarded by a twisted, rusted fuel pump half-wrenched from the earth. Auguste and two others head towards a partially destroyed café nestling between a bombed-out hotel and shop. A woman wheels a barrow into the square and tips her load of bricks into a crater. She's wearing a British issue great coat and has a French carbine slung around her shoulders. She retraces her steps along the lane and disappears into the forest of blackened, dead trees that ring the village.

Desperate for water, I skirt a crater and head for a water trough outside the café. I grasp the pump's handle. It's seized solid, so I scoop up a handful of water and raise it to my lips. A dark haired woman with piercing green eyes and porcelain skin, grabs my wrist and shakes her head. Like everyone else she wears assorted fatigues and is armed.

"You want me to die of thirst?"

"The water is not safe to drink!" Auguste shouts. I drop the water into the trough and watch the ripples work their way across the surface. The disturbed water smells putrid. The woman hands me a canister and enters the cafe. I throw off the stopper and drink.

Minutes later, the two motorbikes arrive. The Harley rider approaches me peeling off his goggles and scarf. I scarce believe my eyes.

"Look like you've seen a ghost, old chap," declares Timmings.

CHAPTER FORTY-ONE

"Welcome to the Zone Rouge," Timmings says with a sweep of his arm. "A swathe of northern France so poisoned with lead, mercury, arsenic and unexploded ordnance, the frogs thought it easier to abandon than reclaim. But on the bright side nobody thinks to look for us in here." He gestures to the FN rider. "Matilde, come and meet my pal, Douglas Rudge."

Matilde walks towards us, her blond hair trailing from her cap. She takes off her goggles and weighs me up while unbuttoning her French army tunic that runs several sizes too large. She's screws her pretty, bold features into a frown. "We raced last year. You rode a Triumph." I remember. The girl aboard the FN in Mons. "Auguste wants to speak to you."

Slapping me on the back Timmings says, "We'll have a chinwag later. What are the odds?"

I follow Matilde towards the café, its torn, striped awning flapping in the breeze. We step inside, passing stacked tables and chairs. The rear wall has been blown out and replaced with a tarpaulin. A portion of a once fine mirror hangs behind a mahogany bar littered with bottles and glasses. The floorboards have been swept, but the smell of damp brick dust dominates. In a smoke-filled anteroom, Auguste and four others sit around a table studying maps. I recognise the two gendarmes from the assizes and the woman who had offered me her water.

A short, dapper man, wearing glasses, sits at the head of the table. He looks a studious sort but comfortable in his skin. Auguste beckons me closer and says, "C'est Rudge." He looks at the small man, "Etienne?" Etienne takes off his glasses, rests them on the maps and glances at me. "Non," he mutters.

He keeps quiet as the others argue. Voices are raised, the table sometimes thumped. Auguste speaks passionately, pointing at himself and at me more than once. When he's finished speaking he points to the woman who gave me the water and says, "Sonia?"

"Non," Sonia answers.

"Octave?" The welterweight also answers, "Non."

"Maxime?" The slender man answers, "Non."

Octave lights a cigarette and says something which Maxime finds funny. Auguste steps towards him, but Sonia holds him back.

"Why should we trust you?" Matilde asks me.

"Je suis Anglais." They laugh. Octave mocks my accent. I lift my tunic to reveal the bruises and scars handed out by the Ostend police.

"Who did this?" Matilde asks.

"The police."

"Why?"

"Because I wouldn't betray your pal."

They start talking again, only calmer this time. After a few minutes, Auguste raises his hand and everyone bar Etienne follows suit. Auguste says, "Welcome, Rudge."

"And if they'd said no?"

"You would have been shot."

∘ ∘ ○ ○ ∘ ∘

Light floods through the church's shell-damaged roof, which some brave soul has tried to patch, without much joy judging by the puddles on the worn flagstones. The walls are daubed with slogans and hammer and sickles. On the altar stands a large, warped photograph of a stern, bald, bearded man.

"Meet comrade Lenin," says Timmings pointing at the picture.

Beside the altar stands a wrought iron cauldron hanging over a fire. The injured driver sits nearby jerking and wincing as an older woman stitches his wounds.

Timmings dishes up two plates of stew from the pot and leads me to a pew. "Just keeping us fed and watered is a monumental task," he says, tucking into his nosh. "Nothing is safe to eat or drink within a twenty mile radius. I'll never moan about army rations again. Who knew a fresh carrot would make your heart soar? And what I'd give to see a Charlie Chaplin film."

Matilde rummages through a stack of crates beside the font. She holds a jar of coffee aloft and shouts, "Voila!"

"Good. Fresh coffee," Timmings says. "You may be surprised to learn that my boyish charms have failed to work their magic on the fair Matilde. By the way, are you still pining for Celestine?" My heart skips a beat, but before I can deny Celestine, the wheelbarrow woman walks past us and helps herself to a bowl of stew.

"Malaphonse. Oddball, but a brilliant hunter. Only speaks to Matilde," whispers Timmings, "Goes out on patrol for days at a time. Knows the woods like the back of her hand."

Malaphonse picks at her food while watching the nurse douse the grimacing driver's arm with iodine. Timmings tips his plate, slurps down the stew's gravy then wipes his mouth with a grubby cloth. He sets his plate on the pew, tamps a French cigarette against the back of his hand and lights it. "So now your belly's full, tell me what happened in Ireland. Did you end up siding with the Shinners? The Comrades go for that sort of talk."

I eat the last of my stew unsure how much I should tell him. "They thought I was a Shinner sympathiser. Had to run for it."

"And were you?"

"Course not."

"Forgotten what a stickler for king and country you are." He takes a drag. "So like the prodigal son, you return to me. People will talk, Rudge."

"Heading for Mons."

"Back to your beloved Chinamen. Remember Petain? Poor bugger struck a grenade. Lost his right arm. Mind you, we could use the coolies round here to dig out the dead. Last week the earth churned up a headless torso just outside the cafe. I think he knew you were coming old chap. The dead are drawn to you."

"*He's onto something Tom.*"

"Why aren't you in Montevideo, married to Ursula, with a nipper yapping around your ankles?"

"Remember that bowler hatted chap in Mons?"

"Yes."

"Ursula wed him after telling me that she couldn't leave Mons. Must say it burned for a while thinking about the pair of them sneaking around behind my back. After that, Montevideo's appeal waned." He laughs, and stubs the fag out on his plate. "Affairs of the heart, hey, old chap? Both of us poor blighters afflicted now."

"So you became a bank robber to fix your broken heart."

"Truth be told, I've always been a wrong-un." He smirks but looks uncomfortable. Exposed. "When I was younger, I nicked the odd farthing from Nanny's purse and cartridges from Father's shotgun. Small things, but theft thrilled me even more than evading discovery. In school I'd steal the other boys' tuck, conkers, rugger boots, anything I could lay my hands on. But I was undone when I nabbed some chap's pocket watch. Said watch was found under my mattress. Very nearly got expelled. Thankfully, Father put a stop to that. But the buggers stopped me playing cricket."

"You've suffered."

"Could say that." He lights another cigarette. "When I found about Ursula and Mr Bowler Hat, I beat him to within an inch of his life. Any man worth his salt would. Hoped it would staunch my anger. It didn't. Had to scarper after that. I hid out in Mouscron, arriving the day this mob filched from a bank there. The police shot one of them, tall fella, something of the night about him. The gang left him behind. He told me about the Zone so I brought him here. At first its stench scared the bejesus out of me, thought Satan himself must be shacked up in here. So, desperate to be rid of the place, I charged along without the foggiest where I was going. Ended up ploughing head first into a dirty great crater. Broke the poor chap's neck." He taps his cigarette against the edge of the plate. "The crater's walls were too sheer to climb and I lay in poisonous sludge for a day and a night until Malaphonse came across me. She drew a bead but thankfully recognised her dead comrade and hauled me out. Etienne wasn't keen on me, but Auguste thought my DR skills would come in handy."

"Even after riding into a crater?"

"Surprised me too. Within days I was sucked into outlaw ways. Imagine what the chaps in the battalion would say if they knew. We're all a mass of contradictions. I see myself as the Jesse James of Flanders. Although among this crowd, I'm more Robin Hood. They pass their loot to Russians in Paris, to buy arms, fund newspapers, pamphlets anything that will spark their precious revolution. But most of the frog Communists have been gaoled, whilst Mussolini and his thugs are strangling Italy. The revolution is miles off, probably isn't going to happen, but these underfed basket cases think it's imminent. Balderdash of course, but against all the odds they've survived. Sonia's the ideologue. Hard woman. Doesn't suffer fools. Parisian chemist by profession, married to a Hun so left for Berlin when the war broke out. Her husband died during the Berlin Spartacist uprising a year or two ago. She fled to Paris and found her way here. When the others lose heart, she's the one who stiffens resolve. All I know about Matilde and Malaphonse is that Auguste found them and another girl, Elise, after they'd been left for dead by the Bosch. Sort of thing the blighters would do. Spanish flu did for Elise. Octave and Maxine haven't a revolutionary thought in their thick skulls. They're thieves who'll slit your throat as soon as look at you. They were in the same prisoner battalion as Auguste and followed him here. That's Etienne and Auguste's conundrum. Having to use scum to create utopia."

"What's utopia?"

"Not this place. After the armistice they numbered over two hundred. Frogs, Belgians, Huns, Tommies, Yanks, even a Moroccan chap. But the Spanish flu decimated them. Now they struggle to make up a rugger team. Auguste holds everything together. That's why they broke him out."

Stubbing out the cigarette on the plate he says. "Got something to show you."

○ ○ ○ ○ ○ ○

Reaching the garage, Timmings lights an oil lamp hanging from the door, and goes inside. The thin streak of orange light bounces off a row of FNs, Harleys and Indians. "Beauties, aren't they? We use them in the raids. It's my job, and now yours, to keep them in good nick."

"In Ostend I built a bike faster than Mercury."

"Mercury? Good lord, Rudge, you've become a scholar. Where is this chariot of the gods?"

"Still parked outside the bank in Ostend, as far as I know."

He sets the lamp down and mounts an Indian V Twin. "We used the Ostend races this summer as cover to plan the bank raid. Auguste, Sonia, Matilde and I went as courting couples. Separate rooms naturallement. Lots of chaps from England were competing. They had a high old time of it. Women, wine, not to mention the racing. Something to aspire to after this caper has run its course. Auguste even nabbed third spot."

"What about you?"

"Held seventh, scrapping with a Sunbeam when my drive belt snapped. Can't wait to get my hands on a chain-driven bike. Much sturdier than these belt-driven donkeys." He pointed to three sidecar combinations wedged against the rear wall. "Recognise them from the Mons raid? They're no longer used. The MO is now what you saw in Ostend. Fast in and fast out. Hit hard. The bikes and loot are loaded onto lorries parked nearby and we return to the forest. The police look for motorcycles, not lorries. Works like clockwork."

The choking air catches in my throat, making me cough.

"You'll get used to the air," Timmings mutters, "Even if it brings on inflamed lungs and pleurisy. Matilde will sort you out a gas mask. She's the quartermaster."

We step outside and see Auguste and Etienne talking by the water trough. Timmings offers me a fag and says, "Etienne taught mathematics in Marseille. Intellectual type. Never saw service though. Only speaks with Auguste or Sonia. As our numbers dwindle, his paranoia increases. Your arrival will have spooked him."

Auguste beckons Timmings over.

In the church the other gang members are gathered around the coffee pot like expectant children at Christmas. Matilde pours me a cup. I take a sip and savour the taste, although tea would have been nicer. Timmings returns. "You're honoured, old chum. Augusts wants Matilde to teach you French."

"I've no need of French."

"Your new comrades can't speak English."

"Why not?"

"They're foreigners."

"They should learn."

"One day I'm sure they will. The natural order of things, English. Anyway, the Russians have been in touch. We're off to recce the next job."

"Where are you going?"

He taps his nose and says,"Can't tell you old chap. But it must be big. Auguste, Sonia, Octave and Maxime are coming along as well."

CHAPTER FORTY-TWO

Dad loops the noose around my neck as the gunner inserts Celestine's luger into my mouth. Celestine dances a reel. "Patriot!" shouts the gunner while cocking the pistol. The noose tightens.

I wake with a start and struggle for breath. Alabaster saints peer down at me, their faces screwed in anger, or maybe ecstasy. Wondering if Saint Waltrude is among them, I draw the blanket over my head and try to go back to sleep but the ghouls refuse to leave me in peace.

It's still dark as I tramp across the pitted square towards the café for my first French lesson. Gripped by another coughing fit, I begin to doubt if my lungs will see the week out in this air. The café's tarpaulin ruffles in the breeze as I enter. Bedsprings squeak in the anteroom. I wait outside for Matilde, half-expecting a cloud of mustard gas to leak through the trees, it's yellow fingers blistering everything it touches.

It's not until daybreak that Matilde, wrapped in her great coat, arrives carrying two gasmasks and a long cardboard tube. She hands me one of the masks. From her furrowed brow it's obvious that she hasn't volunteered to teach me French. I follow her inside, lay the gas mask on the bar, and light a cigarette.

"You cannot smoke." I stub the fag out and lean against the bar. "Stand up straight." I straighten. "I have to teach you French."

"Only need the King's English."

"You are of no use if you cannot speak French."

"Not planning on staying."

"Then why are you here?"

"Had no choice. Either one of your lot or the Belgian police would have done for me."

"So you do not believe in the revolution?"

"Nope."

"Marx said the revolution would begin with the English working class."

"Got that wrong then, didn't he."

"Maybe in England, but the old order has been swept away in Russia and the workers are recasting society into something bold and beautiful. Here we live with comradeship and hope to see a world where every worker is equal, given a home, bread, work, and dignity. We will be free, not vassals."

"Bit of a long shot if you ask me."

"As you please. But while you are here, your job is to keep the bikes running and for this you must speak French."

"You can translate."

"No man tells me what to say."

"That's you stumped."

She opens the tube and unfurls the scale drawing of a Harley that sits inside. After weighing down each corner with ashtrays, she points to the front wheel with her revolver and says, "Roué avant."

"Sorry?"

"Roué avant. Front wheel. Repeat, Roué avant. Front wheel."

"Roue avant. Front wheel."

She points at the tyre. "Pneu."

"Pneu."

She taps the front forks. "Fourches avant."

"Fourche savant."

She points at the headlamp. "Phare avant."

"Phare."

Matilde didn't look impressed at lesson's end. She'd spent most of the half hour muttering under her breath and about five minutes in, I thought she was going to box my ears as I stuttered over translating mudguard. I'd barely learned a dozen words and even they had left my head spinning in a funk of confusion.

I return to the garage, crouch beside an FN and practice the few French words I've managed to learn. The driver, his right arm in a sling, appears. We share a cigarette and through hand gestures and pidgin French, I learn he's from Lyon, was a butcher before the war, had survived Verdun but consumption had claimed his wife. He kindly spent the next hour teaching me more French names for bike parts. I recited these words long into the night until I had them off pat. And when the nightmares forced me awake, I blocked them by reciting these odd-sounding words over and over, annoyed with the French for being too lazy to learn English.

The next morning a glowering Matilde stood at the table with the Harley diagram already unfurled. I point at the exhaust pipe and say, "Tuyau d'échappement."

Surprised, she points to the drive belt. "Courroie de transmission," I blurt. She's suspicious. But for the first time I detect a glimmer of warmth in her eyes. "Well done, Rudge."

"San Fairy Ann," I answer, with a hint of cockiness.

"Pardon?"

"It means, it don't matter, all us Tommies said it during the war. It's

French."

"Ca ne fait rien?"

"That's right, San Fairy Ann."

"You have much to learn, Rudge."

At the second lesson's end I returned to the garage and stripped a Harley engine. But it proved a struggle as my thoughts kept landing on Matilde, her frown, her smile, her disappointment in me. I'm lost in thought when the driver appears at the door wearing a gas mask and ordering me to put mine on.

My sweat-stained mask stinks of aged, perishing rubber and has a faded French infantryman's name scrawled inside. The mask brings back the suffocating panic of the phosgene attacks and watching men claw at life. Panicking, I tear the mask off and go outside, only for the nurse to order me to put it back on.

○ ○ ○ ○ ○ ○

In the following days, my French improves to the point where I can say my name, where I come from and what I eat for breakfast and dinner. I can buy meat from the butcher, vegetables from the greengrocers, bread from the baker and offer directions to the train station. Proud of my stuttering efforts, I hope Matilde will praise me. But she doesn't.

Being able to talk their lingo gains me the others' acceptance, despite them falling into fits of laughter at my mispronunciations. Most mornings the driver stops by for a chat, the nurse speaks ten to the dozen, none of which I understand, and I even drew a smile from Malaphonse after repairing her wheelbarrow. I've grown to enjoy her fitful but solemn, silent, company.

But it's Matilde's acceptance I want above all else. She remains cool and keeps her distance, never suffering any japery or tomfoolery, while being quick to chide. Sometimes her hard edge slips, usually at my French, and I glimpse a tender, warm soul. She's pretty too. Very pretty, now I think of it. But hidden under a stern shell.

She crops her frostiness listening to me pass on Fletcher's bodges for overcoming compression problems, blocked carburettors and the like. Sometimes her questions stump me. But I enjoy dwelling on these puzzles as they help me stem the night terrors and more importantly, keep her in my thoughts. Our time together has become the highlight of my day.

She now visits me in the garage. At first she'd stay for a few awkward seconds but now they stretch to half an hour. We hardly speak. The truth is I don't want to sound stupid in front of her, but when I catch her scent or feel her breath on my neck, my mouth dries, butterflies fill my stomach, and my spanner work becomes half-arsed. If we catch each other's gaze, we both look away sharpish and I redouble my ham-fisted efforts on the task in hand.

Lust saw me trek all over Belgium in search of Celestine. But with Matilde I'm gripped by different feelings that I fear and bask in but don't understand. I've fought on two continents, ridden motorbikes in the shadow of the pyramids, lost my best pal to a German sniper, and witnessed the slaughter of good, innocent men, but now it's all I can do to stop myself telling Matilde the truth about Douglas Rudge and Tom Casey. But the awkwardness between us denies me, while making my cravings all the stronger.

If only I Florrie were here. She'd know what to do. After all, she's probably read a book or two on the matter.

∘ ∘ ○ ○ ∘ ∘

Arriving at the garage, Matilde says, "No lesson today Rudge, we will take the FNs for a run out."

"Just hope you can keep up," I answer.

"Stay close and follow my line," she replies while slinging a rifle over her shoulder.

Leaving the village we head south along a lane marked by shattered trees, the sulphurous air scorching my eyes and chest. After a mile of twisting pavé, we ride over unmarked open ground littered with debris and rusting, unexploded shells. We ride slowly, alert to danger.

For several miles we amble along a narrow gravel track, the morning sunlight struggling to pierce the forest's eerie, charred remains.

"Banshee's lurking, Tom,"

Clearing the wood, Matilde accelerates up a hill and falls from view. I crest the hill but there's no sign of her. Below me stretches out a bleak cratered landscape sliced by a latticework of abandoned, waterlogged trenches edged by buckling, rusting sheets of corrugated tin. Sprouting tree saplings reclaim the land whilst in the near distance a silvery river threads its way towards the sea. Seems strange so many died for this land.

"Even the wind seems fearful of this place, Tom."

Off to my left an engine revs. I turn into a gravel path and follow the

180

sound. The track runs out. I dismount and treading lightly on the uneven ground, walk towards the noise. Moss lined craters intersect each other. I snag my boots on strands of needle-sharp barbed wire camouflaged by sprigs of new growth and skirt trenches marked with painted signs warning of mines.

Up ahead there's a motorcycle, an odd-looking contraption, with wicker baskets strapped to its front and rear. Further on, an old man wearing a grubby, patched Belgian army great coat leans over a half-buried shell. The copper casing will fetch enough to feed him for a month. Grunting and cursing, his white breath curling skywards, he rocks the shell backwards and forwards, levering it from the earth.

The explosion flattens me and I'm showered in black, rancid earth. Bewildered, I sit up and look towards the spot where the old man had been wrestling with the shell. He's vanished, his motorcycle now a contorted wreck. I stand and lean against a tree, slicing my hand on a fragment of hot shrapnel embedded in the bough. I slip and fall headfirst into the fresh crater. Fearing this vengeful land is plotting to take me, I grab an exposed tree root and haul myself up.

"The Banshee's lurking, Tom. Ready to claim ye."

Grasping another overhang I scramble over the crater's lip and like the serpent in Eden, I crawl away, snaring myself on rusted barbed wire and churned shrapnel. I reach the gravel path. Florrie is sitting on a motorcycle. "Why are you here?" I ask her.

Aiming a Luger at me she answers, "No closer."

"Didn't mean to kill Alf, Florrie. Honest. Didn't know my own strength. Tom Casey's been running ever since. But I did my duty. Saw the world too. That's all I ever wanted to do. You know that. Hope my contrition is enough."

I slither into another crater, sinking beneath its putrid waters. The underworld beckons. I claw my way to the surface, gasping for breath. Two masked creatures dressed in fatigues, rifles slung over their shoulders, stand at the crater's lip, shouting muffled commands. Gloved hands with slender fingers inside thread a rope under my arms and haul me out.

○ ○ ○ ○ ○ ○

I'm careering along a fog bound boreen. Chatta Singh steps from his pyre as Sabra kisses Saint Waltrude's statue. But wherever the delirium wants to take me, Matilde shepherds me to safety.

THE STEAM CATCHER

The alabaster saints and Lenin are watching me. I'm half deaf and shivering, despite the heavy blankets covering me. I ache all over, have a burning thirst and my chest is tight. Matilde lays a damp cloth on my forehead, whispers soothing words, and holds a cup of water to my lips. After I drink she asks, "What do you remember?"

"We were riding the FNs. I lost sight of you. I saw an old man. There was an explosion."

"Malaphonse and I dragged you clear then brought you back to the village. You have been asleep for two days. Rest now, Rudge. Or should I call you Tom Casey?"

CHAPTER FORTY-THREE

It's a week later and I still feel woozy and off-colour. Thrice daily, the nurse takes my temperature and barks commands, none of which I understand, much to the driver's amusement. Malaphonse keeps her distance.

It's just a matter of time before Matilde denounces me. And when she does, I'll be shot. All I can do is make a run for it.

I pocket a revolver and then struggle to wheel the Indian V Twin from the garage. "Where are you going?" Matilde asks, wearing a wary, almost vengeful look.

"The Indian needs a run out."

"You are not fit to ride."

"Finish her off, Tom, keep your secret safe."

"Had enough of being cooped up."

"I will come with you." I don't argue. With luck she'll lead me to safety. She wheels out her FN and stifles a laugh listening to me curse the Indian for not starting. Of course, the fuel tap.

Leaving the village we roll north along a series of lanes, shrouded inside the dead forest. With every mile I feel stronger and more alert and revel being in Matilde's company. We pull up at a forked junction. A sign warning of mines hangs from a chain barring entry into the left fork.

"There is a village a few kilometres further on," she says, uncoupling the chain. We take the left fork, and climb a furrowed uphill track, the Indian slewing from stock to stock as I wrestle its heavy steering. Matilde rides with a lightness of touch, sometimes standing on the footrests to absorb the vibrations when her bike bottoms out. The surface improves as we ride through another abandoned hamlet and swing north. After ten minutes we enter a village, still intact. Some windows even sport panes of glass.

Leaving the bikes on a stone bridge straddling a coal-black stream, we enter the village square. For once my lungs aren't burning and there's occasional birdsong. The sun breaks out. Inside a bakery sits a dust-coated counter decorated with a set of ancient scales, its weights stacked in a lopsided tower beside it. Above the counter hangs a slate board advertising prices. Next door is a butcher's, its floor still matted in sawdust. Meat hooks hang from white tiled walls and a scored, bloodied chopping block sits idle. I half expect to see people shopping, gossiping or enjoying a coffee in the nearby café.

"The French army fired gas onto the village a week before the armistice,"

Matilde tells me as we look inside the café. "They were firing on the German lines, but the co-ordinates were out by two degrees. Many of the villagers and soldiers stationed here were killed or wounded."

I follow her along a narrow, crowded lane until we stop outside a fine two-storey house surrounded by railings. Two steps lead up to the front door.

"My old home," Matilde says. She opens the front door. Two crows fly out, startling us. We step in. The house smells of damp. Everything has been stripped out, even the floorboards.

"Are your family still alive?" I ask.

"My father died of consumption when I was a baby. Even the waters of Lourdes could not revive him. But he was remembered with fondness for being kind to his tenants and generous to those in need. Influenza claimed Mother after her evacuation to Amiens to recover from the effects of the gas attack. I had a brother, Cedric. He died at Verdun. His body has yet to be found. One day, hopefully. It was Cedric who taught me to ride." Her guard slips and there's a sad, lost tone to her voice. I offer her my water canister. After drinking, she walks along the exposed joists towards the front room's ornate mantel, which someone has tried but failed to rip from the wall. "All those broken bodies and minds. People haunted by loss and grief." She pauses. "Forgive me, I did not bring you here just to see me cry for my past."

"Don't fret. Do you have any other family?"

"I have an aunt. She lives in Tours. We used to visit before the war. The train took forever. But I would have liked it to have taken even longer."

"Why?"

"My aunt's youngest daughter was a year older then me. Suzette. She had everything; toys, ribbons, even a dog. She looked down on me, laughed at my clothes, shoes, my accent." She giggles, her face lighting up. "We fought like wildcats. Once she bit me on the arm. See?" Pulling up the right sleeve of her tunic she points to a scar on her forearm. "I was always blamed when we fought. Mother always took my cousin's side, saying I'd shamed father's memory. Within a day of arriving I wanted to go home." Rolling her sleeve down she says, "Sometimes I think how nice it would be to see them again."

"Why don't you?"

"The forest is my home now, a place where I can choose my own fate. It is dangerous but shelters us. Like a fairy tale."

"And you ride motorcycles."

"Mother thought it most unladylike. She raised me to be decorous, good

 184

marrying-stock, teaching me to sew, play the violin, and speak English because my father had always admired the English for their nobility. I inherited his stubbornness and refused to listen to Mother's objections. Cedric often challenged me to a race, which I usually won. He claimed I took short cuts or tampered with his bike, refusing to accept that I was the better rider. Sometimes when I'm out on the bike I hear Cedric whispering, "Slow down Matilde, or Pothole, Matilde." She falls silent and steps across the joists. Without looking at me she says, "You remind me of him."

"How?"

"Serious, quiet, and happiest when riding a motorcycle." She turns and looks at me. "You are different to other men. You have not pawed or belittled me. Even Malaphonse values your company."

"Why doesn't she speak?"

"The past was no friend to her. She is happiest in silence now."

"You'd get on with my sister."

"In what way?"

"She has ideas, beliefs, certainty."

"She sounds strong."

"Good right hook as well."

"When did you last see her?"

"Years ago. Can't go back now though."

"Because you killed that boy?" Her remark flummoxes me. "You spoke of it when we pulled you from the crater. Is that why you changed your name?"

"Have you told anyone?" I reach for the revolver.

"No. We all have secrets. Why else would we be here?"

"What's yours?" I loosen my grip on the pistol. She looks uneasy, ill-prepared for the question. "You don't have to tell me."

"It is not that. I have not spoken of them in a long time, hoping silence would lay them to rest."

"You knowing my secret is a weight off my shoulders. Makes me trust you all the more."

"That is nice to know." She reaches the stairs and sits on the bottom step. Lost in thought she wrings the life from her gloves. "If I tell you, please do not judge me."

"I'd never do that Matilde." The space between us shrinks a touch more. She pushes a loose strand of hair behind her right ear. "Before the war I worked as a governess for a doctor's family in Lille. They were bourgeois but nice, the children lovely. But when the Germans occupied the city, the doctor was shipped to a concentration camp and the Germans cast his wife and daughters out. With no chance of returning home, I found work in the Bosch officers' casino, first as a waitress, later as a croupier. That is where I met Gustav." I bridle at the name. "He was an adjutant in the Lille kommandatur. A kind man more suited to teaching than being a soldier. We went to the theatre, fine restaurants, once even to Berlin. He liked to talk of poetry, of home, family, things that war cannot destroy. At the time I never saw the Germans being driven out of France. Having a German captain as a lover offered food, shelter, and safety." Reading my thoughts she continues, "I did whatever it took to survive."

"I know the feeling'."

"When the British marched into Lille in nineteen eighteen, Gustav and the rest of the Germans fled. Within hours the round-ups began. That is where I met Malaphonse and Elise."

"Why were they arrested?"

"They were prostitutes."

"No shame in that. The girls we saw made good money."

She stiffens, regret replacing anger. "Is that what you think? Does it make you feel better believing a woman would enjoy having a dozen men rut on her everyday? That she sits waiting for you to return, the gallant Tommy Knight defending her freedom and liberty, fawning over *you*, a man who lives under a false name."

"They had a choice is all I'm saying."

"The Germans stole our homes, food, even our loved ones. Many women had no choice but to sell themselves. But with the war at an end, people had to blame someone. It helped them accept their own accommodations with the Bosch. So picking out prostitutes and concubines gave cover to much grander betrayals."

"I didn't realise." It dawns on me how little I knew Celestine, how infatuation smothers the truth.

"We all lived with one eye closed during these times." She gathers herself. "We were herded outside the train station, spat on, beaten, our hair shorn. Ropes were slung over lampposts. Two men, profiteers I think, were hanged. Then the mob bayed for Elise, Malaphonse and me to be hanged." She looked away, wiping her eyes. "Such hate, Rudge, such pure, clear hate. You could taste it. I saw the doctor's eldest daughter in the crowd and begged her to help me, to remember the fond times we shared, that I was no traitor. But she turned her back."

I hold her hand. "You don't have to tell me anymore."

"A squadron of British soldiers arrived the moment the nooses were threaded around our necks. They fired over the crowd. Some fled, but the ringleaders rounded on the soldiers, telling them French people should settle their own affairs. Not wanting a riot the officer, young, not much older than me, ordered his men to stand aside and let a group of men throw Malaphonse, Elise and me into the back of a butcher's wagon. We were driven to an abandoned farmhouse outside the city. The men took turns to rape us, all the while laughing and joking that because we were whores we were enjoying the punishment. I felt numb, shutting out their stink and grunts as they lay on me, telling myself to live and that my ordeal would soon end. But it never does." She's distant, her eyes intelligent spark dimmed. "Auguste found us the next morning half-naked, whipped, and tied up like beasts. He untied us, gave us food, and told us we were free to leave or we could join him in the forest. It was not a difficult decision. Return to a place that hated us or seek a new life. So, after four years away I returned home with Elise and Malaphonse. We were three sisters, sharing the same soul." My Three Sisters loom through the Kerry mist.

"That is how we survived by sharing our sadness and rage. Women are strong, much stronger than men. Now, follow me." I follow her upstairs to a small room where she stands by the window and looks out."As a young girl, I would stand here imagining the people and lands laying beyond the village. I dreamed of marrying a man who would cherish me, a knight in shining armour."

"I used to dream of going to the South Pole with Captain Scott."

"There is still time."

"Not with my sea legs." I hated myself but had to ask, "Do you miss the German?"

"Sometimes, although not so much these past few weeks. But I hope he is happy. Alive at least. What do you miss?"

"My mum, my sister Florrie and my brother Stanley mostly. My best pal Jack too. Him and Florrie were sweethearts. I hope they're together as it'll mean Jack got home in one piece. They're made for each other. Hope to find something similar one day."

"Perhaps you have found it, Tom Casey." She slips her hand into mine. I grip her fingers. The space between us has vanished.

"I always wanted to get away from Gloucester. Managed to, after a fashion. Seen the best and worst of mankind. Takes its toll, seeing the world through violent eyes. What about you? What do you miss?"

"My mother, brother, the village and forest as it used to be. Elise also.

She always said I should not close my heart to love." She laughs. "I also miss dancing. Life in the forest is not suited to such folly."

"Fancy a reel now?"

"Why not." We hold each other and sway in time to the silence. For a few frail moments my world stops turning as her left hand rests on my shoulder and her right hand clasps mine. Every movement seems connected, meant. "Why did you kill that boy?" she asks.

"He was going to hurt my brother."

"Why run?"

"Running's all I've known. If I'd stayed I never would have got a fair crack of the whip. Gave a false name to join up. Vanishing's easy. Remembering who you are is the hard part."

"Or a lunatic."

Matilde presses against me and my mind swims with excitement and fear. We kiss. All my life I've been waiting for this moment. She pulls away, chiding herself in French. But within seconds we're tearing at each other's clothes.

"Tom Casey," she whispers as I enter her.

∘ ∘ ○ ○ ∘ ∘

We're in each other's arms sharing a Players. I run my hand along her cheek while she strokes the Sacred Heart tattoo on my chest. She mutters my name. "Why do you keep saying my name?" I ask.

"Tom Casey is a comforting sound. Tom Casey."

"We could make for Tours. Start a new life down there." Her mood changes.

Fool.

"I cannot leave. These people are my family. We have endured by being true to each other." She sits up. "The coast is just five kilometres away. You can be in England by tomorrow."

"Do you think I'm leaving now?"

"You must, Tom Casey."

"Five seconds ago you were whispering my name. Now you want me to scarper? I've been running for years, from madness, bullies, and war. Running from myself as much as anything. Figured out why I've been running all this time. To find you. Fate has brought us together."

"There is no such thing."

"Course there is. Why else did we end up in this God-forsaken place?"

"Do not make me choose." She dresses quickly, cursing as she struggles to lace up her boots. She gives up and storms out, her laces flapping around her ankles. I dress and follow her. We hurry to the square in silence. The buildings now look twisted and deformed, broken by loss. Saplings sprout through chimneystacks, paint peels from walls and shutters hang from rusted hinges. Reaching the bikes I grab the FN's handlebars. "Matilde, I'm not leaving you, as sure as God's in Gloucestershire I'm not."

"You do not belong here. You need faith to survive here."

"Timmings copes well enough."

"He is a robber, you are not. I have heard your cries in the night, the nightmares haunting you, your terror at wearing a mask. The air poisons all of us, but you most of all."

"I love you."

"Then if you do, please leave. Calais is half an hour from here. Go home to your family."

"I don't understand. When I'm with you, I see a future."

"That cannot be."

I let her take off. By rights I should head north for Calais and home. *"Do what's right, Tom."*

I follow Matilde.

○ ○ ○ ○ ○ ○

Matilde ignores me after I make it back to the village. Her scowl makes her feelings plain. That evening she stays close to Malaphonse and the nurse, while I spend the night in the garage, tormented by frustration, anger, and lust. Unable to sleep I chain smoke, mulling over my situation. She couldn't be more than thirty yards away but may as well be in the shadow of the Great Pyramid.

The garage door inches open. She stands in the doorway, partially lit by the streaming moonlight. A strong dose of colly-wobbles courses through me. "I don't understand," I whisper.

"Be quiet." She lays down next to me. "Personne n'est redevable a personne".

"What does that mean?"

"No one is beholden to anyone."

CHAPTER FORTY-FOUR

For the next few days I'd follow Matilde from the village towards an abandoned barn or farmhouse to snatch an hour, maybe two together. One time we tried to fuck astride her bike and I managed to burn my shin on the hot cylinder block and hopped around the barn in agony as Matilde looked on in fits of laughter.

Each day I drown a little more in her, allowing Tom Casey to resurface.

When she scolded me in front of the others, I felt bewildered, cut adrift. Yet the next day as we clung to each other and she repeats my name, my jealousies faded to nothing. I lay pressed next to her watching her sleep, her arm draped over my chest, her soft breaths calming and perfect.

"The nurse suspects us," she tells me while dressing after we'd snatched an hour in a roofless barn. "She talks about the importance of love in our lives, then in the next breath warns how difficult it would be to raise a child in the forest."

"You're not pregnant, are you?" My heart skips a beat.

"No!"

Relieved, I light two Players and hand her one.

"But if I were pregnant, what would you do?"

"Marry you and take you to Tours to start afresh."

She kisses me. "I will never be a man's chattel."

"Don't expect you to be. Just want you to know that I'll always do right by you. Wherever we end up, whatever we do, I'm yours, Matilde."

"Thank you, Tom Casey."

"For what?"

"I promised myself never to love another man. But you have made me break my oath." We kiss. She pulls away giggling.

"What's so funny?" I ask. Without answering she tears two loose threads from the hem of her fatigues and wraps one each around our wedding fingers. "There, Tom Casey. We are betrothed."

○ ○ ○ ○ ○ ○

Returning to the village my heart sinks. Timmings, Auguste, and the others are back. We roll towards the garage. Timmings waves. Parking the bikes up, Matilde and me steal a kiss. "Auguste must not find out," she whispers.

Brushing the cotton thread on my finger she whispers, "Forever, Tom

Casey."

I squat beside the Indian to examine the cylinder head, already missing Matilde. Timmings steps into the garage. "How were things in my absence?"

"All right. Bikes are all in fine fettle."

"Good." He sits on one of the FN's and grips the handlebars. "This next raid will be the biggest one yet. A "Spectacular" is how Auguste described it." I reconnoitred the length of the Boudewijnkanaal that links Bruges to Zeebrugge, whilst Auguste and the others plotted the fastest routes in and out of Bruges. They won't divulge anything more as France and Belgium are crawling with informants. The French have even set up a special squadron to catch us. I'll be off after this caper."

"Where you headed?"

"England, then Montevideo. Fancy it?"

"Not sure."

"Would that have something to do with the fair Matilde? A little bird tells me she has cast her spell on you. Tupped her yet?"

I square up to him. "Don't talk about her like that. She's suffered things that you can't imagine."

He raises his hands. "Didn't mean to upset you, Old Thing. Message understood. Be quick though. If you love the girl, do the decent thing by her."

"Who said I loved her?"

"You, by threatening to crown me."

"Just the way I am. Can't help it."

"You're needy, Rudge. Reckon you were dropped on your head when you were a tot. But what a tale you'll have to tell your feral offspring. War hero, marries a beautiful mysterious Bolshevik woman in the Zone Rouge." He laughs. "Ever think you'd end up part outlaw part Romeo?"

"More to me than meets the eye."

CHAPTER FORTY-FIVE

I lift the flap and the freezing air sucks the breath from me. Mist shrouds the land making our spot four miles north of Bruges feel even more desolate. Matilde, Malaphonse, Timmings, Sonia, Maxime and Octave are crammed together under the covers still asleep while the driver and Auguste sleep in the cab.

I jump from the wagon and land in fresh, ankle-deep snow and survey the fog bound, featureless landscape scarred by drainage channels with only the harsh squawk of crows for company. I light a cigarette and enjoy a peaceful smoke.

Finishing the fag, I draw back the snow coated tarpaulin covering the bikes. They're bone dry but I'm worried the snow will make the handling tricky, so lower the tyre pressures. Auguste pokes his head from the cab window, coughs, and then spits. He looks as bedraggled as he did during our time locked up in Ostend. "Does the snow change anything?" I ask. He shakes his head.

As the others stir, I start both bikes, leave them to idle and return to the wagon for a breakfast of cold coffee, stale bread and jam. We eat and smoke in silence, bound up in our own thoughts, like Tommies preparing to go over the top. Only our objective isn't some Hun trench but gold bullion spirited out of Petrograd before the Russian revolution and stashed in a Bruges bank. When the Russians learned of plans to ship it to Stockholm, they ordered us to steal it back.

"How much gold is on the barge?" I ask Timmings as he checks his bike.

"Enough to build a workers paradise, Old Thing."

"Keep Matilde safe."

"Of course."

Matilde has barely said two words to me since the recce party returned. She threw herself into preparing ordnance and running through practice drills with Timmings and Malaphonse. I spent fretful nights in the garage in a desperate fug waiting for her to come to me. When she didn't I became a resentful, snapping pup, earning regular bollockings from Timmings and Auguste for my shoddy workmanship and slack, couldn't care less, demeanour. Fuck 'em. But most of all fuck her. I should have followed her advice and taken my chances back home.

"Allez! Allez!" shouts Auguste, slapping the lorry's bonnet. Timmings and Matilde examine and then holster their revolvers. Octave lashes a machine gun to each bike as Timmings shoulders the canvas knapsack containing the grenades.

"Remember comrades," Auguste says to them. "The road convoy is a decoy, designed to trick people into thinking the gold is being transported to Zeebrugge by road. All you have to do is draw the gendarmes into Bruges and away from us. Fast in. Fast out. Understood?" They both nod.

Timmings smokes and Matilde hides her nerves by fettling with her bike. I squat by her and say, "I've lowered the tyre pressures. Stay in a low gear."

"I know how to ride in the snow."

"All the same, keep your wits about you."

"I trust the bike. And the mechanic." She brushes my hand and whispers, "When this is over, if you still want, we can go to Tours."

"Thought you'd grown tired of me."

"Sorry if you thought me cruel, but it was the only way I could think of protecting you. Protecting us. Tomorrow we can leave. To start over." I look at her, befuddled but in rapture. "Tom Casey," she whispers.

"Fast in. Fast out."

She nods, lowers her goggles and laces the scarf around her face. She leads Timmings out onto the snowbound road. Both bikes snake as the power feeds through. Matilde's plaits dance around her shoulders. Within seconds they're swallowed by the mist, but I stay rooted to the spot listening to the engines until Auguste tells me to board the lorry.

After a few grinding minutes, we pull up. I jump down and join Auguste, who hands me a machine gun. Snow-coated trees flicker in the breeze and a flock of crows take flight as we tramp alongside a drainage channel.

We reach the snow crusted embankment overlooking the Boudewijnkanaal. The canal's slate grey waters still and partially iced. The thick fog means the far side of the canal is all but invisible. An engine note floats over the water and moments later a dawdling, Bruges bound barge slinks through the fog, fracturing the ice. The barge is over one hundred feet long, making me wonder what a Gloucester bargeman would make of her. A deckhand stands on the prow calling out in Flemish. I cock my machine gun. Auguste touches my arm and gently shakes his head. We sit in silence, the barge's noise waning. "Nervous?" asks Auguste.

"A bit."

"Nerves are good, keeps the mind sharp." The barge horn blows again, scattering more crows. Maybe it's the same flock from a few minutes ago.

"Matilde will never leave," Auguste says.

"What do you mean?" I answer, trying to sound surprised.

Looking over the canal, he clasps my shoulder. "Understand Rudge, our cause runs deeper than love." His cocksure words rile me. He can't know of our plans for tomorrow. I check a childish urge to tell him. "Why are you here?" I ask.

"What do you mean?"

"You've an officer's bearing and have everyone's respect. Yet here you are scraping along with the likes of me."

"A woman. And not in the manner you are thinking." He checks his Webley before continuing. "It is true I am bourgeoisie, a class enemy. My family own collieries in the Alsace. Before the war, I studied mining at university but was more interested in drink and cards than studying. Then, the miners came out on strike in the spring of nineteen thirteen after their pay had been cut. I was outraged. My father was always farsighted in the treatment of his workers, building homes, schools, and churches. So if wages had to be cut, sound reasons must lay behind his decision. More mine owners cut wages. The strike spread. In the third week I hired men to break up a strike meeting in Lens. Just before I gave the signal to attack, a woman by the name of Marie stood to speak. She was malnourished, dressed in rags, but there was something almost saintly about her. Her voice held me in her thrall. Her husband, one of the strike leaders, had been jailed, leaving her and her five children destitute. She had little money or food and faced eviction from her home. Despite such hardships she would always resist the owners and refused to accept that the only life available for her children would be a life of drudgery and exploitation. Her last words were,"Je ne dois pas ceder," – I shall not yield. She spoke to a truth I had never thought of. Before, I didn't see the miners as people but as property. My family's wealth is built upon their toil, not our genius. Only by exploiting them can we continue our lavish lives. My happiness depended upon their destitution."

"The rich always know how to improve the life of the poor, Tom."

"I asked my father to restore the miners' wages. The next day, a squadron of dragoons enter the miners' village. One of the horses struck Marie. She died two days later. Hundreds attended her funeral. Such solidarity. Her death taught me that my father would do anything to protect his interests, even murder. Days later the dragoons appeared again. This time I stood with the miners and fought back, unseating the dragoon captain and killing his horse. We then set the mine ablaze. I was charged with sedition and sentenced to ten years hard labour. Father disowned me, but I had honoured Marie's sacrifice and the millions like her who suffer and starve because of capitalism. I had found my destiny." His face wore the convert's certainty.

"Why are you telling me this?"

"There is more to this robbery than I can say." For the first time since we'd met Auguste has doubt etched on his refined features.

"Sounds like you need to confess."

"To a priest perhaps. Certainly not you."

"There's a man back home who'd set you right in no time."

"After today I shall need him." He checks his watch. "Allez."

We set off. The fog is lifting and the wrought iron arch of the Herdersbrug swing bridge looms before us. The bridge's swing section is open to allow a Zeebrugge bound barge to pass through. The two men standing on the bridge wave to the barge's crew. After the barge clears the bridge, both men lean into a tall double-handled pole and turn it anti-clockwise. The swing section clatters to a close and the men drop large steel pins into position to secure it.

One of the bridge turners beckons our lorry over the bridge and then joins the other man in a small, whitewashed wooden hut on the canal's eastern bank. A gaggle of geese swim in the barge's wake. A cyclist, hunched against the cold, pedals along the western towpath towards Zeebrugge.

The lorry disappears from sight. Minutes later, two hundred yards or so upstream, a slight, well wrapped up figure scrambles down the eastern embankment. "Malaphonse," Auguste whispers. "The barge carrying the gold is minutes away." Timmings and Matilde will have begun the assault on the Bruges convoy.

On the eastern bank Maxime approaches the bridge turners' two-storey house. An aged dog lounging outside barks as he enters but is silent when a few moments later, Maxime leaves the house carrying a wireless set. He drops the wireless into the canal before taking up his position on the bridge and setting up his Vickers to face north. Octave sets up the other Vickers to face south. To complete the enfilade Sonia stands under the bridge covering both towpaths.

I follow Auguste onto the bridge. We stop halfway across and gaze at Bruges' towers and steeples a mile or two to the south. The bitter breeze cuts through me. I breath on my hands to warm them, my gaze flitting between the bridge and canal. I know I should have my mind on the task in hand but all I can think about is Matilde.

Another Zeebrugge bound barge approaches. Our lorry reappears and reverses down a cobbled slipway towards the towpath. The driver drops the tailgate and takes up a covering position. As the geese swim under the bridge, Malaphonse ambles down the towpath, alongside the barge.

Auguste whispers, "Allez." We don the tank driver masks and run towards the hut, our boots clattering over the swing section. Auguste kicks open the hut door. The smell of frying bacon greets us. An elderly man, fat, with fine whiskers, drops the skillet. His confused pal looks over the top of his newspaper. Auguste hollers in Flemish. I smash the hut's wireless set, then bind, gag and blindfold them both.

We sprint towards the swing section's turning point and insert the turning pole into the pivot head. We keep our heads down as we turn the pole clockwise. The swing section creaks opens and a crewman balancing on the barge's prow, bellows instructions while waving his arms. The barge slows.

With the barge yards away we begin to close the swing section. The barge ploughs into the bridge. Both Vickers open up, tearing into the barge's hull and splintering its wheelhouse and cargo pens. Stray bullets skip along the canal forcing the geese to take to wing, with several dead in the water.

Auguste lobs a grenade onto the foredeck and pulls me to the floor. Shards of splintered wood spill from the forward cargo pen. Auguste leaps down onto the foredeck and charges towards the wheelhouse. Bullets strike the bridge's ironwork as I leap from the balustrade onto the foredeck and drop behind a pile of ropes. The wounded crewman lying beside me pleads in Flemish while clasping the splinter of wood in his stomach. I'm pinned down by rifle fire from two gendarmes inside the forward pen. Amid the gunfire, I hear a woman soothing whimpering children.

To reach me, the two gendarmes must leave the pen. I wonder how brave they are, what sense of duty they carry. The answer comes within seconds when they rush me, only to be cut down by Maxime. The children are screaming. Two more policemen dart from the second pen. Again Maxine drops them.

Keeping low, I run towards the wheelhouse and find Auguste standing over the body of the barge captain. A crewman is at the wheel. "What's he doing?" I ask.

"Bringing us along. When he's finished, make it a flesh wound, shoulder or thigh. The gold is in the rear pen. I'm going forward."

After bringing the barge alongside, the crewman kneels in front of me. He's shaking and muttering a prayer under his breath. Despite a wavering hand, I press the pistol into his right thigh and fire. He collapses on the floor screaming with pain. I step towards him but Maxime drags me outside. We head for the nearest cargo pen. I shoot off the lock. Inside are a stack of wooden crates. I jemmy open the first crate. Four gold bars, each one stamped with a double-headed eagle sit in a bed of straw. We both pick up an ingot and are struck dumb by their beauty. "Dix minutes," he says, pulling me back to the robbery.

It takes the two of us to lug one crate from the pen, across a gangplank and onto the lorry. Malaphonse splits open the crate. For a moment she too is enthralled by the bullion, until Maxime tells her to start stowing the ingots inside an empty oil drum. Octave and the driver arrive with another crate.

The four of us work in silence and lug the crates ashore. Even with two of us to each crate it is tiring, cumbersome work. By the fifth crate, my arms ache and despite the freezing cold, my shirt clings to my sweat soaked back.

Upstream, a barge horn blows. Maxime shouts, "Dix minutes! C'est fini!" We've brought out eighteen crates, seventy-two ingots in total. A fortune.

Octave helps Malaphonse to stash the remaining ingots in a second oil drum. The barge draws closer and a crewman balanced on the prow, shouts instructions backed up with hand signals. There's no sign of Auguste.

I return to the barge just as he steps from the second pen. Inside lays a middle-aged woman and a boy and a girl, both roughly eight years old. A doll has fallen from the girl's grasp. I touch her still warm hand and check on the boy. All three are dead. Shot. Speechless, I stumble outside and look back at the bodies, part hidden in the darkness. Auguste is already ashore. The barge is so close I can make out the crewman's sea-sculpted features. I pelt cross the gangplank, run up the slipway and reach the lorry. Malaphonse helps me to clamber aboard.

"In it up to yer neck now Tom."

CHAPTER FORTY-SIX

Although wrapped in a great coat and balaclava, the cold still grinds my bones as I struggle to scrub the dead children from my mind's eye. We've pocketed a king's ransom, with a tale that by rights should pass into folklore. But I taste no glory, no sense of victory. For all the fine words about freedom and hope we'll be remembered as child killers.

The snow and the weight of gold, slow our progress. Maxime and Octave, their white breaths mingling, train their Vickers along the road. Both are on edge. So much so that when I strike a match to light a cigarette Maxime spins round and shouts at me; but he catches Malaphonse's gaze and turns away chuntering to himself.

All being well, Matilde and Timmings should be haring south along the coast road towards France. From there they'll swing east towards the safety of the Zone Rouge. We'll skirt Bruges to the south travelling along unmarked tracks before swinging west towards the French border and the Zone.

We pass Bruges without incident but become bogged down in heavy snow drifts. Shifting the snow is laborious, backbreaking work with the freezing air burning our lungs. But everyone works like Trojans, the others eagers to reach safety, while I'm desperate to see Matilde.

Gunfire. Auguste urges us on and we redouble our efforts, with Sonia and the driver clawing at the snow with their bare hands. The gunfire draws closer, now joined by barking dogs. Police? Already?

Auguste passes word about the group of men spying on us from a field a hundred yards off to the right. We clear the drift and set off. Fifty yards on, the lorry slides into a ditch.

The men draw near. Several carry shotguns; and a boy and girl about ten years old, carry rabbit carcasses on poles slung across their shoulders. Maxime sights the hunters with his Vickers, as the rest of us with revolvers stuffed in our coat pockets, urge the driver and Octave to get on with lashing a rope to the lorry's back axle.

The hunters are a motley bunch, hunched, thin. Untrustworthy. They mumble amongst themselves and leer at Malaphonse and Sonia. Standing on tiptoe, the young girl tries to peek inside the wagon but Sonia blocks her path despite the offer of a couple of rabbits. The men shoulder their shotguns and take hold of the rope, grinding their boots into the ground. The driver starts the lorry and feathers the throttle. A shout goes up and like a tug of war team, we lean back and haul the lorry clear.

As we board, the two hunters closest to the wagon catch sight of the Vickers but say nothing. We set off with Auguste leaning from the cab door thanking the hunters who look on in silence, hands in pockets, their dogs yapping. Two hotheads run towards us. Maxime fires a volley. Snow spits up before the chasers, stopping them in their tracks. The driver accelerates into the snow covered bend, but this time manages to keep the lorry on the road.

On we crawl, mile after pulverising, freezing mile, certain Madame Guillotine lays around the next corner. Nerves fray each time we have to stop and dig a path through the snow. Octave and Maxime bicker, Sonia curses to herself, and Auguste barks random orders even though nobody is listening. Malaphonse as ever, says nothing.

By dusk, in driving sleet, we reach a metalled road. The worst of the journey is over. With luck we'll be in the village by dawn. As we turn onto the road, Malaphonse beckons me closer and opens her rucksack. An ingot nestles inside. Even mute revolutionaries are tempted by greed, it seems.

∘ ∘ ○ ◯ ∘ ∘

I wake stiff-necked and aching with the cold as the lorry judders to a stop. Daylight floods the wagon. The Zone's toxic stench fills my nostrils. Maxime and Octave, no longer threatening, shifting shapes in the freezing dark, hug. Malaphonse clasps my hand as Maxime draws back the canvas flap. The pristine snow gives the charred forest a peaceful air. Sanctuary. We pass familiar landmarks and jolt over the usual potholes, each one greeted with a cheer.

Several hours later in glorious sunshine we pull into the village. The nurse and Etienne greet us. The nurse carries a pail of fresh water. Etienne smiles as he shakes Auguste's hand. I wonder what sort of man could receive the news of slayed children with backslaps and smiles.

"Matilde?" I ask the nurse as she hands me a cup of water. She shakes her head and says something. As usual I don't understand her.

We stow the gold inside the church confessionals, after which we gorge on bread slathered in butter and honey washed down with hot, sweet coffee. The gang members are exhausted and elated in equal measure. They've proved something to themselves today. What, I have no idea, but it's plain to see on their drawn, tired faces that they're even more convinced their revolution is drawing closer. But not me. Despite Auguste's dismissal of love, I'm desperate for sight of Matilde. She and Timmings should be back by now. We'll have to spend another night here before slipping away tomorrow.

I leave the others to their celebrations and walk to edge of the village. Ignoring the choking wind, I listen out for Matilde and Timmings. Malaphonse, wearing her gas mask, thrusts my mask into my chest. I don the mask and the pair of us wait in this suffocating silence, me fighting the phosgene demons, whilst Malaphonse scours the trees. With each passing minute, my fears grow. Without warning, Malaphonse takes off for the woods. I peel off my mask and gag on the choking air watching her fade from view.

The trees crowd me as the bitter, sly east wind slips between their creaking boughs. Certain the banshee approaches, I kneel down and press my right ear to the ground, just like a red indian scout in one of Stan's cowboy books, hoping to hear or feel approaching motorcycles. But the only sounds are the cracks of twigs and a gentle scuffing on the frozen earth. I look up. Two masked figures step from the woods. Behind them I expect to see near-rotten corpses clad in shredded uniforms.

The two phantoms draw closer, the taller of the two dragging their bloodied right leg. I fumble for my revolver and fire over their heads, the pistol recoiling in my hand. They stop in their tracks.

"Banshee's fearful of ye, Tom."

Lifting his mask, Timmings says, "Still an awful shot." Malaphonse raises her mask. Doubt plays across her face.

"Matilde?" I ask him.

"Dead."

Dumbfounded, a bilious emptiness fills my stomach. *"Tom Casey. Tom Casey."* I touch the cotton ringlet on my wedding finger while searching Timmings face for signs that he's joking and that Matilde will step from the woods laughing about their ruse. But for once Timmings cannot hide his feelings. There's no sign of Matilde. I aim the revolver at him. "You just had to cause a diversion. No need for heroics. She promised me she'd make it back. She promised!"

"Do your best, I'm too tired to care." He sits on a wall, takes a cigarette from Malaphonse, and says, "The Police were laying in wait. *They* ambushed *us*. Matilde was hit. They swarmed around her. Going back for her would be a fool's errand. I had to give it full chat to get out of Bruges with half the Belgian army on my tail. I ran out of fuel ten miles from here and yomped the rest of the journey. They're coming for us. This is serious, Rudge, more than a robbery. What did you do?"

"Auguste killed two children."

"Children?"

Malaphonse's eyes flit between us. "Matilde?" she mutters with an edge of fear.

Timmings and me look at each other. Neither of us wants to be the one to tell her.

"Matilde?" Malaphonse repeats.

Timmings whispers, "Matilde est mort."

"Mort?" She shakes her head. "Non, non, Matilde's est mon souer." She sets about him, with flailing, whirling fists. He doesn't defend himself.

I stumble through the forest tripping over roots, snaring myself on sprigs of abandoned barbed wire. I push on not caring or knowing where I'll end up. I slip into a crater but fall short of the fetid water laying in its floor. I curl into a ball. Stillness. No thoughts. I gather the filthy earth around me, safe in its clutches, understanding why Malaphonse spends so much time out here. Outside some pub in Gloucester, the pastor will be beseeching drinkers to find a new life. I've found mine. Here in this hole waiting for Matilde.

I wake to find Malaphonse beside me. We cling to each other, the forest witnessing our grief. She tries to lift me, but I resist so she draws her revolver and orders me to stand. I relent and clamber from the crater and follow the last of the Three Sisters back towards the village. We stop on the outskirts. Malaphonse kisses me on the cheek and wipes a smear of mud from my chin. Smiling, she whispers in a dry, hoarse voice, "Les trois sœurs veilleront sur toi," and returns to the Forest.

Auguste is sat outside the café, looking a shadow of the man whose guile has brought us this far. Sonia and Etienne stand beneath the frayed canopy deep in conversation. "Matilde is dead," I tell him.

With barely a flicker he says, "She gave her life for the cause."

"Timmings said the police were laying in wait. Somebody betrayed them."

His silence condemns him.

"Who were those children?"

He rolls a mouthful of wine around his mouth before swallowing. "Romanovs, the nephew and niece of the dead Tsar. The Russians issued the order after learning the children were being taken to Sweden. From there they were to be smuggled into Finland to become a rallying point for Tsarists. Action had to be taken." He looks at me, anger replacing doubt." You have no idea of our sacrifices and the debt we owe our fallen comrades.

We owe it to their memory to continue the struggle. I carry their blood in my soul."

"Do you think they would've wanted you to kill children in their memory?"

"They are products of oppression. If they had lived, the opportunity to build a just world is put at risk. We all have choices to make."

"Only the deranged or pitiless will flock to your banner now. The people will want your head."

He waves my words away. "Do you think I worry about the people? They will never be ready for the change they need. They endured the war, yet afterwards sought the old certainties of patriotism and God. We will never seize power by following the false choices Christian piety clings to. We need to sow terror and hate to ensure victory. We are the vanguard of the revolution and if I have to take the lives of a thousand children, so be it."

"But you betrayed your comrades."

"Not when it serves a higher purpose. The police were told in order to increase our chances of success at the bridge. The plan worked."

"So you sacrificed Matilde."

"She gave her life for the revolution. We have achieved our aim. The gold will pay for weapons and the children have been neutralised. A new reality is being forged through violence. There is no room for sentiment."

"You're no better than your father. Marie's words ring hollow in your mouth." He looks stunned. I've spoken a truth he's shied away from for years. He lights a cigarette and with an unsteady hand, pours himself another glass of wine.

"Get some food and then rest. You will see things differently tomorrow."

○ ○ ○ ○ ○ ○

In the church, the unnerved driver hands me a glass of cognac. Its sting jolts me from despair. The nurse orders me to keep the lamp steady as she attends to Timmings who looks washed-out in the thin light. "Think the road has run out for us, Old Thing," he says without his usual sunniness.

"Auguste betrayed you. He tipped off the police."

Disbelief crosses his cowed features. "Always thought there was something fishy about him." He winces as the nurse cleans the wound in his right leg. "Matilde told me about your plans. Never seen the girl so happy. Did my best to protect her, but there were too many of them." He pulls out his Royal Mail steam packet timetable from his tunic pocket. Inside are his passport and a wad of French, Belgian and English banknotes. "Take these and get your arse out of here."

"Come with me."

"I'm crocked. Will only slow you down. I'll take my chances with the comrades. Remember me to Blighty."

I hand the lamp to the driver and leave the church. Auguste, Maxime and Octave are crossing the square. Seeing me, Maxime and Octave level their carbines.

A whining barrage of shells flies overhead. A second later there's a chorus of ear-splitting explosions. The earth shakes. Trees splinter, tongues of flame light the sky as long abandoned ordnance goes up, its percussion setting off a chain of explosions around the village.

Auguste, Maxime and Octave make for the café. Deafened by the fusillade, I take cover in the garage and draw two empty fuel drums over me. A second barrage lands. The earth shudders. Debris showers the drums.

The shelling stops and the high pitched squeal of tracks and the drone of diesel engines fills the air. Crawling to the garage door, I watch two tanks pull up outside the square. A column of soldiers, roughly fifty strong, shelter behind each tank. One tank crosses the square towards the church. The other approaches the café.

The men approaching the café dive for cover as both Vickers open up from the first floor windows. Caught unawares, a handful of soldiers are killed. The tank returns fire, silencing the Vickers long enough to allow a flanking party to move forward.

The second tank rakes the church, shredding the door and stone portico allowing the column of soldiers to get into position. The tank stops firing allowing a raiding party to run forward, hurling grenades. They storm the church with machine guns blazing. Within a minute the shooting stops, save for the odd burst. I fear for Timmings and the others.

Under covering fire from the tank, the flanking party attack the café from the rear. The muzzles of small arms flash in each room. Both Vickers fall silent. Moments later, Maxime, Octave, Sonia, and Etienne are brought out and dropped onto the ground. They're all dead.

Bloodied but alive, Auguste is brought out and set down by the water trough, beside a swaggering officer. The officer looks at Auguste, raises a whistle to his lips and blows.

A convoy of lorries rolls into the square. A familiar face steps down from the cab of the lead lorry. The inspector from Ostend nods to the officer and studies Auguste. Shouting orders, the officer moves towards the church

203

as a shackled woman is lowered from the lead lorry's wagon.

The fight having left her, Matilde struggles to stay on her feet. Her clothes are torn and filthy, her face puffy and bruised. She's no more than thirty yards from me.

I check my revolver. Four bullets. Enough. I snap the chamber shut and step from the garage. Matilde sees me. *"Tom Casey, Tom Casey."*

A single shot rings out. Matilde's head snaps back as she falls. The inspector lowers his revolver.

"No!" I shout. The inspector turns towards me, his face curdling with shock. I fire but miss, first to his right and then to his left. The pistol jams. The inspector takes aim. My time is up. But at least I'll be with Matilde. He staggers forward, the pistol falling from his hand. He raises his other hand to his bloodied mouth and lurches backwards as a second bullet strikes him in the neck. He topples.

Stepping from the treeline, Malaphonse lowers her rifle and shouts, "Matilde est ma sœur!" She slips back into the woods. Several soldiers give chase.

Soldiers leave the church, their weapons shouldered, while the café-raiding party stand outside the café handing bottles of wine among themselves. The sweat stained tank crews clamber from their vehicles to congratulate each other.

The breeze tousles Matilde's matted hair and mud splattered fatigues. Her shackled hands lay outstretched in front of her. She still has the cotton ringlet on her finger.

Matilde is dead.

From the woods there's shouting and the crack of rifle fire. A man screams. Malaphonse is in her element.

Matilde is dead.

Auguste is shackled and thrown into the lead lorry, alongside the inspector. Two soldiers stand guard and share a cigarette. One of the men picks the inspector's hat up from the ground and tries it on for size. Much to his pal's amusement the hat is far too big for him. The other guard tries on the hat. A perfect fit. He stuffs the hat into his ammunition belt. This coward, crouched behind the garage door, can't take his eyes off Matilde.

Matilde is dead.

∘ ∘ O ○ ∘ ∘

In dribs and drabs the soldiers who went into the forest after Malaphonse return, peeling off their gas masks and gagging for breath. Two are carried out. Their hunt has been fruitless.

The soldiers start scouring the village. I scramble beneath the pile of rubble and draw the oil drums over me. Soldiers enter, kicking, and prodding the debris with their bayonets. One stands inches from me compacting the earth with his heavy boots whilst tapping the barrel as another whispers short, cautious commands. After a few minutes, they climb through the blown out rear wall and head on. Near suffocating, I claw my way to the surface, heaving for breath, my eyes dirt-stung, my heart broken.

As two soldiers carry Matilde facedown into the woods. Her bloodied hair and manacled hands brush her sacred earth. *"Run, Tom Casey. Run."*

I've no time for grief. Life is all that matters now.

○ ○ ○ ○ ○ ○

By nightfall, the gold has been loaded onto the lorry holding Auguste and the inspector. At least Auguste is with his loot. The officer and his subordinates have their photograph taken in front of the church by a prissy photographer, who annoys the unharmed soldiers by photographing their dead and wounded comrades. No doubt the pictures will be in tomorrow's papers. Tails of derring-do and another dastardly communist plot foiled.

The dead and wounded soldiers are loaded onto the other lorries. Flares bathe the pitch-black village in a whitish glow. Orders go up. The tanks set off with the lorries following, bucking over the ruptured surface. When the convoy falls from earshot, I step outside into the fetid darkness, hurry to the church and slake my thirst from the font.

Footsteps. A rifle bolt slides. I crouch and pull out my revolver.

Malaphonse squats over the nurse, the driver and Timmings and closes their eyes. She walks towards me. I'm shaking, unable to control myself, thoughts blurred and numb. She holds me and whispers over and over, "Matilde est ma sœur."

○ ○ ○ ○ ○ ○

The Indian's weary engine sings a maudlin, misfiring tune. Sharing the same stern look that Mum wore before clouting me, Malaphonse shouts, "Allez, Tom Casey!" Not sure how far this wreck of a motorcycle can carry me, I offer up a prayer to Saint Waltrude, put the bike in gear and set off, not daring to look back.

THE STEAM CATCHER

The bike snakes over the frozen earth. It's a struggle to keep her true. *"I am with you, Tom Casey,"* Matilde whispers. I accelerate. *"Sharp left, brake, slow, right hand turn, long straight ahead, full throttle. Fast, as fast as you dare. I love you, Tom Casey."* She grips my waist and her breath caresses my neck. I'm in control, alive to every possibility, the bike nimble and responsive. The forest is to be conquered, not feared. I dive into corners, and hare along sections of pavé. *"Faster, Tom Casey! Faster!"* Reaching her village and crossing the small bridge, another headlight punctures the darkness. I glance behind to see another bike closing. I open the taps, but the Indian can only muster a sluggish, deathly growl. The other bike draws level. The rider wears a tattered, rotten uniform, his French infantry helmet sliced along its length. His cadaverous features nod. "Pour Matilde, mon sœur," he shouts. Cedric pulls ahead and guides me through the woods. *"I love you, Tom Casey,"* Matilde repeats,

We pull up at a metalled road on the forest's edge. "Calais," Cedric says pointing west. He fades. I put the Indian in gear and set off but within fifty feet the engine finally gives up the ghost. I lower the bike onto the verge and set off for Calais on foot, each step leading me away from my future denied.

The Steam Catcher—Part 4

The English Channel
February 1920

CHAPTER FORTY-SEVEN

Smoke from the Pride of Kent's funnel drifts across the battle grey sky as the ship ploughs through the Channel's choppy waters towards Dover. I stretch up to try and catch a handful of steam, but the plume flies too high. The ship's horn blows, splintering the flock of seagulls trailing us since Calais. I crave seasickness to rid me of the Matilde's final moments but for once my innards remain calm. "Roué avant. Pneu. Fourche savant. Phare. Tuyau echappement. Courrie. San Fairy Anne."

"No need to show off, Casey."

"Wasn't Matilde."

"You were."

"Should have done more to save you."

"But you didn't."

A hand rests on my shoulder. I turn hoping to see her. An old woman faces me. "Are you all right?" she asks. Behind her stands the pale, shimmering outline of a wounded officer. The woman and her young companion, unsteady in the swell, seem unaware of him.

"Just a touch seasick."

"Visiting loved ones?"

"Yes."

"I lost my dear husband near Ypres and my eldest boy at the Somme. To see all those graves stretching beyond the horizon offers a sadness to last the age." She touches my hand. "If it is any consolation, they never leave you. Not if you want them to." A gust of wind causes her hat to fly from her head, releasing her loose, grey locks which dance around her cigarette-aged face. "Told you to wear a hat pin," says her green-about-the-gills companion.

"Don't fret dear. Besides, I always thought the bonnet too grand for my tastes." The hat, trailed by a pair of nosey gulls, lands in the water. "Remember, only if you want to let go," she repeats. Tidying her hair, she takes her companion's arm and retreats inside. The officer follows.

∘ ∘ ○ ○ ∘ ∘

I'm following Matilde across the Herdersbrug Bridge, flinching as shellfire ignites the morning mist. Bitter foaming saliva spews from my mouth leaving me gasping for breath. Matilde disappears into the fog. The grisly Welsh train guard wakes me. "We're coming into Swindon. You'll have to run to make the connection."

THE STEAM CATCHER

As the train pulls in, I leap onto the platform and dash for the Gloucester train, making it in the nick of time. I sit opposite a young mother and her daughter, who grasps at the air outside. "I'm catching steam," she tells me.

"I used to do the exact same thing," I tell her. "Take care though. It can be dangerous catching steam." I catch my reflection in the window and barely recognise the exhausted, scrawny tramp looking back. "Must've gone ten rounds with a heavyweight," I mutter, now understanding why so many people have shot me queer looks since leaving France.

As we pass through the Cotswolds, the girl delights in showing me her steam collection, carefully explaining the difference between Wiltshire and Gloucestershire steam. We stop at small stations. The churning engine wheezes and clanks as put upon porters unload luggage. Within the hour the countryside gives way to Gloucester's streets, factories, and spires. My stomach churns at the thought of returning, not as a great explorer but a vagrant carrying a tale of murder, robbery, and love. A tale as exciting as it is dreadful.

"Calm yourself," Matilde whispers, "Life awaits."

"This is for you," the girl says. She shares a handful of steam with me as I disembark.

The tannery's stench greets me the moment I leave the soot-stained station. The cattle market teems with livestock being sold for slaughter by a barking auctioneer speaking ten to the dozen. Pubs are full to bursting with red-faced, slurring farmers enjoying their day's haggling, drinking, and story-telling. To my relief, nobody gives me a second look. In Eastgate Street the Hippodrome advertises a film called *The Sheikh* starring Rudolph Valentino, that greasy popinjay the estaminet owner swooned over. Judging by the queue, a fair proportion of Gloucester women share her passion.

I cross the road, forcing a delivery boy on a bicycle to swerve, clip the kerb and fall off his bike. He sits up wincing and rubbing his grazed knee. I apologise while helping him up. Without speaking he gathers up the spilled goods, remounts and rides off.

Ducking into Eastgate market to avoid a copper, I'm stunned by the noise and smell of fish, fruit, vegetables and flowers. A butcher in a bloodied apron cleaves sides of beef whilst his apprentice slices thick pork chops. A pedlar offers to sharpen knives and a hollering costermonger holds pots aloft. The trader next to him hurls piles of crockery into the air, drawing nervous titters from onlookers. At a haberdashery stall, a woman, being pestered by her daughter for a length of ribbon, examines gaily coloured rolls of cloth. Nearby, two women coddle a baby and I earwig their gossip.

"New cap?" A thin man in an ill-fitting outfit asks, "Reckon you're a seven and one eighth." Next to him sits a ghostly naval rating examining his cap's tally.

"Perhaps tomorrow," I reply. The rating sniggers.

"Stop, thief!" a woman shouts. A girl clutching a saucepan scatters onlookers. The costermonger gives chase. Fearful of being drawn into a fracas, I slip away.

Outside the market, a woman is speaking to a small group of people. Probably another hawker flogging more tat. But the voice is familiar. Hard yet soft, and, above all, certain. Edging closer, I recognise the speaker. Florrie. She's standing on a crate with two men behind her holding a crimson banner. Wary of being identified, I retreat to a tobacconist's doorway and look for Mum, Stan, and Jack but can't spot them.

"Homes for heroes?" says Florrie. "Where are these homes for heroes that Mr Lloyd George promised us? Three years since the election and less than one hundred built." There are murmurs of agreement. "Millions on the dole relying on the tallyman or pawnbroker's charity to feed their children or to pay the rent. Was that why so many gave their lives?"

"We did our bit," shouts a man.

"We all did," replies Florrie. "But for what? Idleness? Squalor? Ignorance?"

"We showed the Hun we wouldn't be licked. That's good enough in my book."

"Yes, we freed Europe from the Kaiser's yoke. But why do we, Europe's liberators, still endure damp-riddled hovels, worklessness, and hunger? The profiteers who raised our rents in the war now look to swindle us out of the peace. It is these same hucksters who have cut the men's pay, forcing them to strike."

"They're nothing but communist agitators."

"They are working people just asking for a fair wage. Is that too much to ask?"

"Should never have given women the vote. Only leads to trouble. Besides, why don't you talk about the things that truly troubles the working man?"

"Such as?"

"The pubs still being shut in the afternoons. If you promised to open them, you'd get my vote."

"And I'd be the first to buy you a pint," Florrie replies to laughter. "But before that pint is supped, we must say Enough! to the degradation and misery heaped upon us by capitalism. We must use democracy to advance and win the argument. The path to happiness and prosperity lies through men and women working together to forge a future free from war and want."

"Give us a kiss," the gadfly shouts. Ignoring him, Florrie continues, "We can achieve more through common endeavour than by relying on crumbs tossed from the rich man's table."

"And why should we heed the daughter of a madman?" shouts a woman. Her words sting. Nobody forgets in this city.

"This is not about my family's troubles. Look to socialism to right the wrongs that afflict us all."

"Like them Bolsheviks in Russia?" the woman hollers. "Do you want to slay the king and his family?" I see the two dead children on the barge.

The mood sours, the bannermen grow uneasy. Now with the upper hand, the heckler shouts, "Bet you married a conch. Let others fight and pay with their lives." Florrie lights ups with anger." My husband is at home broken by the war, so do not tell me about what my family have endured. We have given more to the king and empire than most and were proud to do so. You question my patriotism, yet it is my patriotism that compels me to speak out about the intolerable circumstances that is our lot these days. And what do we do? We let the same men with their tired, corrupt ideas decide what is best for us and for that we should be grateful. Waving the Union Jack won't feed your family. Work not the dole, a warm, dry home where the landlord can't turf you out, schools to teach our children, hospitals that treat the infirm regardless of circumstance. A life of dignity."

Riled up, the heckler steps towards her. "Do you like hitting women?" Florrie says, looking him straight in the eye. I recognise the look. From bitter experience. Realising he's lost the crowd, the heckler slides away.

As the meeting breaks up, I slip into the tobacconist's where my eyes are stung by the pungent scent of tobacco. Looking up from his newspaper, the tobacconist asks, "Any particular blend of shag?"

"Just looking."

"How about a new pipe? Plenty to choose from." He picks one from a frame. "Got this beauty in this morning. Pure ivory. Whittled by a Kalahari bushman, if you can believe such a thing."

I examine the pipe from all angles while waiting for Florrie to pack up. With the coast clear, I hand the tobacconist his pipe and leave the shop passing two men, each pushing motorcycles towards the station. The bikes have sleek, rakish lines, their fuel tanks painted maroon with gold leafing and bear the name Cotton.

Reaching the Cross, I turn into Southgate Street where a group of grim-faced, flint eyed men in threadbare clothes swig from bottles. A young woman pushing an aged, squeaking pram stops in front of me. "Set of knives?" she whispers, lifting a blanket to reveal a pile of bric a brac. "Sheffield's finest."

"No thanks."

"How about some crockery. From a very respectable house." She tilts one of the plates towards me, "Lovely etchin'."

"Don't need plates."

"Joint of bacon? Fresh." I shake my head. Tutting, she throws the blanket back over her loot and moves on keeping a close eye on the squabbling drunks. Punches are thrown and a bottle smashes. A man pulls a knife. The others back off. To avoid getting dragged in, I nip down a side street and stop outside a bookshop. Among the books on display is an atlas with its page open on South America. Perhaps I should have heeded Timmings and sought a new life two oceans away. I catch the reflection of a pair of women staring at me as they walk by. The bookseller knocks on the window and tells me to clear off. With no sign of the drunks, it's safe to head back to Southgate Street. I reach the junction. A column of police, some mounted, are bearing down on me.

Voices trip over themselves to denounce me. *"Tom Casey the murderer's come home. Son of a madman. He'll swing when the police catch up with him. Tells a girl in Belgium he loves her but didn't risk his neck for her. He's a coward, plain and simple."*

To avoid the police, I return to the book shop and take a shortcut along a back alley towards the docks.

The facias on the dock warehouses are peeling and faded. Screeching gulls wheel overhead and a stiff breeze whips up the water. Apart from a docked brig out of Antwerp, the east quay stands empty, the freight wagons and cranes idle.

A gang of men, thirty or so strong, stand on the swing bridge, taunting the arriving police. Another cordon of coppers surrounds a band of stevedores lugging sacks from a north quay warehouse to a moored lighter barge. To avoid being spotted, I head back towards the Mariners Chapel and make my way to the canal lock. I stop by the custom house gate to let a lorry pass. The driver looks familiar, but I can't place him.

A brig out of Hamburg lays tied up on the west quay. Beyond her sits the Anselma, now listing to starboard with her masts and rigging collapsed in a charred heap on the deck. Deep scorch marks scour her hull. A 'Keep Out' sign is slung across her gangplank. An old man, a tramp, stops beside me, leans on his blackthorn stick and says, "Snaps the heart to see her reduced to this. Lovely vessel in her time. A queen of the seas. Some nights I swear I hear her groaning with her sorrows."

"What happened to her?"

"Fire, couple of years back. Set the heavens alight." He spits into the water and looks me up and down with his rheumy eyes. "Nobody knows who started it, but two bargemen swore they saw Satan lurking in the rigging minutes afore the flames took hold." His laughter causes his consumptive chest to rattle. "They've sworn off the grog ever since. One's even taken Christ into his heart." Tapping his stick on the ground he asks, "Got a spare fag?" I hand him a Gitanes. He lights it, takes a drag and says, "Tastes funny."

"French."

He looks at the cigarette and says, "If you ask me I reckon the old Anselma was cursed the day poor Georgie Tallow was thrown from her. His folks never got over the loss. His pa took to drink. Got so bad the pubs wouldn't serve him, a rare deed of kindness from the landlords. But the poor fella still managed to pickle himself. Perished three winters ago."

"They ever catch the killer?"

"No, but everyone knows who did it." He beckons me closer and whispers, "Joe Casey's his name. Oddball. Queer as you like. Irish. So no surprise he had a temper on him like a whirling devil. Could snap at the slightest thing. Bastard crippled me. Lost his job over it. He used to wander round the docks at all hours, day or night, barking at the good lord or anyone who crossed his path. Ended up in Coney Hill."

"How does that prove he killed the boy?"

"Nothing like it's happened since." He spits into the water again. "He may be a nutter, but he proved himself cute enough to avoid the noose. The family still live round here, although we all steers clear of 'em. Not keen on catching Mad Joe's affliction. Well, who would be?" He takes a drag. "From round here?"

"Was. Been away a few years."

"Had a chance to leave when I crewed whalers. Fifty years ago that was. Should've set up home in America amongst the yanks. Met the loveliest girl a man could wish for. Never did the right thing by her. Regret it to this day." He cadges another fag. "During the war, three or four ships arrived each day with supplies for the munitions factories. Everyone had a few bob in their pockets." He places his thin, liver-spotted hand on my arm. "Don't get me wrong, I just meant that the place was full of life. Watching them poor lads returning from France in such pitiful states proved a sorrowful sight. Bloody Kaiser. Still, we showed him. Not that a working man has anything to show for it. Homes for Heroes that Welsh windbag Lloyd George promised. Instead he handed us the dole. That's the Welsh for you, liars to a man. Nowadays most ships are unloaded down river at Sharpness or Bristol. 'Cos of that, the Dock owners decided to cut the men's wages by sixpence in the shilling. The lads had no choice but to strike."

"How long they been out for?"

"Week last Sunday." He points to the bridge with his stick."The strikers hold the bridge meaning nothing can get in or out of the docks. Things are starting to bite. The coppers are about to crack a few skulls. I'd make myself scarce if I were you. Thanks for the smoke." He raises his stick in salute and limps away.

The Anselma's spars give off a sour, rancid smell. I run my hand along the charred gunwale, my palm turning Bible-black.

Shouts of "Scab! Scab! Scab!" fly from the strikers towards the men loading the barge. Missiles are hurled but land short in the water. The strikers now turn on the advancing police, launching bricks and torn-up cobbles at them. One or two policemen fall. The strikers charge. Both groups butt against each other in a scrum so dense, the police aren't able to raise their truncheons and the strikers their fists. A union banner twists in the throng and several men leap into the water to avoid being crushed. The police fall back.

"All out together! All in together!" The dockers chant as the mounted police are brought up. The dockers roar their defiance as the horses thunder across the bridge six across and skittle the first lines of men. But the others stand their ground, almost dragging one copper from his horse until he manages to break free. Auguste's story about Marie is being retold in Gloucester.

The horses charge again and this time plough deeper into the strikers. The union banner falls and the pickets retreat and cede their ground, leaving the injured behind. They make one last effort to retake the bridge but the police stand firm, snapping the strikers' resistance.

They flee into the nearby rail yards chased by the mounted police wielding their long batons to bloody effect. Others dockers spill onto the west quay seeking shelter in the warehouses or the graving docks. Some run towards the canal lock, where the police guarding the black legs wait for them. With coppers in front and behind, the strikers are cornered. Heads are cracked and arrests made.

Two constables walk up the Anselma's gangplank. Fearing capture, I open the forward cargo hatch and climb down the near-rotten steps into the pen then draw the hatch lid over me. I gag on the smell of rotting flesh and blunder towards the far wall. I fumble for the brass handle. Finding it, I slide the hatch door open and slip into the middle hatch. I pull the door to and pin my ear against it. The steps creak. "Bloody death trap," complains one of the coppers. "Something's died down here." Torchlight dances around the cargo pen, lighting up old tarps and discarded lengths of rope. "If anyone's fool enough to hide down there, best leave them to fester." The torchlight fades as the coppers climb the stairs. They scour the upper deck and then disembark.

Whistles and shouts go up. I stay put, thankful to the Anselma for hiding me. Something scrapes against the hull, a young boy pleads and there's a loud splash. Fear of Georgie's ghost bests fear of arrest, so I scramble above deck and, keeping low, breathe in the sooty air. The ship yaws in the light swell. *"You ran like a cur from justice, Tom Casey. But you'll swing from the ship's creaking cordage. You'll pay for your deeds. You're no man at all. A coward plain and simple."*

The wind drops and the ship steadies, silencing the voices. A tug tows the loaded barge towards the bridge, now guarded by a phalanx of police. The bridge span rises and both vessels slip through, watched by a knot of defeated men and women.

○ ○ ○ ○ ○ ○

Flemish curses go up, signalling that the Antwerp brig is being readied for sail. Black legs lug sacks of flour, crates of ale and lengths of timber aboard. Tars clamber among the rigging, furling sails. Deciding Belgium is a better bet after all, I leave the Anselma, join the stevedores and board the brig.

"You!" A man is pointing at me. I stop. The game's up. By the cut of his portly jib, he's someone of rank. He hands me a sheet of paper. "Get this release signed in the customs house. We should have sailed an hour ago." I remain rooted to the spot.

"Move, you dolt."

Through one of the custom house's barred windows, I spot Ned Tallow pouring over a ledger. Quiet Ned, making something of himself. Chances are he'll recognise me. Beady-eyed beggar if memory serves.

Belgium or home? Fear or acceptance? I throw the docket away and slip through the custom house gate and out onto Commercial Road.

○ ○ ○ ○ ○ ○

Within five minutes I'm in the alley looking at the back of our house. Little has changed. Rainwater spills from the guttering and the upstairs window is still cracked.

"What you doing'?" It's Old Ma bringing her washing in from the rain. I panic and run but snare myself in a nightshirt hanging on her clothesline. "Them's my under garments you're sniffing. Police! Police!"

I untangle myself and hare along the alley, swerving around a coalman lugging a hundredweight sack of coal and causing his knacker to grow skittish. I reach the road and run. Always running.

CHAPTER FORTY-EIGHT

I stop to draw breath outside the Leopard. No one is following. In the early evening gloom, the pub's lights offer sanctuary and warmth. I take a breath and go in. The barman gives me a wary look as I stand before him drenched, chest rattling, hands blackened by the Anselma's seared timbers. The old tar from the docks is sat by the fireplace, nursing a tot of rum. He raises his glass and says, "Serve the lad, Syd, the boy's a long-lost son of Gloucester. War hero to boot."

I order a pint, drop a penny into the wish bottle and sit at a table facing the door. Three men come in, glance at me and order their pints. "You were on the docks, loading the barge." one of them says to me." Scab bastard."

My chair skids across the floor as I leap up and run outside, skittling a gaggle of children dancing in the rain.

"There he is!" shouts Old Ma. A whistle blows. I dart into an alley and open a privy door, surprising a man wiping his arse. My boots slip on the damp, greasy cobbles as I run on in a blind, wild panic. It was a mistake to come back.

Rounding a corner, I trip and fall, winding myself. A truncheon presses against my throat and I'm ordered to stay put. The chasing copper arrives out of breath and says, "Cheers, Alf. Thought he'd got away."

"Is he a straggler from the docks?"

"No. A pervert."

I'm lifted up and handcuffed. The copper pressing his truncheon against my windpipe looks familiar. The fleshy face, big nose and cold, lifeless gaze haven't changed. But the moustache doesn't suit him. "Alf Fenwick?" I say.

"That's me," Constable Alf Fenwick answers, blinding me with his torchlight.

"That's the one who fondled my particulars," shouts Old Ma, hobbling towards us, "Made me feel all liverish."

"Were you manhandling her smalls?" Alf says, lowering his torch. His features soften a tad. It's taken him a few seconds. "Tom Casey?"

"Mad Joe's boy?" says Old Ma. "Thought he'd perished."

"You one of them perverts now, Casey?" asks Alf.

"Thought you were dead," I answer with relief and regret bubbling through me.

Alf's confused. He never was the sharpest. "This is Gloucester Casey. Fair walk to heaven from here." He punches me in the face."Just remembered.

I owe you that."

"Fine, Alf. No trouble at all." I spit blood onto the pavement.

"You always were off your onion."

"Thought I'd killed you all them years ago on the Anselma."

"My dad leathered me when he found out you were the one who floored me. When did you get back?"

"Today."

"Been away a good while then. Lot's changed since. Not least with your Stan. Been home yet?"

"Was heading that way."

"Your Florrie's there now, shacked up with that big darkie of hers, despite him being a Trembler. Raving all hours of the night. Just like your dad."

"Not anymore though," Old Ma mutters.

"What does she mean?"

Alf clears his throat. "No easy way of saying this, Casey. Your dad's dead. No more than a month ago."

No words come. I'd feared Dad for his madness and hated him for betraying England. But now I'd give anything to see him. I have to get home. For once, Alf does the decent thing and unshackles me. "Best regards to your mum and Florrie. Tell Stan I've got my eye on him."

"What about my smalls?" chimes Old Ma.

"Poor fella's had a shock, Mrs Clayton. Christian thing to do."

∘ ∘ ○ ○ ∘ ∘

I push the back gate open over moss-covered cobbles. Sodden clothes hang from a motorcycle propped against the wall. I hesitate. What will they say? Will they forgive me? The urge to flee returns. I'm twelve years old again.

I open the back door. An Irish lament plays on a phonograph. Murphy looks up and growls. Jack sitting in Dad's chair, looks at me. "Tom?"

"What's that, Jack?" answers Mum standing over the sink, peeling spuds. She's aged, her hair greyer and jowls heavier. Dressed head to toe in black too. She looks at Jack and then at me. The peeler clatters into the basin. She bursts into tears, hugs me and then slathers me in kisses. "My boy's home!"

I fight the tears, relieved to be in her arms. I belong once more.

"Never stopped hoping, Tom."

The front door opens, "Home!" shouts Florrie.

"Got a visitor, Florrie," Mum says beaming at me while wiping her eyes on a towel. Florrie steps into the kitchen, taking off her hat. Tiredness frames her pretty features. "Tom!" She flies into my arms. Again, I fight back the tears. I've missed my wise little sister and don't want to let go of her.

"Never reached the South Pole then," she mutters in a faltering voice. "Just as well, considering what a pickle Shackleton got himself into." After kissing Jack, she hugs Mum and says, "Stan will be pleased to see you."

"How is he?" I ask. All three look uneasy, the happiness of a moment ago gone.

"Why did you run off?" Florrie asks, changing the subject.

"Thought I'd killed Alf Fenwick, panicked and joined up. Saw service as a Despatch Rider."

"You could've sent word you were safe."

"Didn't want to land you in trouble." Now *I* want to change the subject. "Ran into Alf Fenwick. He told me Dad's dead."

"Just a month since," Mum replies. A rueful air settles, their pain still raw. Florrie sat on the arm of Jack's chair and held his hand. "They moved Dad to a sanatorium outside Cardiff in early nineteen eighteen to make room for returning shell-shocked soldiers. But when the war ended, they kept him there. For a while he was on the mend, singing his songs and telling his stories. But the weeks before he died, he fell mute. He refused food and drink and just lay in bed staring up at the ceiling. The doctors called it a catatonic state."

"Tore the flesh from our bones when we got the telegram," Mum mutters. There's a moment's silence. Mum gathers herself. "But enough of sadness. We've cried enough. Today we've something to celebrate. Tom's home." She hands Florrie some money. "Pop to the shop for a fresh loaf and quarter of ham. Don't be fobbed off with anything gamey."

Apart from the phonograph, the kitchen hasn't changed. The yellow-tinged gaslight, the spitting fire, the blackened worn pots resting on the stove, and the cabinet drawers still too swollen to close. Murphy laying by the fire.

A thick, six inch, leather strap sits on the mantelpiece next to the tatty atlas, Mum's Bible, and the Charles Dickens book. There's also a Sherlock Holmes book.

After Florrie heads for the shops, Mum leads me into the front parlour. "I sleep in here now," she says.

"What did you do with the furniture?"

"Had to sell it."

The bed takes up most of the room. Mum and Dad's wedding photo stood on the mantelpiece where the blue and green vases still guard Alice's bonnet, Albie's blanket and an old shirt of mine. Mum picks it up and says, "Kept it close Tom. Always knew you'd come home."

"I should have been here for you when Dad died."

"He was a good man dealt a bad hand. Always remember that."

"Did he ever talk about me?"

"Can't be sure. Before he fell silent, he rambled on about all sorts; bridges, dead forests but mostly about this saint none of us had ever heard of. Walter or Waltrude maybe." Cold elation spread through me. Dad had been with me all along, right up to the day he died.

"He's laid to rest near young Albert. It's a comfort knowing they're together. I'm up there tomorrow and will let them know you're home. Truth be told, that's where I'm happiest these days, enjoying the peace and quiet with my lads."

○ ○ ○ ○ ○ ○

I'm drinking hot, sweet tea, eating freshly cut ham sandwiches listening to Florrie and Mum gossiping. The lament plays over and over on the phonograph. I'm already tired of its maudlin drone. I hadn't expected my homecoming to be small talk, sandwiches and a warbling Irishman. "Haven't you anything more lively?" I ask.

Florrie shoots me a look. "The song helps to keep Jack on an even keel."

I change the subject. "On my way here I saw fighting in the docks. Looks like the war has come home."

Florrie nods. "It's not only the dockers. Everyone's being ground down."

"Tom doesn't want to hear you spouting off, Florrie," Mum warns.

"Change is coming, Mum," Florrie answers. "Over two million voted Labour in the last election. Working people have had enough. There's going to be a rally outside Bearlands where the arrested strikers are being held. The Labour MP for the Forest of Dean is speaking. Fancy coming?"

"Had my fill of politics. Just want the quiet life now."

"We have to demand change."

"You are right, Tom Casey, I do like her."

"You can't change things on your own, Florrie."

"I am millions." I wonder what she would have made of Auguste. Probably give him a right-hander and say violence never pays. "What aren't you telling us?"

"Nothing. Never been one for politics."

"I always know when you're lying. Were you courting?"

She has me. Always ten times smarter. "She died."

Florrie reaches for my hand. "Is that why you've come home?"

"Partly. After losing Matilde I couldn't make sense of anything. Was sick of running."

"We're here for you now, Tom."

"We are," agrees Mum, wiping her eyes.

Jack shakes off his torpor to mumble, "Where were you, Tom?"

"Mesopotamia, France, and then Belgium."

"Where were you?" he repeats. His eyes widen and his breath quickens.

"Quick, Florrie," Mum says grabbing Jack's heaving shoulders. I'd seen these fits before, on shellshocked men. The lucky ones found treatment in hospitals.

His eyes wild and demented, Jack thrashes in his chair. Florrie winds up the phonograph, grabs the leather strap from the mantel and thrusts it into Jack's mouth. He bites down and Mum and Florrie cling to him while reciting the lament's soothing words. I'm told to rewind the phonograph. It takes four or five plays for Jack to calm and he sinks into his chair, sweat soaked and drained. Florrie mops his brow with a damp rag. She kisses him. He drinks her in, desperate to stave off his demons.

Mum wipes down the spit sodden strap and sets it on the mantelpiece. She sits, lights a cigarette and studies her Bible but soon nods off. She stirs to see cigarette ash scattered on the page. Brushing the ash away, she mutters about damnation. Everything is normal but different. Broken and patched up.

"Still attending the Mission, Mum?" I ask.

Her face darkens. "That charlatan."

"Turns out the pastor had been carrying on with two Mission women," Florrie says, taking the Sherlock Holmes book from the mantelpiece.

"Those harlots carried the banner," Mum continued. "And to think they sat at this table studying the scriptures with their minds set on fornication."

"Last we heard he was preaching in the Black Country," says Florrie, opening the Sherlock Holmes book. "No doubt his two-bob words are bamboozling the righteous and sinful alike up there."

"No doubt," Mum says, shaking her head. "His shenanigans sorely tested my faith." She sets the Bible down. "More tea Tom?"

"Think I'll go up to bed Mum. Been a long few days."

I climb the stairs, passing the faded pictures of the old king and queen. My bedroom has received a lick of yellow paint, peppered with black mould fanning across the walls. The gloom is not helped by the double wardrobe partially blocking the steamed up window. Both wardrobe doors are locked. In the far corner a bucket catches water dripping from the ceiling, now sporting a swirling damp patch. The wrinkled remains of Stan's football peek from under the bed.

I reach into the fireplace, feel along the ledge and touch a metal container. Wedged inside the canister a roll of bank notes rest on coins and the shark's tooth I'd lost years ago. All this time Stan must have had it. Too tired for anger, I climb into bed, pull the blankets over me and drift off to sleep with Matilde stroking my hair.

∘ ∘ ○ ○ ∘ ∘

I'm woken by Jack's screams. Florrie sings the lullaby Mum once sang to soothe our nightmares away. I get up and walk across the landing to their bedroom. Jack, sweat-shined, eyes blank, clings to Florrie. Lamplight throws wizened shadows against the bedroom wall. The room smells of talcum powder and damp. On a bedside table beside the lamp, stands a small mirror and their wedding day photograph. Jack's in his Glosters uniform beaming like a Cheshire Cat. Florrie wears a plain white dress and clutches a small posy. She looks fearful.

Florrie whispers, "He'll be fine, Tom. Go back to sleep."

CHAPTER FORTY-NINE

"Morning, Tom." Stan is standing over me. He's no longer a scrawny urchin, but tall, handsome with it and sporting a wispy moustache. Smartly dressed too, collar and tie, ten guinea suit and plush Homburg. I'd seen him yesterday, driving that lorry through the custom house gates. "Heard you were a despatch rider. Must've been exciting."

"Had its moments. That your bike in the yard?"

"Won it playing cards in the Hauliers, but it's only fit for scrap."

"Mind if I take a look?"

"Help yourself."

He retrieves the canister from the fireplace, pops the lid and tips the coins onto the bed. "All yours. Kept them for you."

"Thanks."

"Stayin' long?"

"Not given it much thought."

He returns the tin to its hiding place, slips a coin into his pocket and leaves. Moments later the front door closes. I decide the coins are unlucky, so return them to the canister.

"He's like that with everyone." Florrie says from the doorway. "After you left he spent hours sitting on the front doorstep waiting for you to come home. Like a pining puppy he was. Alf and his mates tormented him to distraction. Since then Stan has played his cards very close to his chest. We've no notion what he gets up to or how he earns his money. But since I lost my job we rely on him."

"What happened?" She went into her bedroom and returned with a newspaper cutting. It's headline read, "Docks Woman Bound Over For Assaulting Constable."

"Late last summer," she said quietly, "Jack was having a seizure. Screaming the house down. Not even his song could calm him. Old Ma fetched the police. Alf Fenwick barged in and threatened Jack with Coney Hill. I got so riled up I punched him." She giggled.

"You punched Alf?"

"Right hander. Good one, too. The magistrate spared me gaol but bound me over for twelve months. But when the manager read about it in the Citizen the next day he sacked me. Two years I worked in the match factory yet it counted for nothing. I've asked everywhere for work, but nobody will take me on. I teach reading and writing to veterans and the unemployed a couple of days a week. Don't get paid, but it keeps me busy. Makes me a hypocrite living on money not earned by honest endeavour, but without Stan, we'd be on the streets with Jack back in Coney Hill."

"If I'd been home, things would have been different."

"Doubt it, Tom. We've always been fair game round here, had to fight for breath sometimes. The shame is you thought you'd no choice but to run."

"When did you and Jack wed?"

"April fifteenth, nineteen sixteen. Even managed a couple of nights in Weston before he went back to France. The following January a shell struck his trench. Jack was the only one pulled out alive. He spent months in hospital in France and then at a rehabilitation centre in Sussex. He arrived at Coney Hill on the day of our first anniversary. When I saw him he was lashed to his bed raving. To my shame I fled. After all that's what we're supposed to do with lunatics, lock them up and forget about them. Mum marched me back there the next day. Jack lay in bed, sedated, repeating my name. Wherever his broken mind had taken him, he'd brought me along. I knew there and then he had to come home. The doctors were happy to release him as they needed the bed." She looked lost, punctured. "It's heart breaking to see him so reduced. But I love him, even if it's a merciless love we endure."

"What about his folks?"

"His Dad's ship was torpedoed by a U-Boat. No survivors. Turns out he had a wife and family in Bristol, who had first claim on the rooming house and his war pension. After they flogged the house we'd no choice but to move in with Mum. His ma moved to her sister's in Weymouth. Not a dickey bird from her since."

Mum comes in, carrying a basin and pitcher of boiling water. The smell of bacon follows her. From the pocket of her tabard she produces Dad's old shaving kit.

"You should be honoured, Tom," Florrie says, winking at me. "Normally we have porridge for breakfast."

"Heard Mr Tallow died!, I say. Handing me the shaving kit, Mum answers, "He got into a brawl in the Hauliers a few years back. Landlord found him in the yard the next morning. They never found his killer. Although it's wrong to speak ill of the dead, it was no great loss. Old sins cast long shadows." There's a bitterness to her words. "Mrs Tallow moved down to Devon to be closer to her family. Took the kids with her. All except Ned, who's making something of himself in the customs house."

"Did she ever say sorry for those things she said about Dad?"

She shook her head. "Suspect any forgiveness she had left was beaten out of her. As long as she's happy." I'm not convinced Mum thinks that. "Breakfast will be ready in a few minutes, Tom." Halfway downstairs she shouts up, "And bring the bucket down. Needs emptying."

CHAPTER FIFTY

The bike is a hybrid with a 3 ½ JAP engine, Rudge frame and Triumph wheels. Not the "Mercury" but good enough. Beggars and choosers and the like. Despite a rotten downpipe and worn cylinder head, I have her roadworthy within a week. Firing her up in the back alley for the first time, Old Ma opens her back gate. She's wearing a grubby dressing gown and unbuckled shoes. Her bright red fingernails are at odds with her twisted fingers. Her dyed hair is thinning and there's a nasty looking sore on her cheek. I suspect she has fewer visitors these days. "Bet your Ma's pleased your home," she says. "Where'd you travel to?"

"Persia."

"Out Worcester way?"

"Five miles south."

"Must 'ave been exciting."

"Had its moments."

"That where you learned your wanton ways?"

"As they say in Persia, San Fairy Anne." I step into the backyard. Mum's hanging out washing and says, "You must have charmed her. She doesn't speak to me at all these days. Only finds solace in funerals, sometimes attends two or three a day. Like the angel of death that one, happy to press on others wounds."

"World's full of people revelling in others misery."

In the kitchen the Irishman is singing, Jack sits in his chair with Murphy asleep beside him. Mum puts on her coat, squeezes Jack's hand and heads out to the shops. I put the kettle on and sit at the table and examine a threaded bolt from the bike's cylinder head. "All right, Jack?" I ask without looking up.

"What happened Tom?"

"What do you mean?"

"I thought we were going to join up together." His words stab.

I better tread carefully. "I meant to, but lacked the guts."

"Thought we were best mates."

I've no answer to the truth. To my surprise he sings:
But if I should die on a foreign land,
and be buried so far far away,
no fond mother's tears will be shed o're my grave,
on the shores of Amerikay.

"Where did you learn that?" I ask.

His breath quickens and the tremors come on. Fearing a seizure, I wind up the phonograph, reset the Irishman and thrust the leather strap into Jack's mouth. As the Irishman returns, I take hold of Jack's still powerful shoulders and grip for all I am worth, hoping this malaise will pass quickly. Jack grips the armrests and thrashes in the chair, his nostrils flaring, the veins thickening on his forehead. "Be all right Jack," I whisper over and over, without the foggiest notion if he will be.

To my relief, by the third rendition, Jack is slumped in the chair gasping for breath. I remove the strap and hand him a cup of milk which he gulps down. He wipes his mouth with a shaky hand. "We were waiting for a Hun assault. Shell bait for hours, we were. Got so bad, this Stroud lad shouts,"Fuck this," and climbs out into no-man's-land. Sniper got him. The shelling lets up. We share the line with an Irish regiment. One of the Micks is singing this verse over and over. "But if I die on a foreign land," There's incoming whizzbangs, so I flatten myself against the trench wall. The next thing it's pitch black. Tons of stinking earth cover me. I'm packed so tight I can't move a muscle."

"And be buried so far, far away." "I can't breathe. I'm not ready to die. I want to head home to Florrie. But my soul's leeching into the dirt. "No fond mother's tears will be shed o're my grave." I'm slipping away, grateful for the peace of mind death brings me. All of a sudden, I'm wrenched into the daylight, babbling like a loon. Ever since I've been trapped between life and death."

The Irishman grows drowsy.

"Some days I wish they'd left me buried." Fearing the worst, I rewind the phonograph. "What good am I to anyone, Tom, least of all Florrie? All I wanted was for her to be proud of me. Perhaps have a kiddie or two. Can't see that happening now. She should've left me in Coney Hill to rot."

"She loves you, Jack."

"Pities me, more like." He runs a finger around the cup's rim.

"Florrie loves you more than life."

"Think so?" There's a rare glimpse of the old Jack.

"Certain of it."

A smile breaks on his lips. "Love her, Tom."

"I know."

He's on the verge of tears. "Worst feeling I ever had, lying in the earth thinking I'll never see her again."

"But you made it back to her." I take his hand. He looks at me proud, yet worn. Somewhere inside him, the old Jack is trying to make it home. "I did, didn't I."

"Fancy a trip on the bike soon?"

He nods. "To the seaside. Weston or Minehead. Be good to see the sea again."

"You're on. We'll give it full chat as well."

"Cheers."

The front door closes. Stan appears. As usual, he says nothing but leaves five pound notes on the table. He goes upstairs. A minute or two later he comes downstairs and leaves, again without speaking.

CHAPTER FIFTY-ONE

Been home best part of two years now. Live the quiet life. Found work in the Railway Carriage Company's foundry; a filthy, noisy, joyless place. I take solace in the odd pint in the Leopard and raised a glass in there last year to honour Mr Shackleton when I heard he'd died.

Clutching a tot of rum the old tar spins yarns about his whaling days before recounting the latest tale he's heard about me. So far I've been a spy for the Japanese emperor, fighting for the Bolsheviks, then against them, a hermit up a mountain in Palestine, and a gold prospector in Borneo.

"What did you get up to?" he once asked.

"Bank robber in Belgium."

He nearly fell of his chair laughing. "Best one yet!"

Other nights I stay home and listen to Florrie read a library book to Jack. Sherlock Holmes stories mostly, but sometimes adventure ones. *Treasure Island* had me harking back to our days leaping around the Anselma pretending to be pirates whilst *Robinson Crusoe* left me feeling sad, adrift, and mourning the life I was to share with Matilde.

As the weeks ticked by, the joy of being home thinned and I found myself missing the Zone Rouge's harsh freedom despite its poisonous air and Auguste's treachery. When the dark mood grips, I try to shake it off by riding around the Forest of Dean. I ride all night and get home the next morning exhausted yet still wistful, my shift at the foundry a struggle. But a day or two later I'm back in the forest, following the headlamp's thin strip of light, hoping Cedric may come alongside or better still, Matilde. Hope, however much it is misplaced, is a cruel drug.

○ ○ ○ ○ ○ ○

Jack and me are outside Eastgate Market watching Florrie address a small crowd; about what I haven't the foggiest. Behind her the Labour Party banner sways in the breeze. Rain is in the air. A constable stands across the road keeping an eye on things. Some Labour supporters shoot Jack queer looks. Although he never lets on, I know the looks wound him.

"What's more," Florrie says, "We're still waiting for the new infirmary. Yet do the great men who lead our country concern themselves with unemployment, starvation wages or exploitation? No! Their only concern is to protect their wealth and their landholdings in the colonies whilst getting shirty with the uppity working class for demanding a better life. They think a few shillings of dole money is enough to keep us quiet. And if that fails they wave the flag."

"Nothing wrong with the Union Jack," a man says.

"You're right, sir. I'm proud to say my husband and dear brother stood behind the flag for four long, terrible years and if needs be they would do so again, like many of you here. The flag belongs to us all, not just those flag-waving charlatans extolling the virtue of pittance wages, damp hovels and half-starved children. Never trust these men. And yes they are *all* men. The patriotic act is to ensure that *every* man and *every* woman, rich or poor, has the means to live a life of purpose and dignity. We, the workers, have the right to forge our own destiny. Remember when every man and woman in this country was valuable, wanted either in munitions or in the trenches? Unemployment banished. Now we see men and women who've fallen off through unemployment. Once fine, upstanding people now dragging along the streets with their hands out for anything they can get. The great mass of unemployed are those who saved us during the war, standing side by side in the trenches, the heroes of Mons, the Somme and Passchendaele. In the war the bosses said, "We must have munitions, rifles, machine guns and shells." As the nation organised for war, so it can be organised for peace and stop the war raging in so many minds and still lapping at so many front doors. Women and men standing alongside each other to allow our nation's children's characters not to be deformed by suffering and privation. It's time to say no to exploitation and poverty. We have it in us to do it. Have faith to believe that real and lasting change can come. From the Labour Party."

Thin applause rings out. A red faced, middle aged man beneath a brolly mutters, "Bloody women getting ideas above their station."

Bridling at his words, Florrie answers. "Our time is coming. Soon all women will have the vote and with that comes power. Power to change our lives for the better."

"My dad would have taken his belt to you. Set you right in no time." Before Florrie can answer, the old Jack, the heroic, fearless Jack, rears over the heckler and says, "My wife's up there talking about a decent world for people while all you do is belittle her."

"I'm fetching the police," the man tells him while backing away. "Darkies can't speak to an Englishman like that."

"Fetch away," Jack whispers, pointing at the copper. The man scuttles towards the policeman but doesn't stop and heads on. An old woman pats Florrie on the back and says, "Don't listen to them naysayers."

231

"I shan't," Florrie answers, "No man can tell me what to say or think."
Taking Jack's arm she asks me, "Like the speech, Tom?"

"Heard it so often it's worn thin," I joke. She punches me on the arm.

It starts to rain, so the three of us shelter in a butcher's doorway. "You planning on buying anything?" the scowling, well fed butcher asks as he hangs a string of sausages in the shop window. We shake our heads. "In that case, bugger off, you're blocking the door."

Stepping into the rain, Florrie announces the last one home has to make the tea. She lifts her skirt with one hand and sets off, clinging onto her new hat with her other hand. Jack gives chase while I dawdle, following a rattling steamroller pressing freshly laid tarmac along Southgate Street. The smell of bitumen catches in my throat, the acrid stink, taking me back to the Zone Rouge.

Most of the houses I pass have black wreathed pictures of men in their front windows. They're nearly all the same. A man chuffed to be in uniform, groomed and polished, every inch the hero with his wife or sweetheart beside them, their eyes unable to hide their fear for his future. An endless grief seeps from these houses, the people living in them exhausted, trying to make ends meet while hoping for better days that always seem to be around the corner.

I arrive home soaked. Florrie hands me a towel. "Tea's in the pot, slow coach," she says.

After drying off, I sit at the table and pick up the book she's been nagging me to read. "Started it yet?" she asks.

"Can't even pronounce the title."

"*The Ragged Trousered Philanthropists*. It'll put some fire in your belly." Moving Jack's mouth strap to make room, she slots the book on the mantel, next to the tatty atlas and Charles Dickens book. Jack wound the phonograph, and dropped the needle on the disc. Marie Lloyd begins singing about her useless husband. I'd bought the disc six months ago. At first Mum and Florrie feared Jack's reaction to hearing a new song, but he soon grew used to it; we now have two songs to play.

"Stanley's been and gone," Florrie tells me. Like the others, I've learned to turn a blind eye to Stan's thievery. In truth I'm a touch jealous of his shady carry-on, which must be more exciting than working in the foundry, if only in running rings around Alf Fenwick and Gloucestershire's finest.

"Elsie's coming for tea on Sunday," Florrie says with that knowing look, I've grown to dislike. Mum nods her approval. "Told me she's looking forward to seeing you again Tom."

Elsie teaches with Florrie at the Chapel. Mum and Florrie have decided that we're made for each other. The first time she came for tea, Mum laid on quite the spread. Ham sandwiches, pickles, fruit cake with tea served in best cups. Elsie was pretty enough, pleasant, and a book worm like Florrie but thankfully didn't get hot under the collar about politics. The next time she visited, Mum added pilchards in tomato sauce to the spread. I was about to ask Elsie if she fancied seeing the new Chaplin film at the Hippodrome, but let the moment pass after Matilde reared up before me.

"You match-making?" I snap.

Mum seems put out. "You've been back for two years now Tom. Yet you've nothing to show for it."

"Happy enough."

"Florrie heard you calling out to Matilde again in your sleep."

"Points to nothing. I'm no Robinson Crusoe."

"Think you are, Tom. Death or heartache stops nothing. Face up to it. Women have had to for years." Nagged and hemmed in, I grab my coat, goggles, and gloves and step into the backyard.

Florrie follows me out. "What are you afraid of?"

Without answering I push the bike into the alley and set off for the forest. With luck I'll find Matilde.

○ ○ ○ ○ ○ ○

I'm standing on the riverbank smoking a Players watching the hand-pulled ferry cross the swollen River Wye. The water calms me. Two passengers, well-to-do-types, pay the ferryman and climb the steps towards the Saracen's Head pub. One of them nods to a group of footsore walkers waiting to board. Lush woodland covers the steep valley slopes.

"I miss you, Matilde."

She doesn't answer.

I drop the cigarette into the river and mount my bike. I'm not sure agreeing to race a man who'd claimed third spot in this year's TT is a wise move, or ten bob down the drain.

"Cotton factory on Quay Street?" my opponent asks. I nod.

We set off along a narrow sodden track that winds up through the forest before dropping to meet the course of the river. Sunshine threads the trees throwing shadow across the road. A skilful rider, my opponent quickly masters the sticky surface and pulls away. But climbing a hill, my JAP engine's low end grunt gives me the advantage and I overtake him and lead through a set of sweeping bends, only to run wide on the last corner and allow him to pass me. He eases away, until carrying too much speed into another corner, he runs off the road and into the woods. Seizing my chance, I accelerate and carry so much pace, crest a small bridge with my front wheel pawing the air.

The forest thins as I reach a near deserted tarmacked road that will take me into Gloucester. I glance behind. There's no sign of my opponent. I cog up and charge, only slowing when I reach Gloucester's outskirts, my eyes peeled for stray dog or dozy pedestrians stepping out in front of me. The clogged roads force me to weave through near stationary Drays and wagons. Any moment I expect to see the Cotton to catch and overtake me just as Lieutenant Chatterton did all those years ago.

But to my relief I reach the Cotton factory gates with no sign of him. In fact I'm on my second Players before he shows up, mud splattered, with a branch lashed across his Cotton's handlebars.

"What kept you?" I ask.

"Hit a tree when I came off the road and snapped the left handlebar." Pointing at the branch he said, "Had to rig this up."

"Shame." I hold my hand out for my winnings.

"How do you get that jalopy to ride so well?" he asks, handing me a ten bob note.

"Was a DR in the war. Learned a thing or two."

"No doubt. Fancy having a bash at a hill climb next week? Over on Cleeve Hill."

○ ○ ○ ○ ○ ○

Mum places the trophy on the mantelpiece and says, "First time a Casey's ever brought a trophy home."

"Beat a score of others, Mum. Better still, Cotton have offered me a mechanic's job. Extra ten bob a week." I don't mention I'll be shipping out to France for the French Grand Prix in a week's time.

"That is good news Tom. Now you're home, take Jack to meet Florrie down at the chapel." She arches her eyebrows. "Elsie will be there." France can't come soon enough.

I find Tours in the tatty atlas. As well as being the town where the French Grand Prix is being run, it's also where Matilde and me planned to head to after the Bruges raid. Sometimes coincidence cheers the soul. Maybe I will find her after all.

○ ○ ○ ○ ○ ○

Murphy follows Jack and me as we stroll along the east quay in glorious sunshine, listening to curses spew from the crew of a docking Irish brig. In the barge arm, three barges are being readied for the journey Up Country. Among the cargo sits a row of gleaming Cotton motorcycles.

Outside the Mariners Chapel, people shake Jack's hand whilst the devout, balding chaplain plays a stirring hymn on the chapel's still wheezy organ. Elsie shares her hymnbook with a tall, earnest man, uncomfortable in his surroundings. I've seen him before, watching Florrie speak. He was one of those uneasy around Jack. Catching sight of me, Elsie flushes, strokes her throat and glances up at her beau.

When the service finishes, the chaplain's spritely nine-year-old daughter asks Jack, "Are you a giant? Do you live up a beanstalk?"

"No, in a house."

"Must have a high ceiling."

"It does."

"Would you have to stoop to go inside the chapel?"

"Shall we find out?" Taking Jack by the hand, she leads him towards the chapel door. Murphy follows. To her disappointment, Jack doesn't need to duck to go inside.

"Hello, Tom," Elsie says catching me unawares as she walks by arm in arm with her suitor.

"Elsie," I answer, brushing the peak of my cap.

"Should have taken your chances," Florrie mutters, watching Elsie and her fella head off towards the dock gates. "Elsie took a shine to you."

"Who's she with?"

"Edgar Troughton, the Labour Candidate for Gloucester in the next election. Smitten with her, by all accounts. A man with prospects."

Wanting to be alone, I cross the swing bridge wondering what Mum will say when I tell her I'm leaving for France. At least it'll put an end to her and Florrie's scheming, even if Elsie for one, has given up on me. I had no intentions for Elsie but seeing her with this gawky, awkward looking Edgar fella, leaves me disappointed and a touch jealous.

Up ahead, two men board the Anselma. One of them looks like Stan. I board the ship but there's no sign of them on deck. I hear a voice, Stan's I think, coming from the forward cargo hold. I reach the open cargo hatch and carefully climb down the near rotten steps, trying not to gag on the reek of scorched decay.

Again I can hear Stan speaking from behind the half-open slide hatch. I creep forward and peer through expecting to see him handing over or receiving money for an act of thievery. Only it's not thievery. They're kissing and Stan has his right hand inside the man's unbuttoned trousers. They break apart. "Hear that?" The man whispers.

"Just the breeze," Stan says, pulling the man back onto him.

What do I do? Walk away and pretend I haven't witnessed this abomination or wring Stan's neck for whoring himself.

Treading lightly, I climb the steps and disembark. Minutes later, the man, red-faced and a touch sweaty, hurries down the gangplank. He bids me good day and heads for the bridge. He's fortyish, slight with a jet black beard half-hiding pocked features. He's dapper too, tailored black suit, newish bowler hat and his silver tipped cane strikes the ground with each stride. Crossing the bridge, he touches the brim of his hat with the cane and stops to talk to a well-to-do couple.

"Amazing what passes through the docks," Stan says leaning against the Anselma's gunwale. "Food, drink, tobacco, even opium. Thought about getting my hands on some for Jack, to ease his burden."

"Florrie wouldn't thank you."

He strides down the gangplank rubbing his blackened hands. Unable to look at him, I light a cigarette and drop the match into the water. I take a deep drag, enjoying the hit on the back of my throat. "In France everyone knew who the poofs were. But as long as they kept themselves to themselves nobody said anything. After all, they could be dead within the hour, so why worry? But round here, you'll be strung up if you're caught."

Unfazed he answers, "Not getting caught is part of the thrill."

"Who is he?" I ask, fighting the urge to throttle him.

"Some posh fella from Cheltenham. Never tells me his name."

"You'll break Mum's heart."

"Like you did? Dad shuttered in Coney Hill and then you disappear. Old sins, new shame. I've heard you screaming at night, just like Jack and Dad before him. Mum and Florrie daren't say anything, but there's an edge to you. You can't see it but you're marked by it. Ever since you came home."

"Didn't have you down as a thinker Stan."

"Seem to remember you didn't have me down as much at all." I grab him by the lapels. My queer little brother smiles. "You as well, Tom?"

I release him.

Tidying himself, Stan says, "After you left, the Alf and his pals never let up on me. Strung me up on the Anselma's rigging, even threatened to slice me. Conscription saved me. Only Alf made it home. The war avenged me. Just left me one thing to do." He flicks his head towards the Anselma. "Torching her was the best feeling ever. Funny thing, though. I'm still drawn back. Maybe some memories are too powerful to burn. Fancy a pint?"

○ ○ ○ ○ ○ ○

The Hauliers' grizzled, addled drinkers, sitting in a haze of cigarette smoke, fall silent when we enter. Stan nods to a group of men sitting at a corner table. There's a hard, steely edge to them. Veterans, with the Somme or Passchendaele still in their blood. The pastor had no chance turning them from drink. A dented brass spittoon sits beneath the bar.

"Perce! meet my brother!" Stan says to the landlord who shoots me a guarded look before offering his hand. "Heard a lot about you," he says, pulling the first pint. "All sorts of capers. Scarpered to China, America, Timbuktu."

"Ireland as well."

He winces. "Makes you either a fool or a hero. Which one are you?"

"Bit of both."

Stan pays for the pints and we sit at a table facing the door. He nods to another group of men. One or two of them I've seen in the Leopard. The atmosphere is tense, unpleasant. Among the company of thieves why would it be any different? I sip my beer. It's rank.

"Don't let Perce see you pulling a face," Stan whispers. "He's proud of his cellar skills." I take another sip and try to keep a straight face as Stan hands me a Players. I hardly know the stranger before me, the annoying little brother who's become the cock of the north.

"How did you fall into all this?" I ask. He shrugs while blowing out the match. "Learned early on there's no point to honesty. Look at you flogging your guts out in the foundry earning nothing but scars. What's more I'm good at it, found my calling. Helps knowing the right people."

"Like who?"

Wary of eavesdroppers, he leans closer and whispers, "Ned Tallow."

I'm dumbfounded. "That stringy little runt?"

Stan nods to a man entering the pub. "Ned knows everything that comes and goes from the docks. Finger in every pie. But he's so quiet and dutiful, nobody pays him any heed. Perfect cover. Years he's been at it, working out who, what, and when to rob. All those chits and declarations passing through his hands in the customs house let him cover his tracks. Even moved his family away."

"To Devon."

He sniggers. "Devon, my arse. He's set them up in a big house in Bristol. Clifton way. Even so, Ned still dresses as if he's on relief and puts up with the merchants looking down their beaks at him while scheming how to rob them. Raked in thousands. Now he's hooked up with gangs in Cardiff, Brum, and Bristol to smuggle booze, fags, and drugs in through Gloucester. Nasty people. Violent."

"Where do you fit in?"

"He needs people to move the loot. People he trusts. Who better than poor Georgie's best mate? Bribe here, bribe there. Easy peasy."

"And the fella on the Anselma?"

"We all have our urges."

"Do Florrie and Mum know?"

"About what?"

"Any of it?"

"Christ, no! They have their suspicions, but turn a blind eye, despite Florrie yakking on about the workers and Mum trying to save my soul."

"They've no choice."

"We all have choice."

"And what happens when you get caught?"

"Don't plan to." He stubs out his cigarette. "Just need to earn enough to ward off Dad's madness."

"Money can't buy sanity."

"Money buys lots of things." He drains his pint and pulls a sour face. "Jesus, that *is* rank." We stand and a dozen pair of eyes watch us leave. Can't say I'll be rushing back anytime soon. The man standing at the bar follows us out and leans against the Hauliers' window. "Just be a second," Stan tells him.

"Come home, Stan. Mum would love to see you."

"Too much sadness there. Besides I've something to collect from that Irish brig. Reckon Ireland owes me a bob or two. I'll have a word with Ned if you want. See if there's an opening for you. Good money. Next to no risk of getting caught. Better than the foundry."

"Going away for a few weeks."

"Where?" His confidence drifts into suspicion.

"France."

"What for?"

"Mechanic for Cotton motorcycles."

"Suit yourself. We'll have a word when you get back."

"We'll see. And Stan."

"Yes?"

"Be careful with the other stuff."

"Sink or swim. That's me, Tom."

As they set off for the docks, Stan slips the man an envelope.

CHAPTER FIFTY-TWO

Barely able to see the buildings and trees lining the road, I latch on to the passing Motosacoche's rasping engine note to guide me through the cloud of chalk dust. I curse my half arsed stupidity for deciding to race the Cotton after Walter, the professional rider, was jailed following an aniseed fuelled fracas with the Tours gendarmes.

Outside the village of Chambray le Tours, the dust is replaced by warped shadows which obscure the cobbles. People hang from every vantage point. A bike draws alongside. I glance across half expecting to see Matilde but instead see a chalk-basted man clinging to his machine for dear life as it runs over the buffeting surface. I cross the finish line and watch him pull away. My race is run. Three laps completed, the start money bagged, softening Walter's jailing. I reach the pits and dismount amidst the sweet, heady scent of Castrol R. Nobody gives me a second look. I'm a motorcycle racer.

The race leader Bennett crosses the finish line followed to the crowd's delight, by a Frenchman aboard a Rudge. Moments later the blurred outline of an FN streaks across the line. Matilde whispers, *"Catch me, Tom."*

I remount and give chase. Why I've no idea. But maybe, *just* maybe. Through dust and sunshine we race in a sealed, private duel with my opponent offering nothing. *"Faster Tom, catch me,"* On the last lap, exhausted and with my hopes fading, the FN runs into a corner too hot and drifts wide. I run alongside, hoping against hope. Hope fades. The FN rider raises an arm in salute.

The shade hides the pothole. The Cotton takes off. Time slows. Only to speed up. Winded on landing, I slide across the cobbles and collide with a row of damp straw bales, scattering the two scrawny boys sitting on one. Dazed by the spill and unable to see through my splintered goggles, I run my hands over my head, torso and legs. Everything is where it should be. The bike lies twenty yards away. Certain I can still catch the FN, I stand, but my legs give way. The two boys help me up and guide me towards the Cotton. Its sheared exhaust pipe lays beside another bale. With chants of "Allez! Allez!" ringing in our ears, the three of us haul the mangled Cotton across the finish line. The boys milk the applause until they're bundled away by a puffed-up steward, deaf to the boos raining down from the stands.

I've run death close, but I want to taste that thrilling, near endless moment again.

The FN's squat, athletic rider, quick to the punch by the look of him,

240

helps me bring the Cotton into the pits. Speaking in a clipped European accent I can't place he says, "You carry speed but also have craft and big balls. I am Josef Zulic." He shares the same cold, hard stare of the Tans gunner.

"Tom Casey." I answer while struggling to light a Players with my cramped fingers. Savouring the tobacco's hit, I listen to a brass band's lopsided rendition of 'God Save the King' in honour of Bennett's victory. Zulic hands me a bottle containing a foul smelling liquid. I take a swig. The alcohol stings but clears my mind.

"Slovenian Plum Brandy," Zulic says wiping his moustache after drinking.

"Where's Slovenia?"

He points to his chest. "Here. I carry it everywhere with me. Here my country cannot be taken from me."

∘ ∘ ○ ○ ∘ ∘

After slathering a bottle of calamine lotion over the smarting friction burns on my arms and shoulders, I sit outside the tent to dry off in the cool, damp breeze. Despite my injuries I'm chuffed to have finished the 1923 French Grand Prix. *Did you see that, Matilde? Did you see me?*

My satisfaction at finishing melts. I've made a fool of myself tramping around Tours hoping to find Matilde's aunt and cousin without a clue as to their name, where they live, or what they look like. And if by some miracle I met them, what would I have said?

Maybe Timmings's tale about this Tantalus fella is true after all.

∘ ∘ ○ ○ ∘ ∘

Decked out in bunting and tricolours, the café where Walter was arrested two nights ago, reeks of cigarettes, brilliantine and beer. Someone plays a jolly tune on a piano. The riders, now in civvies, stand in groups of twos and threes discussing their races in corner-by-corner detail. Some nod to me, telling me I've joined this thrilling world. By the door young women call to the French riders, who wave back and earn excited chatter and giggles from their admirers.

Zulic, already half-cut, hands me a glass of beer which I down in four mouthfuls, grateful to wash the grit from my mouth. A Dutch rider scrounges a cigarette from me and slips a handful of banknotes to Zulic.

"What's the money for?" I ask, as the Dutchman slides away.

"Things," Zulic replies, tapping his nose. "Never trust him."

"Why?"

"He has a moustache." He nods, wipes his moustache and says, "My captain had a moustache. He was a bastard. Turks have them. They are bastards. Charlie Chaplin has one. He is a bastard. Rudolph Valentino has no moustache so I like him. Do you think I look like Rudolph Valentino?"

"You share a likeness."

"You are a liar." I rock back in case he takes a swing at me. Instead he bursts out laughing and says, "People say I have no sense of humour." His handsome features darken again. "They are bastards." Looking at me through drunk, tired eyes he says, "You have the face for a moustache."

As I buy a round, Zulic takes a turn at the piano. Some riders wear knowing looks as he sings a song which in any language speaks of yearning. When he finishes, applause ripples throughout the café.

"What's the song about?" I ask him as a French rider strikes up a more cheerful ditty. He stares into his brandy, his thoughts elsewhere. "It is about three sisters, separated in the Turkish wars." His answer stuns me. *Hear that, Matilde?* The Three Sisters loom through the Kerry mist. "Every night, they each sing this song hoping to be reunited."

"Who were they?"

"Any person from any place. The song reunites us all." Uneasy talking about himself, Zulic sinks his brandy. A manic leer spreads across his face. "Just two things matter to me now. Speed and Slovenian brandy."

∘ ∘ ○ ∘ ∘

Sunshine streams inside the tent. A cat holding a squirming mouse in its mouth studies me from the entrance. Outside, a foreman barks orders to the workers dismantling the race stands. In the already stifling air, my head throbs and I ache all over.

Stretching, I knock over a beer bottle and groan at the memory of being stark naked and leading a conga across the finish line. I light a Players, inhale and cough, causing my ribs and friction burns to throb. The cat runs off with its prize as I crawl outside and slather myself in calamine lotion.

"Morning, Englishman," Zulic is wearing an elegant silk dressing gown and his racing boots. "Breakfast is being served."

As well as his motorcycle, Zulic's lorry heaves with brandy, cigarettes, coffee, butter, and meat. A smuggler as well as a racer. Two silver drums lashed together, rest beside his FN. "Ethanol," Zulic says pointing to the drums with a coffee pot which he then sets down onto a kerosene-fuelled stove. "One drop gives an extra thirty kilometres per hour. I will give you best price. Any man who fought the Turks is a friend."

While frying the eggs, he hums the Austrian army marching song which he'd recited endlessly last night to the annoyance of some riders, unhappy at having wartime memories dredged up. A high backed oak armchair with clawed armrests stands empty. "As you see from my fine clothes and luxurious furniture, I live like a king," he jokes. Easing myself onto the chair, he mutters, "Do not sit there." I freeze, my backside hovering over the seat.

"I am lying," he says. "But do not finish breakfast before me. To me there is no greater insult." Unsure what to do or where to sit, he hands me a newspaper which has a photograph of Bennett overtaking him. With the eggs and coffee softening my hangover I ask, "Who was that girl you were dancing with last night?"

Wiping his plate with bread Zulic replies, "The lovely Beatrice. One dance and I stole her heart. It is usual. Women love me. I am a fine lover. She is good marrying stock too. Her family has money, land, status. Worth thinking about."

"You're not married, then?" His mood sours but in an instant he's all smiles again. "Come to Berne with me. For the next race."

Taken aback, but tempted, I answer, "Don't have a racing licence."

"Walter will not need his for a few weeks. What have you to lose?"

Probably my life.

CHAPTER FIFTY-THREE

The onrushing air ripples my racing leathers, lose fitting on account they belong to Walter, as I follow Zulic around Monza's banked section. I hope my Cotton's handling and low centre of gravity will give me the advantage if Zulic slips up exiting the bend. He did the previous lap but I was too far behind to benefit from it. Maybe this time.

I'd nabbed nineteenth spot in Berne's narrow, twisting streets. The course had suited the patched-up Cotton, and with a few drops of Zulic's ethanol, I managed to pip a couple of fancied riders. Better yet Matilde hadn't badgered me. So when Zulic offered me a lift to Monza, I jumped at the chance. With Walter still locked up and Cotton none the wiser, they agreed to wire more funds to Italy. Better still my new, ginger-tinged moustache was already drawing admiring looks.

Coming off the bank, I hear a yowling Motosacoche closing and seconds later the Dutchman's blurred, reddish outline tore past. I pit, then set off with a handful of other riders, overtaking each one until Zulic hoves into view again. Hearing a thunderous racket, I look behind and see the dust-spattered leaders bearing down on me, each rider moulded to their machines making it impossible to see where the bike ends and the rider begins. Sliding over the back wheel I grip the handlebars and wait. A second later they overtake us. The Cotton stays true, but Zulic slows a fraction, enough for me to pass him. I open the taps around the banking as the oncoming Motosacoche's caterwaul grows louder. The Dutchman shoots by me, but loses control and veers up the banking and flies off the track.

Stunned, I lose control and run onto the verge, barely managing to stop before a low wall. Tearing my scarf away and gasping for breath I watch Zulic ride on.

Returning to the pits, I guess Bennett must have won again because the band are playing 'God Save the King'. Blackshirts prance and strut, issuing diktats to nobody in particular, their thuggish presence unwelcome. I wipe myself down, light a fag, and relive my near miss.

"Any news about the Dutchman?" I ask Zulic.

"Dead," he answers matter-of-factly.

○ ○ ○ ○ ○ ○

That night we drink, sing and laugh like maniacs to honour the Dutchman, each of us relieved he's the one who bought it this time.

"I should have helped him," I tell Zulic. He waves me away, "Never think about death, Casey. Trust me, that will keep you safe. You are feeling sad now, but tomorrow you will want to race again."

"What sort of man does that make me?"

"One starting his future. Racing offers no room for doubt or distraction. All that matters is beating the other rider."

"Did you know his name?"

"Dutchman is enough." He grips my shoulder. "Do you have a wife?" I shake my head. "Just as well. I have a wife and two daughters back home in Maribor. We had a son but he died aged three. Eleven years ago now." His mood shifts. "When I left home to fight, I only wanted to survive. I didn't fight to conquer but to keep things as they were. Coming home I soon learned that the old days were gone forever. In Maribor I lived in anger and disappointment, a stranger to my wife and daughters. The price I paid for surviving was to lose everything. Only racing motorcycles gives me peace. A restless peace, but peace all the same."

"We did our duty, Josef."

"We did." He bellows his regiment's marching song, after which I holler 'The Shores of Amerikay' wondering how I survived the war, Ireland and the Zone Rouge only to risk my neck hurling a motorcycle along cobbled European roads desperate to catch sight of Matilde's ghost.

'But you are free, Tom."

"Thought you'd left me, Matilde."

"Do you want me to?"

"No. Never."

I need to stop thinking. Nothing ever comes from it.

○ ○ ○ ○ ○ ○

Four riders bear the Dutchman's coffin. They follow a brass band playing mournful dirges, marching towards the train that will carry his remains home. The band peter out as the cortege stop beside an open wagon where a small, dapper Italian undertaker takes off his hat, offers soft words of comfort, and helps the pallbearers to load the coffin into the freight carriage.

A bloated Blackshirt steps from a sedan and tip toes over the muddy ground towards us. "Fascist bastards stole Slovenia," Zulic mutters while the fascist speaks. When he finishes, the Italians among us give a stiff armed salute.

THE STEAM CATCHER

The Blackshirt shakes hands with each rider. Reaching Zulic, he whispers something and leads Zulic to his car while the rest of us line up to pay our respects to the Dutchman. It's my turn, I climb the set of wooden steps up to the carriage and step in. The Dutchman lays cross-armed in a tatty ill-fitting suit with rosary beads wrapped around his hands. Vivid bruises cover his puffy, lacerated face. I stand over him, unsure what to do, until a pushy Frenchman behind me tuts and I move on.

We're the last to leave, after which the wagon's door is closed leaving the grimacing undertaker alone with the Dutchman. With a shrill blast from its whistle, the train puffs and clanks away from the platform, shrouding us in steam. I catch a pocketful and as Zulic predicted, set my thoughts for the next race in Berlin.

CHAPTER FIFTY-FOUR

In their quest to make sure no excise duty goes uncollected, every customs inspector, delights in searching a rider's possessions, confiscating the merest of items at the drop of a hat. The inspector in Calais had done just such a thing when he seized Walter's shaving kit, which may have played a part in his troubles in Tours.

Unable to figure how Zulic plans to get his contraband through customs, I was too nervous to revel in the Italian Alps' glorious, spiked scenery as the lorry wound its way towards the Austrian border. Sensing my unease Zulic says, "Do not worry. Mussolini is with us."

Reaching the border, an inspector orders us both from the cab and examines our passports. Another inspector roots inside the wagon. The toe of his boot catches the loose plank. We're done for, a spell in some godforsaken Italian gaol a certainty. Zulic hands one of the letters to the inspector. As he reads, a look of fear and disbelief spreads across his sharp features. He calls to his comrade, who is trying to prise the loose plank free with a knife.

Minutes later we're waved into Austria with our passports and customs carnet stamped. A few miles on we stop to allow Zulic to hammer the loose plank back in place and to snatch a few hours' sleep. By nightfall we reach the German border. A line of vehicles stretches before us. Inspectors with dogs move among the column. By the boot of a Mercedes sedan one of the dogs barks and strains on its leash. His handler opens the boot and lifts out a simpering girl, no more than four years of age. The car driver, busy protesting his innocence, is frogmarched towards the customs post whilst the girl is wrapped in a blanket and taken inside.

"Will make things easier," Zulic whispers.

The fat customs officer raises a lamp and beckons us on. As he studies our passports, Zulic hands him the second letter and the boredom on the guard's face shifts to one of stammering agitation. He calls to his comrades, busy roughhousing the car driver.

"What's in those letters?" I ask after we enter Germany unhindered.

"Power, my friend."

An hour later we pull off the road. From under his seat, Zulic pulls out two Webley pistols. Handing me one he asks, "Do you like Jews?"

"Never given it much thought."

"For the next hours, you hate them."

○ ○ ○ ○ ○ ○

I'm jolted awake. Cramp and thirst are taking their toll. We're driving along a rain-soaked boulevard, bordered by grand buildings bedecked with copper domes and gilded statues. We cross a large square dominated by a train station, its innards belching steam as a handful of people, sheltering under umbrellas, scuttle to and from the entrance, watched by tramps lying in doorways.

"Berlin?" I ask as a cyclist cuts across us and forces Zulic to brake.

"Munich." He says before leaning from his window to swear at the cyclist.

"Thought we were going to Berlin."

"In good time."

Stopping at a junction, I stare at a queue of shabby, poorly shod men and women standing outside a kiosk. Rubbish lays everywhere. Veterans in patched and faded uniforms root in bins. Zulic tosses his fag butt from the cab and three people scrabble for it, the victor taking an eager lungful whilst her disappointed companions look on in the hope of stealing a drag.

"Does the poverty surprise you?" says Zulic. "Don't be. A country where a loaf of bread costs over one billion marks is ruined."

"What caused that?"

"The war and the Treaty of Versailles. The fascists blame the Jews. The communists blame the capitalists. Take your pick. But such desperation creates opportunity. I bring in cigarettes, food, drugs, and barter them for gold, jewellery. Even motorbikes."

"Don't seem right taking advantage of people's misfortune." I know what Florrie would say if she knew I was cavorting around Europe with a profiteer.

"If we don't, someone else will. My brother studied economics in Bratislava. He taught me capitalism. I have what people want but can't get. The more I charge the more they want. It is simple. There is money everywhere. You just need to know where to look for it."

"Where's your brother now?"

"Buried on an Austrian mountainside. Italian shell."

We turn into narrower streets lined with boarded up shops and decrepit tenements sporting rotten mouldings and patched render. Red flags with a strange symbol flutter from a number of windows. "Nazi Swastika," Zulic says. Half-starved people glare at us until their attention turns to a shopkeeper chasing two girls. They are clutching potatoes. Outside a bakery, a baker scrawls the day's prices on a board watched by a sunken-cheeked woman. I offer her a Players. She's wary, so I smile and say, "Please. Take it." As we pull away she snatches the cigarette from me.

"You could have fucked her for that," Zulic mutters.

We drive on and within fifteen minutes, we draw up outside a factory. A man dressed in a twenty guinea suit and holding a clipboard steps from a car, tosses away his cigarette and approaches us with a stiff-backed, military bearing. He seems surprised to see me. "Englander," Zulic replies with a weary sigh, while handing the man the third letter. The man says something which Zulic finds hilarious.

"What's so funny?" I ask.

"He thinks you are long way from Tipperary."

The factory gate is opened and we drive in. The morning light struggles to breach the grubby glass roof. Idle rows of lathes, presses, and smelters stand on the oil stained concrete floor which is embedded with rail tracks. It's cold and the grainy smell of rust and oil linger. Another lorry arrives and parks beside us. A train rumbles passed, shaking the ground.

"Remember, you hate the Jews," whispers Zulic.

With the pistols hidden inside our jackets we step from the cab. A gang of dead-eyed men carrying grappling hooks and crowbars mill around, the left arm of their jackets displaying Swastika brossards. From their ages I guess they fought in the war and like the Italian Blackshirts, each man gives off a spiteful air. Auguste was right. We will be fighting these people again.

The smuggled crates are unloaded and jemmied open. They contain small calibre carbines, Lee Enfield rifles, Webley pistols, grenades, and ammunition. The suited man checks each crate's contents against a list on his clipboard. He holds up two fingers of his right hand. Zulic must have lifted two pistols when repairing the loose planks. Satisfied with Zulic's answer, the man hands him an envelope and orders the resealed crates to be loaded aboard the other lorry.

"Not a word," Zulic says, reversing out from the Factory. He's nervous, desperate to be gone. We retrace our route out of Munich with Zulic constantly checking his mirrors. I grip the Webley. Something feels off.

"Who were those men?" I ask him after we pull into a copse a few miles north of Munich. Zulic wipes his tired, unshaven face and lights a cigarette. "National Socialists. Nazis. They hate Jews, Bolsheviks, and the Treaty of Versailles, but Jews most of all. See themselves as patriots." Patriots. The word Dad had used to describe Danaher. "Now they have a friend in Mussolini, a man whose letters open borders."

"They looked like gangsters. "

"Gangsters and zealots have much in common. But nobody will fall for their lies and thuggery. I am Jewish, on my mother's side. If they knew that they would kill me. But they don't, so I profit from their hate. Adolf Hitler, their leader, thinks himself the Christ. He has a moustache. Makes him a bastard. But he pays in dollars, so I trade with him."

I'm relieved we've got away in one piece.

"Berlin," says Zulic pulling out onto the road and narrowly missing an oncoming motorcyclist. "But first we will stop and rest. I know a place. Very comfortable and welcoming."

CHAPTER FIFTY-FIVE

The soapy water laps around the tub as she reaches for my cigarettes. She lights one, takes a drag, hands it to me and then rests her head against my chest. I close my eyes and listen to the black woman singing on the phonograph.

In the other tub, Zulic's woman giggles and splashes him, sloshing water onto the floor. He whispers and she nods. They step out of the tub, and after robing, she leads Zulic away.

We're alone. I enjoy the stillness and her company. I don't know her name, don't want to. If I did, chances are I'd fall in love. I drop my half-smoked Players into the beer bottle. She examines the ageing friction burn on my right arm. Her touch smarts. She says something in German.

"Motorcycle," I say, guessing at an answer. To help the translation, I do an impression of riding a motorcycle then lean forward and kiss her neck. She speaks again.

"Haven't the faintest," I reply. She hops out of the tub and holds her out a hand. Puncture marks run up her arm.

○ ○ ○ ○ ○ ○

I wake. Rain sheets against the window. I kiss her cheek. She fidgets. I look at the clock on the bedside table. I've only had three hours sleep but feel refreshed. In the room above us, Zulic is still going at it hammer and tongs. She finds his mewling grunts funny.

She gets up and walks over to the phonogram. A moment later the black woman's voice fills the room once more. I sit up, take a swig of beer and watch her dance in supple, measured steps. She doesn't strike me as a prostitute; more a doctor or a teacher. She wasn't as pretty as the other girls and hadn't smiled or simpered when the brothel-keeper paraded them. If anything, she seemed bitter about ending up here. After seeing the poverty in Munich, I guess people have to get by as best they can. Just as Celestine and Malaphonse had to.

"You should be ashamed, Casey,"

"Got me needs, Matilde."

She drags me from the bed. I don't resist. She plants my left hand on her hip, grasps my right hand and squeezes. I like her hand in mine. Not since Matilde. Always Matilde.

We sway to the music even after the black woman slows to a draw:. She kisses the sacred heart tattoo on my chest, and then stands on tip toe. We kiss. Her plump lips part and our tongues entwine. She scratches my burn, pulls away and walks to the bed. I follow, the urge to fuck overwhelming. She wraps herself around me. Within seconds I'm finished.

"Tom," I tell her a few minutes later.

"Charlotte." She leans over me and flicks on a table lamp. I cup her breast. She smiles and opens the drawer of her bedside cabinet. She retrieves a syringe and a phial. "Opium?"

The drug flares through my veins. Charlotte dissolves. But it's just a matter of time before I see her again. For once I am swathed in grace and want this calm to last all my days. I'm free from doubt, fools, and the chastening voices. The black woman drawls. My cock stiffens as I find warm, dry thoughts on which to rest my weary mind. I need to fuck. Time has stopped. A second could be an hour or a day. It doesn't matter. Nothing does, only this soft, yielding moment.

It's cold and I'm gripped by cramps and wretch. Desperate for fresh air, I stumble towards the window, knocking over the phonogram and shattering the disc. I open the window and, ignoring the rain, lean out and throw up again. The sharp, acid bile stings my throat as I try to cobble together the past few hours. The border, the fascists, the brothel. The dollars. The brothel-keeper, a friend of Zulic, hard faced and bitter, eyes shining at the sight of the king's ransom Zulic offered her.

"Any woman you want, Casey," Zulic told me, clutching a bottle of vodka and one of the women. I chose Charlotte. Felt guilty for it. That's not the man I want to be. Matilde, Mum and Florrie would rage. If they knew. I stagger back to the bed heavy-legged, as if clapped in irons. I hear a woman's soft but distant words.

"Matilde?"

"Ja. Matilde," she replies. I look into her glazed, dilated pupils and whisper, "I love you, Matilde." I cling to her and the opium's flame dies.

∘ ∘ ○ ○ ∘ ∘

Zulic is shaking me. I stir, my mind and body leaden. Charlotte has gone. I sit on the edge of the bed and reach for a cigarette. On the bedside table lay two opium phials and a sketch of a man riding a motorcycle. I pick the drawing up and ask Zulic to translate the words beneath the sketch. "Matilde loves you. Find her. Live."

"Where now?" I ask.

"Berlin."

CHAPTER FIFTY-SIX

Zulic sits four rows ahead of me astride his New Imperial, paid for by Herr Hitler. Stirring tunes play over a Tannoy as mechanics tinker with the bikes and nervy looking riders chat among themselves. The opium masks the pain in my cracked ribs that make breathing, let alone riding, seem impossible after my training spill.

Zulic thinks my injuries too severe to risk, but the drugs tell me to ignore him. After all, most riders have raced with morphine pick-me-ups at some point. I just have to complete three laps to claim the start money. I shut my eyes and amidst blank spots, picture the AVUS circuit. Two long straights connected by banked, cobbled hairpins. Flat out from start to finish. A death trap.

The midday sunshine gives way to rain. A maroon arches overhead. The start flag drops and my dosed reflexes allow the bikes behind to first overtake and then blind me with their spray. In this stupor, my every breath and movement is measured, purposeful. Rounding the first endless corner I see him, clear as day, decked out in his Royal Munster's uniform, armed draped around Charlotte. "Open her up, Tom, show us yer mettle," Dad shouts as Matilde overtakes me, her rain-soaked hair splayed around her shoulders. *"Catch me, Tom Casey."* Now everything makes sense. *"Catch me and fend off his madness."* I accelerate. The track narrows to a ribbon of tarmac the width of a tyre. *"Tom Casey, Tom Casey."*

○ ○ ○ ○ ○ ○

I'm lying in a narrow, lumpy bed. A thin reddish-brown rubber tube is attached to the back of my right hand and leads up to a bottle of fluid. A washed-out man in the bed next to me rustles the pages of his newspaper. The smell of bleach stings my nostrils as a cleaner runs his mop under my bed, his wooden stump squeaking on the parquet flooring. Fluttering cobwebs hang from the ceiling's peeling paintwork. I shift and wince with pain. There's a plaster cast around my right leg and bandages wound tight around my chest.

A frowning nurse thrusts a thermometer into my mouth, holds my wrist and looks at her watch. She retrieves the thermometer, studies it and says something in German.

"Englander," I shout. "Proud of it too. Put you lot to the sword. Do so again if needs be."

"I hope not," replies a doctor looking up from the patient in the bed opposite. She's forty with kind, haggard features. She pushes back her thick, greying hair, puts on a pair of glasses and reads the clipboard pegged to my bed. "Thomas Casey?"

"The same."

"Brought in yesterday."

"If you say so."

"You do not remember?"

"Not really."

"What were you doing?"

"Racing motorcycles."

"Not very well, it seems."

She has me. "How did I end up here?"

"A Mister Zulic brought you. Interesting man. Wanted to know if the hospital needed supplies."

"What's wrong with me?"

"Four broken ribs, fractured right ankle and femur, concussion, internal injuries, and assorted lesions."

"Could've been worse."

"Consider yourself lucky. Two riders were killed." She returned the clipboard to its resting place and stowed her pen in the top pocket of her white coat. The nurse rolls up the sleeve of my tunic. The doctor prepares a syringe. Seconds later the pain floats away.

○ ○ ○ ○ ○ ○

A painful nudge wakes me. "You are alive!" Zulic chirrups. He's wearing a fur-collared overcoat and a black fedora hat that makes him look even shiftier. A leather suitcase stands beside him.

"What happened?" I ask.

"You hit standing water and were thrown off. While waving to the spectators."

Dad. "Heard two riders died."

He nods. "A German and a Frenchman. We toasted them long into the night. Everyone knows AVUS is too quick. More so for those riding drugged-up." He shakes his head. "What is that now? Four races and three crashes?"

"Unlucky, that's all. When's the next race?" I pull myself up, groaning with the effort.

"Belgium, in two weeks." My heart leaps. "But you will not be racing. You need two months to heal. So, you will stay here."

"Can't. I'm skint."

"Herr Hitler has paid." He lights a cigarette but the nurse orders him to stub it out. For an instant rage flickers across his face before the charming Zulic returns. "I discovered the hospital pays a fortune for its opium. I have friends in Istanbul who can help. They are Turks so therefore bastards, but I have a chance to turn a profit." He leans closer and whispers, "The Nazis want another shipment of weapons brought into Munich before November. Whatever they are planning will make me rich!"

"Where's my bike?"

"With a friend. He will send word when it is repaired." He shakes my hand, his grip agonising. Ignoring my discomfort, he slides the suitcase under the bed. "Everything you need is in the case. The lining also. Good luck, Tom Casey."

By the ward door Zulic doffs his ridiculous fedora to the nurse and smiles. She is immune to his charm. He steps through the door and I wonder if I'll ever see his like again.

CHAPTER FIFTY-SEVEN

Two nights later, a grumbling porter wheels me into a large, dingy ward crammed with emaciated, wheezing war veterans still stricken by the gas attacks. Certain I'm being punished for being English, I'm afraid to breathe, wary of sharing these consumptives' world. Outside, the crack of small arms fire fills the air. An injured man is wheeled in and parked beside me. The doctor and nurse work like dervishes to save him.

An hour later with the nurse stitching the man's wounds, the exhausted, blood-splattered doctor steps away. "Who is he?" I ask her.

"A policeman. The communists stabbed him after he shot one of their Red Front militia. The mob know he is here. The consumptive ward is the safest place for him. For you also, Mr Casey. As you can see we are still at war in Berlin."

The gunfire is now spiced with the odd burst of machine gun. Flames light up the tar black sky. After a hushed, nervy chat, the doctor and nurse strip the unconscious policeman and cover his face with a mask. Hiding his clothes in the laundry basket beside me, the doctor says, "If they come in, do not speak." She puts on a mask and steps outside. The nurse dims the lights and walks among the patients as outside, the doctor hollers, "Tuberkulose! Tuberkulose!"

The ward door half-opens and curious, fearful men and women peer inside. I cough, as does the nurse and two or three other patients. The door closes and the mob move on, their angry, raucous slogans bouncing off the corridor's walls. The doctor returns and checks on the policeman.

○ ○ ○ ○ ○ ○

The consumptive ward occupies a remote corner of the hospital, near the boiler house and morgue. Nobody receives visitors and only the doctor and two nurses are on hand to care for the men. Despite the doughty cleaner's best efforts, the ward is filthy with mould festering around the windows and ceiling. Even lying in bed, I still feel the cold. The steady flow of death marks time as does the nightly sound of gunfire.

Using pidgin German and hand gestures, I share wartime stories with the ravaged men, while feeding them the thin broth or stew that pass for rations. I sit and listen to a dying man's, sometimes whispered, sometimes raving final words, using the few, hushed German phrases the doctor has taught me to let him know he isn't alone.

To cheer me, the doctor found a newspaper that had the results of the Spa race. There was a picture of Zulic gurning like a simpleton after finishing second. She also gave me a well-thumbed copy of a book called *The Thirty Nine Steps*. I shunned it at first, until one morning, upset at the death of a former Uhlan lancer I'd grown close to, I read the book in one sitting.

Being among the Germans, I started to wonder why we'd fought them with such savagery for so long. After all, we look the same, worship the same God, eat the same food, suffer the same broken hearts, and in this ward at least endure the same lingering, pain-wracked deaths.

Six weeks later, my plaster cast was removed and I began to traipse around the hospital, as the doctor ordered. The cleaner nicknames me "the Englishman in the corridor."

"You should be honoured Mr Casey. Hans rarely speaks favourably of anyone," the doctor told me.

At first, roaming the hospital brought relief, but the sound of clanging pipes, clattering bedpans, and far off cries dredged up memories of Coney Hill. I turned inwards, expecting Matilde to condemn me while the asylum orderlies' boots tramped on the spotless parquet. Stewing in this fetid panic, waiting for the voices to begin, I took to my bed, ignoring the nurse's requests to feed or attend to the dying. At night, desperate dreams pull me deeper into despair. I want to go home and settle down. Find a good woman like Elsie. Fool, Elsie's spoken for. Charlotte then?

I wake bathed in sweat. In between the wheezing and coughing, I hear a set of jangling keys and whispering Englishmen in the corridor. They're coming for me. I throw on the clothes Zulic had packed for me, pick up the suitcase and hurry along dank, deserted corridors towards the hospital's grand entrance, all the time expecting to hear, "Casey! Casey!"

Reaching the grounds, now deadening before the winter, the jarring ache in my right leg forces me to sit. Confused, but aware of the odd looks I'm earning, I raise my face to the morning winter sun and close my eyes.

"May I join you?" asks the doctor. I budge along. "Going somewhere?"

"Just fancied a stroll. Felt a bit stuffy inside." We listen to the birdsong. It's peaceful here, with her. No rush to judgment. No need to run anymore. "Mild winter this year," she says. "The swallows have yet to migrate."

"Good to know."

"Why do you race motorcycles, Mr Casey?"

"Wondering that myself at the moment."

"That is not the answer I was expecting."

"My Dad owned a motorcycle. The first time he took me out for a spin, it was like being on a magic carpet." I shift my aching leg. "For years I dreamed of being an explorer, going on great adventures. My first expedition was to reach the South Pole with Captain Scott."

"On a motorcycle?"

I nod.

"Ambitious."

"Very."

"I was pleased Amundsen won the race to the Pole."

"Scott's a hero," I answer, annoyed with her. "He showed more pluck and courage than any man before or after."

"But Amundsen was smarter, taking the shorter route and using dogs to haul his provisions, whereas Scott's men had to haul theirs. He caused his own downfall."

"Doctor, I'm grateful for all you've done for me, but please, don't taint Captain Scott's memory for me."

"I do not wish to offend you, Mr Casey. Scott was a brave man to the point of recklessness. Sometimes we should look at things differently, if only to challenge the madness around us."

She's given me an opening. "Can a broken heart make you go mad?"

I've surprised her. "A question I have asked myself."

"Did you find an answer?"

She hesitates. The moment reminds me of Matilde's unease speaking about her past. "Grief is a necessary reaction to the loss of someone you care for. It is what makes that person special to us, gives them and ourselves meaning. Love is how we express that meaning. So when we lose a person we love, for a while at least, we lose our own sense of meaning."

"But can it drive you mad?" She mutters in German and grips the seat. "Sorry, doctor. Didn't mean to upset you."

"It is fine, Mr Casey. In all honesty, that is a question I have lived with. You see, the day before the armistice, outside Mons, my husband was wounded by shellfire. He survived because a British soldier carried him across no-man's-land to a treatment station. Why that soldier chose my husband over the other wounded men is a riddle I cannot solve. But I took it as a sign that we were destined to have a long, happy life together." She stifled a sob. "Ludo died in nineteen nineteen. The influenza. I found his death impossible to accept. A stranger had saved him. Then to be struck down..." She tightens with grief and a measure of bitterness. "Why save him only to let him die a few months later? My anger and grief was so profound, so base, that for months, I lost touch with reality, not eating or sleeping. Even speaking seemed a worthless exercise. I only wanted Ludo; to see him, hear him, hold him. I was so stricken, my parents considered having me committed to the asylum." She looks towards the trees. "So yes, a broken heart can drive you mad, or as close as you dare come to it."

"What saved you?"

"Time, people, small acts of kindness. Trying to ease my patients suffering." She held my hand. Hers is warm, soft. Comforting. "You are a *good* man Mr Casey. In time your broken heart will mend and your sense of loss will thin. But not if you break your neck riding motorcycles. There is no coming back from death." She stood. "I am cold, shall we go in?"

Standing outside the ward is a small, distracted bespectacled man wearing mucky overalls. He offers me a card which has *Cotton – Zulic* scrawled on it. He picks up the cardboard box on the chair beside him and hands it to the confused doctor. "Von Herr Zulic," he says, breaking into a gap-toothed smile.

The doctor opens the box. Three straw lined crates of opium phials nestle inside.

○ ○ ○ ○ ○ ○

Against a backdrop of tannoy announcements and whistles, the mechanic and me watch the hungover customs inspector cast a disinterested, bleary eye over the Cotton in Potsdamer Platz station's customs shed. He taps and prods the bike and asks half-hearted questions which the mechanic answers by shoe-horning Zulic's name in whenever he can. The inspection over, the mechanic places an envelope into the inspector's stubby, grasping fingers. The inspector trousers the envelope and then stamps my carnet with a flourish out of keeping with his po-faced manner. Again I wonder how things would have played out if Walter had been a touch cuter in Calais and stayed sober in Tours.

With the Cotton loaded onto the Paris train, I hand the mechanic one of the five pound notes Zulic had stitched inside the suitcase's lining. We shake hands. His are greasy with a rind of dirt under each nail. He wishes me bon voyage then turns and pushes against the throng of passengers surging towards the train.

Finding my carriage, I stow my rucksack and take off the nearly new leather jacket, a parting gift from the doctor. It was her husband's and fits like a glove. The jacket's quality hints at wealth. The doctor's final words to me were, "Good luck, Mr Casey. Please do not become a prisoner to loss."

Steam curls around the carriage. The puffed out, prim women who managed to climb aboard just as the train pulled away, shivers with the cold. At her behest I close the carriage window, but not before catching a pocketful of steam for luck. We leave Potsdamer Platz station to the strains of a brass band playing 'Silent Night'. Christmas must be round the corner.

CHAPTER FIFTY-EIGHT

Mum's on the back doorstep wiping her hands on a towel watching me wheel the Cotton into the yard. Soaked to the marrow, my aching bones crack as I straighten. Her smile masks tired, put upon features. "Good to have you home, Tom," she says squeezing the life from me. "Exciting to receive a telegram."

"Everything all right Mum?"

"Course!" she says, forcing a smile, "Can't I miss my son?"

A new Irish lament drifts around the kitchen as Jack leaves his chair to greet me. The strength in his grip is a surprise. "How you been, Jack?"

"Good Tom. Venture out on my own now."

"He'll be working soon," says Mum, piling up the blouses she'd been stitching at the table. I take off the sodden rucksack and jacket and warm myself by the fire. The air is thick with the smell of treacle and spices and I help myself to a handful of raisins from a jar. Coloured paper chains stretch across the ceiling, above the doors and around the window frame. A nativity crib sits on the mantelpiece, next to the leather strap, Mum's Bible, the tatty atlas, the Charles Dickens book, another Sherlock Holmes story and the Ragged Trousered thingummyjig.

The gaslight throws the same yellow-tinged shadow, the blackened pots sit on the stove, and the swollen cabinet drawers are ajar. As I hoped, everything the same. Until the fire's heat enflames the fleabites I'd picked up in the hovel near Oxford where I'd spent the night. Scratching my left calf, I curse the grasping landlord for charging four shillings for room and board, which turned out to be a mug of cold tea and two slices of stale, mouldy bread.

Mum pours the tea and slices a freshly baked fruitcake. I lay a five pound note beside the blouses. "Your winnings?" she asks, handing me a slice of cake.

"Yes," I lie.

Picking the fiver up, she says, "Things have been a bit tight since Stanley went away."

"Where's he gone?"

"Prison!" blurts Jack. Mum's face darkens to tight-lipped fury as she stirs her tea. "Love the boy to distraction, but he's gone too far. Shredded me of dignity. Had the landlord round threatening eviction, neighbours staring down their noses all high and mighty. Course that old witch next door is enjoying every minute of it." She gathers up the blouses and takes them into the parlour. Moments later, she leaves the house.

"Only a matter of time before his thieving caught up with him," I tell Jack.

"Stan's not in clink for thieving, Tom," Jack answers. "Coppers caught him in the train station toilets with another man. They were doing things to each other. Unnatural things. Gross indecency, the Citizen called it. He got six months hard labour."

The fool hadn't heeded my warnings. I pick up my rucksack and go upstairs. The bedroom's yellow paint has faded. Water still drips from the ceiling into the bucket and the whorling damp stain has spread further. I try the wardrobe doors. They open to the tune of rattling, bare coat hangers. The wardrobe is empty, whatever riches Stan had stowed inside, now gone. The canister hidden beneath the fire grate is also empty. Even the shark's tooth is missing. I stash my passport and money inside the canister and hang my spare shirt and trousers in the wardrobe. They look lonely in such a fine space.

The front door opens. Expecting Mum, but hearing Florrie, I hobble downstairs. She looks bedraggled from the rain, a touch green round the gills too. Hugging me she says, "Good to have you home, Tom. Take it you've heard about Stan."

I nod.

She takes off her hat and kisses Jack, who's still a lovesick pup around her. He lifts the needle from the disc and points to a dozen more discs stacked by the phonograph. "Got all sorts now, Tom." He sets another disc on the platter and a man's reedy voice fills the room. "And Her Mother Came Too," Jack says, nodding along. "Ivor Novello penned it." Him and Florrie sing along but immediately fall silent when Mum comes in carrying a bag of shopping, her edginess at odds with the song's giddiness.

"Still teaching, Florrie?" I ask.

"Three days a week up at the Friends Meeting House. Doesn't pay much but it's rewarding. Thought I'd be sacked after Stan's conviction. Thankfully the Quakers took an enlightened view."

"Don't see why you should have to suffer."

"Remember how we were treated after Dad was shipped off to Coney Hill?"

"That's my only consolation," Mum interrupts while slicing a loaf of bread. "That your father will never know of Stanley's corruption." She butters the bread with angry sweeps of the knife after which she throws on thick cuts of fatty ham. She lays the cut sandwiches on a plate, hands them to me and sets about making another round.

"Labour was elected into government last week," says Florrie, keen to change to the subject.

"For all the good it will do," Mum complains while slathering butter onto the fresh slices. "All the poverty and fecklessness round here. Can't ever see it lifting for clean-minded folk." Florrie bites her tongue. Ivor Novello falls silent. Jack winds the phonograph and is about to lower the needle onto the disc but Florrie catches his gaze and shakes her head.

We eat in an uneasy silence with Florrie, Jack, and me wary of upsetting Mum who seems absent and distracted. Not the homecoming I was expecting, made worse when the flea bites rear up.

To escape the fretful atmosphere I go for a walk. Florrie joins me. It's cold, the lamplick air tinted by the streetlamps. The war dead's photos still stare out from windows, and in the failing light their ageless faces take on a tainted, ghostly edge.

"Evening," Florrie says to a woman and a young girl approaching us.

"Hello, Miss Florrie," the daughter replies. Her mother chides her. A few yards on, another woman ignores Florrie.

"She came to me last autumn, needing help with her landlord," says Florrie.

"Is everyone like this with you now?"

"One or two still speak, but since Stan's carry on, most people give us the cold shoulder."

Another neighbour slights us outside the Goat, the pub's windows rattling with the raucous singing coming from inside. Two men tumble out and collapse in a heap. They haul each other up, apologising to us in German, and stagger off.

"Must be a Hun ship in port," I say. "There's a country on its knees, gun battles in the streets, millions out of work, the money all but worthless. Some of them still stuck their necks out for me though. Doubt we'd help a German lad on his uppers."

"Thought you were going to France."

"I did to begin with. Then I fell in with this fella and we ran all over the place, Switzerland, Italy, Germany."

"Sounds exciting."

"At first. But the war is still being fought over there, or a version of it. Won't end well. Strange thing is though, the more people I met the less I understood why we spent years killing and maiming each other."

Threading her arm through mine Florrie says. "Most days it feels like we lost the war. Everyone scrabbling to earn enough to eat and stave off the landlord. Makes people fearful and angry. That's not right. Never will be. A decent life's not too much to ask for."

"Did that help your lot win the election?"

"Possibly. Despite all the lies in the papers, people want change and make a world fit for their kids to inherit."

"You should write a book about it all."

"Don't be daft."

"How many paupers coffins have passed the house on their way towards the chapel? How many of us died in the war? Why do our kids go without because their parents can't find work? Nobody hears our stories. It's like we don't count. But we do. Just surviving makes us heroes."

"You becoming a socialist?"

"Still a patriot, Florrie. Always will be. But we matter just as much as the king, Lloyd George, and the rest of them."

"Got something else to worry about first." She's tearful but beaming from ear to ear. "I'm having a baby."

I open my mouth, but no sound comes. She laughs. "Found out yesterday. Was going to tell Mum earlier but I can't judge her mood these days. Thought if you knew, you could be happy for me when I tell her. Chivvy her along a bit." We hug. Matilde flits into my mind. A bittersweet moment. "How will you cope?" I ask.

"We'll get by. Jack's much better, his seizures are few and far between now. Hopefully he'll find work soon." But there's little hope in her voice.

"I can help. Earned a few bob while I was away."

"Honestly?" she asks with a sharp look.

"Course," I lie.

From the bridge, lights from the north and east quay warehouses glow a little brighter as night descends. Dockers, shipwrights, and factory workers hurry home or to the pub. "Elsie's engaged," Florrie says while throwing a stone into the water. "She still asks after you though."

"Never thought I stood a chance there."

"You did, but you were too wrapped up in yourself. You can't live on a whim all your life Tom. Look at the pickle Stan's landed himself in." She launches another stone. It skims four or five times across the water before sinking. "I'd no notion of his inclinations. Did you?"

"I saw something once, on the docks."

"You never said."

"Not the sort of thing you talk about. I warned him though."

"Looks like he listened." She hurls another stone, this one a threer. Rubbing her hands for warmth she says, "Made us fair game again. Tomorrow's visiting day. Why don't you come with me." From her tone it's clear I've no choice in the matter.

○ ○ ○ ○ ○ ○

The trees surrounding the paupers' cemetery are winter-bare and laden with perched crows. Most graves are so neglected they're little more than weed-choked patches of earth marked by near rotten crosses. Somewhere Georgie Tallow is laying among them. There's a loneliness here, of lives that never mattered and are soon forgotten, unlike those thousands of well tended graves in Belgium and France. At least those lads will be remembered.

I spot Dad and Albie's white marble headstones close to the boundary wall on ground that shames the plots either side of them. But seeing them leaves me confused. Old, stale thoughts and fears collide. Memories dredged up, refuse to sink.

Albie's engraving reads, "Albert Casey. Much loved son. Cruelly taken." I reach into my trouser pocket and smear a handful of steam over the headstone and say, "There you go Albie. For luck. Sorry I haven't seen you for a while. Florrie said I'd feel better for coming. As usual, she's right."

Strange to think how random it all is. Your brother breathes in the same fetid air but, you survive. Fletcher cops it because he wants to see his pal even though Timmings' name was on the sniper's bullet. Maybe if Georgie had boarded the Anselma five minutes later, he'd have missed the madman and our lives would have taken a different turn. Life's a rag-tag bundle of tiny, accidental events which we try to make sense of. Me? Give it full chat. Head down. Charge on. There's a freedom to that. A purity. I'll keep charging until I find Matilde, even to the Shores of Amerikay. But enough of thinking. Thinking never gets you very far. Better to be, like last night watching Mum burst into tears after Florrie told her she was expecting. Couldn't believe my ears as the silence gripping us over tea was traded for Mum talking the hind legs off a donkey over the new arrival. Jumpers to knit, cribs to buy, toys to make. Hardly came up for air, truth be told. Still, at least she forgot about Stan for a while.

The engraving on Dad's headstone reads, "Jack Casey. Husband, Father. A Soldier of the Empire and loyal servant to the King."

"I've some news, Dad. Florrie's having a baby. I promise they'll know your stories and songs and your love of Ireland. Went over there after the war, to atone for you and to try and forget this girl I got stuck on. Strange place, beautiful yet seething at the same time. Didn't help we were at war with them I guess. Saw the Three Sisters though. A beautiful, mournful sight. Funnily enough three sisters saved me in France. Even fell in love with one of them. Matilde was her name, you'd have liked her. Whip-smart but kind. Pretty too. Understood me. Made me a better man."

I pick up decaying flowers, brittle to the touch that are scattered around both headstones and stand in the freshening breeze. One or two crows squawk. There's so much more I want to tell him, the Zone Rouge, Berlin, the Grand Prixs. Matilde again. Next time.

I pass a patch of cleared land where three freshly dug graves wait for coffins. The grave diggers lean on their shovels, enjoying a smoke. They're the men I saw at Georgie's funeral all those years ago. By the look of things they're still doing a brisk trade. Even on parish rates.

Changing my mind, I walk back to Dad. "One more thing Dad, I climbed the pyramids, sat on the Sphinx and saw the Garden of Eden, only it was more akin to hell than paradise. When Mum told me you mentioned Saint Waltrude, I wasn't sure whether to laugh or cry. Something else as well, Dad. Not sure how to say this, but I hope you can forgive me for not being a better son. Should have stuck by you, like Mum did." I hope for an answer. There isn't one. No surprise really. But I've made peace with myself. Of sorts.

∘ ∘ ○ ○ ∘ ∘

A cloud of stream spirals from the train station. I try to catch a handful but a gust of the wind sends the plume skywards.

In Eastgate Street, the Hippodrome is showing a film called *The Hunchback of Notre Dame*. A poster shows a beautiful gypsy girl cavorting with a repulsive, twisted creature. Idlers skulk outside the market, smoking and chatting, eyeing up passers by. I wonder how easy it would be for some chancer to turn this rag-tag army of the forgotten and angry into something more sinister as in Italy and Germany. At least there's no flags fluttering, slogans daubed across walls or hectoring dead-eyed-zealots. Not yet anyway.

Outside the dock gates pilferers hawk filched wares. One woman holds up a blanket so worn I can see through it. I wave her away and after her, a man selling mouldy potatoes.

To kill time, I head to the docks and watch a barge head Up Country while over on the north quay, stevedores unload grain from a Spanish merchantman, while their terriers doze in the shade. Waterman's warehouse is encased in scaffolding. Answering brickie's calls, hod carriers scamper up ladders while buckets of mortar are raised on pulleys.

A dour-faced bargeman, fag clamped to his lips brings his vessel quayside as two old timers look on.

I pass a German brig out of Kiel, guessing it was her crew I'd seen out carousing last night. It starts to rain so I hurry towards the chapel to find shelter. A pauper's coffin is carried out, no doubt bound for one of the fresh graves. A handful of mourners follow, among them Old Ma, draped in a mangey fox fur, her sour features creasing at the sight of me. The pall bearers settle the coffin onto a horse-drawn dray that rattles over the cobbles as it pulls away. The rain swept mourners follow, except for Old Ma who peels away, her prying satisfied.

Inside the chapel, the scent from extinguished candles and polished pews mingle. I read the Ten Commandments hanging on banners from the rear wall. Must have broken half of them by now. Rain drums on the roof. The chaplain, collecting hymn books, coughs. Time to go.

Hunched against the rain, I head towards the prison. Outside its gatehouse, hard-faced women, wearing drab, aged dresses, grumble to each other about the weather. One or two eye me with suspicion, or maybe covet my jacket. The main gate's sally port opens and a middle-aged man steps into his freedom, heaving a canvas duffel bag onto his shoulder. A butcher's wagon arrives. The main gate opens and the van enters. We shuffle forward but the gate closes. The women complain again.

I bury my hands in my jacket's pockets and run a finger over the toy Prussian soldier, barely an inch tall in the left pocket. It must have been left there by the doctor's husband. For safekeeping, I've wrapped Matilde's cotton ringlet around the soldier. It's a comfort to know she's near. Wedged in the lining of the right pocket is the receipt, dated November 15th, 1919, from something called an apotheke on a Berlin street whose name I can't pronounce.

Florrie arrives. One or two women turn their backs on her. "More pupils," she mutters. The sally port opens, and a warder herds us into a freezing, room reeking of bleach, the only light coming from two small, barred windows set high in the wall. A gull lands on one window ledge and peers down at us, its head bobbing in jagged movements. In the far end of the room, a burly warder sits at a raised table. Affixed to the wall above him is a large clock and plain wooden crucifix.

We sit at our allotted table, number seventeen, shivering, breaths white, fingers already numb. Two warders walk among the tables, their key fobs jangling, their boots squeaking on the stone floor. A middle-aged woman leans towards Florrie and asks, "Who you vistin', Miss Florrie?"

"My brother." Florrie whispers back.

"The Nancy boy?" Florrie flushes. "Weren't natural, what he got up to."

"What he did or didn't do is of no concern to you or yours!"

"As long as he keeps away from my boy."

A warder calls for silence.

The uniformed prisoners enter in single file. Their hard expressions lighten upon sight of loved ones. The room resounds with creaking tables and joyful mutterings. Florrie waves to Stan and he threads his way towards us, eyes cast to the floor, his movements laboured, the swaggering tearaway now gone. He sits but fidgets, eager to be gone. He's stick-thin and has a black eye. A bandage covers his right hand, which he tries to hide by tugging his shirt cuff over it.

"How long you been back?" he asks me.

"Arrived yesterday."

"Should've stayed away." He's annoyed me already. "How's Mum, Florrie?"

"Fine. Sends her love. Looking forward to having you home."

I'm struggling not to lean over the table and belt him, but manage to say, "How you coping?"

"They're hanging a fella next week. Poisoned his wife with arsenic. Quiet man, wouldn't think he'd murder in him. The other inmates say I should swing alongside him."

"Just keep your head down," Florrie says. "You'll be home soon, in time for Christmas. Then we can think about the future."

"Montevideo, Tom?" says Stan, with a touch of desperation. "Where my old football came from?"

"Why not," I lie.

The hour drags. Florrie chitchats away and encourages me to recount my racing adventures. But Stan, consumed by fear, barely listens. "When can we sail for Montevideo?" He interrupts as I recount my spill in Berlin.

"I'll need to make enquiries."

Before I can carry on, Stan says, "You told Mum I was sorry, didn't you Florrie?" He's close to tears, once more the petrified eight-year-old in the backyard tent.

"Hundreds of times, Stan."

"Why hasn't she visited me?"

"She will Stan. She just needs more time."

"For what?"

"To come to terms with things."

To my relief the warder calls time. Slipping Stan a packet of Players, Florrie whispers, "We're here for you Stan. Aren't we Tom?"

I half nod. Not sure I am to be honest.

As Florrie steps away, Stan grabs my arm and whispers, "Ned Tallow's gunning for me, Tom."

"What for?"

"Moved some rum and brandy off the docks without telling him."

"How much?"

"Two thousand pounds worth."

"What possessed you?"

"Got greedy. Remember that fella I met outside the Hauliers?" I nod. "He dobbed me in to Ned."

"What'll Ned do?"

"Dunno. The booze was to go Up Country to Birmingham and then on from there. But he'll have to save face."

"Time," repeats the Warder.

"Speak to Ned for me, Tom. Try and smooth things over. Thirty-seven Hopewell Street. That's where he lives."

"And if I can't?"

"I'm a dead man."

○ ○ ○ ◯ ○ ○

"What's up with Stan?" Florrie asks as we walk home. "Never seen him so fractious."

"Just getting a hard time from the other prisoners. Be all right when he gets out."

"Why was he rabbiting on about Montevideo?"

"Dad always made out Stan's old football came from there. Bit of a running joke between us."

○ ○ ○ ◯ ○ ○

That afternoon, I give the Cotton the once over. The tyres are a little worn but the engine, brakes and exhaust are in good nick. I glance to the back door. The coast is clear. I remove the fuel tank and free the Webley .38 taped to the chassis, grateful to Zulic for his foresight. Takes a thief to know a thief, I suppose.

CHAPTER FIFTY-NINE

Two boys kick their football against the Leopard's public bar door. The landlord comes outside, swots them with his towel and holds the door open for me.

Two men are playing darts and a cribbage school has just settled in for the night. A cloud of cigarette smoke nestles against the yellow-stained ceiling while a barking dog is shushed by his master. The old tar sits by the fire, nursing his drink. I order a pint for myself, a tot of rum for him and drop the penny change into the wish bottle.

"Most kind," he says accepting the rum from me. "Haven't seen you for a while."

"Been away."

"Whole country's gone to the dogs. Got so bad that Labour lot won the election." Shaking his head, he sips the rum. "Havin' a working man in charge goes against the order of things. Like on a ship. Captain's the one in charge, not the ratings nor even the first mate. Has to be a man who knows how to lead. That's bred into him over centuries."

"Thought you supported the strikers."

He nods. "Them lads never got a fair shake. But when it comes to running things, we need men with breeding and education. What does a miner or docker know about affairs of state?"

"They know what's right and wrong."

"That's as maybe. But are they bastards? Bastard enough to send our boys to war, to defend king and empire?" He shook his head. "Even the Irish kicked us out. What's the world coming to when the Micks can defeat the greatest empire known to man? Sorrowful times."

"From what I saw, they had right on their side."

"If you say so," he answers looking surprised. A cheer goes up from the darts match just as three men step into the bar. At first I pay them little heed until the smallest man smiles at me. I half-hoped Ned Tallow wouldn't turn up. He must be worried about Stan.

The other two men stand at the bar sipping their pints while Ned joins me at an empty table and sets a glass of lime cordial down. He's thin, petite as a Frenchman might say, with every movement measured and deliberate while his narrow intelligent eyes weighed me up. His suit may be baggy, his shirt collar frayed and his shoes scuffed but there's a smugness about Ned I've not seen since the prancing Blackshirts. "Been a while Tom," he says.

"Ned. How's the family?"

"Oh you know. Since Dad died, Mum's not been herself. But she's happier down in Devon. Got her sisters for company, for starters."

Lying bastard.

"My youngest sister married a fortnight ago. Nice fella. Taylor. Owns a shop in Tiverton. They're all married off now. Except me, of course. Perhaps I should follow them out of Gloucester. Your Mum and Florrie keeping well?"

"Fine."

"Good. Nice people, very kind to Mum when Dad died." He swirls his cordial around the glass. "Can I ask you something Tom?"

"Course, Ned."

"Did your dad kill our Georgie?" He must have seen the flicker of doubt on my face because he leans back and raises his hands in surrender. "Don't mean any harm. Just wondered what you thought. Friend to friend."

He's testing me. He doesn't care who killed Georgie, just wants to get me on the back foot. To buy time I sip my pint, struggling to read him.

"Dad was many things, Ned. But not a killer."

"My mum wouldn't agree with you."

"Your mum's a good woman, dealt a bad hand."

"Can't argue with that."

"But she's got the wrong end of the stick about Dad. The seeds of his madness were sown during his time in South Africa. They took years to rear up. But he wasn't a killer, more likely to hurt himself, truth be told."

Nodding, Ned wears the same wistful look the pastor perfected. "That's good to know Tom. Always wanted to ask you." Smiling, he leans forward and pushes his glass towards me. "So what was it you wanted to ask me about Stan?"

"He thought you might have some work for me."

"Did he?" He raises an eyebrow. "There's no positions in the custom house."

"He wasn't talking about the custom house."

"What then?"

I push my pint towards him, and whisper, "Moving pinched stuff off the docks." Hie feigns surprise as I continue, "With Stan locked up, I thought you might need someone."

His eyes narrow a fraction, all pretence gone. "Wasn't expecting this."

"What were you expecting?"

"Oh, you know, if I could help out your mum and Florrie while Stan's inside. Be happy to by the way."

"Very thoughtful of you. But I'd rather work than accept charity."

"Course. Always better to graft." He paused to let more cheers from the darts match die down. "Did Stan tell anyone else he worked for me?"

I shake my head.

"Your mum? Florrie?" Again I shake my head. "Good." He blows his nose on a grubby hankie. "'Scuse me, can't shake off this blessed cold. Lingering, that's what it is."

"Sorry to hear that."

"Like your fucking brother." Startled by the venom in his voice, my heart skips a beat. I glance at the door. The path is still clear. "Taken me years to get where I am. Even got rid of my drunken, squalid dad. He was bad for business blabbing all over Gloucester about me as well as making our lives a misery. No hardship watching those two fellas at the bar put an end to the bastard." Again I look at the door and then over to Ned's mates, both looking on while supping their pints. The air is stuffy, the swirling fag smoke stinging my eyes. Contrition has replaced anger on Ned's face. "Let my heart rule my head taking on Stan. Did it for Georgie. Remember how close the pair of them were?" I nod. "Seemed right to help him."

"Was good of you, Ned."

"Stan's smart, diligent. Crafty too. Thought I could trust him." Tutting, he shook his head. "Greed is a deadly sin. But then you'd know that Tom, traipsing round the streets listening to that pastor spout off."

"Guess so."

"Funny carry on with him and those women. Must have been a shock for your mum."

"It was."

"Test someone's faith, I'd wager."

"It did."

"Having a drunk for a dad tested my faith. I learned early on to keep out of harm's way; watching, learning, finding weaknesses and turning them to my advantage. The docks offer a patient man ample reward. All it takes is a slip of the pen here, and a spot of under-counting there. Soon adds up. There's a word to describe it. Incremental." He blows his nose and takes another sip of cordial. "Nice word. Trips off the tongue. Course there's been a few jack the lads who thought they could outsmart me. Specially during the war. None did though."

"Stan's sorry, Ned. He wants to patch things up."

"Heard he's finding prison tough going." He wipes his mouth and sniffs.

"Course if I could, I'd let sleeping dogs lie, for our Georgie's sake, if nothing else. But I can't risk people getting wind of my activities. All these years walking around dressed as a tramp, kowtowing to rich arseholes will have been wasted. That's my predicament Tom."

A shout goes up from the cribbage game. Ned flinches. "See?" he whispers."Even sitting here with you, I'm a bag of nerves. Happiest in the shadows, nobody giving me a second look. Trouble comes when you step into the light." He stands and offers me his hand. It's as soft as a priest's. "We'll speak soon, Tom. Figure something out. Regards to your mum and Florrie." The two men follow him out.

He plans to kill us all.

"Haven't got a fag by chance?" The old tar asks. I hand him a Players. "Ever sailed to Montevideo?" I ask. His face brightens. "Just the once, on a merchantman carrying beef. Place was packed with men nursin' hangovers or broken hearts, sometimes both. On their way to the Devil many of 'em. The women were bold, big, violent. Gouge a man's mortal soul for ten bob. Why you askin'?"

"Might be heading there."

CHAPTER SIXTY

Outside the Leopard, a dog yaps and one of the two boys playing football asks me for a cigarette. When I tell him I've just smoked my last one, he tuts. His mate tells him to scarper. The pair hare off. Another victory cry comes from the pub. "Back home then, Casey," says Alf Fenwick. His moustache still doesn't suit him. "France, wasn't it? Where you raced."

"Other places too, Alf."

"On a Cotton too. Gloucester's finest." Looking towards the Leopard he asks, "When's Stan released?"

"Tuesday."

"Thought so." He looks at me. "Best if he moves on. London or some such. People round here won't put up with his sort." He brushes the brim of his helmet and walks on.

The night presses down as I hurry along the narrow streets with the pictures of the fallen scowling at me from each window. I'd felt safer among the Nazi and communist thugs in Germany. Once home, I bolt the front door and hurry into the kitchen where Mum is peeling spuds and Jack is listening to a song on the phonograph.

"Where's Florrie?" I ask.

"Working. Home soon enough," Mum answers.

Murphy follows me into the yard. There's voices in the alley. I open the back gate and two men run off. "In Murph." The old mutt toddles inside. I bolt the back gate and prop a length of wood against it.

"Still no sign of Florrie?" I ask Mum as I step inside.

"No," she answers. "Why are you so desperate to see her?" There's a knock on the front door. Heart pounding, I step into the parlour and peer outside through the net curtain to see Florrie turning the front door handle.

"Why's the door locked?" she asks after I let her in.

Without answering, I run upstairs and retrieve the pistol from the canister. The chamber is full. Murphy barks. I look outside and see two men hanging about the alley, their fags glowing in the dark. They duck from view and seconds later flames lick the yard wall. I tuck the pistol into my jacket and hurry downstairs and out into the yard, joining Mum, Florrie, and Jack.

Jack pulls the prop away and opens the yard gate, but the fire's heat forces him to back away. Tearing the tarp from the Cotton, I smother the flames. Neighbours look on. Not one lifts a finger to help. "That's what you get for raising a sodomite!" Old Ma shouts from her back gate.

"What about you taking in men for a few coppers a time?" Florrie hollers back. "Half the men in this street have been round to you." One or two wives study shamefaced husbands. For once Old Ma bites her tongue.

"Florrie!" Mum shouts, leading Jack into the kitchen.

Jack grips the chair's armrests, his eyes fixed on Florrie as she thrusts the strap into his mouth. The convulsions begin. Florrie winds the phonograph. Ivor Novello sings. "Hold him," Florrie says taking one arm, Mum the other. I grip Jack's shoulders and pin him to the chair. Florrie sings along to 'And Her Mother Came Too'. Mum and me join in. It's not until the fourth rendition that Jack's breathing steadies and the spasms ease. Florrie pulls the sodden strap from Jacks mouth and he leans forward gasping for breath.

"Been a while since that's happened," says Mum, mopping Jack's forehead. Florrie looks relieved and fearful. Without thinking, she brushes her belly.

"Who'd do such a thing?" Mum asks.

Ned Tallow.

∘ ∘ ○ ○ ∘ ∘

Alf kicks at the smouldering planks piled up against the yard wall, sending up a cloud of cinders. "Any idea who did it?" he asks.

"Could be anyone round here," I answer. Best not to tell him about Ned.

"Told you, Casey. Best for everyone if Stan moves on. Him lingering, puts all of you in danger."

Lingering? Odd to hear that word twice in one night.

Checking Old Ma's back gate, he asks, "Why does trouble always follow you?"

"Circumstance, Alf."

Confused, Alf heads towards the docks his torchlight bouncing off the cobbles and walls. I lock the back gate and replace the prop. A brick sails over the wall and strikes the Cotton. "Don't want that perverted fucker round here!" A man shouts. I go out and he runs off. Fifty yards on, he turns and shouts, "We'll burn you out, Casey!"

CHAPTER SIXTY-ONE

His black eye still ripe, Stan steps through the sally port looking like quarry desperate to go to ground. Florrie hugs him. I chivvy the pair of them along. To Florrie's surprise, we skirt the docks to take the long route home, despite the night descending.

Mum is sat at the kitchen table sewing the sleeve of a blouse.

"Hello, Mum," says Stan with a hint of nerves. Mum bites off the thread, holds the sleeve to the light, tuts and unpicks a stitch. Without lifting her eyes she says, "Tom, show Stan the door."

"No, Mum."

"Then you can pack your bags as well."

"Jack and me will follow," says Florrie. Her threat catches Mum unawares.

"Sorry, Mum," Stan whispers.

"For what? For shaming me? For sinning? Or for getting caught?" She holds the seam to the light and sighs for a second time. Flustered, she attacks the seam but curses under her breath after pricking her index finger with the needle. She throws the shirt onto the table and sucks her bloodied finger.

I sit down beside her. "Let Stan stay for a day or two Mum, until we can work something out. Don't be like your pa. You're better than that."

"Scripture says a man lying with another man is an abomination. I cannot go against God's word." She picks the blouse up and tries to wipes a smear of blood from the collar. "Enough of this footle. I want him gone."

"Stan paid for Dad and Albie's headstones."

"I'll have them torn out. I won't sully their memory. That's my final word." But it isn't, was never going to be. She looks into Stan's sorrowful eyes. Looks to me like she's grieving for something precious but lost. "I taught you right from wrong, Stanley. You know the struggles I've endured to raise you all. I blamed myself for your thievery and I was wrong to turn a blind eye. But I'll never accept this. And there's the baby to think about. A new life as opposed to a corrupted one."

Stones strike the back window. "You see!" Mum shouts. "We're not safe with him here."

Jack and me go outside but we're forced to duck when another volley of stones are launched at the house. Shouts of "String him up!" gather strength. I open the back gate. One or two neighbours I recognise, but mostly they're strangers, drawn by hate and no doubt Ned Tallow's shilling.

"Take Stan out the front," Jack whispers.

"You sure?"

"Need to keep Florrie and the baby safe." Without warning, Jack charges the mob who part and then enfold him. Flailing fists descend upon him but he manages to deck a couple of men. I'm rooted to the cobbles. Help Stan or help Jack? Jack is back on his feet. He drops another fella and looks back at me. A hurled brick smashes the cracked bedroom window.

I go inside, grab Stan, and lead him out onto the street where one or two neighbours look on from the doorsteps. Shouts go up.

We head towards the city.

No guesthouse will give us board. Even the Sailor's Mission refuses us a bed. After another landlord declares they've no rooms, I decide it's safer to hunker down on the Anselma for the night and get Stan away tomorrow.

The docks are quiet, the warehouses shuttered, moored ships still, with only the night watch above decks. A solitary barge sits heavy in the barge arm, a sign that it's leaving in the morning. A light shines from the cabin and a thin plume of smoke rises from its battered chimney.

I leave Stan and cross the swing bridge and hurry towards the barge. I tap on a cabin window and the bargeman's haggard, drink addled face appears. "What?" he slurs in a half-cut, drowsy voice.

"I want to book passage, to Birmingham. For tomorrow." Swearing at his mutt to move, he stumbles towards the cabin door and opens it. Holding a cargo hook in his right hand, he squints at me, his breath rattling, near consumptive. He weighs me up, no doubt wondering what he can charge. The late hour gives him the advantage. "Two quid."

"Two quid?"

"Night, then," he replies in a thick Bristolian accent.

"All right, two quid."

He holds out his leathery hand. I pay him. "Keen to get away eh? Should've asked for more." He goes inside the cabin and holds the notes up to a lamp. Satisfied they're real, he returns. "Push off at five o'clock in the morning, on the dot."

"Can he board now?"

"No." He closes the cabin door, shouts at the dog and douses the light.

Stan's propped against the Anselma's balustrade using his duffel bag as a cushion. "The bargeman will take you to Birmingham," I tell him while lighting two Players. We smoke in silence, the cigarettes half-lighting our faces each time we take a drag.

"Remember all the times we played pirates aboard her?" he says.

"Preferred being a marine," I answer. "Or Captain Scott."

"You and Captain Scott."

"Great man."

"Then you ran because you thought you'd killed Alf."

"We all make mistakes."

"Too many to mention." For once we're easy in each other's company.

"Always seems to start and end on the Anselma," he says after spitting out a strand of tobacco.

"Like what?"

He clears his throat. "I killed Georgie." Dumbfounded, I try to decipher his shadowy features. "We'd been playing football in the alley. For some reason Georgie decides to run off with my ball. I chased him onto the docks and then onto the Anselma. He balanced on the gunwale and started taunting me about Dad. I launched myself at him. Georgie loses his balance and fell overboard, cracking his head on the hull. I stood there, watching him float face down in the water. Didn't know what to do, Tom. So I ran home. As fast as my legs would carry me."

"Why didn't you say anything?"

"Thought I'd be blamed."

"But it was an accident."

He shook his head. "Who'd have believed me? We're outsiders, always have been, always will be, no matter which way you dress it up. They'd locked Dad up, which made me fair game in my eyes. Couldn't bear the thought of that, so kept quiet." He ground out his fag. "Saw the beatings from the Bridge Gang as punishment. Mum's Bible said I deserved to suffer. But each punch, kick, and taunt drove the guilt further into me until it sat so deep, it lay hidden. As I got older I understood they were beating me because they enjoyed it. And when Ned took me on, I figured I'd atoned for Georgie. Even fancying men didn't feel so wrong then. Everything up to that point had been a lie. Torching the Anselma let me destroy the past. Course it didn't. Made things worse truth be told." He wiped his mouth. "Never thought a football bobbing all the way from Montevideo would lead to such heartache."

"Stranger things have happened, Stan."

"Not many."

A church bell rings in midnight.

"There's something I need to do," I tell him. "If I'm not back, make sure you board the barge for five o'clock."

"Where you going?"

"To speak to Ned."

"Be careful. He's clever."

"More to me than meets the eye."

Leaving the ship, I hear off-key singing and make out the swaying old tar, trousers by his ankles, pissing into the basin. "Evenin'," he says, pulling up his britches. "Got a fancy piece on the Anselma?" He chuckles and mutters, "Some fella was in the Leopard earlier, asking after you and your brother. Promised twenty quid to the man who told him where you were. Tidy sum." He rubs his whiskery chin. "Got a fag?" I hand him a Players which he stows behind his ear. "Cheers. Harsh times we're living through, enough to make a man slay a neighbour for a gob full of bread."

I hand over ten bob. "You're a kind hearted soul."

"And you're a grasping old bastard." He flinches.

"I've no mind to tell anyone I've seen you, I swear."

Stan is surprised to see us. The Old Tar squirms and tries to free himself from my grip. "Please, Master Casey, I meant no harm, just the drink talking that's all. Loose lipped when I've drink inside me. Caused me no end of trouble down the years. I can be as quiet as a lamb or the grave. Both if you want."

After binding and gagging him we ignore his muffled pleas and lower him into the forward cargo hatch.

∘ ∘ ○ ∘ ∘

Reaching the back alley, I open the yard gate. Bricks lay scattered everywhere with the Cotton a charred wreck. Murphy barks and scratches at the smoke-streaked back door. "Who's there?" Florrie asks.

"Tom." She opens the door. Murphy stops barking. Florrie falls into my arms. *"The baby Tom Casey, you must save the baby."*

"Thought we were going to be burned out. We were only saved when the police chased the mob off."

"Is Jack all right?"

"Bit shook up but all right. Is Stan safe?"

"Yes. He's leaving for Birmingham first thing."

"What we going to do?"

"I'll deal with it."

"On your own?"

"We've no choice. The police won't do anything. Never have. Never will. Only one way to stop this."

The parlour door is ajar. The net curtain flutters as Mum stares through the smashed front window. She's holding Albie's shirt. Never seen her look so afraid or broken, not even the day they took Dad away. "That you Tom?" she calls.

"Yes, Mum." Seizing my hand she whispers in a cracked voice, "What you said earlier was right. I should have shown more compassion towards Stanley. He's as precious to me as you and Florrie. But it's not safe for him here. For any of us."

"Stan's safe, Mum. He'll be gone by the morning."

"Good. Seems like the whole of Gloucester has turned into the asylum these past months. So much anger everywhere. Hate, too. Too much hurt in this place."

"Don't think the war has left us yet."

She hugs me. "Tell Stan his mother still loves him."

I go upstairs and fish out the canister from beneath the fire grate. Zulic's money is still inside, but the pistol is gone. I pocket the money, shake out the last of the soot-stained coins and scour the room for the pistol.

"Gave it a clean," says Jack standing in the doorway, the revolver in his hand. His jaw is swollen and he sports several cuts about the face. "Saw you take it from the Cotton. I knew Stan hid his valuables in the fireplace. Figured you would too."

"How you feeling?"

"Few aches and pains, but it'll take more than a few diddy coys to down me."

"You're on the mend, Jack."

"Looks that way. Just hope I'll be a good Dad."

"You will."

Handing me the pistol he says, "One to the chest, then one to the head."

"There's an old man tied up aboard the Anselma. Raise the alarm tomorrow morning."

"Good luck, Tom."

"Cheers. Look after Florrie and the baby for me."

"Will do."

I go downstairs and find Florrie sitting at the kitchen table clasping a cup of tea while staring into the dying fire. Like Mum, she looks washed out. I lift her book from the table. *Far From The Madding Crowd.*

"It's to do with love, obsession and death."

"Spent years living with that stuff. No need to read about it."

She reaches for my hand. "Scared, Tom."

"We'll be all right, Florrie."

"Scared for the baby."

"With you, Jack, and Mum he'll want for nothing. He'll be extraordinary. Maybe even end up an explorer."

"Just like her uncle, then."

I hand her the money. "This will keep the wolf from the door for a while." I fight back the tears and whisper, "Thanks, Florrie."

"What for?"

"Everything."

Clasping me tight she says, "Don't forget us."

"No danger of that. Say hello to the baby for me."

CHAPTER SIXTY-TWO

"Fast in. Fast out. Chest then head."

Standing in an alleyway four doors down from number 37, I try to ignore the cramp in my right leg. I crave a smoke, but daren't give my position away. Time drags. I'm not cut out for this malarkey. But I'll keep my promise to Dad. A stray mongrel looks at me and trots away.

Light still bleeds around number 37's front curtains even though it's almost four o'clock in the morning. I check the pistol and hum 'The Shores of Amerikay' for the umpteenth time.

The dog returns. As I shoo it away, a man, buttoning his overcoat, steps from number 37 and turns to speak to a woman in the doorway, their breaths spiralling into the night. The man moves off. I slink into the shadows as Alf Fenwick passes me. The bastard.

I wait five, ten, minutes running over my plan. Kill Ned then run like fuck. Fool-proof. Made easier from all the comings and goings tonight. Probably people keen to earn themselves twenty quid with news about Stan and me. For all his caution, Ned has given me a chance.

"Chest then head."

The woman sees another man off who he bids her goodnight in Flemish. "On the Antwerp brig?" I ask, stepping from the alley towards him.

"Ja," he replies, straightening his cap. "Sailing in the hour."

The woman draws her shawl around her and studies me. She's in her early forties and wears too much make-up that in this murk gives her a hard, salty edge. "Getting late, my love," she says. "Come back in the morning." She tries to close the door but I place my foot in the jamb. "What you doing?" she says. A heavyset, scarred bruiser, reeking of sweat and fags, brushes past her to stand before me.

"I know where the Casey brothers are."

Her interest pricks. "Best come in then."

"Chest then head, then run like fuck."

She leads me along a gaslit hallway into a parlour bedecked with a thick carpet, plush drapes, and a roaring fire. Christmas decorations hang from the ceiling and sprigs of holly and mistletoe decorate the mantelpiece. Paintings of men o'war hang from the wall. There's something else though. The dense, leaden tang of opium. Another, younger, woman sits in an armchair beside a phonograph, the needle crackling as it strikes the end of the disc's groove. She casts me a drowsy, doped look.

Ned is slumped on the opposite settee. The woman shakes him from his fug. Muttering to himself, he rubs his eyes, smooths his hair and looks at me. "You?" he says with disbelieving eyes. I raise the pistol. *"Chest then head, then run like fuck."* I fire. The woman screams. I fire again. Ned stares at me through dead eyes.

Ears ringing, I run along the hall. The bodyguard stands before me, knife in hand. I fire and he crumples into a heap clutching his left leg, screaming with the pain. I leap over him and throw open the door. The woman's cries follow me outside as I set off for Barton Street as fast as my gammy leg will allow. Dogs bark. Front doors open. People peer out. They go inside.

Reaching Barton Street, I cross the road, hop over the tramlines and duck into the first alley I come across. I stop to draw breath. Nobody is following. I set off down the alley towards a dead end, hoping my tuppenny map of Gloucester is accurate. At the end of the alley I scramble over a wall and drop into the sprawling railway marshalling yards. I give silent praise to the map maker and ignoring the pain in my leg, I set off across the yard.

Ten minutes later, I'm walking along Commercial Street, mingling with dockers on their way to work. Gloucester jail looms grey and harsh. Spiteful. The dockers give this gasping, limping stranger a wide berth. One or two mention there's been some trouble over on Barton Street. A shooting or some such.

I slip through the custom house gate and follow the dockers towards the Antwerp brig, where a gangerman is picking men for a day's work. I peel away and slip aboard the Anselma. "Where you been?" asks a nervous Stan.

"No time to explain," I answer. We cross the bridge, our eyes fixed on the narrow boat. "Get yer arse into gear," the bargeman shouts.

I turn to Stan and say, "Send word to Florrie when you reach Birmingham. It'll be safe to come back in a month."

"Don't have your faith, Tom."

"Find some." I hand him two fivers and the coins from the canister. "Always knew you'd end up with them."

"See you in Montevideo." He steps aboard the barge and ducks inside the cabin. I untie the narrow boat and watch the bargeman manoeuvre her into the basin and on towards the northern lock. Minutes later the barge is pootling Up Country towards Birmingham.

Stevedores lug crates of whiskey, sacks of grain, and flexing lengths of steel piping aboard the Antwerp brig. I grab two crates. The sailor I'd seen leaving number 37 stands by the forward cargo hold bellowing orders in Flemish. To avoid him recognising me, I shift the crates to my other shoulder before climbing down into the hold. Once inside I stack the two crates and help another stevedore do the same. A growling terrier backs out from another stack, throttling a rat. The docker pulls the dead rat from the dog's jaws and throws it to the floor. The terrier barks, unhappy at having to leave his breakfast behind. The docker picks him up and climbs out.

Now alone, I squeeze between the stacks and drag them around me. More Flemish orders are hollered above decks. The hatch lid closes but opens again. Fearing the worst I inch further into the stacks. There's a soft thud as a length of rope lands on the hatch floor. The lid closes but the odd slither a daylight pierces the hold.

The ship's engine turns over and seconds later, the propeller churns. Above me muffled Flemish shouts ring out. The turbines work harder, and the hull's vibrations cause the bottles to rattle. The ship's horn blasts.

° ° ○ ○ ° °

I wake heavy-lidded and dry-mouthed and stretch my stiff, cramping legs. The ship yaws and the crates teeter. Rinsed by seasickness I crawl from my hiding spot and throw up. The dead rat stares at me.

"Some sailor you make."

"Shut up, Dad."

Craving the hangman's noose over the barrelling waves, I dry heave and wonder how long my agony will last.

"I love you, Matilde." She laughs.

"Quiet Tom," the Three Sisters whisper as one.

A puzzled deckhand shakes me and says something in Flemish. Another sailor peers into the hatch, whispering to his shipmate. The deckhand points to me, shrugs his shoulders and helps me up. I climb out and suck in the crisp, salty air. A thick curling mist crowds the juddering ship. I grab a handful for luck.

In the wheelhouse, a helmsman releases the ship's horn every few seconds to warn other vessels of our whereabouts. The captain has his back to me and is examining the charts spread before him. Feeling queasy, I hold onto a rail for support.

The crewman clears his throat and says, "Kapitein." The captain turns. She has plain, sea weathered features and can be no more than thirty. But there's an air of calm authority about her. "Why are you on my ship?" she asks with jaded interest.

"Had a skin-full last night. Got the better of me this morning. Laid me head down for five minutes. Next thing I know, your lad here wakes me."

"Please, the truth only."

Too seasick for more lies, I mutter, "I was escaping."

"From where?"

"Gloucester."

"Why?"

"A man threatened to kill my family. I couldn't let him do that. Haven't been much of a son or brother to be honest, the war saw to that. But last night I'd no choice."

"You killed this man?"

"Yes."

"Did he deserve to die?"

"I'd say so."

She takes a sip of coffee and says, "A man who deserved death. In my experience most men do."

"Some truth in that."

She smiles. "How can I believe you? What proof do you have?"

"None, except my word."

"Why should I accept the word of a fleeing murderer?"

"No use for this anymore." I hand her the pistol. She sniffs the barrel and empties the chamber. The spare cartridges clatter on the deck. A hobbled old man dressed in soiled whites and carrying a coffee pot, struggles to climb the steps from below decks. He pours the captain a cup of coffee while weighing me up with a sharp, cagey eye. He turns to the captain and mutters to her in a lingo I've not heard before. The captain sips her coffee, grimaces, and stirs it. The second sip is more to her taste. "What is your name?" she asks.

"Tom Casey."

She sets her cup down and lights a cigarette. "We reach Zeebrugge in two days. I will decide what to do with you then, Tom Casey."

"Please. I served in the war. I helped to free you from the Germans."

"I am German."

Shit. The cook reappears carrying a length of rope. He and the helmsman take me to a storeroom beneath the wheelhouse where I'm lashed to a reel of heavy chains and locked inside.

○ ○ ○ ○ ○ ○

Sepp, the ship's cook, holds a cup of water to my lips. I drink it down, desperate to slake my thirst. The ship has stopped. The captain wearing a greatcoat and woollen hat, looks on from the doorway with two crewmen either side of her. Sepp cuts my ties and helps me to stand. Stiff-legged, I stumble into her. She steadies me and says, "You can thank Sepp. That and the fact that I need to catch the evening tide for Kiel."

"I don't understand."

"If I hand you over to the Belgians they will ask questions and wish to inspect the ship's manifest and customs declarations. I do not want that. There is profit in irregularity. And Master Tallow would not thank me."

Saved by Ned Tallow. Who'd have thought?

"And Sepp?" I ask.

"He killed a man once. Probably more than one, but I think it's better not to ask too many questions. His lack of scruples means he is a good judge of character. He tells me you have sorrows and harbour fears, but you are not someone who takes pleasure in killing. You are free to leave."

"Thank you."

"Just thank the profit motive and a smuggler's instinct."

Dawn has broken, but fog still cloaks the ship. Gulls chime. Overboard I can hear shouting men, straining cranes, and clanking chains. The mist lifts to reveal large brick warehouses and men scurrying about a quayside. "Zeebrugge," Sepp mutters. He hands me a woollen overcoat.

CHAPTER SIXTY-THREE

I jump down from the cab and thank the lorry driver. "Joyeux Noel," he replies and carries on his way. Two saloons pass me, both drivers surprised to see someone standing in this desolate spot.

In the low sun, the coating of fresh snow gives everything a pure, untainted look. Birdsong fills the air. Fear mixes with excitement as I fling the rucksack over my shoulder, draw up my coat collar and step back into the poisoned peace of the Zone Rouge, recalling Matilde's words, *"It is dangerous, but shelters us, like a fairy tale."*

Moving south, I pick my way along the lips of snow-filled craters, trenches, and narrow tracks guided by signs warning of mines, shells, and poison. I look out for landmarks, a tree, a ruin, anything familiar, all the while treading softly for fear of coming a cropper on a mine or disturbing the unclaimed dead.

The forest has thickened with sprouting saplings and fresh undergrowth. Life is reclaiming death. But the further I trudge, the snow and new growth cannot temper my growing disquiet at returning to this blackened, splintered world whose air is still fetid. Reaching a clearing, I stop to catch my breath and to eat one of the sandwiches Sepp had made for me, a disgusting but filling mash of lard and pork rinds. After eating, I smoke one of the foul Belgian cigarettes, another gift from Sepp, to lose the taste of lard. I head on in the fading light. I hear footsteps.

"Shittin' yerself, Tom?"

"Thought you were dead, Dad."

"Told ye, I'd never leave yer side."

A raw wind picks up. The footsteps are off to the right this time. I step lively, scanning the trees for sight of my pursuer. For a brief, mad moment I wonder if it's marsh Arabs hunting me. I was a fool for handing over my pistol to the Captain.

Panicking, I bolt through the freezing near darkness my fear of the unknown trumping the danger underfoot. I catch myself on branches, trip over twisted roots but stumble on through a perishing, swirling blizzard, which at least hides me from my pursuer.

Up ahead are the dark, glowering outline of buildings. A village. A bridge over a coal-black stream takes me into a snow-coated square. Minutes later, I force open the front door of Matilde's old home. The remains of a fire, still warm to the touch, sits in the hearth and throws a thin reddish orange glow over piles of brass shell casings, rolls of rusted barbed wire, and other foraged material.

But the fire means I cannot stay here. I step into the storm and trudge towards the square. Looters have ransacked the bakery, taking anything of value, even the oven's cast iron doors. Flattening myself against the stairwell, I climb the stairs and enter the bedroom overlooking the square. It's empty, but the windows have been put through leaving the freezing room coated in a six inch layer of snow. I cross the landing and enter another room. Again it has been ransacked, save for a wrought iron bed frame. I lay on the squeaking frame, curl into a ball, pull my coat tight around me and light another foul Belgian cigarette.

A howling banshee funnels down the chimney.

○ ○ ○ ○ ○

The rifle's barrel pricks my cheek. From the tail of my eye I make out a short figure wearing a French infantryman's great coat several sizes too big. A tank driver's mask covers his face. He presses the barrel deeper into my cheek.

"Je suis Anglais," I tell him.

"As if that'll make a difference."

The bolt action slides. Time slows. At least I've made it back to her. "Matilde," I mutter. Time to make peace.

The looter lifts the rifle and beckons me up. I stand before him, hands raised. He's small. Half my size. No match. Break the fucker's neck. After all, killing comes easy to me now. The looter peels of his mask.

As usual Malaphonse wears neither a frown nor smile and avoids my desperate attempt to hug her. She offers me her water canister. The water tastes of rust but is refreshing enough. Two brass shell casings are strapped to her back.

"Allez,' she whispers. I follow her downstairs. We step outside into a glorious sun-drenched winter's morning and move off at a fair clip. The poisoned air means I struggle to keep up. Malaphonse shows little sympathy but hectors me with short, barked commands.

By mid-morning a derelict church spire appears, the sight of it draining my tiredness. I've made it back. Never thought I would. But here I am on a fool's errand.

The forest has swallowed the village's outer buildings and creeps towards the square. The rusted hulk of the upturned lorry now shorn of its wheels, still lays outside the remains of the café. "Seul?" I ask, wondering why Malaphonse stayed on, hacking life from the forest. She nods.

I flinch watching her unhitch the shells from her back and lean them against the church's bullet scored portico. She loosens the chain wrapped around the door handles, pull the doors open and goes inside. Snow covers the floor, pews and altar, upon which Lenin's half-hidden picture again rests. Rubble is piled up against shell-damaged walls and a tarp hangs between the two pews closest to the altar.

Malaphonse crawls beneath the tarp and reappears carrying firewood, which she stacks beneath the altar. Within minutes the fire's flames drift through the roof space heating coffee and a pot of vegetable broth.

With time to kill before eating, I wander around the church noting the once brave slogans and running a hand over the jagged remains of the alabaster saints. In the sacristy the café's torn awning covers an FN. Apart from a missing seat, grips, smashed headlamp, and flat tyres, the bike seems in reasonable nick. I remove the fuel tank cap. Petrol sloshes inside.

Restored by the broth, I smoke, stretch out, aware how a king lives. At that moment the most dangerous place on earth feels the safest. I marvel at Malaphonse's stoicism for living in a place damned by God but not her.

Rusted, deformed Indians and Harleys lay amongst the garage's rubble. I twist the perished throttle grip of a Triumph and poke around the dented fuel cans, shorn engine parts, and rusted spanners. With night descending I return to the church examining the links on a drive chain.

Near the portico Malaphonse uses a hammer and chisel to split open the two shells she's scavenged, using a cloth to deaden the impact of each hammer strike. Her deft touch reminds me of the Dingle fish gutters. Even so, expecting the worst, I take several steps back.

After splitting the shells, she carries the fuses and charges into the woods. Returning, she bid me enter the church and closes the doors, winding the chain around each handle. The fire dims, drawing the cold night air in. Malaphonse ducks under the tarpaulin and beckons me inside. She hands me two blankets and hunkers down for the night, with a pistol by her side, answering any ideas I may have had about making a pass. I arrange my bedding, draw the coat around me and fall into a dreamless, but peaceful sleep.

○ ○ ○ ○ ○ ○

The tarp sags with fresh snowfall, but despite the tightness in my chest, for the first time in days I wake free from the fear of capture or weighed down by the troubles of others. I crawl outside to be greeted by the smell of coffee and frying bacon.

Malaphonse hands me a woollen scarf and hat. I rummage in my jacket pocket for the Prussian solider. I unwind the cotton ringlet, loop it around my marriage finger and hand her the soldier. "Not exactly a girly present. Beggars can't be choosers and all that."

She holds the soldier up to the grey light, looking as excited as any six-year-old on Christmas morning. We wolf the bacon down and take our time sipping the strong, sweet coffee. I can't remember a finer Christmas dinner.

After eating we trek through the forest and stop in a clearing, criss-crossed with animal tracks. Eight graves, each one marked with a roughly hewn wooden cross, stand before us. We pay our respects to Timmings, Etienne, Sonia, Maxime, Octave, Lucette the nurse, Albert the driver, and finally Matilde.

"Matilde," Malaphonse says reaching for my hand. "Mon souer."

"I loved her, Malaphonse. With all my heart I loved her." She squeezes my hand. Her calloused fingers tell of a life cut from the earth. "Matilde t'aimait."

∘ ∘ ○ ∘ ∘

The weeks pass in easy, graceful silence. Even when the east wind blew, the rush to don gasmasks grew less urgent. Malaphonse demands nothing of me and spends her time foraging for anything of value. When she's collected enough, she treks to the nearest town to sell her finds and returns with provisions. I wonder what the townsfolk think of this mute, unkempt hermit who emerges from the forest to trade with them.

I set about restoring the FN, working by candlelight long into the night, under the tarp fiddling, sawing and bolting different parts from different bikes together. The rebuild becomes a monument to Matilde and when she's not patrolling the forest, Malaphonse looks on with a keen eye, once returning with a pair of second hand tyres from one of her sorties into the town.

Finally, with the spring thaw, I wheel "Matilde" from the Church. I check the plugs, tap the carburettor and paddle. Nothing. I rock her back and forth then push her across the muddy square and jump aboard. Still nothing.

After examining the carburettor, magneto, and plugs, I can't figure why she won't start. I smoke a fag to calm myself. Malaphonse squats by the engine and turns the fuel tap.

I try another bump start, this time with her help. The bike nearly tips over but a tar-black smoke pierces the exhaust pipe's seam. **Matilde lives.**

We head north west along a mud clogged track with the nervy Malaphonse gripping me around the waist. The bike slides and weaves but I press on, once again a DR pushing through the Flanders mud. We stop by **the graves.** The trees, sprouting new foliage, sway in the light breeze as we stand in silence over our fallen comrades.

Kneeling beside Matilde's grave, Malaphonse scrapes away the earth at the base of the cross and retrieves an oblong object wrapped in a stained cloth. She peels away the cloth and hands me the gold ingot she'd helped herself to at Hederbrug. Astounded, I catch my golden reflection and brush the bevelled eagle motif. *"Take it, you deserve it,"* temptation whispers. Such a fortune would let me strike out for the mysterious Orient, Montevideo, even the South Pole. Anywhere. Everywhere.

"You are better than this, Casey." Matilde whispers.

Memories of the dead Russian children baulk my greed. I'll be tainted with their blood if I take the ingot. I hand it back. Twice more Malaphonse offers the ingot to me but each time I refuse. Accepting defeat, Malaphonse wraps the ingot in the cloth and returns it to the grave and tamps the soil down with the heel of her boot. I wonder what stopped her from putting this fortune to good use herself. She looks up at me and tries to speak, but the words won't come. Wiping tears from her dirt stained cheeks she strokes Matilde's cross and mutters tender, sweet words, at odds with the poisoned barbarity surrounding us. But I understand. Malaphonse will never leave her sister. I unwind the cotton ringlet from my finger and wrap it around Matilde's cross. At least some part of me will stay with Matilde too.

"Allez!" Malaphonse shouts, shouldering her rifle.

We set off for Calais but the cold and snow means we barely get above walking pace for long stretches. We pass through Matilde's village but press on and reach the forest's edge by the afternoon.

I kill the engine and we dismount and stretch our frozen, aching limbs. Reaching inside her baggy great coat, Malaphonse hands me a thick bundle of French and Belgian francs. I can't refuse her again. She breaks into a rare if wistful smile and I glimpse another side to her; happier, at peace with the world. I wish I had the French to thank her for saving me and for standing guard over Matilde. But all I can say is, "Merci, Malaphonse." But it's enough.

Without fanfare Malaphonse returns to her forest and within a handful of steps I lose sight of her. Despite all the hardships, she's found her own freedom in the Zone Rouge, shorn of men; her silence, stealth, and patience protecting her. Outside, such silence would earn her the straitjacket.

"Allez, Tom Casey!" The last of the three sisters shouts. "Tu est mon frère!"

"Mon soeur!" I shout.

I start Matilde, point her south and set off for Montevideo.

CHAPTER SIXTY-FOUR

June 1928 - Pau, Southern France

As usual when leaving the caravan, I catch a pocketful of steam funnelling from the steam engine working the merry go round. Squealing, delighted children grip their brightly coloured steeds except for one terrified little lad who clings on for dear life and ignores his waving parents. I understand. These prancing horses and their sinister grins drive the fear of God into me as well. The sight of a charging Uhlan never leaves you.

At the ticket booth a suited Scotsman struggles to buy a ticket from Claudette. Not a surprise. Even locals struggle to buy tickets from her. Again I can't figure why Bernice keeps her on.

"How many tickets?" I ask him.

"Just the one."

Claudette rips a ticket from the reel and hands it to the smartly dressed Scotsman after he pays over the five francs entrance fee.

"Where you from?" I ask.

"Hawick, in the Scottish borders."

"Long way from home."

"Here for the Grand Prix."

"What are you riding?"

"Works Norton. What about you?"

"A few years ago maybe, but you've just paid to see me. Douglas Rudge." I offer him my hand. "Jimmy Guthrie," he says.

"Enjoy the show," I tell him as we shake hands.

Outside the tent, Bernice hollers through her red megaphone, "Mur de la mort. Mur de la mort." Punters stop to listen to her proclaim the derring-do about to unfold inside. Passing her, I pat her belly to wish our unborn baby well and again wonder why such a remarkable woman fell for me. But I'm glad she did. She's fixed me, even if she knows just half my story.

I descend the stairs one step at a time, wincing from the pain in my leg. I duck down to enter the barrel, and sit on the slim bright red Indian Scout. Taking the envelope from my jacket pocket I study the neat handwriting, "Douglas Rudge, Poste Restante, Pau Poste Office, Pau, France." I unfold the letter and read it for the umpteenth time.

THE STEAM CATCHER

"Hello Tom,

So you didn't make it to Montevideo then!

The Quakers passed on your letter. It was a thrill to hear from you. We are all well. Mum's hip is playing her up and this wet weather doesn't help. But she was pleased as punch when I told her you'd written.

Jack is fine. He's working at the match factory. Been there a couple of years now. Hasn't suffered a seizure since that night of the fire, although he needs peace and quiet to keep him on an even keel. He's outside at the moment with Elizabeth. I can't believe she's turned five this year. Chip off the old block is Elizabeth, won't take any nonsense from anyone. I wonder where she gets that from! Matilda is asleep in her cot. Mum reckons there's a lot of Dad in her. The right side, I hope.

Stanley came back from Birmingham a month or so after all that business with Ned Tallow, but he couldn't settle so headed off for London. He's still there as far as we know. Once in a while he writes to say we're not to worry and that everything is tickety-boo with him. I hope so. Be nice to see him someday.

Any money he sends, Mum leaves in that old can of yours. Stan may need it when he comes home, she says.

Alf Fenwick told me that they didn't look too hard for Ned's killer, "Good riddance to bad rubbish," is how he put it. Turns out Ned was up to all sorts of things on the docks, smuggling, prostitution, bribery and even piracy believe it or not. By all accounts he killed a few people as well. And him quiet as a mouse too. It's always the quiet ones you have to watch.

In another life Tom, you'd be treated as a hero for what you did. But you'll always be a hero for sticking your neck out for us. Dad would have been proud. He'd have even sung a few songs in your honour!

Well, it's getting close to tea time and if she's not fed at four o'clock on the dot Matilda roars the house down! I hope one day you can meet them. They owe you their lives. As will their younger brother or sister. I'm sure it's another girl. Just imagine, three sisters in the same house!

Take care and when you can please write again.
Florrie

PS Mr MacDonald has become Prime Minister again. We're hoping for great things. The Tories still hold Gloucester. One day we'll get them out!

Returning the letter to my jacket I spot Guthrie, quiet, assured, taking everything in. As always, people look down on me. But at least they have to pay for the privilege these days.

296

I button up the worn, creased leather jacket, close my eyes and run through the routine as I've done thousands of times before. I like this moment of stillness, the nerves and excitement building.

I start the Indian and its thundering exhaust note bounces around the thirty-foot diameter barrel. I set off anti-clockwise, listening to the tyre patter on the rail sleepers that form the barrel. I build up speed on the banked section and then mount the vertical wall. Round and round I go snaking up and down, thrilling and scaring the audience in equal measure, catching the bike's echo until the wall and crowd became a confusion of noise, movement and speed.

I should be terrified, but the wall lets Tom Casey chase his fate, if only for a few seconds nine times a day. Twelve on Saturdays. On I press, the speed bearing down on my neck and shoulders.

There's the FN, ahead of me, its rider crouched over the handlebars, her blond hair streaming over her shoulders. I accelerate, but as always Matilde stays out of reach. *"You'll never catch me, Rudge,"* she shouts. *"Or is it Casey?"*

She fades as I decelerate. I'll try to catch her again in an hour's time, but as usual I'll fail. Doesn't stop me trying though.

Douglas Rudge comes to a stop. Guthrie gives me the thumbs up. Next to him Bernice holds Florence. "Papa!" My daughter shouts, and then giggles at the booming echo of her voice.